Gracie Jenkins runs a Marathon

Penny Mirren is the pen name of Samantha Pennington. Sam writes light-hearted, uplifting fiction and romantic comedy. She was selected for the inaugural Kate Nash Literary Agency Mentorship Scheme in 2020 and is a member of the Romantic Novelists Association. Sam lives in rural North Essex and when she's not writing, enjoys being first mate on her husband's tiny fishing boat and reading books for her wine club. *Gracie Jenkins Runs a Marathon* is her second book with Avon.

Gracie Jenkins runs a Marathon

Penny Mirren

avon.

Published by AVON
A division of HarperCollins*Publishers* Ltd
1 London Bridge Street
London SE1 9GF

www.harpercollins.co.uk

HarperCollins*Publishers*
Macken House, 39/40 Mayor Street Upper
Dublin 1, D01 C9W8, Ireland

1

A catalogue record for this book is available from the British Library.

ISBN: 978-0-00-873865-5

Set in Minion Pro by HarperCollins*Publishers* India

Printed and bound in the UK using 100% Renewable Electricity at CPI Group (UK) Ltd

This book is dedicated to anyone who has ever run a marathon,
you are ALL amazing.

And also,
for my dad – who knows the importance of an excellent shed.

1

Gracie

Marriage should be an Olympic sport really, mused Gracie as she observed her husband washing up. Bronze for a bloody good effort, silver for surviving it at all and a gold medal for growing old together in congenial acceptance of each other's infuriating traits.

Gracie watched as Andrew tugged a crude homemade attachment from the mixer tap, gave it a quick shake and replaced it under the kitchen sink. Regardless of the fact they'd been the proud custodians of a dishwasher for at least thirty years, Andrew persisted in washing up by hand. Yet, because Andrew was, well, Andrew, he constantly sought ways to improve a process – in this case by fashioning a gadget to both dispense washing-up liquid and rinse dishes simultaneously – completely overlooking the fact that Bosch, Hotpoint and countless other designers of domestic appliances, had perfected the art decades ago.

'Another job jobbed,' said Andrew, drying his hands on a tea towel, then pirouetting ungracefully in time to the beat of 'Boogie Wonderland', which played on Radio Essex, and landing in front of Gracie, just as she adjusted her affectionate smirk into a wide smile. She might spend a good proportion of her day being vaguely irritated at her husband's eccentric ways, but he could always make her laugh.

'We could do without you falling over and buggering up the other knee, dear. The stairs are enough of a bother as it is. Cuppa?' she asked, flipping on the kettle and reaching into the cupboard for their two favourite mugs: his – a gift from their son Nathan celebrating their favourite football team, hers – a botanical printed souvenir from a long-ago holiday to Portmeirion (she no longer remembered *whose* holiday, might it even have been theirs?).

'Point taken, light foot-tapping only from now on. Oh, hold your hats, here we go. . .'

Picasso's ears stood to attention, and her golden tail wagged furiously.

Banksy read the room, meowed in disgruntlement, then bolted from the kitchen. The ginger tom had been enjoying a light snooze in Picasso's bed, his most favourite way to piss off their beloved mutt, the hiding of her rubber chicken coming a close second. The mangy object was usually to be found inside a wellington boot or camouflaged in the washing basket.

Gracie tilted her head, a tea bag pinched between finger and thumb.

'I can't hear anything.'

'Mm,' Andrew agreed, 'a rogue banger, perhaps. What time did you say the official display starts?'

Gracie crossed the room to the cluttered dresser and turned the blaring radio down several notches. 'Not for another hour or so yet. Look at her, bless her heart.'

They both looked to Picasso, who was hovering on the brink of a whining session. It was the same every year, fireworks – which were no longer sacrosanct to the fifth of November – transformed their usually placid Border Collie into the canine equivalent of the girl in *The Exorcist*.

All three of them startled when the loud bang came again. *Not* a firework, then, but their door knocker.

'Silly old fool,' muttered Gracie as she padded down the hallway. If he would insist on having a kitchen disco whilst he unnecessarily scrubbed and laboured over the remnants of a full Sunday roast, was it any wonder they couldn't hear the door. The rest of the house could have been burgled before they'd detect an intruder.

'Emily!' greeted Gracie, with delight. 'What a lovely surprise. Come on in.'

The young woman bundled up in a large puffa coat against the chilly evening grinned and followed her inside.

'Have I caught you at a bad time, Auntie Gracie?'

'Not at all. In fact, we were about to have a cuppa. Let's go through to the lounge, the kitchen stinks of cavolo nero. Love the stuff, but it does tend to linger. ANDREW! Be a love and bring the tea? Can you make another for Emily?' She paused mid-holler to check with her niece, 'Milk and one, isn't it?'

'Yes please,' said Emily, unzipping her coat as Gracie relayed the instructions, and hooking it over the banister at the foot of the stairs, before following Gracie into the lounge.

'Not going to the fireworks tonight, love?'

Emily shook her head, bouncy auburn hair shimmering in the reading light above the armchair she'd selected. Gracie couldn't put her finger on it, but something about this young woman always gave her a pang of nostalgia. Even down to the way she immediately tucked her socked feet up beneath her, curling into the chair like Gracie always had – still did as a reasonably fit and flexible woman of seventy-two years (though she normally paid for it with crippling pins and needles). However, the reality was that Gracie and Emily

3

had only recently been getting to know each other properly, so it warmed her heart to see her so comfortable in their home.

'I thought I might wander down to the seafront and watch from there,' she said.

'Excellent idea, that's what we usually do. Great view of the pier, none of the crowds. Or, in my case, students, and even worse than that – parents. Last thing you want mid-bite of a hot dog, with mustard on your nose, is Mrs So-and-So asking for an extension on little Johnny's coursework.'

Emily sniggered. 'I still can't picture you as a teacher. You're nothing like any teacher I had growing up. I bet you were one of the fun, popular ones.'

Gracie gave a snort of laughter. 'I don't know about that. My suspicion is many students saw Art lessons as a nice gentle doss, until it got to their GCSEs and they realised you have to actually do the work.'

'I wish I'd studied Art. I always liked it as a kid, even if I'm not all that good at it, or very creative. Paintings fascinate me – I could spend hours in the London galleries.'

'And that, dear, is what it's all about. The power of appreciation – of being moved, stirred, inspired, repulsed, awestruck – any one of a million responses is valid and makes you just as qualified as the next person when it comes to consuming art. Absolutely no talent or skill required.'

This was a common misconception Gracie always felt compelled to rail against, such snobbery in the arts.

'And anyway,' she continued, 'what are you talking about, you *are* talented. You have a brilliant job and a bright future ahead of you. What I'd give to be starting out again at your age, on the cusp of adventure and promise.'

Emily made a dismissive noise, as though such notions were the stuff of pure fantasy.

And thinking about it, when Gracie pictured herself at twenty-five, as Emily was now, she'd just qualified as a teacher. She didn't know it then, but that would be her destiny right through to retirement, her wild, nomadic days already behind her, future adventures to be crowbarred into the restraints of the term-time calendar. She decided not to voice her thoughts after all.

Andrew bustled into the room with the tray of mugs and a plate of shortbread biscuits, followed by Picasso, who, appearing to have recovered from her earlier trepidation, made a beeline for Emily and nuzzled into her dangling hand.

'Great to see you, Emily love. What brings you out here on this cold old night?' asked Andrew.

'Perhaps she heard the banging tunes and thought we'd opened a secret nightclub to shake up this sleepy little town, dear,' said Gracie, giving Emily a knowing eyeroll.

'Ha! It did sound like you were having a bit of a party, I must admit. Perhaps you've got more in common with Mum than you think – she dances round the kitchen like a loon when she thinks no-one's watching.' Emily grinned.

I can well imagine, thought Gracie, and *especially* when she knows she's being watched. If there was one thing her sister Jill loved, it was an audience.

'How is your mum?' asked Andrew, ever the considerate host.

'Oh, you know Mum. Keeping herself busy. We've been doing a bit of a spring clean today, or whatever the equivalent is in November – a winter declutter. Been in the garage looking through some of Dad's things that we never had chance to sort out in the move.'

Gracie nodded and sipped her tea, conscious that her niece was still in the relatively early stages of grief. Her own interactions with the man had been limited to two separate occasions: a funeral, and an embarrassing encounter on the M6, when she spotted her brother-in-law in a fast-food queue at Corley Services and deliberated over whether to approach. In the end, she was spared the indignity of having to remind him who she was, when he was accosted by a couple of fans. She'd slipped back out to the car where Andrew had been waiting whilst she had a quick wee and spent the remainder of the journey kicking herself for not seizing the opportunity. She presumed Gary's own funeral didn't count as an interaction, though they'd both been present.

'He had some pretty collectable guitars and we're thinking of auctioning them for Alzheimer's Outreach UK. Which brings me to one of the reasons I popped round . . .' Emily gave Picasso a final rub of the ears, then swung her socked feet to the ground. 'I. . .' she said, pausing for dramatic effect, 'have just received confirmation that I've got a place in the London Marathon!'

Gracie slapped her knees in surprise. 'Really? Wow, Emily! I had no idea you'd applied. That's incredible.'

Emily pulled a face. 'Incredibly scary, you mean.'

Andrew, from where he sat beside Gracie on the sofa, stood abruptly.

'Well, I don't know about you two, but I think that calls for something a little stronger than tea. Bloody well done, Em.'

Gracie had to agree. 'Good call, there's a bottle of fizz in the fridge, Andy.'

Andrew left the room and Gracie shook her head in astonishment. 'Well, well. What a thing, isn't it incredibly difficult to get a place, or a *bib* – isn't that what they call it?'

Emily slurped her tea. 'Mm-hmm. I didn't think I'd get in to be honest, but with some of Dad's old contacts pledging support, and what with him having had Alzheimer's, I guess that really strengthened my application for a charity place,' Emily shrugged.

'Now all I've got to do is, er, train hard enough to actually be able to complete it. No pressure.' She let out a slightly manic laugh.

'I have every faith in you,' assured Gracie. 'Besides, don't you run already?'

'Yep, but I'm still only a beginner really – Saturday mornings here, with the local running club. I'll have to start running in the week now too. They reckon allow at least six months to train from scratch so hopefully there's enough time.'

Whilst Emily lived and worked in London, and shared a flat with two other young professionals, it seemed she chose to hop on a train most Friday evenings to make the two-hour journey to Frinton-on-Sea and stay with her mother until Monday morning, before heading back into the city and to her job as a market researcher for a bank. In the short time Gracie and Andrew had been getting to know her after a long period of estrangement, she seemed increasingly disillusioned with the corporate world, her career choices and her living arrangements. This was of growing concern to Gracie because although Emily was a quiet and serious sort, and perhaps not suited to city living, the split lifestyle she'd adopted wasn't healthy either. A girl of her age needed friends and a support network and perhaps above all, fun.

Andrew reappeared with the bottle, three champagne glasses and a distinct limp, which pricked at Gracie's conscience. He'd overdone it today, a short walk before dinner, then all that standing around in the kitchen. She should have insisted he sit down and made the tea herself.

'Will you join a running club in Hackney too?' asked Gracie, taking a tall flute of fizz from her husband.

'Probably not. But I don't mind running alone, in busy areas obviously. It'll be nice to switch off from the chaos of the office.'

Gracie could relate. There was simply nothing she'd loved more after a long day teaching adolescents, than to get down onto the beach for a mess around with one of their much-loved four-legged companions and there had been a few, over the years. The wide-open space and sea air clarified the mind.

'Right then,' said Andrew, having distributed the wine. 'Cheers to you, Emily. I've no doubt you'll smash it and raise lots of money for a brilliant cause in the process.'

The three of them clinked glasses and Gracie sipped at hers thoughtfully. Jill must be so proud. And rightly so – for all her faults, she'd raised a kind, sensitive and intelligent young woman, who Gracie had no doubt at all would make her mark on the world. Even if, for now, she seemed a little lost in it. She'd felt like that too, once upon a time, and knew that sometimes you needed to work out *who* you were before you could work out what or where you wanted to be.

'Oh, I just remembered,' said Emily, placing her glass on a side table and reaching for her bag on the floor beside her, a vibrant green and white striped canvas tote that bore a little badge stating *I used to be a deckchair*. This was another trait Gracie hugely admired in her niece, her commitment to living a cleaner, simpler, more sustainable way of life. 'When we were clearing out the garage, I came across a shoe box that Mum keeps lots of little mementos in. Like, my first shoes were in there and this gross lock of hair. But anyway, I found these and thought maybe you'd like to see them. Mum didn't think you'd be interested, but have a look. . .' She pulled a brown envelope from her bag and passed it to Gracie.

Intrigued, Gracie opened the flap of the envelope and pulled out a small stack of postcards, banded together with a fluorescent pink hair bobble, the elastic so perished it snapped and pinged across the rug.

Recognising the first postcard immediately, or rather, the faded depiction of Machu Picchu upon it, she let out a small murmur of surprise.

'Goodness.' She looked up at Emily. 'Your mother kept these all this time?'

Emily met her eye. 'That surprises you?'

Well, frankly, it did.

'It was a long time ago. You expect these things to be lost,' she countered, deflecting away from any notion of animosity on her part. As far as she was concerned, it was *Jill* who had made it clear in the past where her priorities in life lay. And that wasn't with the family – which made the fact she'd moved to the area even *more* puzzling.

'What have we got here then?' asked Andrew, leaning in.

'What we have,' replied Gracie, swiping her husband's glasses from his nose and placing them on hers instead – the prescription was far too strong for her, but adequate for reading – 'are relics from another life. Long before I met you or settled down to live on the Essex coast, of all places.' She turned the card over and recognised her own lazy, looping script. A shiver ran through her. An echo of a thrill. An instantaneous yearning for the nomadic existence she'd lived that year. For the *adventure*.

'Mum said she was nine when you went off travelling?' asked Emily. 'And that you sent her postcards from all the places you visited so she could picture where you were.'

Gracie nodded, scanning the message she'd scrawled to her little sister. She remembered writing this one. She'd been staying in a hostel with another single female traveller, and they'd intended to hike the famous trail the next day together. As it happened, Dominica got food poisoning and so Gracie had to set off alone, leaving the other poor woman to spend a miserable day retching into a bucket. She wondered whatever happened to Dominica. No mobile phones back then, of course, and she'd never got her address. She also found herself wondering what happened to that version of Gracie. Had her adventurous spirit upped and left at some point, like an exorcised ghost? No, she knew it was still there, tapping her on the shoulder occasionally, and whispering teasingly into her ear. But such ambitious exploits were now consigned to the past, a place unsuited to lingering; life was fleeting enough as it was. Even if her restless nature did crave invigoration.

As if reading her mind, Emily said, 'It's so cool that you visited all these amazing places on your own. Wasn't it scary, to be a lone female traveller back in the seventies, before mobile phones and Google?'

Gracie considered for a moment. 'I wasn't on my own that often, actually. You meet others along the way, like-minded folks who are interested in the same places, same cultures, same artefacts. Lots of Art History graduates, like me, hoping to follow in the footsteps of the greats. I spent most of my time in Florence and Paris, before I got the travelling bug and ventured further afield. And then, of course, I got the hiking bug, which let me tell you – once it gets its teeth in you, never quite lets you go.'

Andrew found Gracie's hand and gave it a squeeze, which made her heart contract for the man who had been by her side for nearly fifty years of treks, hikes and hill climbs. Until osteoarthritis crumbled his left knee and put paid to the gentlest of ambles and their life-long love of rambling. His shoulder was starting to go too. It woke her in the night sometimes, the wince of pain and his crackling joints when he rolled over onto his better side. The doctors had said it would never get better, that he could expect deterioration with time.

'Oh, don't mind me, Andy,' she hastened to reassure him. 'Just enjoying a little stroll down memory lane. I'm sure it's high time I hung up my walking boots anyway and took up something a little more age-appropriate, like cribbage or gin rummy. Cynthia's always on at me to go to her local history group. If I guzzle a gallon of coffee beforehand, I'm sure I'll stay awake.'

Emily gave a hoot of laughter. 'Mum said you've always had bags of energy, far more than her, even if she is fourteen years younger. Hey—' she stopped suddenly, and her lips broke into a mischievous smile '—perhaps you should join the CPR too, Auntie Gracie!'

'CPR?' Gracie frowned.

'The Coast Path Runners. Why don't you come with me on Saturday morning? You obviously love to keep active, all those long walks on the beach. It would be fun.'

Gracie blew out her cheeks. 'I think expecting me to join the likes of you youngsters for a *run* might very well end up with CPR of a different kind!'

Emily tutted. 'It's not like that. People of all ages and abilities go along, and anyway you can go at your own pace – there's quite a few of us who take it slow, it's more of a light jog really.'

'I think that's a brilliant idea,' piped up Andrew. 'You could take Picasso along too. Run off all that excess energy.' He gave Emily a big fat wink.

Gracie looked between them, at their smirking faces.

'Excuse me!'

'The dog, of course I meant the dog,' he laughed.

As if to prove a point, a sudden gunfire burst of fireworks punctuated the moment and Picasso leapt into the air, before commencing to circle the rug as though her tail were on fire and speed alone could extinguish it. No sign of Banksy, of course, the cat was probably hiding under one of the beds. Jolly good idea, if Picasso's current display was a sign of how the evening would progress.

Gracie checked the time and rose to stand. 'Well, I don't know about you, but I think that's our cue to get our coats. The display starts in ten minutes.'

Half an hour later, they huddled together in the biting cold on Gracie and Andrew's favourite bench overlooking the sea, watching the crescendo of an aerial display that illuminated the sky in vibrant streaks of pink, purple and gold. Gracie watched Andrew with a deep swell of affection, as each crackling rainfall of sparks lit up his face. He'd leaned heavily on a stick to walk down here, a recent necessity when leaving the house, but he was damned if it would stop him, even though she knew he was in pain. They were still here, still living. She didn't need to be hiking a Lake District fell or scaling the South Downs to experience life in all its glorious technicolour. Everything she needed was on her doorstep, even, in a plot twist she certainly hadn't seen coming – her sister, these days, and Emily too, who beamed back at them both as the final shower of colour exploded against a deep indigo sky.

Maybe she *would* pop along to this running club, see what all the fuss was about – after all, it was just putting one foot in front of the other, something she'd been doing all her life.

Did it really matter if the ground beneath was the familiar and well-trod territory of home?

2

Jill

'There you go love,' said Jill, placing a steaming mug of hot chocolate in front of Emily. 'That'll warm you up.'

Emily blew on her hands, then wrapped them around the mug, her pale, freckled skin illuminated with a rosy glow that extended to the tip of her nose.

'Thanks, Mum.' She lowered her face to the steam and breathed it in heavily.

Jill turned back to the kitchen worktop where she'd been busy frosting a carrot cake.

'Been anywhere nice?' She kept her tone casual, even though she was deeply curious as to where her daughter had been until ten o'clock on a Sunday evening, because it certainly wasn't the beach-clean she'd gone to early that morning. Yes, she may be a twenty-five-year-old woman who left home several years ago, but to Jill's knowledge Emily's routine of staying with her at weekends was simply habit, a hangover from when Gary was ill that she hadn't yet felt able to shake, not because of a thriving social life in Frinton-on-Sea. Jill had only moved to the small town earlier in the year, and was still finding her feet herself, so it wasn't as if the place was teeming with Emily's old school friends; it wasn't like 'coming home'. Besides, Emily had *never* had a thriving social life, no matter where she'd lived. She wasn't the sort – she certainly didn't take after her parents, Good-time Jill and Mad Gaz, as they'd been affectionately known, back in the day. Jill had to work hard at remembering him like that, as the man she'd married, rather than the man he'd become by the end. And the move had helped with that, a fresh start on the so-called Essex Sunshine Coast. Some joke that was, it never stopped raining.

But, even though Gary had been gone over a year, Emily was *still* jumping on a train from London every Friday night and spending the whole weekend with her, as she had done in that last year of caring for him. Something wasn't right; she knew that deep down yet hadn't the first clue how to approach it. For all her reputation as an extrovert, when it came to talking to her daughter, words somehow eluded her.

'Actually,' began Emily, bending to take a long slurp of the full-to-the-brim mug and surfacing with a chocolate-coated top lip, 'I watched the fireworks with Uncle Andrew and Auntie Gracie.'

This brought Jill up short.

'Oh,' she said, fussing with a palette knife to spread the icing evenly and trying to hide the jolt of disappointment behind a bright tone. 'How lovely. In town, or. . . somewhere else?'

And why wasn't I invited, for that matter?

'Down at the seafront – we watched the display off Walton Pier. They were pretty good. It's been ages since I saw a proper firework display. Remember the ones Dad used to do in the garden at the old house,' she giggled, 'they always went wrong.'

At this Jill smiled too. Gary had been one of life's optimists. A dreamer with a heart of gold. You'd think that someone who played lead guitar in a band all his life would have at least some technical knowhow, but instead he subscribed to the 'it can't be that hard' school of thought, which whilst serving him well most of the time, tended to bite him on the arse sometimes – and in the case of an unsecured Catherine wheel one year, quite literally.

'I know,' agreed Jill wistfully. 'But you can't say he didn't throw a cracking party.'

Emily's eyes drifted skyward, and Jill pretended not to notice. She couldn't understand why her daughter had never appreciated the musical household she'd grown up in, never picked up an instrument herself, or ever shown much interest in her dad's (rather short-lived) status as a heartthrob in an eighties pop band. She supposed she should be grateful really. Grateful that Emily had never been destined to run off and live on a tour bus, high on life, and other substances, with her older punk rock lover, as she herself had done at seventeen.

'And how are Auntie Gracie and Uncle Andrew?' Jill enquired tentatively.

'For heaven's sake, Mum. They asked me the same thing about you. You know, they do live only five minutes down the road – maybe you could go and see for yourself sometime? I mean that *is* why you moved here, isn't it?'

Jill plonked the palette knife on the counter and spun around to face her daughter.

'And a fat lot of good that did. I moved a hundred miles away from all my wonderful friends, to be spitting distance from my sister, yet why do I get the feeling Gracie wouldn't spit on me if I walked past her in the high street with my tits on fire?'

'Oh, don't be so dramatic. You know that's total rubbish. And maybe your *wonderful* friends could visit some time. Honestly, you're both so stubborn, and so similar, it's actually funny. I can't

15

believe I never saw it. Not that I ever had the chance to get to know her before now, of course. Are you cutting that cake or what?'

Jill frowned, decidedly ignoring Emily's comment about her friends. And the dig about never having had chance to get to know her aunt. But seriously, her and Gracie, similar? Surely it wasn't possible for two biological sisters to be any more different if they'd grown up on separate continents. Although, to be fair, for some of Jill's childhood Gracie *had* been on a different continent.

'What? Oh, no, sorry, it's for the café. There's a packet of Jaffa Cakes in the cupboard, your favourite.'

'Now you're talking,' said Emily, pushing back her chair. 'I was going to offer to save the poor souls from a fate worse than hunger but looks like they're on their own.'

Jill tutted. 'Bloody cheek. I don't get any complaints, I can tell you.'

Emily rammed a whole Jaffa Cake into her mouth and shrugged, amusement crinkling the corners of her eyes.

When she had finished munching, she said, 'I took those postcards round to show Auntie Gracie. It must have been strange seeing them again after all these years, but she seemed pleased. And maybe also a little bit sad?'

Jill harrumphed. 'Sad that her age has finally caught up with her, you mean? Sad she can't go gallivanting off around the world anymore, acting like some kind of hippy?'

A memory flashed through her mind. She would have been maybe seven or eight years old. Gracie had been away at university but was home for the summer break. Jill had adored her older sister and loved having her home. She always brought exciting things home in her suitcase, like that beautiful red velvet beret and a waistcoat fringed with tassels, all of which she let Jill parade around in, along with high wedged sandals that her toes peeked out from like shy mice. She enthralled her with tales of smoky bars and cinemas, dance halls and lecture theatres, all of which sounded thrilling and made Jill long to be a grown-up. One hot July afternoon, Jill had wandered into the garden and found Gracie lying face down on the lawn, reading a book, large sunglasses shielding her eyes from the sun.

'What's your book about?' Jill had asked. The front cover had an enticing image of a window thrown open onto a vista of rolling hills.

Gracie had lowered her sunglasses and taken on a dreamy, faraway look.

'I think it might be about me, Jill.'

Jill hadn't understood, of course. What seven-year-old could possibly grasp the captivation of a book like *A Room with a View*. But many years later, when she'd watched the movie adaptation as a lovestruck woman of eighteen, she'd recognised something of her sister in the character of Lucy Honeychurch. Yet it hadn't been something as elusive as love calling to Gracie through E. M. Forster's words back then, it had been the pull of Florence itself – and the romance of *adventure*. Gracie was an inquisitive, passionate woman, and passionate people made things happen; they commanded their own destiny.

'Or. . .' countered Emily patiently, pulling Jill back to the present, 'maybe because she was thinking about how close you were back then. She wrote to you all the time – from every place she went. I've read the postcards; she was constantly thinking about you back home and chiding you to keep up with your schoolwork and to be good for Nan and Grandad. What changed, Mum? What *is* it between you? Why is it *so* weird?'

'Oh, I don't know, Em. Maybe some are always destined to be *inside the gates of life*, whilst the rest of us have all the fun with the riffraff on the outskirts eh? I know which side I'd rather be on.'

Emily smacked her own forehead.

'Seriously? Not that again.'

When Jill made the knee-jerk decision to move to Frinton-on-Sea after Gary's passing, and, more prudently, after her own mother's death, which removed the primary obstacle to her setting so much as a foot in Essex, she had been unprepared for the long list of quirks attached to the Edwardian seaside town. Number one of which was the deeply embedded commitment to preserve a certain way of life for those who resided inside the boundary of the railway crossing – or, *inside the town gates*. This way of life, for a good many years, prohibited the presence of a public house, for instance, among other dens of hedonistic delight – such as fish and chip shops. Coachfuls of tourists were also banished, along with any notion of beachfront amusements. Thankfully, in the twenty-first century, many of these rules were relaxed. Honestly, the very idea of living in a town without a pub! Gary would turn in his grave.

And whilst Jill and Gary had owned a mock-Tudor three-bedroomed home in Hemel Hempstead, it had not fetched enough to snag one of the desirable *interior* properties of Frinton, but had secured her a lovely, modern semi-detached on the newly built estate just across the road from the proverbial town gates. Number fourteen Lavender Way was smaller than their old house, certainly, but living close to the sea offset any shortcoming on space. There was plenty enough to live on, with pensions and music royalties, so it had felt like the right thing to do. The *only* thing to do if she were going to make up for all that lost time. She just needed to work out how.

'What?' asked Jill, innocently. She examined her nails, which were painted a deep glossy pink. 'I'm just saying.'

'You're behaving like a spoiled child, Mum. Auntie Gracie and Uncle Andrew aren't minted, you know, they were secondary school teachers for heaven's sakes. Properties didn't used to cost the

18

equivalent of a Polynesian island forty years ago when they bought their dormer bungalow. Maybe you should be more grateful that you have this very nice house at all, in this very nice part of the country, because I can't even dream of buying a beach hut, let alone a flat, here or *anywhere* for that matter. The world's gone insane.'

Feeling slightly chastened, Jill folded her arms across her chest, which was easier said than done, as she had plenty of it.

'Look, love, I *am* grateful, truly. We might not be as close as we used to be, but I do love my sister, and I love living here. I've fitted in like a glove, haven't I? Look how busy I am with the café, all the baking, and there's the charity shop too. Did I tell you they asked me to do another day? Cynthia has rehearsals with the Christmas concert coming up, so naturally I said I'd take on extra hours. I don't know how I'll keep up with the housework, I'm busier than ever. But I just think Gracie could have been a little more welcoming too, that's all I'm saying.'

It wasn't the whole truth. But it was as much as she was admitting.

'I know, Mum,' sighed Emily. 'You're doing well. I'm happy for you. Really.'

This would be the time – the perfect time – to ask Emily if *she* was doing OK. But somehow, those words would not come.

'Right,' said Emily, crossing the kitchen to peck her mother on the cheek, 'I'm heading to bed. If I don't see you in the morning, have a great week and I'll see you Friday, OK?'

Jill nodded, turning to find a tin for the cake, ready for tomorrow. She couldn't disappoint her customers with dried-out icing now, could she?

'Night, love,' she called, knowing she wouldn't see Emily in the morning. Why would she want to start her already achingly long day at 5 a.m.? Though she knew she'd lie awake anyway, listening to the soft, hushed sounds of Emily as she dressed, cleaned her teeth and slipped from the house, leaving her alone in it for another four days.

After Emily had padded up the stairs and the tell-tale sounds of the toilet flushing and her bedroom door closing signalled that she was in bed, Jill reached into her handbag and pulled out her bright pink diary and the glittery ballpoint pen she kept with it and opened it on the worktop to examine her scrawled notes for the week ahead.

Monday, 4th November	*Café 10 a.m. – 6 p.m.*
Tuesday, 5th November	*Shop p.m. Fireworks?*
Wednesday, 6th November	*Call Sharon?*
Thursday, 7th November	*Shop a.m.*
Friday, 8th November	*Lorraine's Birthday. Keep Free*
Saturday, 9th November	*Café 10 a.m. – 2 p.m.*
Sunday, 10th November	*Invite G. & A, for lunch?*

She chewed the end of her pen, before making some alterations.

Monday, 4th November	*Café 10 a.m. – 6 p.m.*
Tuesday, 5th November	*Shop p.m.* ~~*Fireworks?*~~
Wednesday, 6th November	~~*Call Sharon?*~~
Thursday, 7th November	*Shop a.m.*
Friday, 8th November	~~*Lorraine's Birthday. Keep Free*~~
Saturday, 9th November	*Café 10 a.m. – 2 p.m.*
Sunday, 10th November	~~*Invite G. & A. for lunch?*~~

The fireworks display had, it seemed, come and gone and no-one had said a word about it. And she'd called Sharon last week on a whim, but it had gone straight to voicemail, so she'd left a message. Sharon hadn't called back. And Lorraine always celebrated her birthday in style, sometimes with a spa day, sometimes with a party, only this year she'd apparently celebrated it early. The photos had been all over Facebook this week. Sharon had been there, of course. No need to keep Friday free for trips to Hemel Hempstead. She was gradually being erased from their lives, not that it surprised her much; they'd been the wives of Gary's friends, after all. She'd been kidding herself to think they were her friends too.

And as for Gracie and Andrew, was there any point in wasting her breath? She'd invited them for lunch twice since moving here and both times they had been 'busy'. No reciprocal invite, of course, which was perhaps to be expected.

However, Jill was a resilient woman. She was Good-Time Jill, after all. She'd moved here for a reason and something as trivial as a little historic animosity wasn't about to get in the way of her game plan to make amends. Not if she had anything to do with it.

3

Gracie

The greensward was coated in a film of dew and the sea was a ribbon of grey. On a crisp autumnal morning like this, with no-one around but a lone dog walker and the overhead squawking of gulls, Gracie couldn't imagine a better place to be. She stopped at the kerb and bent to retie the lace on a pair of ancient Reebok trainers that may have been on her shoe rack since she and Andrew went through a phase of playing badminton with the Cartwrights back in the late nineties. That had been a by-product of marrying another teacher, all the extra-curricular invitations and expectations. Andrew had never been a social butterfly, only ever really in his element when exploring new terrain with Gracie, or pottering in his shed, a pursuit he had embraced in retirement with the fervour of a crazed professor.

She stood, then crossed The Esplanade to make a beeline for the iconic blue seafront pavilion, which was the designated meeting point for the Coast Path Runners.

'Auntie Gracie,' called Emily, spotting her approach, then walking towards her.

Behind her, a buff-looking fellow in leggings and absurdly chunky neon green trainers was performing one-legged squats. Another was stretching his calves. The poster girl for fitness stood beside the squatting man and tapped things into her watch with manicured talons – she had a vaguely familiar look about her, Gracie thought. This had been a mistake. She should turn back right now, apologise and say she was feeling a bit dicky.

Emily drew her into a hug when she drew level. 'You made it,' she said, beaming.

'Well, I hardly had far to come now, did I?' she said instead, not wanting to disappoint her niece.

Sixth Avenue, where Gracie and Andrew had lived for the past forty years or so, ran parallel to the seafront, or The Esplanade, as it was named, and was a humbler and more recent offshoot to the prodigious leafy Second, Third, Fourth and Fifth Avenues. Door to beach was usually no less than a five-minute walk, double that with Andrew on a good day.

'True,' replied Emily, blowing on her hands to warm them up, the vapour from her breath ballooning into the cold morning air. 'It's a nippy one today. Hope the others hurry up – we need to get going before we freeze to death.'

Gracie smiled to herself. It was a perfect morning as far as she was concerned. The kind of bright, clear day she loved to spend down on the beach with Picasso – made all the better for being out of season and free of day-trippers. Besides, it was only November and Emily was already in a woolly hat. How would she fare in January, when the wind off the North Sea sliced into your cheeks like razor blades?

'How many runners are there in the group?' she asked, glancing over at the pavilion, where one of the men had begun bouncing on the spot.

'Um, there's usually about six of us, give or take. Oh, here comes

Ray, you'll like him. He's ace.' Emily nodded to the road and Gracie turned to see a well-built chap, in a hi-vis vest, jogging along towards them. 'He runs here from Walton would you believe, only for us to turn around and run straight back there. Says it warms him up.'

Gracie mumbled, 'So much for being a beginner.'

'You'll be fine. And I told you, I'm still a beginner myself. Yes OK, I'm doing the marathon, but as far as I'm concerned, my only goal is completing it, even if I have to walk it.'

'Morning, ladies,' greeted Ray, jogging across the grass towards them. 'Been out recruiting, Em?' He nodded and smiled at Gracie.

'This is my aunt,' said Emily proudly. 'Ray, meet Gracie.'

'Pleased to meet you,' he said, a twinkling smile lighting up his eyes. 'Always good to see fresh blood, keeps us on our toes.'

Gracie laughed. 'I think, with the best will in the world, there's precious little about my person that could be described as *fresh*. But thanks for the vote of confidence. I'll need it.'

'Nonsense,' said Ray. 'You'll be right as rain, girl.'

There was an incredible warmth about the big man, who hadn't a hair on his brown-skinned, shiny head. Gracie liked him immediately.

'Let's go and meet the others,' said Emily, turning and leading the way.

'Here we go,' muttered Ray, 'bolster yourself for some dick swinging.' Then he swiftly followed up his remark with, 'If you'll excuse my language.'

Gracie raised an eyebrow, out of curiosity, rather than offence, because there was really rather little that could offend or shock a woman of seventy-two years who'd spent over half of them teaching in secondary schools.

'You'll see,' said Ray.

'Everyone, this is my auntie, Gracie,' said Emily, and Gracie noted a flush of pink promptly warm her cheeks. In the short time she'd spent with her niece, she'd noted how she hated being the centre of attention, *so* unlike her mother. Emily motioned to each of the assembled crew in turn. 'Ray, you've already met. This is Malik. . .'

A softly spoken young man in a baggy grey hoody embroidered on the shoulder with the word 'NewTek' nodded at Gracie. 'Pleased to meet you.'

Next, Emily indicated he of the luminous shoes. 'And this is Giles, and this is Kat.'

Each of them had smiled in greeting, all except for the poster-girl, Kat, who, if Gracie wasn't wrong, actually sneered down her perfect nose. It wouldn't be difficult to remember *her* name, her plucked and plumped features were positively feline. Presumably Gracie wasn't the kind of participant Kat expected to see within her running club, especially if, as Gracie was starting to suspect, she may be an ex-student of hers. It was bugging her that she couldn't place her.

'Just waiting on Oliver then,' said Giles. 'Al-ways wait-ing on Oliver,' he added in a lazy sing-song tone.

'Oh, didn't you see his WhatsApp message?' asked Malik, stuffing his hands into the pockets of his hoody. 'Done his hamstring. Won't be running for a while.'

There was a WhatsApp group? Lordy, what was she letting herself in for? She'd only just extricated herself from the constant pinging of Thorpington High Alumni and its bountiful teacher tittle-tattle. Gracie had cherished her years at the school, but did she *really* still need regular updates on the deputy head's halitosis? She had her old friend Linda to reminisce with over the good old days when overhead projectors and the staff smoking room were still the order of the day (not that she'd ever smoked herself, but it had been the nerve centre for only the very juiciest gossip – who was having an affair with whom, and suchlike). Although Linda had moved to Wales last year and she did miss their coffee catch-ups.

Giles scoffed. 'Right. Well, that's what you get for skipping cool-down.'

'Not sure that's completely fair.' Malik frowned. 'He pulled it playing five-a-side.'

'Whatever. All I know is he always gets in his car at the end of a run and expects to be fine. If you're serious about running, you do the cool-down. End of.'

'Well, I don't know about you guys, but I cool down just fine in the pub,' said Ray, effortlessly diffusing the conversation.

'On a Saturday morning?' asked Gracie in surprise.

'Not usually, no, although on a hot day that's sorely tempting. We run on Tuesday evenings too. On *Tuesdays* it's the pub.' He winked at Malik, indicating his usual partner in crime.

'What's all this I hear about the pub?' came a lilting Irish accent from behind.

They all turned to see a woman with a night-black pixie haircut who looked to be in her early thirties striding towards them with purpose.

'A run *and* a pint?' she asked. 'Now that's my kind of running club.'

'Sophia?' enquired Ray, tilting his head in question.

Aha, thought Gracie. *Another newcomer. Excellent stuff.* Nobody liked to be the new girl.

'The one and the same. How are ye?'

'Sorry, who's this?' asked Kat, somewhat rudely.

'Does *nobody* read their messages?' asked Malik, exasperated. 'Sophia contacted the CPR Facebook page and asked about joining the club. Ray added her to the WhatsApp group last week with an introduction.'

'Oh, I muted the chat ages ago, when Oliver kept forwarding those stupid memes. Last thing I want to see when I'm practising meditative yoga are pictures of beer-bellied football fans,' sniffed Kat, as though messages sent to her phone were automatically transmitted to her temporal lobe.

Malik shrugged. 'I thought they were quite funny.'

'Welcome, Sophia, it's lovely to meet you,' said Emily, her good manners prevailing. The others all followed suit, apart from Kat who merely looked her up and down.

I don't know about dick swinging, thought Gracie, but from where I'm standing, there seems to be an awful lot of pouting going on.

'Let's head off then shall we,' said Giles, running on the spot and checking his chunky watch. 'Anyone aiming for a PB today?'

'Obvs,' replied Kat.

Giles flashed the group a smug grin, then began to jog backwards. 'See you on the way back then, guys.' He saluted, then fell into a sprint, Kat falling into his slipstream, her pert derrière flexing beneath trendy, neon Lycra.

'If you're into smart watches and PBs, stick with them,' said Ray, pointing at their retreating forms. 'The rest of us are here for the moral support.'

'Oh, I'm just here to counteract the litre tub of Ben & Jerry's I hoovered up last night,' said Sophia. 'You'd think as a nurse I'd really know better, but to be sure I'll be doing it again, so this is going to have to be the payoff.'

Everyone chuckled and as Ray led the way, they all set off on a gentle jog towards the steps that led down from the greensward and onto the promenade.

As Emily fell into step beside her, Gracie discreetly whispered, 'And what, might I ask, is a PB when it's at home?'

'Personal best,' replied Emily. 'They're *obsessed* with beating their own run times.' Emily shielded her mouth with her hand. 'But personally, I think Kat's more obsessed with Giles than she is with her run times. It's embarrassing to watch. *And* he's a married man.'

The beach-hut-lined promenade stretched out before them, a pathway Gracie had traversed a thousand times, although probably never at more than a brisk walking pace. From here, with just the seawall separating them from the sandy beach, the path continued all the way to Walton Pier in one direction, whilst back the other way, it connected Frinton-on-Sea with the small village of Holland-on-Sea, and beyond that the larger tourist resort of Clacton-on-Sea.

'How far do you usually run?' asked Gracie, already feeling breathless and slightly concerned for her blood pressure.

'Just the length of a Park Run – to the pier and back. The others tend to run further, but *we* call it a day at that.' Emily gave a tight laugh. 'Although I guess I seriously need to up my game now and work towards being able to run twenty-six point two whopping miles, which is um. . .' she counted on her fingers '. . . blimey, eight and a half Park Runs!'

'Golly,' remarked Gracie, who had previously thought little of hiking ten or fifteen miles, but who was fast realising there was a considerable difference between rambling and running.

'Everyone alright back there?' called Ray, who was effortlessly bouncing along in long, lazy strides.

'Yep,' called back Malik, who lagged behind him.

'Just. . . grand,' gasped Sophia, puffing out her words. 'Jesus Christ, we've only just started, and I'm wheezing like a stovetop kettle.'

'You'll be fine,' said Malik. 'Think of all the ice cream you can eat tonight.'

'I'll be lucky if I can even make it to the freezer at this rate!' she retorted. 'Perhaps that's the point of it.'

Emily grinned at Gracie and mouthed the words *told you*. Feeling only partially reassured, Gracie gave a thumbs-up, having decided that giving a speech may be too ambitious at this early stage, and hunkered down to concentrate on breathing steadily in and out, with each pounding footstep.

It wasn't long before even the chilly breeze coming straight in off the water wasn't sufficient to cool Gracie's burning cheeks and she regretted her decision to wear a pair of leggings. For pretty much six months of the year, she lived in shorts, loose linen shirts and her favourite battered Birkenstocks. She had never been one for vogue and trends and had been somewhat amused to find herself considered 'cool' by students when the feted footbed sandal experienced a tidal wave of popularity. She'd been wearing them since her twenties for comfort, not style, and fifty years on, if you overlooked the salt and pepper tones scattered throughout her long hair, which she normally wore in a practical braid, and accounted for her well-weathered, tanned and wrinkled skin, she looked pretty much the same. Next time, if indeed there was a next time, she was wearing her shorts, even if it was November. Heck, she might even wear her swimming cossie too and wade out for a cold-water dip on the way back, the icy water was that tempting.

Somehow, and with several gasping walking stops along the way, during which Emily jogged on the spot until she'd caught up, Gracie made it to the pier at Walton-on-the-Naze, where Ray was casually chatting with a customer waiting at the little beach kiosk to be served.

Some way back, Giles and Kat had sailed past them in the

opposite direction, Giles with a smug grin, Kat looking as though she'd stepped from a sportswear photoshoot, complexion as fresh as a daisy, not a streak of sweat in sight.

'Caffeine, now *that's* an idea,' panted Sophia, veering off towards the kiosk.

'Uh-uh, not so fast.' Ray waggled a finger at her. 'Good things come to those who wait. Back we go, gang.' He twirled a finger in a 360-degree motion.

The man he'd been chatting with laughed and took his take-out hot drink from the server. 'See you tomorrow, mate.'

Ray raised a hand in acknowledgement, already leading the way back towards Frinton.

'Alright, *Dad*,' muttered Malik, pushing his glasses back onto his nose and sucking in a bolstering breath before falling back into a jog.

Gracie smiled to herself, enjoying the easy banter between this small group, who, until thirty minutes ago and with the exception of her niece, she'd never even met.

As they set off on the return journey, Ray slowed down to let the others pass, then fell into step beside Gracie and Emily.

'Hope you don't think I'm too bossy,' he said. 'Someone's got to keep these slackers on their toes and I'm afraid old habits die hard.'

'Ray used to be a firefighter,' supplied Emily.

'Really?' Gracie could well imagine it. He was a big man, in good shape, difficult to guess at his age.

'Yeah,' he said, his voice rich and gravelly. 'London Fire Brigade for twenty-five years, before tapping out.'

'Tapping out of the fire service? Or the city?' asked Gracie.

'Both.' He smiled. 'All this sea air and none of the stress. Best decision I ever made. Although I should credit the old man with that. He wanted to move here to live out his days beside the seaside,

30

so I followed him.' He shrugged as though such a big life choice had been decided on the flip of a coin. Gracie admired that kind of attitude; it spoke to her young self when the world had been at her feet.

'How long have you been here?' asked Gracie, panting between words, any benefit from the brief pitstop at the pier vanishing fast.

'Five years now. Almost long enough to consider myself a local, I reckon,' he laughed. 'Right, see you back at the ranch. Final sprint for me.'

With that, he accelerated and overtook the others, along with several dogwalkers who had braved the fresh November morning.

By the time they arrived at the familiar stretch of beach close to home, Gracie's legs were like jelly, but somehow, she managed the steps to the top without collapsing into a heap, which as far as she was concerned was a triumph.

'Well, how was it?' enquired Emily, as they approached the pavilion once more.

Gracie considered. Her lungs, which had been screaming, had now quietened to a hum but perhaps most unexpectedly, she felt rather invigorated. Not, as she'd imagined, ready for a soak in the bath and a restorative nap, but alive and ready for the day.

'Surprisingly good,' she said. 'But I know jolly well you were hanging back to keep me company, dear. Next time you go on ahead. I won't be responsible for hampering your training.'

Emily grinned. 'So, there *will* be a next time. Brilliant. I knew you'd get the bug.'

She'd walked into that one. Andrew would be most amused, and based on this morning's experience as she grudgingly got ready, she was sure to face a never-ending stream of his comedic quips, such as 'Can't remember what day it is dear, can you jog my memory?' And, as she'd sank onto the bed with a sigh and a pair of thick socks in hand and seriously debated bailing, 'What's that?' He'd sniffed the air. 'Surely not the smell of da feet?' The memory made her smile. He always had such a positive outlook, her husband, even though she knew he was often in pain. Yes, she decided, there would be a next time. She'd do it for Andrew, if not for herself, for all the runs he'd now never do.

'Right then, folks,' said Ray, rubbing his hands together, 'who's up for some of the good stuff?'

Gracie looked to him in question.

'Liquid refreshment of the non-alcoholic kind,' he was quick to clarify, 'and a hefty dose of calories on the side. Little Saturday morning perk.' He winked. 'Oh, hold up, here come the others.'

Giles and Kat sprinted across the grass, having extended their run in the other direction.

'Eight miles and a PB for me,' said Giles, fist bumping the air.

Over double the distance in less time, marvelled Gracie, her thrill of achievement ebbing away. *What have I just been doing, crawling?*

Damn her competitive nature. At her age she was lucky to still be active, let alone running.

'Well done. Coming for a cuppa?' asked Ray.

Giles said he had to get back and Kat didn't even furnish Ray with a response before marching away from the greensward.

'I'll see you next time, guys,' said Malik, peeling away. 'Mum's got the kids, better dash.'

'Are you coming?' Emily asked Sophia, who shrugged in bemusement. 'If there's cake, lead the way.'

'Where's everyone going?' asked Gracie, slightly puzzled at a group of runners keen to indulge in tea and cake straight afterwards. It seemed counterintuitive.

'Victory Hall. You're coming too, right?' asked Emily, her expression earnest and hopeful, but with a hint of caution.

In all the decades Gracie and Andrew had lived in Frinton, Victory Hall – the small red-brick community building – had been a familiar fixture in the town centre and the backdrop of many memories. When Nathan had been young, he'd attended Boy Scouts there and performed in the Christmas concert along with his primary school classmates. There had been regular jumble sales, craft fairs, exercise classes, children's parties, meetings of the history club, WI, art group and parish council consultations, as well as being home to Seashells Amateur Dramatics Society. Victory Hall was old and draughty, and some organisations now chose to use the more modern out-of-town Community Hub instead, but it was still the perfect size for more intimate gatherings and had bags more character too, with its arched windows and heavy red curtains.

On Saturdays and Mondays, it was also home to the Be Together Café, a community initiative she'd recently learned her sister had become involved with, since moving to the area.

If it was possible to grimace on the inside, whilst smiling on the outside, that's what Gracie did. Because she'd just been put on the spot and no amount of running was getting her out of this one.

'Sure,' she replied bouncily. 'Of course I'll come.'

'Brilliant!' beamed Emily. 'Mum will be so thrilled.'

Gracie gave an involuntary snort of disbelief, which she hastily disguised with a cough.

Because being thrown together with her sister after decades of distance between them. . . This wasn't going to be awkward in the slightest.

4

Jill

By the time it became clear Pink Silk were not going to reach the heady heights of Spandau Ballet, or Wham!, Jill had realised two things: one, she'd left school without so much as an O Level and her career choices were sadly limited, and two, she loved Gary deeply and couldn't give a flying fig about fame, or the knowledge that he would grow old ahead of her. When Jill was twenty-five, Gary was turning forty. His temples were streaked with grey, and Pink Silk had become the stuff of working men's clubs or the occasional cruise ship stint – work Jill hated for the periods of time she would spend alone. Band members were replaced, as their lives took them down new paths. Eddie, the original drummer, became an estate agent. Jonno, the keyboardist, fell in love with a Scottish lass and moved to the Isle of Skye to rear sheep on her father's farm, whilst Logan, the bass guitarist, found fame on a whole different level. Only Gary remained true to the original band, subsidising quiet spells by offering local guitar lessons, and occasional appearances on low-budget quiz shows, though his status as a celebrity even at the peak of Pink Silk's success was bordering on questionable.

For Jill's own part, she took a part-time job at the local primary school, working as a dinner lady. As far as Jill was concerned, the modern term 'midday assistant' did not do justice to the role she felt she'd carved out at the school, that of agony aunt, mother hen, friend, colleague and caterer (her Rocky Road was the stuff of 'legend', or so the kitchen staff said anyway). Personally, she tried to cut as much processed sugar from her diet as possible. Crisps and cheese were her usual downfall; her nemesis in the dieting trenches.

Another reason she'd taken the job was to gain some sense of affinity with her older sister. They would have something in common at last, a deep well of school-ish anecdotes to draw upon when they chatted on the phone, which never happened quite as often as Jill would have liked and was often cut short at Gracie's end by the arrival of a surprise visitor or a meal being ready, even when she phoned outside of usual mealtimes.

Her old job was one of the things she missed when she moved to Frinton nine months ago. The increasing level of care Gary had required before he passed away, had kept her busier than any job ever could, and now that he was gone and she was starting again, Jill sought out new ways to fill her time.

First came the voluntary job at the charity shop in the high street, which was where she met Cynthia. Cynthia was a robust woman, rosy-cheeked like a farmer, wearer of jerkins and lover of floaty scarves. One of those pillar-of-the-community types with fingers in pies and an ear to the ground, but also incredibly well liked. All the staff of Help the Hospice were primed to pluck the prettiest silk and chiffon scarves straight from donation packages on arrival, for her first refusal. Jill soon discovered the formidable woman, quite apart from being church warden and chair of the WI, had also founded the place where she now most loved to spend her time, her second volunteering position, and where she was currently listening to two octogenarians squabble over a proper noun – the Be Together Café.

'Eugene, if "zod" is in the Oxford English Dictionary, I'll get up on that table and do a tap dance,' said Harold, leaning back in his chair and crossing his arms across his chest as though the final word had been spoken.

'Well of course it won't be in the *Oxford* dictionary. But it will be in *a* dictionary – who said it had to be the *Oxford* dictionary? And a triple letter score too, huh?' Eugene rubbed his hands together and picked up the biro to write down his score.

'Uh, uh,' said Harold, reaching across and swiping the piece of paper away. 'Not so fast.' He tutted, as though scolding a naughty boy. 'It's *not* a word. You can't go around putting down any letters you like and calling it a word, that's cheating my man.'

Eugene pointed at the three yellowed tiles he'd placed on the board. 'Z. O. D.' – he spelled it out as though Harold was deaf, or stupid. 'Superman's arch enemy? Did your boys never read *Superman*?' He clapped himself on the head, squashing down his flat cap in a display of forgetfulness. 'Silly me, it was probably the *FT* for them at bedtime. Stocks and shares were far more interesting than kryptonite, I expect.'

Jill smiled to herself as she spooned sugar into mugs over at the kitchen hatch. It was the same every week, these two bickering away like schoolboys, causing havoc and hilarity.

Harold shook his head and with a weary shrug removed the tiles, pushing them back towards Eugene. 'Peter's an accountant and Patrick's a tax inspector. They are *not* stockbrokers. And you're *not* allowed to use proper nouns. Isn't that right, Jill?' he called, bringing her into the disagreement.

Jill put down the teapot and raised her hands in defence. 'Don't ask me, my love. I couldn't tell you the difference between a vowel and a vole. School was not my forte.'

Eugene's face broke into a twinkling grin. 'But, woman, you sure know how to bake a cake. What delectable delights have we on offer today?'

At this, Jill preened. The kind, cheeky gentleman with his freckled, wrinkled face, boyish charm and lilting Caribbean accent had won her over the first time she met him. He resided at the Beachcombers Retirement Village across the road but liked to complain at length that his fellow residents were like stuffed dummies, only with less conversation. He and Harold, a widower and ex-train driver, had discovered a mutual love of competitive board games, though today's choice was clearly contentious.

Harold muttered something under his breath about fillings and teeth and Eugene's smile widened.

'Sorry,' she said, cocking her head, 'didn't catch that, Harold?'

He straightened the tiles on his stand without looking up. 'Oh, just that it's a good job I don't have a sweet tooth, or I'd be fat as a pig coming here twice a week.'

Eugene winked at Harold then picked his rejected tiles back up.

Catching the gesture, Jill gave a tinkling, unsure laugh. Sometimes it felt like she was back in her old job supervising sniggering eight-year-olds in the school dining room, but she loved it all the same.

'Two teas and one portion of Death by Chocolate coming right up then,' she said, loading the mugs onto a tray and reaching for the cake tin.

'And what a death,' said Harold with feeling. 'Right then, Eugene, it's still your turn.'

After Jill had served the two men their refreshments and done a sweep of the room for other requests, she began wiping down one of the trestle tables when the doors to Victory Hall swung open.

'Hi, Mum!' Emily waved at her across the room, trailed by the usual motley crew she ran with on Saturday mornings, including Eugene's son, Ray.

Jill raised her hand to wave back, when someone she wasn't expecting appeared in the doorway too.

What the blazes was her sister doing here?

Generally speaking, the customers of the Be Together Café tended to be elderly, lonely or both. It was a community initiative to provide somewhere for people to go for a bit of company, a cuppa and a sandwich or a slice of cake at heavily subsidised prices. Ray popped along most Saturdays to catch up with his old dad and usually joined in a game of chess or draughts with anyone without a playing partner, such was his generous nature. Lately, Emily had been coming along too, and sometimes that nice young man from the running club, Malik. Today there was another new face besides Gracie, a wild-looking, flushed young woman with jet black spiky hair, whose gaze snagged on the jumble of board games as she passed them, exclaiming, 'Monopoly – jeez, that takes me back. Sweetest way to wage war among my family come Christmas time, that game.'

Gracie laughed and followed the group, which was when Jill spotted her sister was wearing trainers. She was *with* the runners. Gracie had been running.

Back behind the small serving hatch where Cynthia was cutting a cheese sandwich into triangles, Jill rinsed her cloth under the tap and eyed the runners. Ray introduced the newcomer, an Irish woman called Sophia, and Gracie to his dad and Harold, then there was the scraping of floorboards as they all pulled out chairs.

'Ah, what a lovely surprise,' crowed Cynthia, looking up. 'Your sister's here. *Such* a wonderful woman,' she added. 'Brilliant teacher too, my two liked her enormously.' She tilted her head and squinted as she took in Jill's bleached layers, rose-pink lipstick, animal-print tunic and leather-look leggings, then contrasted the ensemble with Gracie's utilitarian braid, make-up free, sun-kissed complexion and trim figure. 'You're really not alike, are you?'

Jill eyed the damson scarf encasing Cynthia's sagging throat, which reminded her of a chicken's crop, and had a fleeting urge to tug on the knot, despite being enormously fond of the woman.

'*Retired* teacher, actually,' she remarked, 'and no, we're not alike. I'm the younger, prettier one.' Jill took the plate of sandwiches from Cynthia. 'Table by the piano, yes?'

Cynthia nodded, her mouth quirking in amusement, and Jill turned to make her way over to the lone woman in the corner with the stained raincoat and unbrushed hair, who she hadn't seen at the café before.

'Cheese sandwich?' she asked, placing the plate before her.

The unfamiliar woman looked back at her with a blank, bewildered expression before seeming to remember why she was there.

'Yes, thank you', she said, sliding her handbag towards her and retrieving a small, zipped purse. 'How much is that?'

'One pound please, love. But I can throw in a slice of Death by Chocolate for an extra fifty pence?' Jill added.

The woman nodded, then slipped long, bony fingers into the purse and pulled out two coins before dropping them into Jill's upturned hand.

Jill looked down at her palm and saw one pound coin and one shiny gold button, the sort you would find on a smart wool coat, in place of a fifty pence piece. She was about to correct the woman on her mistake, but she was already munching hungrily on one of the small sandwiches, so she decided against it. Probably had deteriorating eyesight too, a treat Jill discovered she'd also been blessed with upon turning fifty, almost overnight.

'Thanks,' she said with a smile, 'I'll bring over the cake.'

On her way back to the kitchen, Jill made a show out of stopping to greet her sister with a bosom-squashing hug.

'*So* good of you to pop by, Gracie. We need all the support we can get. These cakes don't make themselves you know, and none of us knows when we might need a little company and a kind ear ourselves; we're all getting older, after all.'

At Gracie's po-faced expression, she gave a manic little laugh and inwardly kicked herself. Why could she never just keep her trap shut? Now her sister would think she was calling her old and decrepit and in need of friendship, when in truth it was Jill who wanted the company. Why else would she give up her Saturdays to serve hot drinks and referee games of Scrabble?

'I'd heard you were doing some volunteering, Gillian,' Gracie said with a perfect, polite smile. 'Good for you.'

'Auntie Gracie came running with us today,' chipped in Emily. 'You should come along sometime too, Mum.'

Anyone else might have been surprised at a seventy-two-year-old woman suddenly taking up running, but Jill knew Gracie of old. She was fitter than most people three decades younger and had that annoying habit of being generally good at most things she tried.

'Now who would feed these rascals a never-ending supply of tea and cake if I came running with you then, hey?' she asked, quirking a brow in Eugene and Harold's direction and making light of the invitation. *Running?* She'd rather sort through endless bags of soiled undergarments, which was her own personal idea of hell and a more frequent occurrence at Help the Hospice than anyone would like. *Who* honestly thought it was OK to drop off bags of dirty laundry at a charity shop?

There came the sound of muffled laughter, as Ray bopped his dad on the shoulder at something he'd said. Such a doting son, and a bit of a looker too, rough around the edges, with cheeky rogue vibes. Jill subconsciously sucked in her tummy and plucked a notepad and pen from the pocket of her tunic.

'Right then, gang, what can I get you?'

With a long list of drinks, snacks and surprisingly more requests for Cynthia's bland sultana cake than her own decadent chocolate creation, Jill retreated to the kitchen, just as the Irish woman said, 'So, Eugene, you know how to play Twister, right?' to raucous squeals of delight. Gracie's gravelly, gut-deep laugh rang out loudest of all as she settled down with her new friends. 'I'm kidding. I meant Jenga. Of course I meant Jenga. Shall I set it up?'

A dribble of disappointment trickled through Jill's gut. This tiny comfortable corner of a new community that she'd carved out for herself suddenly felt awkward and strange. As though it was no longer hers. And it was an achingly familiar sensation.

5

Gracie

Over the course of the next few weeks, Gracie kept running.

Emily had been right, which surprised her, it *was* somewhat addictive. She never especially felt like going, especially as winter closed in, but Picasso drew one of them from bed early each morning anyway, so on Saturdays, she decided, it may as well be her.

On the second run, she'd taken Picasso along too. This seemed like a good idea, until the dog developed a fascination with Malik and constantly tripped him up by circling his ankles to sniff out her new friend.

'I don't get it,' said Malik, 'dogs usually hate me. I don't particularly like them either. Why is this one so obsessed with me?'

'Sure you're not slathering your balls in peanut butter, Mal?' called back Sophia, who had taken the lead.

Malik had retorted, 'Last time I checked, it was definitely shower gel in the bottle. But with my kids, quite honestly, you just never know.'

'Enough with the testicle talk, please,' panted Gracie. 'I've always rather liked peanut butter, and this conversation is quite putting me off.'

That had been the last time Picasso joined the CPR in any official capacity. However, the duo had partaken in a little extra-curricular burst of jogging some mornings with no-one around to distract the mutt from her focus on the horizon. Gracie had discovered something revelatory – that the simple act of bounding from one foot to the other, for no other reason than she could, made her feel purposeful and free.

One frosty early Wednesday morning, on the return leg of a brisk walk along their usual route, Gracie heard her name.

A familiar figure sat on the step of an open doorway to a sherbet lemon-coloured beach hut, nursing a tin mug.

'Ray!' she greeted him in surprise. 'I didn't know you had a beach hut?'

He smiled warmly back at her. 'Couldn't afford a seafront property when I moved here, but I part-own this with a mate. I love watching the sun come up in the morning, can't beat it.'

He tilted his head to the golden glow of a low winter sun cresting above the grey-blue water. It had a deceptive warmth to it when the clouds parted. 'Can I make you a brew?'

'That would be lovely, thank you.'

Ray pulled himself to standing and reached inside for a folding chair.

'Sit yourself down and I'll stick the kettle on.'

Gracie did as instructed, and settled down into the camping chair, already knowing she'd regret it when it came to getting her legs going again, but for now she would enjoy the pitstop and a cuppa, and Picasso would enjoy it too.

On cue, Ray brought out a small saucer which he placed on the ground next to Picasso and poured from a water bottle. She lapped at it thirstily.

'I'm curious. Are all your pets named after Cubist painters?' he asked.

'Not at all,' she laughed. 'We have a cat called Banksy and our last dog was Renoir. Andrew fancied Toulouse-Lautrec, but I convinced him it was a mouthful. Ex-art teacher here,' she explained, pointing at herself. 'Do you have any pets?'

Gracie had enjoyed chatting with Ray on their runs but still couldn't get the hang of spitting out more than a few words at a time without gasping for breath, so conversation was sparse.

'Nah. Wouldn't be fair in my flat. Besides, I'm out and about so much, what with Dad and the lifeboat, I'd barely find the time for dog walks.'

'Oh, I didn't know you volunteered with the RNLI?'

Ray shrugged, ever the humble gent. 'I like to keep busy, and it seemed like something I could do, after all the years on the job.'

Gracie nodded, recalling that he used to be a firefighter. She'd hazard a guess he was late fifties at most, a similar age to Jill. Must have taken early retirement. She was about to ask him more about his former career when he clapped his hands and said, 'Right then. Tea.'

He retreated inside, calling over his shoulder, 'Sugar? Milk? Biscuit?'

'Just milk please, better pass on the biscuit as Andrew's making breakfast.'

'Here you go.' He handed her a mug then settled back down on the step.

'Not too shabby a view, is it?' he asked, looking out at the expanse of blue. 'I remember coming here as a kid. The church used to organise these coach trips to Clacton, and it was the highlight of the year for me old mum. I think that's why Dad was drawn here. Somewhere she really loved to come.'

'I think it's wonderful that you moved here to be near him; you both seem very close,' said Gracie, who had observed their easy company and playful banter. In some ways Eugene reminded her of her own late dad: warm, gentle and with a great sense of humour. The total opposite of her mother who'd been strait-laced and reserved. But love worked in mysterious ways, for they'd seemed happily married on the whole.

Ray laughed. 'He certainly keeps me on my toes. But yeah, it's working out well. And how about you? Didn't your sister only move here recently? It must be nice to have her around.'

'Oh, yes, quite lovely.' Gracie nodded a little too eagerly, then buried her face in her mug.

After a few beats, Ray said, 'Tell me to mind my own business, but why do I get the feeling you're not quite as enthusiastic about that as you're pretending to be?'

Gracie rolled her eyes. 'Whatever gave you that idea?'

She had continued to frequent the Be Together Café each Saturday morning, and despite the initial minor awkwardness between her and Jill, had enjoyed getting to know the others over coffee. They really were a fabulous bunch. Of course, Giles and Kat never rejoined them after a run, apart from to gloat about their run times before slipping away to look beautiful somewhere else. Kat was a Pilates teacher, apparently. Probably performed planks and toe taps in the very place they supped coffee and cake each week. It had taken a couple of sessions, but Gracie had placed the woman eventually. Ironically, it was a customer in the Be Together Café who had provided the missing piece of the puzzle, a slight, bird-like woman whom Gracie recalled from parents' evenings as being the subdued, shamefaced mother of Kathleen Banks, or Kat, as she now went by. The poor woman had been dragged into school repeatedly over Kathleen's truancy and unacceptable behaviour. She'd broken down in tears once after Gracie described her daughter as frustratingly talented, yet resolute in disrupting class. She'd been referring to an incident involving Kat, printmaking ink and another girl's folder of coursework which had not ended well. Despite Kat's cosmetic enhancements, a coldness lingered in her eyes that Gracie couldn't forget.

Ray laughed. 'Dunno. Could be the giant iceberg in the room whenever you and Jill are sharing airspace. I keep thinking we'll all be dragged overboard at any minute.'

Gracie chuckled, although it really wasn't a laughing matter. How best to summarise their strained relationship?

'Jill can be. . .' She paused, searching for the right phrase.

'A lot?' supplied Ray, with a kind smile.

Gracie looked at him and nodded. 'Don't get me wrong, I love her dearly. Zaniness and all. We just have a little history; that's the best way I can put it. I'm sure we'll work it out.'

'Ah,' said Ray knowingly. 'We all have suitcases full of that. Well, I hope you resolve it one day. But, for what it's worth, I think she's solid, and you know Dad worships the ground she walks on right?' He grimaced. 'Even called her a "fine figure of a woman" the other day.'

Gracie spluttered on her tea.

Ray chuckled. 'I'm serious! You should hear him when her back's turned. It's all "Jilly this" and "Jilly that". He even likes her cakes! Or, at least, pretends to.'

At this Gracie laughed out loud. En route to Victory Hall that first Saturday morning, Emily had warned her, 'Whatever you do, don't order the Death by Chocolate. She made it last night. Whichever other cakes are on offer, choose those. Same goes every week. I'll give you the heads up. Forgo these tip-offs at your peril.'

Thoroughly bemused, Gracie had ordered fruit cake instead and found herself watching the bird-like woman across the room, Kathleen's mother, as she absently forked great lumps of Jill's sticky, brown chocolate cake into her mouth. She didn't know what she was expecting, the poor woman to start foaming at the mouth or something, but instead she'd finished what was on her plate and then retrieved a tissue from her handbag and used circular motions to wipe it clean. As though she were simply at home, doing the dishes.

'It's a really good thing she's doing,' said Gracie. 'The Be Together Café is a wonderful idea. I hate to think of anyone being lonely. Don't know what I'd do without my Andy.' She sipped at her tea thoughtfully. Did he resent the amount of time she was spending with her new friends? Was he lonely at home without her, stuck with pottering around the house and tinkering in the shed whilst she racked up the miles on her still healthy legs?

'You should get him to come along to the café too. He could meet us there after our run,' said Ray, tipping the dregs of his tea from his mug and ruffling Picasso's fur.

'Perhaps I will.' That wasn't a bad idea, thought Gracie, not a bad idea at all.

Two weeks before Christmas, and weighed down with bags, Gracie let herself in the front door.

'Bloody hellfire. I've never seen so many people queuing to get in the butcher's. Anyone would think we're on rations. Do any of these people realise you can eat turkey all year round? It's called chicken. Never have been able to tell the difference. Give me a good beef rib any day and judging by the queue, I'm glad I ordered ours last week. . .' Andrew appeared in the kitchen doorway with the phone under his chin. 'Sorry!' she mouthed. 'Who is it?'

Andrew raised a palm, signalling she'd find out in a moment.

'Yes, well I get your point, but you really needn't worry. She's absolutely fine. Fit as a fiddle in fact.'

He put his hand over the mouthpiece. 'Nathan,' he mouthed. 'Had to cancel.'

At this, Gracie's heart sank. She let go of the handles of her shopping bags and they sagged onto the doormat.

It had been two years since his last trip home and Gracie had been counting down the days to Monday, when their beloved son and his beautiful antipodean family would come strolling into Arrivals and she'd wrap him in a hug so tight she'd crush them both.

'I know, I understand. Listen, your mother's just walked through the door, let me hand you over.' Andrew said his goodbyes and passed the receiver to Gracie, who stared at it blankly for a few seconds then took a fortifying breath.

'Nathan,' she said, regretting the coolness in her tone immediately and not for the first time wishing she could reach through the phone and touch his cheek. Reassure him she loved him, that she always would. At least it wasn't a Facetime call. At least he couldn't see the disappointment written across her face, because she knew it would be as obvious as war paint.

'Hi, Mum,' he said, his adopted Australian drawl even more pronounced after fifteen years of living there. 'Yeah, so the girls have both gone down with chicken pox, and Beth's never had it, or her jabs, so she's isolating for a bit. We booked flexible fares, thank God, so for a fee we can still use them another time.'

At this, Gracie's heart lifted. Perhaps they could come later in January instead, once the girls were better – wouldn't that be a way to see in the new year.

'Are they OK, the girls?'

'Liv's pretty crook, but Charlie feels fine. Sorry, Mum. I know how much you were looking forward to it. We all were.'

Gracie had her doubts that Beth had been looking forward to a bitter, grey Christmas in Essex. She'd much rather be celebrating on the beach with her own sprawling family back in Queensland, but these are the sacrifices one has to make when one marries an Englishman with a heart of gold.

'Obviously we're disappointed, but these things can't be helped. The most important thing is that you're all safe, sweetheart,' she assured him.

'Right, well I'm glad you think that because I've just been chatting to Dad about this fitness lark of yours.'

Gracie wondered if she'd heard right.

'Sorry? What fitness lark?'

'The running club, or whatever it is. Look, I know Park Run is a big thing over there. It's big over here too. But – and don't take this the wrong way – aren't you a little old to be pushing your body like that? I know you've always liked walking, and you could probably out-hike the lot of us, but running? That's a totally different bag. You could fall, Mum. At your age you don't just bounce, you know. You could break a leg, a wrist, your ribs. Worse. What if you fell and there was no-one to help? How would Dad cope with you out of action?'

Gracie, who was normally a woman with much to say on matters, found herself lost for words. Maybe it was the shock of someone pointing out unpalatable facts; *at your age, you could fall, how would Dad cope?*

In all honesty, she had never even considered that she could fall. When she moved, on her steady, trustworthy feet, she felt like a child again. Free. Without limits. Untethered from the tedium of retirement and a life unspooling in the rear-view mirror. When she ran, she only looked forwards. She was going somewhere. It had never occurred to her she was being reckless. Was she? Or was Nathan worrying unnecessarily?

'Well, firstly, it isn't about fitness, Nathan. It just feels good to get out there. And secondly, I'm hardly Mo Farah. I go for a light jog, dear. Barely more than a brisk walk. And more to the point, I'm not on my own, which is, I'm sure you'll agree, the entire point of a *club.*'

Andrew, who'd been lurking in the kitchen, pretending to water the houseplants with an empty watering can, gave her a thumbs-up. Bless that man. Always on her side. Not that there needed to be sides when it came to how she used her body.

'OK, OK,' placated Nathan, who had perhaps picked up on the doubt in her own conviction. 'All I'm saying is, please be careful. I worry about you, that's all.'

The conversation moved on to lighter topics, such as Nathan's recent promotion and his work in renewable energy, which he could enthuse about for hours, but the niggling feeling remained that her son viewed her as old and redundant. As someone who needed coddling, whose adventures were numbered, as were her days. In Gracie's agile mind, all those things couldn't be further from the truth, but was he right?

When Saturday came around – the last meeting of the Coast Path Runners before Christmas – Gracie laced her trainers thoughtfully. She'd long since ditched the leggings and embraced the stinging cold on her bare legs, galvanised by the knowledge that within minutes she'd be grateful for it. This week she was first to arrive at the pavilion, which stood proud and inviting against a stark white winter-heavy sky, its blue and white clock tower showing her she was ten minutes early. She ducked inside to shelter from the chill and watched a sailing boat as it zipped along the horizon, carried by the same biting breeze that whipped through the branches of bare trees along The Esplanade. So far, they'd been lucky with the weather, a perk of living by the coast, for it was rare that heavy snow made an appearance, but it wouldn't be long before wintry conditions hampered their morning routines. She might be bloody-minded, but she wasn't stupid. The hard of the promenade would be a deathtrap in such conditions. She'd ask the others what the protocol was when rain or ice stopped play.

A sound like ripping Velcro alerted her to another, just as Kat rounded the corner, adjusting the fluorescent snap strap on her upper arm.

'Oh, it's you,' the younger woman said, not even bothering to disguise her disdain as she joined Gracie inside the hut.

'How are you, Kathleen?' enquired Gracie, seizing the opportunity to engage with the woman who had thus far snubbed them all. She may well be choosing to ignore the fact that Gracie had been her teacher, but that didn't have to work both ways.

'Fine,' she snapped, her voice nasal and tiresome. 'And I go by Kat now.' She began tapping away on her watch, pointedly turning away from where Gracie sat on the wooden bench.

Gracie was having none of it. She got up and wandered over.

'So, tell me about this thing,' she said, indicating the bulky wrist piece. 'What does it do besides tell the time? Can it predict the future?' She risked a joke, then regretted it when Kat's lip rose in the corner.

'It's a *Garmin*.' She said the word as though Gracie was soft in the head. 'It does everything. GPS. Heart rate. Pacing. There's no point even thinking about taking running seriously without one. Not that anyone here does anyway. Except for Giles, that is.'

Ah, well she walked into that. So much for thinking a little one-to-one time might break through that acrylic exterior, which extended far, far beyond her razor-tipped nails.

'Oh, I don't know, Emily certainly takes it seriously.' Gracie gave a friendly laugh. 'After all, it doesn't get much more serious than the London Marathon, does it?'

Kat looked her in the eye. '*Anyone* can run a marathon. It takes real training to break three hours though, that's what Giles is going for. I would be too if I'd got a place in the ballot. But there's always next year.'

'I didn't know Giles had a place?' Gracie said, surprised. Nobody had mentioned it to her, at least.

'What's that about Giles?' asked Malik, appearing, breathless, at the entrance. 'Sorry I'm late, couldn't find Theo's left shoe.'

51

'It's only us so far,' said Gracie. 'Everyone else is probably busy with it being so close to Christmas. I was just saying to Kat, I didn't realise Giles was running the marathon too.'

Malik clapped his hands together. 'Oh yep. Running the marathon. Climbing Everest, have you heard about that one? And last I heard from Theo, he's going into school to give a talk about the riveting world of being an investment wan — sorry banker. I bet Year Three will be unable to contain themselves in their haste to whizz through the remainder of primary school, high school, university and secure themselves a spot on the Square Mile.'

Kat made a noise of disgust. 'You're so pathetic. Will you ever get over the fact his son built a better rocket than yours?'

Malik's eyes widened. 'Um, I think you'll find *Giles* built that rocket? The homework was set for the seven-year-olds to do, not their egomaniac dads.'

Gracie looked from Malik to Kat and back, marvelling how two full-grown adults could behave with little more maturity than most of her ex-students.

'Alright, children?' asked Ray, leaning against the doorway.

'It's way too claustrophobic in here,' said Kat, elbowing her way past Malik and out onto the greensward.

'Goodness,' said Gracie. 'And to think I ever thought running would be boring.'

'Never a dull moment around here,' grinned Malik, who had clearly enjoyed winding Kat up. He tugged his phone from the zipped pocket on his sleeve and swiped the screen. 'OK, well it looks like this is all of us. Giles is away for Christmas with his family. Nothing from Emily so far and nothing from Sophia either.'

Was that Gracie's imagination or did a little of the buoyancy leave Malik's tone at the end of his sentence. It was a shame if Sophia couldn't make it; she liked the girl immensely and had Christmas cards for them all back home, which Andrew was bringing to the café afterwards.

Ray tipped his head. 'Shall we wait for Emily or get going? Its unlike her to be late.'

'Let's go. She'll catch up, or meet us later,' said Gracie, knowing her niece wouldn't expect everyone to wait around.

Outside on the grass, Kat loitered at the fringe of the group. Without Giles there to preen over, or talk of personal bests, Gracie wondered if she would deign to run with them, or steam ahead on her own. Otherwise, what was the point of even coming along? It was hardly a running club if you never actually ran with the club.

Kat looked up and pulled a face, before letting out at a bitchy cackle. 'Who on *earth* is that?'

Everyone turned to see Emily streaking across the grass, trailed by a voluptuous woman in a riot of psychedelic colours. It was as though she'd ransacked a string of charity shops for the most garish ensemble of ill-fitting sportswear conceivable and teamed the outfit with the closest approximation to running shoes she owned, which happened to be a pair of sheepskin Uggs.

'Sorry we're so late,' called Emily. 'Mum wanted to come along, but we had to drop the cakes off at the hall first.'

'Yoohoo,' called out Jill, crossing the green behind Emily in what could only be described as a waddle, owing more to the slack footwear than any physical limitation. She held a phone in one hand and a plastic bottle in the other. 'I've got "Born to Run" on my playlist and a Powerade at the ready! Let's do this!'

Please God, no.

Gracie smiled back through gritted teeth. 'How lovely.'

6

Jill

Four days later, the chorus to Band Aid's chart-topping hit played out as Jill surveyed the room. They might not exactly be feeding the world, but they were doing their best to give these Frinton residents a Christmas dinner and some laughter.

Eugene was dapper in a cream shirt, V-neck jumper and a burgundy bow tie, even eschewing his trusty flat cap for the occasion, to reveal a halo of smooth scalp fringed with tufts of steely grey afro. His companion for the day was his son, Ray. Harold had been collected by his eldest son that morning for two days at their home in Billericay, and even though Beachcombers Retirement Village was laying on a decadent three-course Christmas feast for their residents, Eugene had apparently insisted he'd prefer the more humble festive offering of the Be Together Café. Volunteers Cynthia, Jill and Emily had been hard at work since the early hours to provide the turkey roast, with a cameo appearance from Cynthia's husband Roger in full Santa costume, as he handed out small gifts, made by the local WI. This, apparently, was a role Roger took most seriously, and was to be found throughout December atop a chauffeured sleigh, ringing a bell and ho-ho-hoing.

'And, what, pray, am I to do with this?' Eugene remarked, holding up his unwrapped gift, a hand-knitted tubular object, embellished with buttons, beads and ribbons. 'Aha, I see – it's a legwarmer! But, why only one? How do I choose which leg I wish to keep warm? Do they have to take turns?'

'I don't think it's a legwarmer, you daft old git,' laughed Ray. 'Although, I'm not quite sure *what* it is – perhaps Jill can enlighten us?' he asked with a mischievous smile.

Jill recognised what it was immediately and did her best to stifle the sadness that streaked through her. She'd hoped that being here today, on the first Christmas Day since losing Gary, she would be distracted from the gaping hole in her life.

'It's a twiddle muff,' she said softly. 'The elderly can find them comforting. As well as those with dementia. It can help to calm the mind, keeping the hands occupied.'

'Oh, well,' Eugene blurted, puffing out his cheeks in protest. 'Best we give this to someone else then, because I'm neither eld—'

'*Dad*,' warned Ray, cutting off his outburst. 'I think maybe what you *meant* to say was thank you.'

'Why don't you try this instead,' said Emily, coming to the rescue with another gift from the small bag of spares Cynthia's husband had left behind for any latecomers. 'I've a feeling this one might be more up your street.'

She handed Eugene the wrapped gift and they watched as he opened it to reveal a jar of homemade whisky marmalade, which put a satisfied smile on his face.

Jill took the twiddle muff and tucked it into her bag. She'd take it along to the charity shop in the new year.

'Right, you two, sit yourselves down, I'll hold the fort,' instructed Cynthia, brandishing a fresh jar of cranberry sauce and a steaming jug of gravy. The guests had all been fed, and Cynthia had made a big thing about spending the evening with her family and not wanting to spoil her appetite, so now it was Jill and Emily's turn to eat the reheated roast.

'Thank you, this looks amazing,' gushed Emily, as Cynthia placed two hot plates in front of them, piled with sliced turkey and shop-bought pigs in blankets for Jill, nut roast for Emily, three anaemic roast potatoes, several Brussels sprouts and a dollop of red cabbage.

'*Bon appétit*,' she said, rubbing her hands together with a flourish and disappearing back to the small kitchen.

'Hmm,' said Jill in hushed tones. 'I think *amazing* is a stretch. Adequate, maybe, for £2.50.'

'Well, I'm starving, and it smells great.' Emily fixed her with a smile. 'I've really enjoyed being here today, Mum. I think you're awesome giving up your Christmas Day to be here, helping others.'

Jill reached across and gave her daughter's hand a quick squeeze. What she didn't say, as she glanced along the trestle tables, which had been pushed together and covered with red tablecloths, encouraging the customers to integrate, was that she didn't have anywhere else to be. A few seats away, the timid woman with the unkempt hair was picking through the torn remains of a Christmas cracker. Her name was Rita, Jill had learned, and she'd been dropped off at the hall by her daughter, that ghastly runner who'd looked down her nose at her the other day, and who was spending the day with friends. What sort of daughter offloaded their mother into a day centre run by volunteers on Christmas Day, then buggered off with friends? The thought brought a lump to her throat as she watched her own kind darling girl cut into a potato. She was so lucky to have her.

'I wonder what Gracie and Andrew are doing today,' she said, her mind straying to departed family, lost through death. . . or other means.

'Auntie Gracie said they were having beef. They'd ordered an enormous joint apparently, because Nathan and the others were meant to be here. She was joking that they'd be eating it until next Christmas.'

'Charming,' exclaimed Jill. 'Drowning in beef but don't think to invite us. Not that you'd eat it of course.'

'Ssh,' hushed Emily. 'They knew you would be here, helping out – I told them.'

'She didn't mention it on Saturday, when we saw her for the run. I could have rearranged, changed my plans.'

Emily's cheeks flushed. 'Mum! Keep your voice down. How could you have rearranged Christmas Day – it only happens once. What would all these people have done?'

Chastened, Jill put down her knife and fork. 'I just meant, perhaps we could have gone over in the evening or something. That might have been nice.'

'I *am* popping over this evening, actually. I've got them a small gift. Come with me,' said Emily, washing down her food with a glug of the cheap wine they'd bought from the cash and carry.

Jill thought back to the last time she'd seen her sister. Running along the promenade, with her strong, lean limbs and easy banter, whilst she had heaved, wheezed and sweated before stopping dead and doubling over breathless after only ten minutes. Gracie hadn't even noticed, just carried on running. So much for trying to find common ground and ways to reconnect; she was only thankful she hadn't found the actual ground, with her face. It had been a humiliating morning, reminiscent of PE at school, and she had absolutely no desire to repeat the experience.

'No, I don't think so,' she said. 'Not without an invitation.'

'Mum, don't be so stubborn. I don't have an invitation. Since when do you need an invitation to pop by your own sister's house and wish her Merry Christmas?'

Jill gave a small, mirthless laugh. 'Clearly you don't know my sister very well.'

'And *that*,' said Emily, jabbing the air with her fork, 'is exactly what I'm trying to change. They're both lovely, Andrew and Gracie. As you'd know, if you gave her a chance.'

Oh, the irony, thought Jill. As if everything she'd done this past year hadn't been about second chances. Just what was it going to take to get Gracie to notice her efforts; her need to put things right.

There came the distinctive tinkling sound of a metal teaspoon against glass from the other end of the table and gradually the chattering room descended into quiet.

'I think a toast is in order,' declared Eugene, pushing back his chair noisily on the polished floorboards.

'Hold up, Dad,' said Ray, hurrying round to his side of the table. 'I've been counting the sherries and you're on about number five.' He helped him unsteadily to his feet.

'I would like to wish everyone here a very Happy Christmas and a prosperous New Year, and to thank these angels from heaven for bringing us all together today and for the delicious food. To Cynthia, young Emily and the lovely Jilly, Merry Christmas.'

Jill kept a smile plastered on her face, whilst inside her heart squeezed. Gary had been the only one to ever call her *Jilly*.

The diners murmured Merry Christmas and got back to the more important business of scraping bowls clean of custard and brandy sauce.

Rita, who had barely spoken a word, turned to the woman next to her.

'That poor man has lost his mind,' she stage-whispered. 'He thinks it's Christmas!' She shook her head, bewildered. 'I bet it was his idea to serve us this. . .' she poked at the remains in her bowl '. . . brown stuff with custard, can't think what it's called.'

Emily caught Jill's eye and gave her a sad, understanding smile. One of the things they had found hardest as the horrible disease took hold of Gary, was when he had no longer recalled that he'd ever been a musician, a facet of his character as permanent and distinct as his DNA. And yet, if a guitar was placed in his hands, a familiar tune would eventually emerge from it, and Jill could close her eyes and pretend.

'A Merry Christmas to all of you too, it's been an absolute pleasure to spend the day with you,' chimed Jill, raising her glass and managing, as ever, to also raise a cheery smile.

Ray returned the smile, but there was uncertainty in it. Perhaps he had overheard Rita's remarks, or perhaps something in Jill's face had betrayed her sadness. It had only ever been Gary who'd really known what lay behind Good-Time Jill's smile. Everyone else took her at face value, which was hardly surprising, since she'd become so very accomplished at putting on a front. She must make more of an effort in company.

That evening, feeling like a teenager being dragged to Sunday School, Jill waited on the doorstep whilst Emily rang Gracie's doorbell.

She could probably count on one hand all the times she'd stepped over the threshold. Still, at least there was no danger of bumping into her mother now, even if the reach of her scorn did extend well beyond the grave.

When the door opened, it was Andrew – adorned with an orange paper hat – who stood on the other side, a box of Trivial Pursuit cards in hand.

'Oh, you've got company,' said Jill at once, already stepping backwards, 'we won't disturb you.'

Emily grabbed hold of a wodge of her mother's coat, keeping her firmly planted beside her.

'Merry Christmas, Uncle Andrew,' she said with all the cheer of a doorstep carol singer, whereas Jill's fa-la-la-la-las were snuggled up on the sofa back home with the Terry's Chocolate Orange she'd been fantasising about all day.

'What a lovely surprise. And a Merry Christmas to you both too! Nope, nobody else here, just us and our annual tradition of seeing who can remember the most answers, seeing as we've played this so many times.'

'Who is it, Andy?' came Gracie's voice from the lounge.

A light of recognition sparked in Andrew's eyes. 'Robert de Niro,' he called over his shoulder, then stepped back and opened the door wide. 'The actor who starred in *Taxi Driver*. Knew I knew it.' He tapped his head. 'Come in, come in. Gracie will be thrilled to see you.'

Ever the optimist, thought Jill, who had always found Andrew to be a kind, if puzzling, man.

In the hallway, Emily stood on the backs of her Converse to remove them without unlacing them, divested herself of her coat and sailed through to the lounge before Jill could even unzip her own high-heeled ankle boots. Clearly, her daughter felt quite at home here.

Jill followed Emily and Andrew into the lounge, where a coffee table was laden with Trivial Pursuit, a small bowl of nuts, two glasses and a half-drunk bottle of Rioja. A repeat of *The Vicar of Dibley* played out on the TV in the corner and a ginger cat was asleep on a rug beside the fireplace, where a log-burner flickered, illuminating the room and its tasteful, eclectic wall art, in a warm, soft glow.

Gracie's eyes widened in surprise. 'And your mum too, how lovely!' She scrambled to her feet, from where she'd been sitting up against the sofa, the head of their friendly old mutt resting in her lap.

How did she manage to sit cross-legged on the floor like that? Jill had trouble bending down to cut her own toenails these days.

Gracie wrapped Emily into a welcoming hug, then to Jill's surprise pulled her in close too, giving her an affectionate squeeze.

'Merry Christmas both of you. How was it at the hall?'

'It was actually really fun,' said Emily, demonstrating with a wide smile, which made Jill's heart soar, just how much she had enjoyed their day together. 'How about you two? How was your day?'

'Oh, you know. Same as the last twenty or so. Never quite the same when the little 'uns grow up.'

There was a rose-tinted sadness staining her cheekbones. Perhaps she'd quaffed too much wine.

'I got you both something,' said Emily, handing Gracie her gift, which was neatly wrapped in brown paper and tied with a red bow. Emily recycled literally everything. Even the annoying hanging loops most people cut from tops and dresses; everything could be repurposed. 'It's for both of you.'

'You shouldn't have done that, love,' said Andrew, limping over to his wife. That knee had got a lot worse since the last time Jill had seen him, his gait now bow-legged and sluggish.

Together, they peeled back the paper to reveal a beautiful scented candle, an assortment of seashells pressed into the wax.

'It's made of soy, so it's kinder to the environment and all the decorations were foraged on the beach.'

'Wait, you made this?' asked Gracie, astonished.

Jill glowed with pride. She'd received a similar candle from Emily, as well as a stunning pendant necklace formed of aquamarine sea glass she'd collected while on her weekly beach cleans.

'I make all my gifts,' said Emily. 'I hope you don't think that's cheap.'

'I think it's wonderful, and you've no business saying you're not very creative – this is a piece of art,' gushed Gracie, taking the candle and giving it pride of place on the mantelpiece. 'So thoughtful too. Thank you, darling.'

Slightly embarrassed by the distinct *lack* of thought she'd put into her gift, a last-minute scan of the sideboard that had yielded an unopened bottle of Baileys, but supposing it was better than nothing, Jill thrust it at them. 'Happy Christmas.'

'Terrific. Andrew likes a tipple at Christmas don't you, dear?' Gracie said, passing it to him, indicating that she herself hated the stuff.

Magic. Another deficit in the brownie points column there, Jill, you're doing well at this.

'We got you both a little something too, actually,' said Gracie, crossing the room to the small Christmas tree in the corner and reaching down for two wrapped gifts.

Excellent, thought Jill, who had done the same thing herself countless times before, in the days when Gary would have forgotten to tell her that so-and-so and you-know-who would be popping by for drinks. Always best to have a stash of 'spares' under the tree, inexpensive generic gifts to suit all – tins of Scottish shortbread or bottles of port. Logan had always been partial to port and you really never knew when he'd pop up, only that when he did, he'd be in for the long haul. And now *she* would have to be the one to feign delighted surprise and gratitude at receiving such an impersonal gesture.

But as Jill peeled back the Sellotape under Gracie's watchful gaze, careful not to tear the paper so it could be reused as Emily had taught her, it wasn't to find a random box of confectionery at all.

It was to the ear-thundering rush of a blast from her past.

'Do you still like it?' asked Gracie, doubt having crept into her tone. 'I can return it. I just thought. . .'

'No, I love it. Thank you,' said Jill, a torrent of emotions coursing through her.

'Wow! That's so retro,' said Emily, peering into Jill's hands. 'Let's have a sniff.'

Feeling she had little choice in the matter, Jill removed the lid from the small bottle of Body Shop White Musk and squirted Emily's wrist.

Jill consoled herself that as far as her older sister knew, it had been her favourite perfume and was a kind, nostalgic gesture. She wasn't to know that it carried with it the stench of 1981 and a period of her life she'd rather forget.

7

Gracie

For restless, active people like Gracie, the interminable period between Christmas and New Year dragged like no other. Andrew was unfazed, drifting between small DIY jobs he'd started but never finished, and the long list of projects that drew him to his shed for hours on end. He thrived on the freedom retirement afforded, content to work on his latest hare-brained invention until midnight, if the fancy took him, with no regard to timeframes, appointments or responsibilities, beyond any engagements he had with his wife.

For Gracie, school holidays had always been about frantic packing; the finding of mislaid maps, torches, gloves, flasks and the loading of their car to get on the road and enjoy their break as fast as possible. She'd had it down to a fine art by the end, never a minute to be wasted. When Nathan was little, they'd holidayed at beach resorts or castle-strewn coastlines. Then, as he'd grown older and more inquisitive, they'd revisited some of the destinations from Gracie's past: European cities and rural villages, off the beaten track. Inevitably, Nathan had grown up with a love of travel, and caught the bug himself. Until one day he never come home after falling in love with an Australian backpacker on a year-long tour of south-east Asia.

She hated all this endless free time and felt like a caged animal now the bad weather was drawing in. Thankfully Emily felt the same, and since the Coast Path Runners were taking a short break for Christmas, she'd enlisted Gracie to be her running buddy as she gradually amped up her training schedule in preparation for the marathon.

It had been nearly eight weeks since that first Saturday morning run, and Gracie was inordinately proud that she could now run to the pier and back with just one small break halfway.

'I'm keeping going, Auntie Gracie,' panted Emily when they reached the pavilion. 'I'm going for 10k.'

Gracie gave her the thumbs up and slowed to a stop; even though she was managing 5k herself these days with relative ease. Next time, she decided, she'd push on a bit further, see what she was made of.

'See you tonight,' Emily called back. 'And remember, sparkles!'

Gracie sighed. How had they got themselves roped into a New Year's Eve party? It had never really been her thing, all that queuing for drinks, fighting for a seat and strangers kissing you on the cheek. But still, lots of her new friends from the running club would be there and it would be nice to drag Andrew away from the automatic toothpaste-squeezing device he'd been designing, which had so far resulted in the loss of her pasta-making machine and two sets of her kitchen tongs, as he'd perfected each prototype.

Gracie crossed the greensward and instead of heading towards home, she turned right and strolled along The Esplanade until she reached Connaught Avenue, the town's main thoroughfare and home to Frinton's high street shops. Thankfully she'd slipped her debit card into her back shorts pocket this morning, because she'd entirely forgotten the brief, 'to wear something sparkly'. The closest thing in Gracie's wardrobe to sparkles was an emergency foil blanket, kept on the top shelf with other old camping gear, and she wasn't sure that counted. *Well, if I can't find something in here. . .* she thought, spotting the bubble-gum pink and white sign for Adele's Accessories and crossing the street, *I might just have to resort to it.*

Six hours later, and after eventually coaxing Andrew away from his project, Gracie pushed open the doors to the Sail and Anchor. As with most other licensed establishments in Frinton, it wasn't an old-fashioned inn, trading on centuries of tall tales and boozy myths. It was twenty years old and used to be a building society. But whatever the pub might lack in oak woodwork soiled with the patina of time and grime and horse brasses on the wall, it more than made up for in atmosphere.

'Gracie! Andrew!' came a deep voice, soaring over the tops of revellers' heads and slicing through Queen's 'Don't Stop Me Now'.

'There they are,' said Gracie, shouting into Andrew's ear. 'Oh good, looks like they've got a table.'

They pushed through the jolly crowd to where Emily and Jill sat at a round table, along with Sophia and Ray's dad Eugene. Ray was at the bar, giving his order to a harassed bartender.

'What are you having?' he called over to them. 'My round.'

'A G and T,' called back Gracie, resorting to mouthing the words and forming the shapes of the letters with her fingers when it became clear he couldn't hear her above the din. Andrew mimed the pulling of a pint.

Predictably, Jill was head to toe in sequins. Even her shoes were metallic, horribly pointy things that made Gracie's toes throb just looking at them.

'Nice tiara, Gracie,' said Sophia.

'Why thank you,' said Gracie, reaching up to check the diamanté-encrusted monstrosity was behaving itself atop her head. 'It was the most sparkly thing I could find.'

'You look like you raided a Disney princess's dressing-up box,' said Jill, laughing, until she saw Gracie's face and then picked up her drink and buried her face behind it instead.

'I'll have you know Adele of Adele's Accessories told me all the girls wear these to prom. Ridiculous tradition that is. What was wrong with the good old-fashioned school disco? Back in my day you had a quick snog behind the bike sheds, then got home in time for cocoa. None of this ball gown and Bentley bollocks.'

Sophia let out a squeal of laughter. 'I bloody love your aunt,' she said into Emily's ear, though everyone could hear, 'mad as a box of frogs but top class.'

Emily grinned back at her. The two girls were fast becoming good friends.

'No Malik this evening?' asked Gracie, ushering Andrew in to sit beside Jill and taking a seat herself next to Eugene, as Ray returned with the drinks.

'He has the kids. I don't know how he puts up with that ex of his, putting her new baby and her new bloke before her own children time after time. They haven't stayed with their mum in weeks, so he told me.' Sophia shook her head in distaste.

'Ah, but we can never know what goes on behind closed doors,' said Eugene sagely. 'Everyone has their cross to bear.'

'I'll drink to that,' said Jill, downing the rest of her glass and placing it back on the table with a thud before picking up the fresh drink handed to her by Ray.

Was that a dig?

Gracie inwardly sighed. She thought genuine progress had been made between them, especially after Emily did such a sterling job in getting Jill over to their house on Christmas evening, a plot cooked up between them by text message during the day. And she'd seemed to like her present. It was one of the things Gracie had loved about having a much younger sister all those years ago, being able to treat her to the latest fashionable garment, cassette or make-up item when she was still a teenager. How she had droned on about that damned perfume. *Everyone wears it,* she'd pleaded, *it's not even expensive, why won't Mum let me have it?* Eventually, Gracie had encouraged Jill to get a Saturday job so she could buy her own little luxuries. But she'd still loved to spoil her. Until everything changed. Until Jill shunned their mother, then drifted away from the rest of the family, leaving Gracie to wonder what they'd ever done to deserve it. And now, she was here, levering herself back into her life, which both delighted and perplexed her. It just didn't make sense.

'Is that Kat?' asked Ray, motioning across the room. 'She looks different.'

'Maybe because that strange gaping thing in her face is a smile,' said Sophia. 'Don't think we've seen one of those before. It's a transformation to be sure.'

Gracie spotted her, standing with a small group, near the back of the room, glass of Prosecco in hand, hair blow-dried to perfection. She caught her eye and gave a little wave, but Kat simply turned her back.

'Cow,' muttered Sophia.

A little while later, Gracie got to her feet. 'Right, folks. Our round, same again everyone?'

Andrew made to stand too, but Emily jumped up instead. 'Stay there, Uncle Andrew, I'll help.'

Living in the same area where you've taught all your life *can* have its drawbacks. Gracie and Andrew met as newly qualified teachers at a school in north London, but after falling head over heels in love, both she and her nerdy science teacher fiancé realised they disliked the city immensely. There followed a relocation to Essex and new jobs for each of them, with Gracie taking a post at a local secondary school whilst Andrew commuted much further afield to Ipswich. Essentially, what that meant was, Gracie couldn't buy loo roll without someone hollering 'Miss Jenkins!' whilst Andrew could have traversed the high street in his dressing gown, and no-one would utter a word. He'd just be that likeable, mildly eccentric chap who hums to himself in the post office queue. No nosy students or suspicious parents on *his* patch.

However, at times like this it was a boon.

'Miss Jenkins – quick, squeeze in here!'

It was Max Tavistock, a giraffe-like ex-student with a flair for graffiti and spliff-rolling. He was well turned out now though; handsome, in fact.

'Go in front of me,' he said, giving her a sheepish grin. 'You'll be here forever otherwise.'

'Why thank you, Max,' said Gracie, sliding herself past him and yanking Emily through the gap before it closed. The queue for the bar was five-people deep.

Beside them, arms folded on the bar top as he waited to be served, was Giles.

'Hey,' he said, with a nod. 'Busy in here tonight, huh? Not really my thing but the wife fancied it.'

'It is, but it's a great atmosphere,' said Gracie, who was relaxing and starting to enjoy herself. Perhaps she'd avoided public places, or rather students and parents, for too long. 'Did you have a good Christmas?'

'Lovely, thanks. You?' asked Giles.

Gracie assured him she had, whilst also noting this may have been the longest conversation she'd had with the man yet.

'How's the training going, Emily?' he asked, as the bartender placed a glass of wine in front of him and began to pour a pint of lager.

Emily pulled a face. 'OK, I think. But I need to work much harder; April will be here in a flash.'

Giles nodded. 'I hear you. Let me know if you want any tips; this will be my first full marathon, but I've done the Milton Keynes Half and it's not for the faint-hearted.'

'Cool,' said Emily, 'thanks. I've been extending my run times but need to work on tempo.'

'It can be tricky,' agreed Giles. 'Believe it or not, I don't steam off to avoid everyone,' he laughed, 'it's just a pace that's comfortable for me.'

Beyond the bar, Gracie watched Kat watching them. She was probably only here to spy on Giles, hoping for a moment alone with him, even though he was here with his wife. Were they already having an affair? she wondered. Or perhaps it was wishful thinking on Kat's part. From what Gracie remembered of the girl, she'd been a devious minx.

Back at the table, as the clock inched its way closer to midnight, conversation moved on to more serious matters, such as just what *was* the best Christmas song of all time. Andrew fancied Nat King Cole (ever the romantic softie), whilst Sophia was fiercely advocating for Irish punk band The Pogue's 'Fairytale of New York'. Then, in quite possibly the most serendipitous moment ever, two things happened. Firstly, Sophia's gaze drifted upwards from Ray's where he'd been arguing for East 17, and her face lit up with a wide grin.

'Alright, guys! Mum and Dad are watching the kids. Not too late, am I?' said Malik, prompting everyone, now many drinks in, to break into rowdy, backslapping cheers.

Secondly, the final bars of Elton John faded out to be replaced by the distinctive piano melody and gravelly, drawled opening lyrics of 'Fairytale of New York'. Everyone got to their feet with a loud whooping and began swaying along. Everyone but Andrew, who Gracie shuffled up next to, placing one hand on his good knee.

'Are you alright, love?' she asked, painfully aware of how limited he must feel, surrounded by all these youngsters. Even Eugene, who was a good ten years older, was up and grooving on down.

'I'm absolutely fine,' he assured her with a warm smile. He checked his watch, squinting to read the time. 'Five minutes to go. So then, any New Year's resolutions for you this year? I'm considering taking up micro-brewing.' He lifted his glass to his lips. 'Plenty of willing guinea pigs round here.'

Gracie laughed, watching them all sing their hearts out.

'Actually, yes. I'm going to run 10k. Then when I've cracked that I'll work towards 15, that's my resolution.'

Andrew shook his head, laughing. 'Now, coming from the woman who trained each year for the parents race at Nathan's school sports day, why doesn't that surprise me?'

Gracie tutted. 'Don't exaggerate; I merely did a few stretches.'

Yet she couldn't resist a smile at the memory of sailing past the other mums to victory, four years in a row.

'How long have we got?' asked Emily, appearing in front of them. 'I'm desperate for a wee!'

'About thirty seconds,' called Andrew.

'Bum, can't hold it. Gotta go!'

Gracie watched as Emily, cute as a button in a sequinned short jumpsuit, black tights and silver pumps headed towards the ladies' loos. She watched as her niece turned sideways to shimmy past a group of partygoers, oblivious to the platform-sandalled foot that pinged out at a ninety-degree angle, striking Emily across the shin and sending her plummeting, head first down some steps and out of view.

All around them, people stood and began chanting the annual countdown.

'Ten. . . Nine. . .'

Gracie jumped to her feet and yanked hard on the sleeve of Jill's sheer blouse, making her spill her wine, then tore off in Emily's direction.

'What the hell?' came Jill's outraged voice above the chants as she followed after her.

'Seven. . . Six. . .'

Emily lay flat on her back on the floorboards outside the door to the toilets. Her tights were laddered down one leg, and her foot pointed in a disturbingly unnatural direction.

'Emily!' gasped Jill, clapping eyes on her daughter and dropping to all fours beside her. 'What happened?'

Emily looked back at them both, bewildered, then closed her eyes. A single tear began to trace its way down her cheek, just as the pub erupted into a chorus of 'Auld Lang Syne'.

'I'll get my phone. Stay there,' barked Gracie.

Fighting her way back to the others, Gracie batted away the streamers that rained down upon her and shrugged off a handsy chancer who leaned in for a kiss.

'What's happened?' asked Sophia with concern as Gracie grabbed her handbag.

The others looked on, confused.

'Emily's hurt,' said Gracie, turning on her heel.

Half an hour later, as the last of the revellers trickled away and fluorescent strip lights transformed the pub into a stark, sticky space littered with empty glasses, Gracie and Andrew watched Emily be stretchered into a waiting ambulance. Jill climbed in beside her, shrouded in Ray's grey wool coat, which he'd insisted on lending to her before walking Eugene home.

'Call us as soon as you know anything,' entreated Gracie, shivering on the pavement.

'I will,' replied Jill.

Then the ambulance doors closed, and it drove away.

'Are you sure yous will be OK getting home?' asked Sophia from beside them.

Sophia had been a godsend, her knowledge and experience as a district nurse coming into its own as she took control of the situation and asked Emily gently, but firmly, to describe her level of pain. She'd taken the phone from Gracie and could be heard telling the emergency call handler that she suspected a broken ankle, and possibly cracked ribs.

'We'll be fine, you get yourself off home,' said Andrew, leaning into his stick. 'We're only five minutes up the road. Thank you for everything you've done, dear.'

Sophia waved his thanks away. 'I'm just so sad to see the evening end like this. Poor Emily, what rotten bad luck.'

Gracie said nothing.

But she knew perfectly well there had been nothing unlucky about Emily's fall. Emily had been tripped on purpose, and she'd watched Kat do it.

8

Gracie

Two weeks into January, Gracie accepted that Nathan wasn't coming. They'd spoken on the phone twice, at Christmas and on New Year's Day and not once had he mentioned their postponed visit. In fact, he spent a good amount of time telling her all about an upcoming work trip to Dubai in February they planned to turn into a family holiday and the charity they had chosen to offset their flight's carbon footprint against. She wondered if they'd simply upgraded their postponed UK flights, but didn't like to ask. She ran a finger over his present which sat on the sideboard, along with Beth's and her grandchildren's, their small artificial Christmas tree long since packed away and stowed back under the stairs. The gifts were starting to gather dust.

'Not running tonight, love?' asked Andrew, appearing in the doorway with a tea towel in hand and a saucepan.

Gracie had begun running with the CPR on Tuesday evenings too in the run-up to Christmas, but now that Emily was out of action it had sadly lost its appeal. Not to mention the fact that if she saw that beastly woman Kat again, she wasn't sure what she'd do.

When Gracie had confided in Andrew about what really happened in the pub that night, her charitable husband had sat back in his chair and blown out a long, cautious sigh.

'I'm not saying your mistaken, Gracie love. But are you certain malicious intent is what you saw? Because that's a pretty damming accusation.'

Gracie, who was by nature level-headed, had taken a moment to gather her thoughts.

'Well, Kat was with a small group of women in that corner, and she was perched on a bar stool. I know she was wearing sandals, because I remember thinking to myself who in their right mind goes out on a bitter winter's night in bare toes. Who else would have deliberately stuck out their foot to trip up our Emily? She's a jealous, vindictive cow who absolutely hates the fact Emily is, or rather *was*, running the London Marathon with Giles.'

'That's all as may be,' Andrew had said, ever the voice of reason, 'but if you didn't actually *see* that the foot was attached to Kat's leg, then you can't be absolutely certain it was her. And even if it *was* her, it's your word against hers that it wasn't an accident. It may *well* have been an accident. Think about it.'

Gracie had thought about it. She'd done little else in the days that followed, especially after she'd gone along to Jill's house to see Emily, fresh from hospital with a cast up to her knee and crutches.

'Six to eight weeks,' Emily had said miserably. 'Six to eight weeks with this cast on, and then physio for another month. My marathon is well and truly over.'

Of course, Jill was content to fuss around after her, and it was decided that Emily would stay in Frinton until she was off crutches at least. Her employer had been supportive, offering the opportunity to work from home until she was fighting fit.

And so, with Andrew's diplomatic words ringing in her ears,

Gracie had shown up that first Saturday morning in January, resolved to keep running for Emily's sake, and to show her support for the group. Everyone had crowded around, keen to know how Emily was faring and offering their good wishes. Including, to Gracie's outrage, Kat.

'It's just sooo awful,' she'd crooned, forehead wrinkled in faux concern. 'Poor Emily, I know how much she was looking forward to the marathon, such a shame.'

Behind her back, Sophia had raised an eyebrow.

'Is she serious?' she'd asked as they'd fallen into step, Kat motoring off ahead after Giles. 'She wouldn't know jack shit. I don't think she's ever said so much as hello to Emily, let alone had a conversation.'

That had done it, as far as Gracie was concerned. She simply couldn't stomach being around the vile woman again. Even if it did mean giving up a hobby she'd come to love and losing touch with people she'd come to admire. That, she'd decided, that Saturday morning, after kicking off her trainers on the doormat, had been her last run with the Coast Path Runners.

Dragging her attention back to the present and trying to ignore the niggling knowledge that her friends would at this very minute be getting ready for their Tuesday night run, Gracie waved a hand at the wall. 'Do you think we should redecorate in here?' she asked, ignoring her husband's question. She'd now missed two sessions, and had studiously been ignoring WhatsApp. She gathered up the unopened gifts, drawing a line under Christmas. 'How about a nice bright colour, freshen the place up for spring?'

'I think,' said Andrew, wiping around the pan in his hand and slinging the tea towel over his shoulder, 'that if you got outside for a run, you'd realise you couldn't care less about the walls. Never have done in forty years. Always said you'd rather sit in a field and look at nature's palette than line Mr Dulux's coffers.' His eyebrow quirked. He was quite right of course. Gracie had always been far too practical for interior design. Stick her in front of an easel and she was in her element, relishing the glide of a paintbrush across canvas, but put a paint chart in front of her instead and there was simply nothing more mind-numbing.

'I can't stand to even look at her,' replied Gracie, aware she sounded like a slighted fourteen-year-old and feeling about as mature.

Andrew limped into the room and pulled her into a hug.

'I know, love. But what about your other friends, huh? Bit unfair, leaving them all to suffer Jill's cakes alone, don't you think? And I'm rather missing my card games with Eugene and Harold.'

At this Gracie laughed into his shoulder. His jumper smelled of sawdust and solder, with an undertone of yeast. That shed of his would be a tinder box, all that drilling, sawing and now fermenting of hops too. Good job he didn't smoke.

Andrew was quite taken with the Be Together Café and had already fashioned a non-slip device to help Harold open jars and bottles, ignoring Gracie when she told him there was already a gadget on the market for exactly that purpose.

Gracie pulled away and looked at her watch. 'I might just make it.'

'Off you pop then,' said Andrew, tapping her lightly on the bum. 'Best to take it run day at a time.'

Gracie shook her head at his lame pun and went off in search of her trainers.

'Gracie!' cried out Sophia, her flashing armband strobing across the gloaming. 'We were wondering where you've been.' They stood beneath the Victorian splendour of the former Grand Hotel. The magnificent building, now converted into luxury flats, stood watch

77

over the pavilion across the road, which could just be seen in silhouette, and beyond that, the sea.

'Hey, Gracie,' chimed in Ray. 'Everything OK?'

'Everything's fine. Are we fit?' she said, inhaling the cool air deep into her lungs as though it were medicine. Behind Ray, Giles was stretching, no sign of Kat. She raised a hand in greeting.

'Absolutely. Let's go,' said Malik. 'Great to see you, Gracie.'

They set off in single file, tracing the pavement that ran adjacent to the seafront, before bearing right into residential streets. On Tuesday evenings, the group took a well-lit route, the inky promenade too dangerous to navigate in darkness. Their modest circuit, most conveniently, terminated at the Sail and Anchor, where they slowed to a stop outside the pub, their breath forming clouds beneath the streetlights.

'I'll stop for a quick lemonade,' said Sophia. 'I did twelve hours straight today, so you'll have to prod me if I fall asleep.'

'You did twelve hours and *still* came out for a run?' asked Malik, incredulous.

'What can I say? I'm committed.' She pushed open the door to the pub.

Gracie had her suspicions as to what precisely drew Sophia out on a freezing cold night after a twelve-hour shift, and she was pretty sure it wasn't just the running. The younger woman complained with every other footstep, even though she was getting better, faster, and somehow, she always seemed to end up running beside Malik.

Gracie had realised tonight, perhaps more than ever, that she was committed too. She loved every minute of it. Every last stinging breath and aching muscle made her feel alive and *not* running for the last two weeks had been a kind of agony.

'I'm doing another loop. Catch you all on Saturday,' said Giles, sprinting away.

Seated at the same table they'd all shared on New Year's Eve, Gracie's thoughts turned to her new year's resolution.

'Anyone fancy trying to hit 10k with me on Saturday?' she asked, before taking a sip of her orange juice. She had a doctor's appointment in the morning and didn't fancy stinking of booze.

'Sure,' said Ray. 'I could do with pushing myself. Why not.'

'What, are you after running the marathon yourself now, Gracie?' laughed Sophia, taking a large gulp of her drink.

Gracie tutted. 'Of course not. I'd just like to see if these old, wrinkly legs will carry me that little bit further, that's all.'

'Away with you. You're fitter than most of us put together,' said Sophia, then added, 'Apart from Giles, and Kat. Possibly your man Ray too.'

'But not me. Charming,' said Malik.

Gracie laughed out loud, happy to be back with her friends and their lively, well-meant banter.

The next day, Gracie rapped on Jill's blue front door, taking in the neat front driveway and garage doors which were still adorned with fairy lights. Although knowing Jill, they were likely a year-round fixture.

Eventually, Emily got to the front door, crutches in hand.

'Hello, love, is your mum not in?'

'She's doing an extra shift in the charity shop. Something about Cynthia having bell-ringing practice.'

Gracie nodded. 'Ah. Yes, she likes to spread herself around, does Cynthia.'

Emily grinned. 'I think Mum's in competition with her to be best all-round busybody. She taxied someone from the café to their chiropodist appointment yesterday.'

'That was good of her. Brought lunch.' Gracie held up a shopping tote. 'How does mac 'n' cheese sound?'

'Bloody fantastic. If I have to even sniff another mini spring roll, I think I'll die. Mum must have bought the entire canapé freezer section in Iceland. Who did she think was going to eat it all? She didn't even invite anyone round over Christmas.'

'I'm sure she wanted to be prepared, that's all,' said Gracie, following Emily and closing the door behind her. 'She's a social butterfly, your mum.'

'Hardly,' snorted Emily. 'She hasn't seen any of her old friends since leaving Hemel Hempstead. I don't think she goes anywhere apart from the charity shop and Victory Hall, or running errands.'

Interesting, thought Gracie, who had always had quite a different impression of her sister.

'How are you feeling? Still in pain?'

She waited until Emily had settled back into a deep blue velvet armchair and helped to prop up her leg with cushions. It was only the third time Gracie had been inside Jill's home, and she took in the clean, bright space with its new, modern furniture. It was a home still undergoing its stamp of authenticity, as though the occupant were experimenting with colour and style but couldn't settle on a theme.

'It's not so bad now. I'm just so frustrated I can't get out and run.' Emily looked anguished. 'It's suffocating being stuck here. I hadn't realised how much I loved it.'

Gracie squeezed her niece's hand. 'I get it. I feel the same. It gets under your skin, doesn't it?'

'The worst thing is letting all those people down. All that money pledged for the Alzheimer's charity, and it was just the start. I feel like I've failed my dad.' Emily picked at a loose thread on the cut-off section of her jean leg that finished above her cast.

Gracie perched on the arm of the chair and wrapped an arm around Emily's shoulders. 'Now that's complete nonsense, darling, and you know it. None of this can be helped, and people must have to withdraw from the marathon all the time. Nobody is going to think any less of you for it. And as for your father—' she forced Emily to look her in the eye '—do you think he would be anything other than proud of you? Of the kind, caring young woman you've become? Of course not. He'd be bursting with it, love. We're all so proud of you.'

Emily attempted a small smile, and it tugged at Gracie's heart. She did not deserve this injustice and worse still, she didn't even know her accident was likely not an accident at all. Well, Gracie certainly wasn't going to enlighten her. Best to let her think she tripped and fell; the truth would only eat away at her, tarnish her with its venom.

'I had a message from Kat the other day,' said Emily, bringing Gracie up short.

'Oh?' She tried to keep her face neutral. Had the ghastly woman actually owned up? Nay, apologised?

'Yeah. She told me something.'

Gracie braced herself. 'OK.'

'Apparently, if you're running for a charity, there's a chance you can swap your place with someone else before the cut-off date for confirmed participants in January. But they'd have to be running for the same charity.'

'Oh, is that right?' asked Gracie.

'Yeah, I checked online. Apparently, I could even defer my place to next year if I wanted to. Or. . . I could just let Kat have my place. She offered to take it, which was good of her.'

Whatever Gracie had been expecting, it had certainly not been that.

How would Kat even know that, unless. . .

The answer, of course, presented itself to her with all the

ceremony of a marching band. Sabotaging Emily's race hadn't been impulsive, or spiteful, it had been deliberate and strategic.

Disgust rose, like bile, in Gracie's throat. Surely to goodness that wasn't what this was about.

Had Kat purposefully hurt Emily with the intention of taking her place?

How could anyone even contemplate such a thing? Gracie considered Emily's reasons for wanting to run the marathon in the first place: in memory of her father, and to raise vital funds for the charity that had supported him and the family. The motives jarred so starkly with any selfish reason Kat may have, it made the situation ten times more deplorable.

Heck, there were about a dozen better reasons why Gracie should run the marathon herself, instead of that despicable woman. For starters, she was family and for another thing she had more fortitude in her little finger than Kat would ever know.

Emily was still talking; something about letting Kat take her place and trying again next year, but Gracie was no longer listening. She'd been sidetracked by a heart-stopping notion. An idea that bloomed quickly, warming her cheeks and setting fire to her blood. Adrenalin spiked through her, laced with rage. How *dare* that woman? There was no way on God's green earth she was getting away with this. Gracie couldn't tell Emily what she knew to be true; she couldn't break her heart like that. But there *was* something she could do. Kat's scornful words that day as they'd waited in the pavilion drifted back to her: '*Anyone* can run a marathon.'

Is that right, now, Kathleen.

How about we put your theory to the test. And how about Nathan's concerns whilst we're at it? Let's see if anyone's ever *too old* to run.

'Do you know what, Emily,' said Gracie, the plan solidifying in her mind by the second. 'I don't think that will be necessary,' she said, raising her chin and fixing Emily with the full force of her conviction. 'No need to bring Kat into it at all. We'll still raise all that money for Alzheimer's, Emily. In fact, we will raise more. Because *I* will take your place, dear. I would like to run the London Marathon, and you are going to help me.'

Emily stared back at her as though she'd lost her mind.

'Sorry, what? Auntie Gracie – you can't run the marathon. That's insane. You know every year people *die* doing it. Heart failure or exhaustion. I don't even know if I'd have managed it, but I'm nearly fifty years younger than you. It's not safe.'

Gracie got up and stood in the middle of the room.

'I can assure you, it's perfectly safe. I've been to the doctor's only this morning, for one of those OAP-MOT things they insist on summoning us to every couple of years. Do you know what Dr Montague said? She said I had the heart rate and fitness of someone nearly half my age. All those years of active holidays and daily dog walks on the beach have clearly paid off.'

'But. . .' Emily started.

'But nothing. I will train, properly. Starting right away. I'll get a self-help book or something. And you're sitting here. You're sitting here, unable to get out and run, but you *can* help me put together a training programme, work out a pace that's right for me.'

'But there isn't enough time. It's just three months until the marathon. I've already been training for ten weeks.'

'And what do you think I've been doing on Saturday mornings and Tuesday evenings? Paint by Numbers? I've been running too, and I can see the results. I don't have to keep stopping any more to catch my breath. I didn't stop at all last night. The others send their regards, by the way.' Gracie became aware she was pacing the lounge, the idea scrambling and circling around in her mind like a tropical bird, desperate to break free and take flight.

Emily fell quiet, rubbed at her face.

'I can do this, Emily. *We* can do this. I don't know why I didn't think of it before, although from the sounds of it, swapping bibs isn't quite as straightforward as it sounds and there are no guarantees of course. But this is an opportunity. Something good can still come of your awful injury. Say you're in. That you'll help me do it.'

With a great sigh that spoke more of resignation than determination, Emily looked up.

'OK. OK. I'll email the organisers tomorrow; we've got just under two weeks until the cut-off date so hopefully there's still time. But only if you're absolutely certain.'

Gracie nodded, a tentative, adrenalin-fuelled smile tugging on her lips. 'Oh, I'm certain. Our secret then, for now at least.'

Gracie left Jill's house and took the long way home, strolling the wide and leafy Edwardian high street with its clean, straight lines and enviable selection of shops. Once affectionately dubbed the Bond Street of East Anglia, Frinton's high street had so far resisted the small-town inevitability of fast food outlets, bookmakers and Poundstretcher and still proudly boasted a fishmonger, butcher, baker and a wonderful independent bookshop, as well as small clothing boutiques and numerous eateries. But it was January, and the small businesses were feeling the bite of winter and the loss of passing trade. The hardware store that usually sold buckets, spades and rubber rings from its shopfront, looked naked minus the colourful trappings of summer. Luigi's, the popular Mediterranean bistro, lacked appeal without its humming street-side tables and chairs, the perfect spot for a latte and a touch of people-watching.

Like many, Gracie found the winters long and the days short and, as so many of the older generations also complained, she'd begun to feel the effects of the biting cold on her skin, her joints and her mood. Had noticed a shift in her routines, especially since retirement; more hours spent in bed or huddled up on the sofa, more wishing away of a dreary day and hankering after spring. At her age, of course, the wishing away of *any* days was completely unacceptable. Running had changed her outlook completely. Running galvanised her in body and mind and it had given her a purpose, so that now even on the days she didn't run, she felt more inclined to try new things.

Was she completely out of her mind? Or deluded perhaps? Was she really going to attempt to run a marathon on little more than a whim, outrage and woefully little training? And what on earth was Andrew going to say about it?

'Of course, you'll need sunscreen, and a hat,' was, it turned out, what Andrew had to say about it. 'It can get jolly hot in April you know. Remember that Easter we were in Tintagel? I got burnt to a crisp climbing up to the castle.'

Gracie fixed him with a look. 'Andrew, there's three months to worry about factor fifty creams and headgear. What about the more immediate question, namely – do you think I've taken leave of my senses or is this a good idea?'

The more she'd thought about it, taking the longest route home possible to delay the inevitable reckoning, the more she'd convinced herself that Emily had been right to object. Aside from the fundraising side of things, was this simply little more than an ego trip? Of course, Emily didn't realise she had the added motivation of thwarting Kat's horrible plan. But had she an overinflated idea of her limits? Perhaps she was simply in denial about her age and what her body was capable of. This imperfect, yet reliable body that had carried her across continents, endured childbirth, a lifetime on her feet in class, withstood illness, injury and pain.

'Do you know what I saw on Anglia news the other day?' Andrew answered with a question. 'A one-hundred-and-two-year-old woman from Suffolk did a skydive. A *skydive*, Gracie, for charity.

And do you remember that programme we saw last year, the one about Devon and Cornwall? Remember the woman who was a champion surfer back in the Sixties? Gwyn Haslock? She's in her late seventies and at the time of the programme, was still surfing the beaches of Newquay most days.' Andrew tilted his head and smiled. 'Do you think those women have taken leave of their senses? Or are they incredibly spirited and determined, a bit like you.'

Gracie choked out a laugh, feeling strangely emotional. 'Bloody-minded, probably.'

Andrew drummed the kitchen worktop, providing a feeling of finality to the discussion. 'That settles it then. My bloody-minded but brilliant wife is going to run the marathon. Now, what shall we have for tea?'

9

Jill

Jill watched from the doorway of Victory Hall as Rita wandered away. It was way past closing time, and they still had the clear up to do before the hall was let out again for a children's birthday party. They'd practically had to push the woman out the door. Jill hoped she'd be OK getting home.

'Did she pay this time?' asked Cynthia, beginning to stack the chairs against the wall.

'Oh, yes,' Jill lied breezily. She'd paid for Rita's refreshments herself and added the buttons to a collection in her pocket that was growing as steadily as her unease when it came to the sparrow-like woman. 'Is this necessary, won't they be needing the chairs out again anyway?' It always seemed pointless, the restacking of chairs and tables, when within the next half an hour they would likely be shifted straight back into the centre of the room.

'Rules are rules now, Jill, we can't go bending them at will,' Cynthia sang, as though she got no greater enjoyment than when heaving large items of furniture.

Except, being the keyholder to the hall, likely meant if anyone could, Cynthia could. But there was no use arguing with her, so Jill grabbed the end of a table and together they pushed it back into its usual home, beneath the colourful display of painted handprints, created at Mums and Toddlers.

Emily was behind the serving hatch in the small kitchen-cum-storeroom, leaning on one crutch and using her free hand to slide the board games back onto a shelf in the cupboard, labelled 'Be Together Equipment'.

'I can do that, love, you go and sit down,' called Jill.

'I don't want to sit down. I do nothing but sit down,' she complained. 'Do you know, I'm so bored I actually read the instruction leaflet for this today.' She held up 'How to Play Scrabble'.

'Excellent stuff. You can teach Eugene and Harold; they're always cheating.'

Though she teased, Jill's heart went out to Emily. She'd been stuck there all day, having got a lift with Jill and unable to make her way back home. At least the running group had brightened her day.

Once everything was shipshape, and Cynthia had handed over the hall to two beleaguered parents, weighed down with helium balloons and shopping bags, they made their way to Jill's parked car.

It took some doing, levering Emily into the two-seater sports car, which only just accommodated her crutches, for the short drive home. Even that was easier than getting one of the café's customers into her car the other week when she'd taken him to his hospital appointment. Her ancient turquoise Mazda MX-5 simply wasn't suited to seventeen stone gentlemen with hernias. Perhaps it was time she traded it in for something bigger.

'Gracie and Ray were late today,' ventured Jill, who missed nothing. 'They came in a good half hour after the others. Was everything alright?'

Emily was scrolling absently through her phone, a riot of colour and soundless video content entreating her to read this, buy that, wear this, eat that.

'Hmm, oh fine. They're just training harder. Do you think I should cut my hair like this?' she asked, thrusting her phone into Jill's face, who was more concerned with keeping her eyes on the road.

Training? Training for what?

'I think your hair is lovely as it is, but it's your hair, love. What are they training for? Ray is already incredibly fit – um, what I mean is, with his job he had to be, I guess,' Jill hastily clarified. She'd spent enough time surreptitiously drinking in the man's firm biceps and shoulders to appreciate that much. Not that she was admitting that to anyone and certainly not to her daughter.

'Not Ray. He's just keeping Gracie company. But do you think a fringe would suit me?'

'Emily? Why is Gracie training? She's a seventy-two-year-old woman with a disabled husband at home, what can she possibly be training for?'

Emily clamped her mouth shut, turned her face away.

'Em?'

'She asked me not to say anything,' she said, in a tone indicating she'd already put her foot in it.

Jill turned into their paved driveway and pulled on the handbrake. She turned to her daughter.

'If Gracie is up to something, I should know. I might not have been around for the past few years, but I'm here now and I want to be a good sister. I want to help.'

Emily sighed and dragged her hands across her face.

'She's going to kill me for telling you. I promised.'

'She'll understand,' maintained Jill, not even believing it herself but determined to get to the bottom of it.

Emily shrugged. 'OK. Auntie Gracie is going to take my place in the London Marathon. Nobody else knows. Ray thinks she wanted to extend her run and push herself to 10k. I'm helping to put together a training programme, so she'll start to extend that even further each week.'

Of course. She should have seen this coming. Why hadn't she seen this coming? Age, experience, safety, none of those things were obstacles in Gracie's eyes. Just like when she'd buggered off to the arse end of God knows where with nothing more than a rucksack.

Jill opened her car door.

'Aren't you going to say anything? Are you mad?' asked Emily.

Jill leaned back in and smiled.

'Darling, I know you've not known your aunt for long, but surely by now you've realised she's a stubborn old boot who thinks the rules of this world do not apply to her. What would be the point of being mad? On the contrary, I think this could be an opportunity.'

Emily's puzzled words followed her as she circled the car and opened her door. 'An opportunity for what?'

She tugged the crutches free and offered Emily an arm.

'Your aunt might be good at some things. She's practical and outdoorsy, a brilliant artist too. But I, my dear, am an excellent planner.'

The following morning, fortified with four cups of coffee, as she'd been awake since the early hours, Jill rang the Jenkins' doorbell and braced herself.

'Hi, Jill,' said Gracie, surprise registering on her make-up-free face. 'Is Emily OK?'

Jill supposed it was rather irregular, her showing up unannounced like this, and up until now nearly all interactions between them had revolved around Emily in some way.

'She's fine. Sat at the kitchen table turning pebbles into animal faces. Must get her artistic streak from you.'

'I don't know,' said Gracie, mischief dancing across her eyes, 'I seem to remember you being the creator of several striking works of art in your youth.'

Jill gave a long-suffering sigh. 'Really? You're going to bring that up again?'

She'd rather not hear one of Gracie's favourite sisterly anecdotes, brought out at weddings, funerals and christenings, which involved a lipstick, a bottle of red nail varnish and their parents' cream bedroom carpet. In her defence, she'd been about four. And besides, her mother had never let her forget it.

'Come in, Andrew's in his man cave. Fancy a coffee?' said Gracie, beckoning her inside.

'Oh, go on then. I think my bloodstream is already pure caffeine, so another won't hurt.'

'It's decaf, actually. That alright?'

Jill smiled. 'Perfect. That's one thing ticked off my list.' She tapped the pearlescent pink cover of the hardback notebook in her hand and followed her sister into the kitchen.

Gracie and Andrew's kitchen was a cosy space, simple Shaker-style units elevated with colourful porcelain knobs, plain white walls adorned with an arresting mix of art; small, framed family photographs interspersed with postcard prints and ceramic plates. A large butcher's block trolley housed a collection of wine bottles and sprawling house plants hung from macramé potholders, the overall effect being that of a mismatch of favourite things and collected artefacts, rather than a curated design concept.

'What's that then, your list of new year's resolutions?' asked Gracie, flipping on the kettle.

Jill swallowed and straightened her back.

'No. Actually, they're a list of yours.'

Gracie cocked an eyebrow.

'Not resolutions, exactly,' Jill clarified. 'More of a lifestyle revamp. If you're really serious about running this marathon. . .' she held firm as Gracie sucked in a sharp breath '. . . then you're going to need my help. And. . .' she held up a hand to stop Gracie's protest '. . . I know what you're going to say. That Emily is already helping you, well, I'm afraid, sister dear, that's not going to cut it. You see, I've been doing my research and you're going to need a whole lot more than a spreadsheet. Emily can't even walk. You're going to need a training partner. Someone to help with diet, exercise, motivation and pacing. *I* can be that partner, Gracie.'

The kettle boiled away noisily, vibrating violently on the worktop until Jill thought it would never turn itself off.

Eventually, Gracie flicked the switch.

'Blasted thing needs replacing,' she said. 'Andrew keeps saying he'll fix it.'

'So, what do you say?'

Gracie sighed. 'Look, Jill, I really don't want to hurt your feelings, but how can you be my training partner when you hate running? You even went as far as to say you'd rather have your toenails plucked out one at a time than to ever try it again, in fact.'

Jill folded her arms across her chest.

'I don't think I put it quite like that. Merely that it was about as pleasurable as having one's toenails plucked out. My boobs hurt, my thighs chafed and my pants disappeared up my bum so often it was a wonder I didn't get thrush. Even my *eyeballs* hurt, all that bouncing around in their sockets, it can't be good for you.'

Gracie's lips twitched in amusement.

'We can't *all* excel at everything, now, can we?' Jill continued. 'You're fit and athletic, whilst my talents lie in other areas. I have no intention of *actually* running beside you – believe me, even the memory makes me wheeze – no, my part in this would be in more of a mentoring capacity.'

Jill was gabbling, she knew it. But she was almost beside herself with anticipation. This could be it. This could be the thing that finally bonded them after all these lost years; a real chance to grow closer and get to know her sister again.

'I'll think about it,' said Gracie.

Jill hugged the notebook to her. Allowed herself a small moment of triumph. Gracie had been a teacher all her life, as well as a mother. First rule of diplomacy, you *never* said maybe, unless the answer was going to be yes.

'Can I show you what I've got so far? Then you'll see. I might not be an academic, sis, but let me tell you, after managing Gary's band for twenty years and in the early days getting them to gigs on time, sober or at the very least upright, I learned a few things about stamina and the importance of sticking to a schedule.'

This was no understatement. Jill might have been just seventeen when she hooked up with Gaz, but she'd to grow up pretty quickly. Especially when it became crystal clear as far as her family were concerned, she'd made her bed and she'd have to lie in it, dirty sheets and all.

Gracie poured out their drinks and pushed a mug towards Jill.

'OK. But I'm not making any promises. And more to the point, you are not to tell a soul. I've no desire to be the town laughing stock, some gallivanting granny that everyone spots coming a mile off. Because I'm taking this perfectly seriously. Agreed?'

Jill nodded furiously. 'Pinky promise?' She offered her little finger.

Gracie looked pointedly at the proffered digit and rolled her eyes in a manner that screamed, *Seriously? You just did that?*

Brushing her hand briefly against Jill's, she said, 'Why don't you just show me what you've got, before I change my mind.'

10

Gracie

It was three weeks since Jill had shown up on Gracie's doorstep with what resembled one of her ex-student's homework diaries; all colour-coded bubble charts and heavily underlined mantras written in purple felt-tip pen. Since then, a stack of library books had materialised in a transparent bag on her doorstep, presumably borrowed under Jill's membership. Gracie threw up a prayer of thanks to the gods of late and irregular postal services when she discovered them before Jason delivered the mail – her marathon would have been all around town, once the over-sharing postman and former pupil of class 10J had spotted *Preparing Your Body for a Marathon* and *Running a Marathon – Your Way*. The volumes included all kinds of helpful advice on running post-partem and adapting your training plan to fit your menstrual cycle, which thankfully were no longer concerns of hers, though she had digested some unpalatable facts about chafing and bleeding nipples, which were, apparently, a stalwart complaint of the long distance runner.

Despite Jill's sloppiness, Gracie had somehow managed to keep her marathon hopes under wraps from all except Andrew, Emily and

Jill. On Tuesdays and Saturdays, when she ran with the CPR, she kept to her normal routine. On Tuesdays it was the small loop, which was now starting to feel like child's play, topped off with a drink in the pub and on Saturdays she ran the extra section with Ray and joined the others afterwards at Victory Hall. She'd felt particularly bad about keeping the news from Ray, but just couldn't face the extra pressure the revelation would put her under, intentional or otherwise.

Gracie now also ran on Thursdays, which gave her alternate rest days and she had been using the secret solo run to gradually build on distance. This week she'd completed her first 15k, which had thrilled her, even if her calves had screamed in agony. Until that was, she'd calculated it to equate to just over nine miles and remembered the marathon was *twenty-six* miles. Twenty-six point two, to be more precise.

The next morning, Andrew presented her with a gift.

'We don't normally celebrate, do we?' she asked, conscious that she had no gift for him, not even a card. They both long ago agreed to dismount the merry-go-round of commercialism which had nothing to do with romance and everything to do with landfill.

Andrew looked perplexed.

'Valentine's Day?' she prompted. 'Fourteenth of Feb. Which is today, dear.'

'Ah.' He pulled a face. 'More of a "well done". For all your hard work, but given with heaps of love, of course. Happy Valentine's Day, darling.'

She offered up her cheek for a kiss, then tackled the bulky object which had been crudely wrapped in Christmas paper and sealed with duct tape.

Inside, she found what looked to be some kind of harness: long straps made of black webbing, secured to a plastic box-like compartment.

Quite practised by now in the perplexing mechanics of her husband's mind, she held the contraption aloft and quirked a brow.

'Are we to take up S&M in our dotage, Andy? Or have you some other fun pursuit in mind for this leash. Walkies on the beach, perhaps?'

From somewhere within the depths of the house, a frantic barking ensued, followed by the panting arrival of Picasso, who skidded to a halt at her feet and Gracie realised her faux pas. Drat. Now she'd have to take her out, again, or deal with the beseeching eyes and forlorn wagging of a hopeful tail for the rest of the morning.

Andrew tutted and took the object from her outstretched hands. 'Allow me to demonstrate.'

He took both straps and threaded them around the front of her arms, as though she were donning a rucksack. There was the adjustment of straps and the soft click of a plastic catch, then he fished his phone from his trouser pocket.

'We'll use mine for the moment. You just slide it into place like so,' he said, fiddling around behind her, 'and voila, you can carry your phone hands free on a run. Even plug in earphones if you fancy a tune or two. There's room for a house key too, some coins, a bank card et cetera. Take a look.'

He led her into the hallway and spun her around so she could see her back reflected in the mirror.

She looked like she was either wearing the world's most microscopic rucksack, or required a battery pack to operate, like a robot, or garden power tool.

Gracie nodded slowly.

'I see. How very resourceful of you. Just one question – how am I meant to retrieve my phone to take a call or select a song? Without first dislocating my shoulders, I mean?'

Andrew pursed his lips. 'Obviously, you take it off first, Gracie.

The whole point is that you don't need to touch it. That you can run as usual without even knowing it's there.'

Gracie very much knew it was there. She felt like the Hunchback of Notre Dame for one thing, or a two-year-old in reins.

She decided not to enlighten him that there were a good many gadgets and garments on the market with enclosures for phones and essentials, that nay, an entire consumer industry had been built around the sport of running, as she was fast learning through Jill and her never-ending lists and podcasts. Instead, she took her thoughtful husband's bearded face in hand and kissed him on the lips. He didn't want her running without a phone, not now she was out on her own some mornings, before anyone else was around. He had a point, she conceded.

'Thank you. Now how about our favourite restaurant for dinner tonight. A little not-Valentine's treat. After all, Jill keeps on at me to up my carbohydrate intake, and I'll take any perk I can right now, which happens to be that my body needs constant refuelling, and I, for one, am only too happy to oblige.'

The following morning Gracie regretted the suggestion, when she began to run and had to contend with acid reflux. A combination of red wine, garlic ciabatta and anchovies were conspiring to scorch her oesophagus as well as mow down anyone in a six-metre shared-oxygen radius.

'You alright there, Gracie?' asked Malik, who had noticed her lagging.

She forced down a burp and gave him the thumbs-up.

'Late night,' she offered, instead of the truth, which was that she and Andrew had rolled into bed at nine stuffed to the gills with Luigi's spaghetti puttanesca. How could she compete in a marathon if she couldn't even last until ten o'clock on a Friday night out in

Frinton, which had to be one of the sleepiest towns in Britain. Best add a bottle of Gaviscon to her next shopping list, she made a mental note.

If she'd worn Andrew's ridiculous contraption, she could have carried a couple of Rennies with her, she mused, before pushing away the idea and resolving to eat more sensibly instead. She would find a tactful way to tell Andrew his invention needed refining. And by that, she meant, binning. He was good like that, taking her advice on the chin and getting back to the drawing board.

Somehow, she struggled to the pier and back, then found herself alone with Ray for the final leg.

'So,' he said, their footsteps falling into synchrony, as he shortened his long strides to match hers, 'Dad told me something the other day.'

Gracie waited for him to elaborate, wondering whether Eugene was ill or if he had some other unpleasant news.

'He said that *you*, Gracie girl, plan to run the London Marathon.'

Gracie swore under her breath. Blooming Jill. She should have known she couldn't keep her trap shut. She had been foolish to trust her.

'Uh-huh,' she replied, not wanting to add gravity to the gossip. 'And what of it?'

Ray spluttered a laugh. 'What of it?' He shot her a sideways look. 'I knew you were up to something. I've seen you, you know, early in the morning. From the lifeboat station. Pretty good view of the coastline from there. I've seen you pounding the promenade like your life depends on it. Much faster than this too.'

'I told Jill to keep it under her hat,' she huffed. 'Not make a big song and dance.'

Ray broke his stride and slowed to a stop.

Gracie slowed up too.

'Gracie, I'm not being funny, but it really *is* a big song and dance,' Ray said, his jovial face turning serious. 'Your sister is so proud of you. We all are.'

'All?' Gracie winced.

He checked his watch. 'Give it about five minutes, and they'll know. My old dad is not known to be a shining soul of discretion.'

'They'd make a good pair then,' Gracie harrumphed.

At this Ray grimaced. 'Don't encourage the man, please. He already thinks the sun shines out of her arse.'

Gracie put her hands on her hips and shook her leg. Giles might be a bit of a tool, but he was right about the cool-down. Her calves cramped like a devil if she didn't stretch them after a run. She lived in eternal fear of getting shin splints, a common runner's injury that could see her marathon over before it had begun.

'I knew I couldn't keep it secret for ever,' she acquiesced. 'I just don't want all the "Are you sure about this?" remarks, as though it isn't the first thing I think about when I wake up in the morning and the last thing when I go to bed. I can't explain it. But the fewer people who know as possible, the less likely I am to fall short.'

Ray seemed to be weighing up her words, his gaze drifting out to sea and alighting on a windsurfer scooting across the water.

'The way I see it, we're your friends. We're also runners. We get it. You're doing something most of us haven't the balls to even attempt, except for Emily, bless her. We want to support you, be your cheerleaders and. . .' he paused for effect '. . . share in the glory at the finish line.'

This was something Gracie hadn't even allowed herself to imagine. The journey between now and that elusive goal felt as distant as a pot of gold at the end of a rainbow.

'Anyway,' added Ray, 'there's fundraising to be done. And if I've got even half the measure of Jill, she'll have a plan for that.'

That's what I'm worried about, thought Gracie, trying not to let her feelings show on her face.

True to Ray's prediction, by the time the pair rejoined the others at the Be Together Café, everyone in the room knew of Gracie's news. Even Rita commented as she passed, 'You're the lady who's doing the running, aren't you?' then shook her head, wild-eyed as though even the thought of it was exhausting. She didn't seem to recognise her as Kathleen/Kat's teacher, although Gracie supposed it had been over twenty years ago.

'I can't believe you've kept this to yourself,' exclaimed Malik, who was making a rare appearance for coffee, as his children were seeing their mum. 'This is amazing. I'm in awe of you, Gracie.'

'Now come on,' she batted away the compliments. 'It's just running. Any of you could do it.'

Sophia let out a guffaw. 'Excuse me? I've been in this club as long as you and the only improvement I've seen is managing the seventeen flights in Beachcombers without having an asthma attack.'

Eugene rolled his eyes. 'You do exaggerate. There are only three floors. And we have lifts.'

'Lifts make me panicky,' retorted Sophia, 'and besides, if *you'd* walked the length of Colchester General Hospital before breakfast, then visited a hundred outpatients, *you'd* find any amount of stairs a bother.'

Malik said, 'Then, I'm in awe of you too. I don't know how you do it, all those sick people. And needles.' He visibly shuddered.

Sophia tugged up the side of her t-shirt, revealing the inky swirls of a beautiful botanical tattoo on creamy white skin. 'Needles don't bother me so. It's handkerchiefs I can't stand. Who decided that folding a piece of cloth covered in snot and stuffing it back in your pocket was a great idea? Or even worse up your sleeve. Check out your woman Cynthia over there – see the lump there near her wrist? Everyone over seventy has them. Brings me out in a sweat.'

'Ahem, not quite everyone,' laughed Gracie, even as Harold looked down at his tweed jacket and pushed something ivory-coloured firmly back inside his top pocket.

'Better for the environment though,' said Emily, sparking a debate about the devastating effects on the ocean of so-called flushable wipes, and relaying staggering statistics about paper products and deforestation, somehow convincing even Sophia that the hanky had its merits. In all honesty, her niece was wasted in the corporate world; she should be using her skills to help save the planet.

Gracie looked around the Be Together Café and experienced a spark of pride for what her sister was doing. Over the past couple of weeks, they'd been in touch more frequently, since Jill also insisted on sending her links to the latest article she'd read on prepping for a marathon or daily motivational quotes via WhatsApp, such as 'You never regret a run'. Although surely anyone who'd sprained an ankle sorely regretted theirs?

The old hall was abuzz with chattering customers, young and old, alone in this world or otherwise, and from all walks of life. Jill was partly responsible for making that happen and Gracie realised there was so much she didn't know about her. So many years unaccounted for.

'Alright, Gracie?' asked Jill, approaching the table with her notepad and pen. Gracie detected a hint of mischief dancing about her eyes and realised the outing of her marathon attempt had been 100 per cent intentional. Insufferable, interfering woman. Though it was hard to be annoyed, with so much goodwill and encouragement in the room. Gracie was amazed by how excited everyone was for her, which far from filling her with doubt, had given her a much-needed injection of resolve. She would not let these people down.

'What can I get you?' Jill asked.

There were two cakes on the counter. One looked to be some kind of sponge, the other a pile of cupcakes, each of them topped with generous swirls of icing. Both looked appealing.

'We have Victoria sponge or lemon cupcakes,' she added, nothing in her tone of voice giving away which had been her own creation.

Gracie looked to Emily for help, but her niece was deep in conversation, the small plates scattered among the group empty of all but unidentifiable crumbs.

Bugger. This had the potential for disaster. If she chose incorrectly, she was destined to suffer the consequences under Jill's watchful eye. Surely her baking couldn't be that bad, could it?

'I'll go Victoria sponge,' she decided, thinking it was perhaps the safer bet.

Jill merely smiled.

'Oh hello, what's she doing here?' murmured Ray beside her, and Gracie looked up at the open front door to see Kat peering through. 'I would have thought the likes of us in a place like this were far too lowly.'

'Ah. Not here for the refreshments, I think you'll find,' replied Gracie. 'That's her mother.' She indicated across the room at Rita who was staring blankly at a hand of playing cards.

Eventually, realising her mother hadn't seen her and that she'd have to enter the building, Kat slipped through the door. Her movements were careful and stilted, everything in her body language screaming, *Get me out of here now*.

'Hey, Kat!' called out Malik, raising a hand to catch her attention, as though she hadn't immediately spotted them all and simply chosen to ignore them. But Malik was far too nice to notice such things. 'Come and join us.'

Kat stopped in her trajectory to her mother and, perhaps realising all eyes were upon her, flashed him a smile.

'Hi Malik. I didn't see you there. Oh,' she said, lips forming an O as though she were the prom queen entering a ballroom of worshipping teens, 'you're *all* here! How sweet!'

How *sweet*? Is supporting the community you live in whilst enjoying a criminally cheap cuppa sweet? Gracie wasn't sure she could contain the contempt rising from her gut much longer. It burnt hotter than the repeating pasta.

'Did you hear the news?' Malik continued, oblivious to Kat's sarcasm and feigned delight. 'Our Gracie is running the London Marathon. Isn't that cool?'

Whilst Gracie inwardly swooned at being referred to as 'our Gracie,' she watched, fixated, as Kat's smile slid down her face like melted candlewax.

'Yeah, she's taking Emily's place,' he blundered on, 'seeing as the only running she's doing these days is the bath tap.'

'I thought you'd chosen to defer,' Kat snapped, directing her question accusingly at Emily.

'Um,' Emily floundered, looking cornered. 'Well, I *was* thinking about doing that, until I realised Auntie Gracie was keen. And, you know, what with her being family, the charity were really happy with the substitution.'

As if she has to explain herself to you, thought Gracie, gritting her teeth to keep her tongue in check.

'I told you *I* was keen too.' Kat's top lip curled upwards. 'I also think the charity might have preferred a participant who stands a good chance of completing the course, don't you?'

The bloody cheek!

'Well now,' interjected Sophia, shooting Kat a disgusted glare, 'it's a good job they've passed the mantle to Frinton's finest then, isn't it? Because Gracie won't just complete the course, she'll *kill* it, and we'll all be there to watch, won't we, chaps?'

'Absolutely!' said Malik

'Just try stopping us,' said Ray, smiling good-naturedly.

Kat managed a fake, fixed smile when she realised nobody was going to agree with her. 'How wonderful,' she said.

Gracie drew a tiny measure of satisfaction from knowing the deadline had now passed for confirmed entries for the marathon and if you're name wasn't already down, so to speak, you weren't getting anywhere near that starting line. Which was a good job really, because she wouldn't put it past the dreadful woman to find some creative way for Gracie to become suddenly indisposed. It certainly came to something when you suspected your fellow runner capable of inflicting grievous bodily harm. *Was* she simply being paranoid? Should she give Kat the benefit of the doubt and chalk Emily's awful accident up to coincidence?

Then Kat turned away and made a beeline for her mother.

'I told you to be ready, Mum, you'll make me late for my class.'

Rita looked up at her blankly, before seeming to register that she was waiting for her, then she tucked the playing cards from her hand into her bag, rather than back with the pile on the table, and began fastening her coat.

Beside Gracie, Sophia muttered, 'I see she doesn't reserve her charms purely for our own pleasure.'

'Here you are. An extra big slice for the elite athlete,' said Jill, breezily, swooping in to place an Olympic-stadium-sized piece of Victoria sponge in front of Gracie. 'Got to replace those calories!'

11

Jill

A week later, over breakfast on Saturday morning, Jill resumed her marathon training research, which had begun to feel like the theory part of an upcoming exam, and she was damned if she'd be doing the practical assessment.

'What do you know how about cross training, Em?'

Emily was sitting across from her at the kitchen table, also tapping away on her laptop. And whatever it was she was doing, she was being mightily secretive about it, because when Jill crossed the room to make a cuppa, she abruptly closed her browser and instead pretended to be checking the weather forecast.

Was she venturing into the world of online dating? wondered Jill. It was possible, because every now and then a small, furtive smile would break across her face, something highly unlikely to be triggered by any of the gloomy news headlines on the BBC website.

'Hmm?' she said distractedly, then looked up. 'Why? You're not thinking of joining a gym are you, Mum?' Emily reached down to scratch her foot again, which seemed to have become a compulsion since her cast removal on Friday.

Jill tutted. 'There's no need to sound *quite* so alarmed! No, not me, your auntie. I'm reading about how cross-training can really help to strengthen other parts of the body and build fitness alongside the running. And stop scratching, you'll give yourself a rash.'

Talk about low expectations. She was perfectly capable of using a gym thank you very much and had done in the past. Still had nightmarish flashbacks to the spin classes Lorraine had invited her to several years ago.

'I can't help it. It itches!' Emily complained. 'But, yeah, swimming's meant to be really good, and Pilates, or yoga, anything really that uses different muscle groups and works on improving cardio fitness.' She looked thoughtful. 'And, seeing as you're meant to be Auntie Gracie's training partner, that's something you could actually do together, isn't it? Maybe I could come too; I should definitely be working on building my strength back up.'

Hang on. . .*what?* That's not where Jill had been going with this at all.

Emily continued. 'In fact, doesn't Kat run a Pilates class at Victory Hall?'

Jill squirmed. The idea of a Pilates class full stop was unappealing, particularly in February, when the last thing you felt like doing at night was venturing outside in flimsy Lycra and lolling around on a dusty floor. And that was before adding Victory Hall into the equation, where she went to work and *knew* people, not to mention a decidedly frosty fitness instructor with the bedside manner of Medusa.

'Mm, I'll look into it.' She aimed for noncommittal, then changed the subject. 'Also, take a look at this.' She angled her screen for Emily to see the Google map image she'd been studying of the familiar stretch of Essex coastline she now called home. 'You see this marker here, in Walton-on-the-Naze, and this one, further along, just beyond Jaywick, well this stretch of coast, which is practically all beachfront promenade and footpaths, also happens to be exactly half a marathon. Well, twelve point three miles to be precise, but there and back plus a little bit is an entire marathon. In lockdown, when everything was cancelled, including the London Marathon, this became a virtual marathon route. There's an official course mapped out on the Runners' Routes website; it's been properly measured and everything.'

'Cool,' said Emily, nodding along with interest. 'That should make the long-distance training runs easier, no busy roads to navigate, or muddy fields.'

'Exactly my point. I'll show Gracie later. Speaking of which,' said Jill, snapping the lid of her laptop shut, 'I'd better get going. Are you coming?'

Emily sighed. 'Well, it's not like I can do anything else, so I may as well come along.'

Jill gave her a sympathetic smile, before offering her hand to help her up. Poor love was going stir-crazy sitting around, when she wanted to be out there training for this marathon herself.

At half past ten, Andrew arrived, breezing into the hall and choosing a spot at a table with Eugene and Harold. He seemed to rather enjoy the Be Together Café since he'd started coming along and had slotted right in with the naughty boys' corner, as Jill liked to think of them.

'Morning, Uncle Andrew,' called Emily, hobbling over to their table.

'You look like you could do with one of these,' he said, tapping the handle of his walking stick.

'The doctor said I have to try and walk on it now,' she said, wincing. 'But it blooming hurts.'

'Perhaps you two should start up your own club,' grinned Eugene. 'The Seafront Shufflers.'

'You can't say that,' said Jill, approaching the table too. 'That's disabled list.'

See, Emily might think she was in a world of her own, but she was more clued up than her daughter thought.

'It's "disablist", Mum,' corrected Emily. 'And technically, neither of us are disabled, just the walking wounded. And you'll be fine once you've had your op, won't you, Uncle Andrew?'

Andrew nodded enthusiastically and declared in an appalling attempt at a Scottish accent, 'Aye, and with a new knee, there'll be nay stopping me.'

Jill knew from a conversation with Emily that the osteoarthritis plaguing Andrew's joints would only get worse, not better. Not that Gracie had said anything about it. She rarely opened up about anything much, always with that guard up, keeping Jill at bay. What would it take to break through it, she wondered.

'I take it Gracie is running today?' asked Jill, when Sophia arrived alone and pulled up a chair next to Eugene.

'She is,' said Andrew, in a way that indicated that wasn't the whole story. He lowered his voice. 'Needed a little encouragement getting out of bed this morning, mind, so I told her if she didn't put her trainers on and get going, I was going to tell Cynthia she was free on Sunday evenings and had always fancied a spot of campanology. That did the trick, I can tell you; she shot out of bed like a scrambled fighter jet.'

Emily burst into giggles and Jill floundered. Why did it always feel like she was on the outside of a joke? If anyone knew anything about camping, it was Gracie and Andrew. She'd always hated it herself, shower blocks and bugs, damp towels and sleeping bags, though she failed to see why Gracie would need to teach Cynthia anything about it, of all people, especially on a Sunday evening. Cynthia was the last person she could picture spending a night under canvas, far too fond of her bone china and petit fours.

Before Jill could enquire further, the door flew open, and the remaining Coast Path Runners entered, bringing with them the smell of outdoors.

'The peace is over,' declared Eugene.

'It's a beautiful day out there today,' said Ray, his snug-fitting grey t-shirt damp around the collar. 'We should get you out for a walk later, Dad.'

Eugene gave a sniff of indifference, then moved a chess piece, causing Harold to curse under his breath.

'Where's Gracie?' asked Jill, scanning the room for her sister.

'Not sure, I thought she was behind me,' said Ray, looking up.

Andrew tapped out a tune on the table. 'You can ring my b-e-l-l, ring my bell,' he sung, a mischievous look on his face.

Emily snorted.

What the devil was going on today. Was everyone going mad?

Emily leaned in and whispered to Ray, 'Uncle Andrew told Auntie Gracie if she didn't get out there running today, he'd tell Cynthia she'd always fancied bell-ringing. She's been trying to recruit everyone in town apparently.'

Ray's face creased up in amusement and Jill mustered a smile too, mainly in relief that she hadn't voiced her camping thoughts.

'Ah, here she is,' said Andrew, as Gracie came into the hall.

'Sorry,' she said, 'I was just chatting with an ex-student I bumped into outside.'

'I gather it was a struggle to get out there this morning, Gracie?' said Jill. 'You know, even when you might not feel like it, you're going to have to learn to push through.'

Gracie stuck out her chin, and it was a defensive gesture Jill recognised of old. Whilst Gracie had left home when Jill was still very young, she did recall some of the stubborn disagreements between her older sister and their mother. What she didn't understand was

109

how Gracie had always managed to stand up to her, when somehow, she had never been able to.

'Since when did you become the expert on endurance, Gillian? Besides, it's not a chore. I *like* exercise,' asserted Gracie, matching Jill's own passive-aggressive tone.

'Glad to hear it. Me too. Which is why I've booked us into a Pilates class on Monday evening. It's not all about the running you know. We need to work on core fitness and cardio as well as mental strength.'

Gracie looked slightly taken aback, which was nothing compared to Jill's own surprise at hearing such a fib spew forth from her mouth.

'Oh, right. Er, thank you. I should be free.'

She didn't sound enthused, but then neither was Jill. And she only hoped the class she'd seen advertised in Clacton when scrolling earlier was accepting new bookings. Dammit. Now she was going to have go out and buy some appropriate gear because the charity shop's mismatched offerings she'd cobbled together for her one and only run had left much to be desired, *or supported* for that matter. Scaffolding may even be required.

'And Mum's done some research on a fab training route too, haven't you, Mum?' said Emily, prompting Jill to wonder if her daughter was being genuinely encouraging or merely exercising a little diplomacy between the two clashing personalities. 'Why don't you show Auntie Gracie.'

Jill reached into her pocket for her phone, just as Cynthia came over brandishing her notepad.

'I'll be right with you, Cynthia, just need a quick word with Gracie about the marathon,' said Jill, hoping the older woman would take the hint and bugger off. As much as she'd come to count on Cynthia as a friend, there was an air of prim righteousness that tended to follow her around like the Lily of the Valley she wore, not to mention she was also thoroughly nosy.

'Oh, please, do carry on,' she tittered, 'it's all so terribly exciting; we were chatting about it at WI this week in fact, having a little think about how we can help with drumming up community support. Now, I know we've never managed to entice you to our meetings as a member, Gracie, but how would you feel about being a guest speaker?'

At the look of abject horror on Gracie's face, Jill scrambled to rescue the situation.

'I think perhaps Gracie's looking to keep this all a bit more *low-key*,' she said, hoping her slightly saccharine tone would convey the gently-gently approach required with her sister. She crossed her fingers behind her back; it was already too late for 'low-key', with the wheels she'd set in motion.

'Thanks for the offer, Cynthia,' said Gracie, ignoring Jill's intervention, 'nothing against the WI, but public speaking isn't really my strong suit.'

'Noted.' Cynthia nodded, pulling an imaginary zip across her mouth. 'You're a modest woman, but I'll say no more about it. Now what can I get you all?'

As Cynthia trotted away with a list of refreshments to prepare, Jill showed Gracie the route she'd found.

'Apparently, this route has been properly measured, so it's perfect for training. We have our official virtual marathon route.'

'For one thing, there's absolutely nothing virtual about running twenty-six-point-two miles, and for another, what's all this *we* business,' snapped Gracie, 'as presumably *you* won't be taking up the challenge?'

Gracie seemed well and truly miffed with Jill. Perhaps she should have known better than to ambush her in front of the others like this. But at some point, she was going to have to accept this wasn't a challenge to be taken lightly. She would need help, with the training *and* the fundraising.

'Ooh,' cried Sophia, 'you know what we should do? We should all get t-shirts printed up, like official kit for the CPR with Gracie's name on. It would be great advertising, whenever we're out for a run, or even just out and about.'

'I think that's a fantastic idea,' said Ray. 'Turn it into a real community event.'

Jill squirmed in her seat. No, no, no, this wasn't helping. It was the whole 'event' part that needed playing down. Any minute now Gracie was going to call time on this whole conversation, insist that she wasn't some sort of town mascot, to be paraded around like Pudsey Bear, and all her work will have been for nothing.

But Gracie always did have the capacity to do what you least expected.

She nodded at Sophia, a grin starting to spread across her face. 'We'd have to include Giles's name too; it's only fair if he's also running the marathon. But we could make them as loud as possible, rainbow colours perhaps, and insist *all* members wear them. I'd pay good money to watch Giles and Kat sprinting around town with my name on their back.'

On Monday at half past six, Jill ran outside to where Gracie was waiting in the car with Emily, engine running impatiently.

'Sorry I'm so late,' she said, climbing into the back. 'Eugene went to the gents' forty minutes ago and we thought he was still in there,' she added under her breath, 'you know, *having trouble going*. But it turns out he'd snuck out through the back door to avoid getting stuck with one of the other regulars who likes to drone on about his hernia. I only know because I rang Ray and suggested he might want to check on his dad, only to be told he was sat with him in the residents' lounge at Beachcombers looking at cruise brochures, can you believe.'

Gracie and Emily exchanged a glance in the front, then Emily snorted with laughter.

'Maybe TMI, Mum?'

Gracie's mind, however, didn't appear to have snagged on Eugene's possible constipation, but something else Jill had let slip.

'You have Ray's number?' she asked, indicating and pulling away.

Jill batted the question away. 'Just for emergencies, you know, next of kin, that sort of thing.'

'Really? Do you have the numbers of next of kin for *all* your customers?' asked Gracie, raising an eyebrow at Jill in the rear-view mirror.

'Not all, but, yes, some.' Surely it wasn't outside the bounds of possibility that Eugene might suddenly be in need of his strapping son. Well, Ray hadn't batted an eyelid when she'd asked for it, anyway. Jill decided to change the subject. 'So, did you read the article I sent you this morning?'

Gracie nodded. 'Uh-huh. Top ten performance running shoes. What a captivating read that was.'

Jill blew out an impatient sigh. 'It's important! I've seen the trainers you run in, and they look as though the laces are the only thing stopping them from falling apart. If you're going to invest in anything, it should definitely be new shoes.'

'I don't see why I need to invest in anything,' shrugged Gracie. 'I've been doing perfectly fine so far. What will these so-called miracle shoes do? Fly me to the moon?'

'Well, funny you should say that, because apparently the Nike Vaporfly, which are top in their class, caused a bit of controversy a few years ago due to the advantage they give their wearers. More spring in your step apparently. Now that's got to be appealing, surely?'

'Not really,' said Gracie, 'it sounds suspiciously like cheating!'

Jill shrugged. 'Hardly. But I do think you owe it to yourself to invest in some better-quality running shoes as a bare minimum. In fact,' she said, leaning forward and tapping Gracie's seat, 'I think a spot of retail therapy is in order. What are you doing on Wednesday?'

Gracie sighed. 'Nothing I can dream up on the spot to get me out of it, so I guess I'm all yours.'

'Excellent.' Jill grinned.

Emily sighed. 'Wish I could come too. I have a riveting Zoom meeting on Wednesday about macroeconomic trends. But I'm looking forward to this – it'll be fun to do something just the three of us.'

'It will, dear,' agreed Gracie with a smile.

Fun wasn't perhaps the word Jill would have chosen, though she couldn't help but agree. This *was* nice, being all together. As though they were a normal family.

Emily twisted in her seat. 'Although can someone tell me why we're going to Clacton for a Pilates class? I thought there was one in Frinton?'

'There is,' said Jill, 'but it's run by that awful woman in your running club and I'm not overly struck, truth be told.' She might enjoy a gossip as much as the next person, but it didn't feel right to mention her concerns about Rita just yet.

Gracie made an audible sound of approval, then fell oddly quiet for the remainder of the short drive.

As feared, they bustled into the community hall where the class was being held, ten whole minutes late. Which was late enough to have the embarrassment of making everyone shift their mats along to make room for theirs, and having twenty-odd sets of eyes on them as they shrugged off coats and hurriedly laid down to join in.

Never had Jill so regretted her healthy breakfast choice of muesli and prunes, as she battled through forty-five minutes of uncomfortable pelvic floor exercises whilst holding in trapped wind. At last, after an excruciatingly lengthy cool-down process, the instructor led a round of self-congratulatory and hearty applause, and she was able to facilitate its inaudible release. The relief was clearly so apparent on her face that both Emily and Gracie mistook it for delight.

'I'm pleased you enjoyed that, Jill,' said Gracie as they buttoned their coats and filed outside. 'Though I can't say it's really for me. Perhaps we could try swimming instead next time.'

Oh terrific. So, she'd just put herself through that for nothing. What was it Gracie had said about her not being an expert in endurance? At this rate, she begged to differ. But needs must and it was all part of a wider plan, so endure she would, even if it did mean feigning enthusiasm for another activity that was far from top of Jill's list of fun things to do.

'Hang on a minute,' said Gracie suddenly, staying both Jill and Emily with an arm as they crossed the car park.

'Ooh,' said Jill, following her line of sight to where a woman in high heels and a short fur coat emerged from the cinema opposite, looping her arm around a man as they strolled away. 'Speak of the devil.'

'Oh,' said Emily, realising who they were looking at. 'That's Kat! Who's she with? I didn't see.'

Gracie's lips hardened into a line.

'That,' she said, 'was Giles.'

12

Gracie

Having accepted that she might possibly benefit from a little of her sister's enthusiasm, Gracie resigned herself to one of her least favourite pursuits, shopping.

'Eugh,' agreed Sophia as she ran beside Gracie that Tuesday evening. 'The only thing I enjoy shopping for is alcohol and that's pretty easy in a pub.'

'Can you really call "asking for a pint" shopping?' called back Malik.

'Why not?' retorted Sophia. 'I browse the various options available, I make my selection and then hand over my debit card. I'd call that shopping!'

'I don't think she's wrong, mate,' laughed Ray. 'I'm quite partial to a mooch round the shops as it happens, or even better, Camden Market. Probably the only thing I miss since moving out of London.'

Gracie had become quite adept at holding a conversation whilst running now, the only tricky part was keeping to a slow enough pace, as it soon became impossible if she ran too fast. On her solo runs she pushed herself a little harder, but the joy of running with the Coast Path Runners was in the chatting and catching up.

As they waited at the kerb of Connaught Avenue for a short stream of traffic to pass by, Gracie found herself next to Ray.

'It must have been a pretty big life change, leaving the city to move out here,' she said. She had to admit to having always been a little curious about Ray. As to why such an outgoing character as him would jack in his career and move somewhere he didn't know another soul, apart from his aged father.

'Well,' began Ray, as they crossed the road and continued on with their circuit of the town, 'let's just say a life change was required. And I haven't regretted it for a minute.'

'Fair enough,' chipped in Malik. 'There's been plenty of times I've thought about moving somewhere new and starting again, but to be honest, without my parents on the doorstep to help me out with the kids, I don't know what I'd have done. I think it's fantastic that you and your dad moved here together.'

Sophia seized her opportunity. 'So just why *is* your ex-wife such a gigantic arsehole, Mal? If you don't mind me asking.'

Gracie disguised an escaped laugh with a cough. She had to hand it to the woman; somehow being as blunt as a baseball bat only made her more endearing.

'I wouldn't say she *intends* to be an arsehole,' he said, veering around a parked car. 'She just has different priorities now, what with the new husband, the new baby and the fancy new house that apparently needs extensive renovations, all whilst being fully documented on Instagram, and after all, I am their dad. Why shouldn't they stay with me?'

'And she's their mother! Or does she think that every time she makes a new one she can consign the older ones to the back of a drawer like an old iPhone?'

Malik gave a defeated sigh. 'She loves them, she's just. . .' He tailed off, and Sophia was only too happy to finish his sentence.

'A selfish tosser? Was that the word you were looking for?'

'Preoccupied, I was going to say.'

'And what about you, Malik?' asked Gracie. 'Do you manage to find time for yourself at all?'

He turned his head, the streetlight casting his face into shadow, but the half of it Gracie could see was screwed into a grimace.

'*This* is my time. If I didn't run, I'd probably start daytime drinking, or eating chutney straight from the jar and sending the kids to school with pizza crusts for lunch.'

Sophia gave a grunt of agreement. 'I'd probably strangle my patients and launch bedpans out of windows. The running's definitely a kind of therapy. Doing feck all for my waistline, mind.'

'Your waistline is just fine,' said Malik, perhaps regretting it when everyone fell silent and left his words hanging there. 'Anyway,' he hastily continued, 'Mum and Dad are going on holiday in a few weeks, so I won't be able to run then. Pray for me. Or better still, pray for the kids because I'll be like a pumped-up hamster without a wheel.'

On Wednesday morning, Gracie and Andrew were eating breakfast when a quick succession of loud car horn blasts from their front drive caused Gracie to drop her buttered toast in her lap.

'What the heck. . .' Gracie jumped up and peered out to see Jill waving at her, all lipstick and grins, behind the wheel of her Mazda. Across the way, Mrs Sands glared from her bedroom window before letting the net curtain fall back into place.

'I knew this was a mistake. The woman's a lunatic – I should never have agreed to it.'

Andrew got up and placed calming hands on her shoulders.

'It will be fine. Two sisters going on a shopping spree and having lunch, what could possibly go wrong?'

It was a question that didn't warrant a response.

'So then,' asked Gracie, fastening her seatbelt and feeling as though she were virtually prostrate in the impractical sports car, 'where are we off to – Colchester?'

'Chelmsford. More choice and some specialist running shops too. Plus, I've heard about this new keto restaurant I thought we could try for some inspiration.'

'OK,' said Gracie cautiously, aware she didn't want to sound ungrateful, 'that sounds lovely, but I'm not a *huge* fan of sushi, or Japanese food generally.'

Jill glanced sideways and beamed. 'There was I thinking you were the educated one in the family, sis. *Ketogenic diet.* Low carb, but high fat. Something to do with the chemical your liver produces. Definitely worth investigating, to introduce some protein-heavy meals into the diet plan.'

Oh perfect. And here she'd been imagining that the highlight of this insufferable shopping day would undoubtedly be Pizza Express or Prezzo, where she could bury her face in a carb-loaded pizza and guzzle a fortifying glass of wine. That was what runners needed, wasn't it – carbs, carbs and more carbs? And what was all this about a *diet plan*?

Gracie muttered, 'I think you're forgetting Andrew's the one with the science degree, Jill. I was always more interested in Vermeer.'

Unfazed, Jill continued, 'I've been doing a lot of reading up. Ketosis is the process where your body no longer has carbs to burn, so instead burns fat. It could have benefits on long distances, if you've loaded up properly beforehand.'

'Sounds like one of those faddy weight-loss diets to me,' said Gracie, not convinced.

'They're not *fads*,' said Jill defensively, 'they're just not for everyone.'

119

'Like that Atkins diet, or whatever it's called, where you eat nothing but cow. Or the Jurassic one, where you eat leaves and seeds like some sort of Neanderthal.'

Jill expelled a gust of breath through her nose. 'Honestly, Gracie, do you need to be quite so scathing? It's called the Paleo diet actually and is based on simple unprocessed foods available to people in the Stone Age. It's also rather effective.'

'Sounds like you know first-hand,' said Gracie.

'Are you trying to say I'm fat? That I need to go on a diet?' asked Jill snappily.

'No!' replied Gracie quickly. Blimey, they were barely out of Frinton, and she'd already put her foot in it. That boded well. 'Of course, I'm not saying that. I was merely commenting that you seem quite knowledgeable on the subject. It's something I know little about.'

Tread carefully, Jenkins. It's going to be a loooong day.

Jill loosened her grip on the steering wheel, her shoulders seeming to relax.

'Well, what can I say. Perhaps I'm not just a pretty face, eh?' she said, her confident bluster doing little to disguise her insecurities.

The irony of it was, Jill had always had a pretty face. She was beautiful, in fact. Blessed with apple-shaped cheeks, a wide smile and strikingly clear, grey-blue eyes. Whereas Gracie had always found her own visage to be plain, angular and unremarkable. She wasn't a vain woman, but the truth was she'd never been comfortable using cosmetic products. Whenever she'd used mascara, or swept blusher across her cheeks, she felt like a child playing dress-up, like how she remembered Jill as a child, when she'd pranced around in too-big shoes and smothered her mouth in their mother's lipstick.

'Quite far from it,' agreed Gracie, then adding, 'do you mind if we put the radio on, it's Woman's Hour on Radio 4?'

'Sure, if you want,' said Jill with a shrug.

An hour and several hair-raising encounters on the A12 later, Jill reversed her small car into a parking space in the multi-storey carpark and switched off the engine.

'Right then,' she announced with all the gusto of a holiday park entertainer, 'first stop, Planet Run. Let's get you sorted with some proper gear.'

Gear? What was she, an army cadet?

As it transpired, Planet Run delivered exactly what it promised, an entire cornucopia of gadgets, gizmos and paraphernalia to do with the simple art of moving from one foot to the other, quickly.

'We advise an AeroTechnic tank as the bare minimum in performance wear; their sweat-wicking technology is second to none,' said the sales assistant, an enthusiastic chap clad head to toe in sports gear and looking like he belonged on an Olympic track, rather than in a shop.

'I'm jogging along the seafront, not joining NASA,' joked Gracie, mildly disturbed by the armfuls of clothing slung across Jill's arm.

Choosing to ignore her comment, he continued, 'And when it comes to compression shorts, we swear by GlowFit Endurance – great on the glutes and chafing, although of course, you have to go commando. Huge range of colourways too.'

Gracie blinked in astonishment. Compression shorts, nipple tape, hydration vests, around a thousand different types of leggings, anti-sweat this, anti-chafe that, and she was expected to run without underpants?

'We'll just try these for now, thank you,' said Jill, ushering Gracie towards a fitting room.

Inside the cubicle, a poster on the wall advertised the store's revolutionary gait-analysis technology, to help with selecting shoes. 'We match your natural biomechanics to find the ultimate in fit and comfort.'

What the heck were biomechanics and since when did you need a machine to see if a shoe fitted? The Cinderella story would definitely lose something in the retelling these days, mused Gracie.

'I'll be waiting right here. Shout me when you're changed,' said Jill, swishing the cubicle curtain shut and leaving Gracie with the mountain of clothing.

With a sigh, Gracie unzipped her jacket and hung it on a peg, then unbuttoned her cotton shirt. Probably the only fit-for-purpose item of sportswear she owned was the slightly greying sports bra she was standing in now, having had the foresight to wear it in preparation for this exact scenario. She was a small-chested woman, not as blessed as her sister in that department, but she'd soon realised the error in judgement of not wearing one, back on her very first run. Perhaps these other garments would offer equal benefits. Perhaps she shouldn't be so cynical and accept there was much to learn: biomechanics, ketosis and the like.

By the time they left the shop an hour later, laden with bags, Gracie was the proud owner of a tangerine orange windproof running jacket, with matching leggings and several long-sleeved anti-UV sun-protecting, sweat-wicking tops which she'd argued against and lost. Apparently, her plain white cotton tees would be 'weighing her down with stale sweat', such a charming observation, coming from a young man. She had also procured a pair of eye-wateringly expensive and hideously garish running shoes that proclaimed something terribly scientific about carbon layers and velocity, of which she remained ignorant and suspected was hogwash, but would quiz Andrew about later.

By now it was gone one o'clock, and Gracie's stomach was rumbling loudly. The scent of herby, garlicky loveliness drifted from a Nando's up the street, propelling her legs towards it. Was there anything better than chicken and chips? And did she not deserve the calories?

'Ah here we are!' announced Jill proudly, tugging her to a stop outside a blackboard announcing the small café's special of the day to be a salmon, avocado and broccoli salad. 'Lunch.'

'Mmm,' said Gracie, feigning delight. 'Can't wait.'

The next day, Gracie and Andrew were startled awake by the doorbell.

'It's still pitch-dark,' hissed Gracie angling her phone towards her. 'Six o'clock. Who the heck is that?'

Andrew groaned and swung his legs from the bed, leaning heavily on the mattress as he levered himself to standing.

'I'll go. You stay there,' he said, and before she could argue, he'd grabbed his dressing gown from the back of the bedroom door and headed downstairs, leaving Gracie rubbing at her eyes in irritation.

The doorbell sounded again before he got there, so slow was his progress and Gracie cursed whoever it was at this ungodly hour.

However, after a few moments, Andrew called up the stairwell.

'Gracie? It's Jill. She's here for your training session, love.'

'Here for my. . .' Gracie trailed off.

She'd been dimly aware of Jill blathering on over lunch about the importance of strength training, leg lifts, squats and core work, along with all kinds of advice on interval running and tempo, most of which had sailed over Gracie's head. Then Jill had pushed a piece of folded paper towards her when their plates had been cleared – 'The schedule for the next eight weeks, to take you right up to Marathon week,' she'd said. But Gracie had been debating the merits of the dessert offerings on the menu and wondering whether a chocolate brownie made from courgette could possibly ever deliver, and shoved it into her handbag without looking.

Wearily, she got up and trudged downstairs, pulling her own dressing gown on as she went.

Jill was standing at the kitchen counter, unloading a shopping bag.

'Kale is packed with vitamin C and perfect for a pre-run smoothie,' she told Andrew, as she unpacked vegetables and fruits. 'And she's going to need a good protein source for post-run recovery, like almond milk-based shakes,' she said, placing a carton on the worktop. 'Beetroot's another superfood, its brilliant for. . . Oh, Gracie, there you are. Why are you not in your workout gear?'

'I didn't know you meant we were starting the schedule *today*,' she said. 'I was in bed. We were in bed, asleep, like most normal retired people at six o'clock on a Thursday morning.'

Jill tutted loudly. 'That's why I drew up a schedule.' She said it as though Gracie were dumb. 'Not all of us are ladies of leisure, you know. I do have other responsibilities.' She tugged out her own sheet of paper from her bag, a duplicate, presumably, of the one she'd given Gracie. 'As you can see here,' she said, pointing at the colour-coded chart, 'I work in the hospice shop on Thursdays from half past eight, so we have to start work early. Honestly, I'm shocked you aren't already up at this time anyway. Don't all you runner types like to get your run in first thing in the morning, before the world and his wife are up and about?'

'Generally, I like to run when I can see more than two feet in front of me,' replied Gracie, trying and failing not to let her frustration come out in her tone. 'And I'm not a lady of leisure, I'm retired – from a forty-year career. I think I've earned a few lie-ins.'

'Well,' said Jill, her mouth settling into a thin line. 'You're up now. Why don't you pop upstairs and get dressed so we can crack on before *I* have to get to work. Then you can go for your *run* at any time of your choosing.'

13

Jill

Jill's role as Gracie's personal trainer had been in effect for several weeks. In some respects, it was going well, and Gracie was adhering to the schedule, as a rule, although her interpretation of some of the sessions was a little fluid. For instance, by week three of her plan, Gracie was supposed to be interspersing longer runs with much shorter runs, to give her body chance to recover, and gradually pushing herself with longer distances one day a week. But Emily had told her Gracie ran ten miles last Sunday, then another eight on Monday, which was supposed to be a rest day. And she was almost certain she was skipping her protein recovery shakes.

'You should just let her do her own thing, Mum,' Emily had said. 'After all, she's been running since November anyway, and she didn't have a plan then.'

'But this is a proven process, it's how the professionals do it,' Jill had argued. 'Building up your core strength and stamina, then tapering off again carefully before the big race.'

'Auntie Gracie just wants to run the marathon; she's not trying to break any records. She'll probably end up walking a bit and running a bit, like so many others do. I think you're getting a bit obsessed, to be honest. It's not *your* race.'

The cheek. She wasn't obsessed, she was thorough. And she was doing this for Gracie, not for herself, to get closer to her.

And, as a plan, that was kind of working. Admittedly, it had got off to a shaky start. There had been a moment, back on their shopping trip three weeks ago, when Jill had nearly thrown in the towel. She'd specifically chosen Chelmsford, as it would mean an hour in the car together, alone, with all that time to chat. Then what did Gracie go and do? Ask to listen to some boring radio programme about a woman who'd jacked in her job and left her family to go and live in a convent. Jill was convinced Gracie did things like that on purpose, just to reiterate *she* was the intellectual in the family. As if that hadn't been thrown back at her a hundred times by their own disappointed mother.

Still, there *had* been progress. Gracie had listened to her about the trainers for a start, and thankfully stopped wearing those grubby old shoes that looked fit for the bin.

There had also been that time in the park, when Jill had timed her doing laps – an exercise designed to help with pacing – and Gracie had caught the hiccups so they'd had to start from the beginning. Only for the same thing to happen again. They'd fallen about laughing and it had been nice. Like it used to be, a long, long time ago.

'I've been thinking,' Jill said, when Gracie sat with the other runners on Saturday morning. 'Perhaps it's time you got a smart watch. Sticking to the schedule is everything now, and I can't be there with you on your runs, as I *think* we've established.' Jill gave a self-deprecating laugh to cover the embarrassment she experienced whenever she thought back to that one disastrous attempt.

'Why would I do that?' asked Gracie. 'I've got a perfectly adequate wristwatch, thanks.'

'It's not the same though. You should talk to Rita's daughter, the oh-so delightful Kat. She has one of those Garmins. I'm sure she'd show you what's what, seeing as she seems to think she's God's gift to everyone.'

Gracie's face shuttered. 'Believe me, I don't want anything from that woman.'

Andrew shifted in his seat. 'Anyway,' he said, clapping his hands. 'What's on the menu today, Jill?'

How curious. What had gone on there? she wondered. Gracie hadn't mentioned anything when they'd seen Kat coming out of the cinema, although she had gone a bit quiet, Jill recalled.

Emily seemed to notice something was off too and pulled a *don't ask me* face at her mum, when Gracie wasn't looking. She'd have to do some digging. Mind you, if the way Kat bossed her mother around was anything to go by, Gracie was probably right to keep her guard up.

Something wasn't right with Rita, that much was obvious to anyone, and Eugene had received a stern look when she caught him making cuckoo gestures behind her back. Yes, the Be Together Café existed to support the vulnerable in society as well as those seeking friendship and company, but Jill got the distinct feeling Rita was more vulnerable than most. She wasn't there today, hadn't been in for a week or two now. Jill hoped she was OK and made a mental note to talk to Cynthia about it, see if she knew where she lived, for a start.

'What's this then, Eugene?' asked Andrew, indicating the glossy brochure next to his mug. 'Going on your hols?'

'Pah,' snorted Harold. 'If you can call it that. Why on earth anyone

127

would want to be crammed into a floating tin can with thousands of other people beats me.'

'You're just jealous, my friend. That I will be sipping a rum punch next to a pool, spoilt for choice with all the beautiful, single women who'll be looking for love on a Mediterranean cruise, whilst you sit here scouring your precious Oxford dictionary for seven-letter words.' Eugene took on a glazed, faraway look, as though he were already living out this vision of the future.

'Ahem,' coughed Ray. 'Are you forgetting something, Dad?'

Eugene sighed. 'Yes, for one moment, I forgot my babysitter will be with me, watching me like a hawk and spoiling my fun. But a man can dream.'

The others laughed at Eugene's playful teasing of his son, even Gracie, who seemed to have cheered up, yet Jill couldn't bring herself to find it amusing. Jill was imagining Eugene and Ray with their cheerful, cheeky patter, and the glamorous, single, hopeful women who would swarm around them like bees around a honeypot. Eugene's humour was infectious, and Ray was an attractive man – together they made quite the double act.

Before Ray could respond to his father's jibe, the doors to Victory Hall flew open and Sophia burst in, carrying a large cardboard box.

'I wondered where you'd got to,' said Gracie, 'could have sworn you were right behind me.'

'I was,' replied Sophia, 'but then I got a text to say my parcel was ready to collect from the post office, so I swung by to pick this up.'

Jill caught her eye. 'Is that what I *think* it is?' she asked.

Sophia grinned. 'It sure is. Are we ready to take a look?'

Gracie looked between them, puzzled.

As Sophia tore at the parcel tape, Jill prayed Gracie wouldn't kick up a fuss. After all, it had *kind* of been her idea.

'Wow,' grinned Sophia, peering into the box. 'These are

FANTASTIC. Gracie, take a look at. . .' She tugged the garment free and held it aloft. 'This!'

The soft, purple t-shirts had been sourced from a company that specialised in bespoke sportswear and had been printed up with the letters 'CPR' in an orange circle, with the crest of a blue wave beneath and the silhouette of a runner in the foreground. It resembled sunset over the water and looked fantastic against the purple. On the reverse of the shirt, in bold orange capitals, were the words:

GRACIE JENKINS
THE LONDON MARATHON

Then in a smaller font:

Please give generously to Alzheimer's Outreach UK

Gracie's hand shot to her mouth and Jill relaxed. Her sister's eyes were sparkling in tell-tale joy.

'Oh my goodness.' She looked to Sophia. 'Did you arrange this?'

Sophia gave a coy shrug. 'I can't take all the credit. Malik designed the logo for the Coast Path Runners and your sister here stumped up the cash. And we decided to leave off Giles's name and plug the charity instead. He's not running for a charity, so there isn't much he can say about that. They're bloody amazing, right? I can't wait to wear mine on my next run. In fact, to hell with it, I'm wearing it now.'

She tugged the t-shirt over the top of her own and proudly gave a twirl, before handing them out in various sizes to the others.

Gracie took the offered garment as though it were a newborn child and held it slightly away from her.

'I can't believe you did this. I thought we were only joking about a running club kit.'

She wasn't disappointed. She didn't hate them. Phew.

Then Gracie got up from her chair, t-shirt still in hand, and circled the group, giving Sophia and Malik a swift hug, before arriving in front of Jill.

'Thank you, Jill. I *love* it. How clever of you all.' She wrapped her arms around her and squeezed her tight. It was the kind of closeness Jill had craved from her sister for over thirty years. A familiar, unwelcome stinging sensation moistened her eyes, and she blinked furiously before stepping back and batting away the praise.

'Just a simple marketing ploy. Got to raise as much dough as possible for the cause. For Gaz,' she added.

Though it wouldn't have mattered if Gracie had chosen The Society of Missing Socks as the recipient of her sponsorship money, Jill would still have pulled out all the stops. That was simply who she was; she only wished her sister could see it. Perhaps, God willing, they were beginning to put the past behind them and focus on the here and now. Although there were still several hurdles to jump first, and some of them, Jill knew with absolute certainty, were not going to be as easy as producing a printed t-shirt.

On Tuesday evening, Jill was upstairs folding a pile of washing, when Emily called upstairs.

'Mum, I'm just walking into town to meet the guys after their run.'

It had been nearly three months since her ankle injury and she had gradually been increasing her walking distances, and taking part in her beach cleans most Sundays. Then she'd announced over dinner the previous evening that as of this Saturday, she intended to start running again. She might only manage a small part of the usual route, but it would be a start.

However, whilst Emily had been making giant strides in a full physical recovery, she had yet to move back home to her London flat.

'You want to be careful you don't turn up there one day to find your room's been let to someone else, and your belongings have gone to charity,' Jill had remarked the other day, half in jest.

'Wouldn't be the end of the world. I have everything I need here anyway; we all have far too much stuff, that's the problem.' Emily had shrugged, as though the fact she was paying out half her salary for living quarters she didn't inhabit was neither here nor there.

It was great that Emily was able to work from home, and had only needed to go into the office a handful of times for meetings, which rather begged the question – why keep the flat on?

'OK, love,' called back Jill, picking up a pair of Emily's jeans from the laundry pile, and beginning to fold them. She faltered. There had to be a reason Emily was avoiding her life in London. Why else would she continue to hang around here? All this time they'd been under the same roof and still Jill hadn't found the right time to talk to her about it.

Seized with the panicked thought that something terrible must have happened, something Emily wasn't facing up to, at work, at home, or elsewhere, Jill imagined months and years trickling by in this limbo state, with both of them dancing around each other and never addressing the elephant in the room. She wasn't going to let that happen again. Not with *her* daughter.

'Hold up, love,' she called down the stairwell, just as Emily had one hand on the front door handle. 'Give us two minutes and I'll come with you. I could do with a walk.'

'Sure,' said Emily, sinking down onto the bottom stair to wait.

Jill ran back into her bedroom and glanced at herself in the mirror. Her hair needed washing, she had on an old pair of leggings and a long fleecy jumper she only wore when lounging around at home and hadn't the time to change. It wasn't the image she usually liked to present. But bugger it, this wasn't about other people. It was about her and Emily. Who said she had to go *into* the pub anyway; she could walk her down there and turn around to walk back.

Jill felt she was good at many things: she made a lovely cake, she was organised and driven, she took good care of her appearance. What she wasn't good at was subtlety. They'd virtually reached the end of the high street and all she'd done was waffle on about her jazzed-up paperback display at the hospice shop, books arranged according to their coloured spines, rather than alphabetically, which had met with some criticism from Cynthia, before the first and only question that slipped from her lips outside the pub was 'Is there something you want to tell me?'

Emily stared back at her blankly. 'Er, you're going to have to help me out here?'

'Anything to do with your London flatmates? Or your work colleagues perhaps?'

'Sorry?' said Emily, her face screwed in confusion. 'I don't know what you mean.'

Jill balled her hands into fists inside her coat pockets. Why was this so difficult? Although, of course, she knew the answer to that. It was all just too close to home.

'What I mean is, why don't you want to go home? Back to London.'

Understanding seemed to dawn then, and her daughter's beautiful pale face tightened into something rather unattractive.

'Ah,' she said grimly. 'I get it. I've overstayed my welcome. OK.' She nodded and pushed on the heavy door. 'It's OK, Mum. I'll sort it. Funny thing though, I'd kind of thought this *was* home. My mistake. Are you coming in or what?'

Jill opened and closed her mouth as the door swung shut and Emily disappeared inside. Jill scanned the street in both directions to see if anyone had overheard, her overriding instinct, as always, being to plaster a smile on her face as though it had all been a jolly good joke. But there wasn't anyone to have seen or cared. It was just her and the creaking overhead pub sign, swinging in a gentle breeze, like a scene from a Western, right before the shoot-out.

She couldn't leave it like that. Couldn't have Emily thinking that. She'd have to get her on her own and explain; assure her that that wasn't what she meant. She smoothed back her windswept hair, took a deep breath and pushed on the door.

Inside, Emily was already seated at a table with Gracie and Ray, looking all cosy in the corner, whilst Malik and Sophia chatted at the bar.

Gracie threw her head back and hooted with laughter at something Ray said to Emily, all wind-flushed cheeks and bright eyed, with light-catching silvery strands escaping from her plait that always looked so stylish in a not-put-together way. Most probably, they were ridiculing her. Having a good old laugh behind her back.

'Gracie,' she said as she approached the table, the accusatory edge in her tone causing them to all look up. 'What is that?' she asked, pointing to the pint glass in Gracie's hand.

'Er, my drink?' said Gracie, eyebrows pinching together in confusion. 'Sit down, I'll get you one. What are you having?'

'I can't believe you're not taking the nutrition plan seriously. Your body is taking a hammering and there's only five weeks to go. How are you going to hit twenty miles this week if you insist on swigging alcohol instead of the appropriate nutritional fuel you need?'

'Are you kidding, Jill?' called Sophia from the bar. 'There's more nutritional content in that pint of Guinness than in one of my mam's roast dinners.' She turned back to Malik. 'Although to be fair, that wouldn't be hard. Mam's idea of a balanced meal is equal parts roasties and gravy. You could sail a catamaran on one of her dinner plates.'

Malik grinned. 'Sounds like the perfect roast to me.'

Jill's skin prickled hot. Why did she always feel like this? As though everyone was in an exclusive club, and she didn't know the secret password. How did everyone else always manage to seem so easy around each other?

'Sit down, Mum,' said Emily, nothing in her tone to suggest she was annoyed with her. 'Ray was in the middle of telling us about a callout he had on the lifeboat today. Apparently, someone tried to paddleboard out to sea on an ironing board; luckily no-one was hurt. I'll get your drink. The usual?'

Jill conjured a life-and-soul-of-the-party belly laugh from somewhere, causing a few bemused faces, before sinking into a chair and trying to appear rapt at Ray's anecdote as he continued actively avoiding eye contact with her sister. All the time wondering, how was it her own daughter could read her like a book, yet *she* couldn't even begin to work her own self out.

14

Gracie

Sunday, 30th March, as well as being Mother's Day, marked four weeks exactly to the London Marathon. It was also the point in the training schedule at which Gracie should be peaking in terms of distance, before tapering back down again and resting (according to Jill).

So far, Gracie's longest run had been twelve miles, or 19 kilometres, all the way from Frinton to beyond Jaywick, where she'd dropped onto the sand in an exhausted heap and telephoned Andrew to come and pick her up. Galvanising her limbs to get to the car had damned near finished her off, never mind performing cool-down stretches. But still, she reminded herself, as she forced herself to do Jill's abominable morning exercise routine, it was three times the distance she had been running back in November. And yet it still wasn't even half a marathon. She would have to push herself today, rest day or not.

But first, there was something far more important to attend to.

'Nana! Look, I lost a tooth!'

Gracie's heart contracted as the red-headed six-year-old with pigtails and a distinctly feral look loomed into view on her iPad screen and showed the cavernous inside of her mouth.

Olivia was Gracie and Andrew's youngest and loudest granddaughter, whereas twelve-year-old Charlotte, or Charlie as she preferred to be called, was somewhat more reserved and hated appearing on screen. It was funny, mused Gracie, how in her experience, two siblings were rarely alike. They might share cannily similar physical traits, might share the same values and core beliefs, but their characters were so often wildly different, as though nature provided the DNA equivalent of aloe vera to cool a hot head. She wondered which sister she would be in her own analogy, the after-sun lotion, or the sun. The one who burnt, or the one who got burnt? Probably best not to dwell upon that. Anyway, at present it was her calf muscles that burnt like hell. She reached down to rub at her left leg, whilst beaming back at her granddaughter.

'What a brave girl you are, Liv. And was the tooth fairy kind?'

Liv nodded furiously. 'She paid me five dollars! I'm going to save it up for. . .'

'Right then, Olivia,' called Nathan, swooping off the sofa to grab his daughter from behind. He planted a kiss on her cheek. 'It's way past your bedtime, young lady. Now say goodnight to Nana.'

Liv's face clouded over in a clear signal that she was about to protest, when Beth's arm shot out from where she must have been sitting on the sofa all along, just out of view. So nice of her to say hello, thought Gracie, hating the fact she had to conduct her conversations with her family like this, as though she were the teacher at the front of a class, aware of unseen gestures and whispers each time she turned her back.

'Come on, munchkin, let Daddy have a chat with Nana. Let's go brush the rest of those teeth before they all fall out! We don't want to bankrupt the Tooth Fairy.' Beth took Liv by the hand, then together they gave a little wave at the screen. 'Night, Nana. Love you, Nana.'

Once they had left the screen, Gracie ventured, 'Five dollars for a baby tooth, eh? I seem to remember you being happy with twenty pence.'

'Cost of living crisis,' he smirked. 'Ice creams don't cost what they used to. Anyway, what's wrong with your leg, why do you keep rubbing it?'

Gracie withdrew her hand immediately. She'd sworn Andrew to absolute secrecy about her marathon attempt. As far as their son was aware, she was still stubbornly running on a Saturday morning with the club, and he'd given her enough grief over that. Doubtless he was also behind the most recent of Andrew's inventions – a tracking device that fitted to her shoe. She couldn't decide if the bulky rectangular object made her feel more like a tagged prisoner, or the pet of a zealous cat owner.

'Nothing's wrong, pins and needles, that's all. Anyway, thank you for the gorgeous flowers, darling, they arrived yesterday. Brightened up the kitchen no end.'

Nathan smiled. 'You're welcome. Happy Mother's Day! I only wish I could have delivered them in person, but I guess that might have bumped up the postage cost a bit.'

The slight tightening of his brow was a life-long gesture and betrayed the sadness behind his bright chat. Gracie knew him well enough to know the distance between them weighed as heavily on him, as it did them. But it was her job to reassure him his decisions were for the best. That the lifestyle was better for their family, even as it broke her heart.

'Where's Dad?' he asked.

'Do you need to ask?' She jerked her head in the general direction of the shed. 'Working on something revolutionary, apparently. . .'

She only hoped it wasn't another dratted contraption intended for her. If he weighed her down with anything else, she may as well throw on a grey mac and call herself Inspector Gadget.

Nathan gave an amused snort. 'Keeps him out of mischief. How is he? Really?'

This, Gracie understood, translated to *How much should I worry about him, Mum? How much longer do I get to spend bodyboarding with my girls and enjoying hot, lazy days with friends, mending fences on Beth's folks' farm whilst the girls feed the chooks and working in a job I love, before I must consciously choose this lifestyle over him.* If only she could make him understand, there was no choice to make.

'He's OK,' she said kindly. 'Shouldn't be waiting too much longer for the op now, then he'll be right as rain.'

He'd never be right as rain. The other knee was starting to disintegrate, and his right shoulder was giving him increasingly more jip. But with a few small adjustments, he was leading a normal life. To Gracie that seemed to be what getting older was all about – small adjustments and a lot of tall orders.

After the video call with Nathan, Gracie popped her head into the shed, which was really more of a small industrial warehouse taking up at least two-thirds of the garden, and waited patiently, until Andrew wasn't wielding an angle grinder, to cough and announce her presence.

'Alright, love?' he asked, pushing up his goggles.

Lord only knew what he was making now, but it looked like Armageddon, his workbench littered with what looked like the insides of an old laptop, wires protruding like torn arteries, tools scattered everywhere and the air thick with the stench of fermenting hops. He had three plastic barrels on the go, stacked against the wall on an old metal trolley; pipes, funnels and other equipment stacked underneath.

'Off for a run,' she said. 'A long one.'

He nodded. 'Have you got your—'

'Debit card? Telephone? Water bottle? Hat? Sunscreen, even

though it's still March, oh, and my GPS tracker? Yes, Andrew,' she snapped, tapping various parts of her body for effect, 'got all those. What I don't have is much strength left to actually lift my legs off the ground.'

Andrew's face fell and she regretted her tone immediately. He was just being his normal, caring, kind self. He certainly didn't deserve her taking out her frustrations on him. It was her own stupid idea to take up this ridiculous challenge.

She stepped further into the cabin of creativity and kissed him on the lips.

'See you at teatime. If you're good we're having steak and chips.'

His face brightened. 'Onion rings?' he ventured.

'Big bag of them in the freezer, the beer-battered ones, your favourites.'

And what would Jill make of that, she wondered, closing the shed door behind her and waiting until she was off the drive before breaking into a jog. Processed food, oven chips and slow-to-digest beef, washed down with a good Malbec. If she followed Jill's schedule, she'd be eating nothing but bananas, sweet potatoes, eggs and avocados. She also wouldn't be running today, which was supposed to be a rest day, yet how else was she supposed to improve if she didn't keep at it? Her yellow trainers glowed radioactive in the mist coming off the sea, distracting her even though she focused straight ahead. It was like having one of these pesky dancing spots in the corner of your vision from staring too long at a light bulb. There were just four weeks to build up her stamina and she *had* to know if she could do it. The thought of failing, of having to abandon the race – it had her waking at night in a cold sweat. So, whilst Jill had only good intentions, Gracie was going off script. Today's run would rack up the miles, and the thought of the steak and chips would help her get there.

'You ran how many?' asked Emily that Tuesday evening as they jogged through the streets.

'Can't be sure, as I don't use a Smartarse-watch or FitGit like some, but I managed to get to Lee-over-Sands, then back as far as Clacton Pier.'

Emily looked at her in awe. 'Auntie Gracie, that's got to be like fifteen miles or something?'

'Mmm, fourteen according to Google. But it's certainly the furthest I've ever managed.'

'That's incredible. I've never managed anything like that,' said Emily, shaking her head in wonder.

'My darling, you never got the chance. Not this time, but there's always next year.'

She made a noncommittal sound. 'Perhaps.'

Emily was making huge progress with her ankle, and at a slow steady pace was managing the CPR Saturday morning and Tuesday evening runs. It was absolutely clear to anyone though that she was in pain by the end of it and had to spend a good proportion of the week continuing with strengthening exercises. Kat had done an extremely thorough job. Of course the intolerable woman continued to blithely ignore them, buzzing around Giles instead, like a persistent wasp. She had proclaimed herself to be Giles's pacer, a running partner with the sole purpose of *setting the optimum running pace*, so as to avoid early burn-out, according to Giles who was still intent on a sub-three-hour finish time.

'But what about on marathon day?' Gracie had asked him the other day. 'Kat won't be there with you then.'

He'd tapped his watch. 'Does it all. As I told you at the start, best investment you could have made. Such a shame. Far too late now to change bad habits. . .' He'd offered a conciliatory smile, as though she'd already failed before reaching the starting line.

Jumped-up little twat.

'Sounds like Kat might be your bad habit,' she'd muttered under her breath as he sprinted away. And bad habits die hard when you try to kick them, so you'd better watch your neck, was the advice she perhaps should have given.

'Can't stop, guys,' said Malik now, as the pub came into sight. 'And I won't see you at the weekend either. Mum and Dad are off to Sri Lanka first thing and the ex is in hospital having a small op.'

'Oh, that's a shame,' said Sophia, then seeming to realise she'd said it out loud, added, 'I mean, that sounds full on. What about work?'

'Well, I'm sure I won't be the first IT support guy to talk their client through a system reboot whilst their kids merrily pelt each other with a NERF gun in the background,' he said with a resigned shrug.

Emily said, 'Poor guy looks exhausted already,' as he walked away.

'You're not kidding. I've no idea how he does it,' agreed Sophia.

Gracie had nothing but admiration for Malik, juggling the demands of a home and career as a single parent. She already knew from a conversation weeks ago that he'd had to turn down a training opportunity; a course that would have meant a pay grade leap and the opening of new doors. 'Too much time away from home,' he'd explained. 'My parents are in their seventies, it's too much for them.'

Sometimes life served you reminders of how lucky you were. Still here, still surviving, no financial worries to speak of. A full-grown child with a family of his own, whole, healthy and happy. It made her own selfish pursuits seem trivial.

'I'll see you all on Saturday,' said Gracie, coming to a halt at the pub door. 'Jill has a gruelling day planned for me tomorrow. Best behaviour and all that.'

Emily hugged her goodbye, then linked arms with Sophia and followed Ray into the pub. They were all becoming firm friends, and this cheered Gracie because this was by far the biggest benefit of any club. Yes, she loved to run, but joining the CPR had filled a hole she hadn't even known was there since retiring from teaching. She'd found a new community.

The following day yielded a series of disappointments.

Firstly, over breakfast, Andrew presented her with a new hat. It was similar to her favourite battered old beige baseball cap, purchased years ago from a popular outdoor clothing retailer and beloved for its comfort and ability to keep her long braided hair from whipping her in the face. Except this one was crisp, pristine and considerably deeper. So deep, in fact, that Gracie knew without picking it up that it would be weighty, and not *just* a hat.

'You know how you always get so hot,' began Andrew excitedly, 'and complain about sweat dripping in your eyes?'

At this, Gracie flinched. She didn't enjoy the idea of her husband dwelling on things like sweaty foreheads and resolved to keep such complaints to herself in future. Why couldn't he present her with a strawberry Cornetto when she got home from a run instead, the universal cure for all sweatiness, surely?

'Well,' he continued, allowing a dramatic pause for the big reveal, 'let me give you the world's first air-conditioned baseball cap. Look,' he said, turning the hat over to show the inner workings, 'this semi-conductor cools the fluid which passes through a heat exchanger, then this miniature fan directs the cooled air downwards onto your head. It's powered by a rechargeable lithium battery and a small pump which you can slot into the running backpack I made you. Nobody will notice the tubes running down beneath your vest, it's incredibly lightweight, see?'

Silently, Gracie took the hat from him and weighed it in her hands. Not *lightweight*, exactly, not in the way an actual, fit-for-purpose hat should be, but not quite the clunky helmet she'd expected.

'You switch it on with this small button here, hidden in the peak, see?' instructed Andrew, demonstrating by pressing on the raised small knob and bringing the whirring sound of a struggling, dust-clogged computer fan to life. 'Some of the parts came out of an old laptop – clever, eh?'

So it was, in fact, the sound of a computer fan she was hearing.

Gracie cleared her throat. 'And what is there to prevent my hair from being ripped clean from my scalp by the blades of this fan?' she asked, in as level a tone as she was able to achieve.

Andrew smiled. 'It's enclosed behind a grille. It's quite safe, I've trialled it several times.'

Gracie looked at the perfectly symmetrical sphere of smooth skin at the back of his head of curly hair, his 'Friar Tuck'. Hmm.

'OK then. Saddle me up.'

Because that's what she was, surely? A pack horse finding itself in the stalls of the Grand National, beside multi-million-dollar thoroughbreds.

Owing to the hat's accessories, it sat a little proud and needed to be fastened with a chin strap to keep it from toppling off, but otherwise, Gracie noted, it was surprisingly effective, delivering a gentle but consistent iciness to her cranium. It would give the well-used idiom 'to keep a cool head' a whole new meaning, because she suspected the wearer may end up with brain freeze.

Next on the agenda for Wednesday morning was the peak point of Jill's training plan, 'the long run', which should see Gracie completing twenty miles, before entering what was known as the taper phase in the final fortnight pre-marathon day, designed to conserve as much energy as possible. Gracie did not feel ready for today's undertaking. She'd already racked up the miles on Sunday, then again on Monday and again last night. Her legs were sore, her mind was tired, her heels were cracked, and she'd lost a little toenail courtesy of the hated yellow trainers which rubbed like billyo. But on the plus side, she had a cool forehead. What was making today's prospect doubly grim was the knowledge that Jill planned to pop up at two-mile intervals, brandishing sports drinks and energy bars in simulation of the big day and to cheer her on, as though the deserted seafront promenade in April was any match for The Mall.

Just as Gracie was downing one of Jill's pre-race smoothies, a recipe she'd modified herself into something that was actually drinkable, rather than the green gunk her sister had served up, her phone buzzed with a text on the kitchen table.

It was from Emily.

Have you seen Malik's WhatsApp message? Poor guy ☹

Poor guy? What had happened? Gracie scrolled through to WhatsApp, which showed seventeen unread messages. She really should switch her notifications back on.

She swiftly scanned through the messages, all of them from the CPR group chat.

Malik   *Heads up to anyone I saw last night. Bad sickness bug this end. Won't go into details. Hope it's not catching.*

Sophia   *Sorry to hear that, Mal. Do you think you should see the doc?*

Emily   *Definitely see the doc!*

144

Malik	Can't leave loo. Sorry if TMI.
Kat	Seriously? I was eating my breakfast.
Sophia	Thought you didn't look at your messages @Kat
Malik	Sorry
Sophia	Don't fecking apologise, Mal. Last time I checked, nobody ever forced anyone to look at their phone whilst eating their breakfast.

At this Gracie laughed aloud. Not at poor Malik's predicament, but at the outrage she could hear in Sophia's tone. God love that girl.

@Kat has left the group

Sophia	Good fecking riddance
Ray	What have you eaten Mal? Could it be food poisoning?
Emily	Are the kids OK?
Malik	Uh-huh. Watching Despicable Me. At least I think they are.
Giles	Kids skipping school. Tut, tut. Two big black marks for you.
Sophia	Oh you can bog off too @Giles. Does nobody give a shit about Mal?

Giles	*I think the whole problem boils down to the giving of much shit. LOL*
Sophia	*Spoiler for the squeamish and stupid – got to go dress a gaping wound in an elderly gentleman's inner thigh right now, but Mal, I'll call you when I knock off this evening.*

'Everything alright?' asked Andrew, coming back into the kitchen and seeing Gracie frowning at her phone screen.

She looked up at him. At her kind, caring husband, always so supportive and positive. A problem solver, who would see a friend in need and instantly understand what should be done.

'Everything's fine. However, I suspect I'm about to set my sister on the warpath by not following orders.'

She gave Andrew a quick hug. 'Change of plan. Popping out for a bit, but not for a run, I'll call you later.'

15

Jill

As the Coast Path Runners bundled into Victory Hall on Saturday morning, Jill's hackles began to rise. No sign of Gracie, or Andrew for that matter.

The marathon was just three weeks tomorrow. *Three weeks.* And yet, it looked to all intents and purposes as though Gracie had decided playing fairy godmother was of far more importance than all the generous benefactors and sponsors who had promised their money to Alzheimer's Outreach UK in Gary's name. Of course, Gracie didn't know the half of it, had probably thought the flimsy form Emily printed out from the official London Marathon website for her to drum up sponsorship from friends and family represented the total pledged sum. It did not.

Jill beckoned Emily over to the serving hatch.

'What's up, Mum?' she said, bright-eyed and radiant in her purple CPR kit.

'Where's Gracie?' Jill hissed. 'Didn't she run today?'

Emily's face shuttered. 'No. She and Uncle Andrew have taken the kids to the zoo.'

'The ZOO?' repeated Jill, her voice shooting up an octave. 'Seriously? What the hell is she playing at? She's supposed to be training for a *marathon*, Em. And instead, she's at the zoo.'

'Why are you shouting?' asked Emily, her cheeks reddening. 'Stop being embarrassing. I think it's really kind of Auntie Gracie to step in and help Malik out this week.'

Jill leaned forward and lowered her voice. 'Shall I tell you what's kind? The Bell and Whistle in Hemel Hempstead having a charity quiz night to raise funds for Alzheimer's Outreach UK in honour of your father. Tony Hadley, for bidding a five-figure sum on your dad's guitar at auction. What should I tell these people, Emily, when your aunt bails at the first mile because she's been babysitting for someone she barely knows instead of putting in the work? Don't you think it was hard enough to convince them someone of her age could actually run a marathon in the first place?'

The look of disappointment reflected back in her daughter's eyes took Jill's breath away.

'I don't know, Mum.' She shrugged. 'Maybe you can tell them your seventy-two-year-old sister is more than just a novelty act? That she has friends and family who she cares about more than adhering to your spreadsheet? Nobody said she wasn't putting in the training; she's just not dancing to your tune. Oh, and for what it's worth, Malik is far more than someone we barely know – he's our friend and a thoroughly decent bloke, someone who's had a rough time.'

Emily went back to sit with the others and Jill pushed down the paranoia that rose up and threatened to choke her every time she glanced over and caught them laughing. *Our* friend.

'What's the matter with you today, Jilly?' asked Eugene, looking up from his game of chess when she appeared at his side. 'You've got a face like an angry bear.'

'Nothing's wrong with me,' she snapped. 'And please don't call me Jilly. Are you having anything to eat?'

She stood brandishing her notepad and pen and suddenly felt ridiculous. What had once been her favourite place to come and chat and have a good laugh with these larger-than-life characters, now seemed cheapened. What had she been thinking? She was nothing more than an ageing waitress who didn't even get paid. She didn't get to sit playing games with them and eating cake. *She* was still on the outside of the gates.

'That depends—' winked Eugene, seemingly unperturbed by her bluntness '—on what you have to offer?'

Was he ridiculing her? She could no longer tell. Never had been any good at telling the difference between those who made fun and those who were simply funny.

She gave a long, weary sigh. 'I didn't have time to bake yesterday, I'm afraid.'

This was a slight fib. What she had actually been doing was pacing her kitchen and getting herself more and more worked up by the fact that Gracie had texted her on Wednesday to say she wouldn't be running for a few days because something urgent had 'come up'. It was only when Emily had mentioned over dinner that evening that her poor running friend was sick with suspected food poisoning and that he had two kids to look after, that things had clicked into place.

'So, it's just Cynthia's cream scones on the cake front, I'm afraid, homemade minestrone soup and I think we have some packets of biscuits,' she added, having the good grace to feel ashamed that she'd let the Be Together Café customers down.

At this a titter rippled through the group.

'Ooh, put me down for a scone please, Jill,' said Ray. 'Easy on the jam. Hard on the cream.' He gave her a playful wink, which took her slightly by surprise.

'A scone for me too please,' said Sophia.

'Count me in,' said Harold, sliding his bishop across the board. 'And that, my friend. . . is checkmate!'

As Eugene contested Harold's move and they descended into one of their usual disagreements, she continued taking orders, her shame deepening as everyone ordered the scones. Hungry customers and she'd let them down, leaving them with only boring old scones to choose from, instead of tasty homemade cakes. She couldn't let that happen again.

A few days later, a message arrived from Gracie.

Hi Jill. Just to say, I'm about to tackle the big run. I know you're working in the hospice shop today, so don't worry about coming down, I'll report back later.

A week later than scheduled. The training plan was completely up the spout.

Well, better late than never, she supposed.

Jill slid her phone back into her pocket and got back to the task of sorting through a donation bag brought in earlier by a customer.

'Any scarves?' enquired Cynthia, poking her head in the stockroom.

'Nothing yet,' said Jill. 'Just more woolly jumpers.'

'Happens every spring,' said Cynthia. 'Besieged by winter clothing, just when folks are looking for a nice cropped trouser.'

She was right. The first days of April had brought glorious sunshine, earlier mornings and later evenings. Spring was definitely in the air.

Jill checked the time. By her calculation, Gracie would be on the return leg of her run in around three hours.

'Cynthia? Mind if I skip lunch and finish slightly earlier today? I need to pop into Clacton.'

At half past three, Jill parked up in Clacton's busy town centre and dashed into Tesco Express. Then she took her purchases and hotfooted it to the seafront, where amusement arcades, doughnut sellers and ice-cream stands were waking from their winter hiatus ready for the Easter holidays and the first tourists of the season. She descended the steps to the promenade and strolled away from the noise of the pier. The sky overhead was a cloudless blue and though there was warmth in the sun, she wished she'd brought her coat from the car, as she sat down, legs dangling over the seawall, and settled in to wait.

Within twenty minutes, a familiar figure appeared up ahead, striding purposefully.

Walking was fine, Jill reminded herself. They'd been practising intermittent running, which allowed the body to recover at walking pace before breaking back into a sprint. Many long-distance runners used this training technique.

However, as Gracie grew nearer, she showed no signs of running. In fact, she looked positively murderous.

'Jill,' she said, tight-lipped as her sister rose to standing. 'What are you doing here?'

'I came to give you this,' said Jill, holding up the energy drink in one hand and a protein bar in the other. 'And to do this.' She pumped her arms in the air as though cheering on her favourite football team, and chanted, 'Grac-ie, Grac-ie, Gra. . .' Her limp patter fizzled out. 'Gracie, why is your hair green?'

Gracie looked fit to drop. Her hair was all frizzy and had escaped its braid, sticking to her scalp in a greenish liquid, which had drizzled down the side of her face.

'This?' she said, with a high note of sarcasm. 'Oh, this would just be the refrigeration coolant my husband built, rather unsuccessfully, into my new hat. I'm thanking my lucky stars it wasn't battery acid.'

Gracie unscrewed the cap of the energy drink and glugged it down in one.

'Thanks,' she said, then, 'have you got the car?'

Jill bristled. 'Yes, but you need to carry on, Gracie, practising endurance is crucial for the big day. I can take that for you.' She held out her hand to take the wet, stained cap that seemed to be attached to a small box with straps.

'I don't need you to take it, I'd just very much like a lift home please,' said Gracie.

'But. . .'

'But *what*, Jill?' asked Gracie, grey eyes flashing angrily. 'I've had enough. I want to go home and soak my ruined feet and my stinking hair in the bath, if that's quite alright with you, Sergeant Major.'

Jill began nodding slowly. 'I see. And that's the thanks I get, is it? For giving up all my free time to help you train, for being your cheerleader, going out of my way to raise money and find sponsors, all whilst *you* decide to be Mary Poppins for the week and look after someone else's children, when I'm sure there were plenty of others he could have called upon to help. If you hadn't kept skipping training and supping pints in the pub with your *mates*, maybe you wouldn't be finding this quite so hard now, eh?'

'Supping pints in the pub?' questioned Gracie, her voice rasping. 'Being my cheerleader?' She shook her head and scrunched her eyes, as though trying to shake off a bad dream. 'Are you *serious*, Jill? Since when have you ever been my cheerleader? You *disappeared* for nearly forty years. And then only popped back up in my life after I'd spent the best part of five years caring for our mother. *Our* mother, Jill. You know, the woman who gave birth to you and who needed round-the-clock care as she slowly faded away. And then *you* have the cheek to criticise *me* for wanting to help out a sick friend with two young children. Well, obviously you were never going to understand that, were you? Because you were always far too selfish to put yourself in anyone else's shoes.'

Jill fizzed with fury.

'How dare you. You've got no idea what you're talking about. You know nothing about my life. It's you who should be grateful to me, for coming here and extending the olive branch, because Lord knows there's plenty who wouldn't.'

Gracie went deathly still, and Jill experienced a frisson of fear. This wasn't how this was supposed to go. She'd wanted to get closer to her sister so they could talk things through. So she could finally tell her side of the story.

Gracie spoke slowly and calmly, delivering her words with icy steel.

'You're unbelievable. Mum knew what you were, but I always defended you and made your excuses. Well, she's gone now and it's too late to make amends. With her *or* Dad.'

16

Gracie

As the words left Gracie's mouth, she knew she'd gone too far.

Jill might be standing there scowling at her in suede ankle boots unfit for the east coast in April and the most garish pink and gold print blouse she'd ever seen in her life, but she was also the wide-eyed, cute little girl who had looked adoringly up to her older sister and hung on her every word. Surely that version of Jill had to still be in there somewhere? Gracie had always found it so hard to correlate her mother's version of Jill with the one she'd known. Yet the facts had spoken for themselves. . .

'So that's what this is all about is it?' said Jill, hurt lancing across her face. 'You've been giving me the benefit of the doubt since Mum died and now – what? I've been found to be sadly lacking? Well, I'm sorry, Gracie, for never living up to the extremely high standards set by you in our family. I'm very sorry for my inconvenient arrival in this world, but you know what, perhaps Mother should have given a little more thought to birth control rather than taking it out on me. Because that's all I ever was to her, a scapegoat. Someone's feet, at which to pour all of life's shortcomings.'

Gracie looked to the sky.

'Gillian, you disappeared! How could you possibly feel sidelined when you were the one who buggered off?'

At this Jill let out a nasty laugh. 'Oh, you're a fine one to talk. And what about when you turned your back on me when I needed you most? Disappearing across the continent to look at crumbling buildings and frescoes was more important to you than I ever was, so don't go getting on your high horse now.'

Exhaustion swept through Gracie, threatening to overwhelm her. She did not want to be standing on Clacton seafront having a screaming match with her sister, and certainly not whilst three feet away a gentleman on a mobility scooter had parked himself up under the guise of looking out to sea, when he was clearly having a good old earwig.

'Look, Jill,' she said, fiddling with the cap of the drinks bottle in her hand. 'Clearly, at some point you feel I let you down. I apologise for going off to live my young adult life and leaving you alone at home. And I'm sorry if I ever made you feel less than. That has never, nor ever would be my intention. But I will never understand what our mother did to deserve your treatment of her. Perhaps you can enlighten me one day, eh?'

Jill's face filled with scorn and her top lip curled. 'Do you know what, don't trouble yourself. It was a mistake moving here. A huge mistake.'

With that, she tossed her blow-dried hair, flailed her arms and turned to leave. Then, she spun around and thrust the protein bar at Gracie.

'For the walk back. And don't forget your quad and hamstring stretches. Unless you want runners' knee.'

And with that, she stomped off, her heels clip-clopping along the pavement as she went, until she turned, ascended the steps and disappeared out of sight.

So much for the lift home.

Slowly, Gracie galvanised her sore, aching feet into moving again.

As she passed the man in the mobility scooter, he gave her a smile and a little wave, as though he'd paid for front row seats at the theatre and was trying to get the attention of the cast.

'Hungry?' she asked, then chucked the unwanted protein bar into the basket at the front of his scooter. It would only be another tasteless piece of cardboard, with chaffs of wheat that got stuck in her back teeth.

Gracie knew that if she just picked up her feet and began to run, she'd get home a damned sight quicker, but she hadn't the energy or the inclination to run another step. Long before she'd encountered Jill on the shore, the spring had left her shoe, along with her other little toenail. She could feel it scratching at her inside her sock. Then the leaked coolant had put a literal dampener on things, and she'd thought to herself, *Why the hell am I doing this?* Why was she forcing her aching, screaming body through this agony, all for the sake of what. . . pride? A moment of extreme anger and a desire to lash back at Kat. . . *You do not get to take this dream away from my niece.*

And then, of course, Jill had so kindly reminded her of her lack of commitment to the cause.

Well, Jill hadn't been the one welcomed into Malik's home by a seven-year-old boy bearing a forehead decorated in permanent marker pen, whilst his father groaned from the bathroom and his nine-year-old sister gawped at *Bridgerton*'s X-rated scenes. Why the heck Malik hadn't set up parental controls on Netflix had been Gracie's first thought, swiftly followed by a mental note to google The Duke. It had been immediately clear, however, that Malik needed help, and with his ex-wife recovering from abdominal surgery and his parents sunning themselves in Sri Lanka, Gracie would have defied anyone not to step up to the plate.

They were sweet kids, actually. And once Gracie had instilled order and called out a GP to see to Malik (plenty of fluids, penicillin and bed rest), they'd settled at the table with her tried and tested child-friendly activity (made all the more attractive with KitKats) – who can draw the best, e.g. dog, cat, house, tree, octopus, and so on. Always a winner among competitive youngsters, and especially effective with drunk adults, only it was packaged into a box, cost fifty quid and was marketed as Pictionary.

The trip to the zoo on Saturday had been great fun too. Donkey's years since she and Andrew had been, and something she frequently fantasised about doing with her own grandchildren.

But perhaps she'd handled the situation badly. In her eagerness to be a good friend to Malik when he was in need, perhaps she'd made it seem to Jill as though she didn't matter. Hadn't considered her feelings. This whole damned situation was completely out of control.

Almost two hours later, and five hours since she set out that morning, Gracie limped back through the front door to find Andrew sitting in the kitchen waiting, his mobile phone in front of him.

'Gracie. Thank God,' he said, getting to his feet. 'Where have you been?'

This was a highly unusual response from her husband, who wasn't by nature a worrier and who had known she'd be out for a good portion of the day.

'What do you mean?' she snapped. 'You know where I've been. Out for a run.'

He looked back at her with concern. 'I looked to see where you were on the tracker, to see how long you might be – it wasn't moving. Then I tried your phone but it was turned off. I thought something must have happened. What's wrong with your hair?'

Gracie huffed out a sigh. 'My phone is off because I was conserving the battery. And this,' she said, plopping the sodden baseball cap on the table in front of him, 'is quite some way off being a patented and marketable product just yet. I'd hold off on the application to *Dragons' Den* if I were you.'

Andrew picked up the hat and grimaced as he looked inside.

'The movement must have caused too much friction on the semi-conductor,' he said, rubbing his chin thoughtfully. 'I think if I just...'

'No, Andrew,' said Gracie, a little more forcefully than she'd intended. 'Please, don't *just* do anything. I never wanted a poxy air-conditioned hat. Just like I never wanted to be strapped into a harness, or made to wear these... hideous, expensive, uncomfortable shoes,' she said, levering them one by one from her sweaty, bloodied, socked feet. 'Oh, and the GPS tracker flew off my foot at some point. It'll make for a disappointing discovery by some poor detectorist scouring the beach for treasure, I expect. All I wanted to do was run. That's all. And now I'm not sure I even want to do that.'

She closed her eyes against the throbbing in her temple.

'I am making a cup of tea, then I am going upstairs for a soak in the bath. I may be some time.'

Gracie went to fill the kettle, trying not to dwell on the look of hurt surprise that had registered on Andrew's face. He didn't deserve her venting her frustrations on him, but she wished he would just stop interfering, however well meant.

In the loaded silence, the kettle boiled itself into a maelstrom of fury, before she flipped it off. That was it, the blasted thing was going in the bin tomorrow; Andrew was never going to get around to fixing it. Not whilst he was so busy reinventing the wheel.

'Aren't you going to ask why I was trying to get hold of you?' he said eventually, from where he was still seated at the kitchen table.

'Sorry?'

'I was waiting to speak to you,' he explained, 'to let you know this came today.'

It was then that Gracie noticed the piece of paper on the table beside his phone.

'Oh?' she said, conflicting feelings flooding her core. Bad news. Had to be, nobody ever tried contacting someone urgently unless it was bad news. Was it Nathan?

Andrew tapped the paper. 'Knee replacement op. I've got a date.'

Gracie forgot her sour mood in an instant, her entire body relaxing with relief. 'Andrew, that's brilliant news. Thank goodness. When is it? When's the op?'

He gave a compassionate but sad smile.

'Well, that's just it, Gracie love. Sunday the twenty-seventh of April. Marathon Day.'

17

Gracie

In days gone by, breakfast would have been a noisy, hectic affair in the Jenkins household; Gracie constantly trying to rescue Andrew's students' homework from coffee cup stains, the feeding of various pets invariably taking precedence over any nutritious breakfast of their own, which usually consisted of buttered toast clamped between teeth, whilst bags, briefcases, keys and books were bundled into cars.

Since retirement, however, breakfast usually began with a cuppa in bed, courtesy of whomever had to give in to their bladder first. Picasso would need a quick circuit of the back garden to complete her own ablutions too and Banksy would be miaowing at his empty biscuit bowl. Then they'd acquired the terrible habit of adding a couple of digestive biscuits to the cuppa in bed, *just to tide them over*, because, until Gracie's training had intensified, there'd been no real urgency to get up. And always, Andrew waited for Gracie to return from her run, or from cross-training, before commencing the first meal of the day, a ritual they'd enjoyed together for over forty years.

Today, however, Gracie had slipped from bed at daybreak, silently grabbed some clothes, then taken them to the bathroom to dress.

It wasn't that she was avoiding Andrew. After a good long soak in the bath the night before, and some patching of her sore toe with a blob of Savlon and a sticking plaster, she'd returned downstairs and joined him on the sofa, wrapped up in her fluffy dressing gown. There had been a nature programme on the telly about migrating birds, which seemed to be enthralling Andrew, so she'd sat there and pretended to be enthralled too, because that was far less energetic than talking.

She scribbled a note for Andrew – *Gone shopping early to beat the crowds*. Then she took his favourite mug from the cupboard, plopped a tea bag in ready, and set two biscuits on a plate beside it.

There was something eerie about being in an empty supermarket. A flickering fluorescent light in the tinned goods aisle gave the place the feel of an apocalyptic movie, and she kept half expecting to see the undead appear next to the tomato soup. Difficult, too, to focus on sprouting broccoli, salmon fillets and wholegrain pasta at half past six in the morning, when all she felt like doing was sloping off to the café for a gigantic latte and a toasted teacake. In fact, what the heck was stopping her from doing just that, she wondered. What *exactly* was stopping her, besides the ingrained rhythm of her life that dictated she and Andrew had breakfast together, with the cryptic crossword and Radio Essex? Would the old Gracie, the one who had once smoked a bong in Laos for breakfast, have been so concerned with a bowl of fruit and fibre and five across (six, four)? She promptly abandoned her trolley next to the basmati rice and strode towards the on-site coffee shop.

Stick that up your jumper, Jill, thought Gracie as she lifted a gigantic, oozy, toasted teacake spread thick with butter to her lips. *I might even have another one.*

'Hello, Miss Jenkins,' came a rich, smooth voice, with a vaguely familiar ring to it.

Gracie looked up to see a man standing by the table he was vacating, dressed in a well-cut navy-blue suit, a newspaper under his arm.

It was only when he smiled that she recognised her former student, the way that one of his front teeth slightly overlapped the other and lent him a hint of devilry. It must have been twenty years since she'd seen him last, and the years had been kind; he was a smart, well groomed, and, dare she say, handsome young man.

'Isaac Hunter,' she said, putting down the teacake and wiping her lips on a napkin.

'You remembered me? Gosh, you've got a good memory. You've not changed one bit, whereas. . .' He pointed to his receding hairline.

'Well, that's teaching for you, most students think their teachers are already old-timers, so it can come as a bit of a shock to discover we're still alive and kicking by the time they're all grown up with mortgages of their own.'

Isaac laughed. 'And are you still teaching?'

'Retired,' said Gracie. 'What about you?'

'Sadly, I'm not retired, yet. . .' he smiled. 'But I'm working on it.'

Gracie huffed. 'Trust me, be careful what you wish for.'

It was coming back to her now. Isaac had been a gifted illustrator; obsessed with cartoons, his powers of observation informing the simplest of pencil strokes with energy and movement. She'd submitted his work to the Young Artists Show at the Royal Academy once – it was that good. He'd won some vouchers if she recalled, and she'd displayed the certificate on her classroom wall.

'Actually,' he began, but faltered when his phone started ringing. 'Excuse me,' he said, pulling it from his pocket. 'Ah, apologies, I'd better take this, so I'll say cheerio. Nice to have seen you again, Miss Jenkins.'

He gave her a warm smile and left the café, leaving her to her breakfast and the memories of a thousand students. It was nice, she decided, to glimpse at a future occasionally, one she'd only ever been able to imagine.

When she returned home with the shopping, there was no sign of Andrew, which usually meant he was in the shed. She unpacked, put the groceries away, then wandered down the garden with a mug of tea.

'Knock, knock,' she said, letting herself in.

Andrew stood up so fast he nearly toppled over and stuffed his phone back into his trouser pocket. He'd commandeered the rickety old wicker chair in the corner, along with a footstool, for sneaky naps, but he hadn't been napping.

Gracie felt oddly wrong-footed. Her husband had the distinctly sheepish look of someone who'd just been caught in the act. The act of what, though?

'Brought you a cuppa,' she said, pushing aside a puddle of screws on the workbench to make space to put it down. 'Picked up a nice quiche for lunch, and a crusty loaf. You'll have to sort yourself out though, as I'm popping out.'

Andrew's face brightened. 'Going for a run, love?'

'No, I'm going to Malik's to watch Theo for a couple of hours whilst he collects his parents from the airport. Poor love's off school with tummy ache. Hope he's not got what his daddy had.'

He nodded. 'That's kind, Gracie.' He seemed to search around, until his gaze alighted on a broken picture frame that to Gracie's knowledge had been perched on top of a pile of old woodworking

163

magazines for at least two years. He hobbled over to the bench, wincing visibly, before masking it conversationally. 'I'm finally getting round to tackling this. Thought you might want to hang that print we bought in Cornwall last year.'

Gracie had nagged him for weeks after that holiday but finally given up. 'It was two years ago actually. Two years since our last holiday.' And she was pretty sure that whatever he'd been doing, it certainly wasn't mending a picture frame.

'Ah,' said Andrew, with regret. 'Right you are.'

Gracie pulled the shed door shut and mentally chastised herself for adding to Andrew's feelings of guilt. She knew he held himself responsible for their slower pace of life and hoped her new-found passion of running had eased some of the guilt he carried. But at what cost? She was always out these days and he was often alone.

These thoughts circled in Gracie's head throughout the rest of the day. There was some respite, like when during a game of hide-and-seek, Theo miraculously recovered from his apparent tummy ache, and vanished into thin air sending Gracie into a wild panic. Perhaps she was getting too old for this childminding lark, it made running 10k seem like a doddle.

By early evening, Gracie was itching to get outside. To feel the cooling air on her cheeks, but also, to be alone. She picked up one of her expensive trainers and sat on the bottom stair, turning it over in her hand. Jill had been so enthusiastic the day they'd bought them, and surprisingly informed, spouting mind-boggling pros and cons about each footwear brand, such as their cushioning-to-weight ratio, or outsole grip. Gracie would wager she'd known almost as much as the sales assistant; she'd been so thorough in her research. Somehow Jill knew everything there was to know about training for a marathon, yet next to nothing about *her*. How could she, when she hadn't been around? She'd turned her back on her family forty years ago, only materialising for weddings and funerals, before popping up like a jack-in-the-box and expecting the red carpet. How was Gracie supposed to feel, after all this time? Where had Jill been when she and Andrew had devoted all their free time to looking after her mother: the endless visits, hospital appointments, cleaning, cooking and eventually at-home care until she passed away two years ago? And it wasn't as though Jill didn't have a compassionate bone in her body, quite the opposite, in fact; Gracie knew from Emily's account how devoted she had been to Gary's care as that awful disease had claimed him day by day. So why had she left Gracie alone to deal with Mum? And why wait until she was gone to reach out? None of it made sense.

Abruptly, Gracie stood and yanked open the door to the small cupboard where shoes, coats, boots and umbrellas went to die; the daily resting place for garments in current circulation being the bedecking of banister, door handles and backs of chairs. She bent down and rooted around, tossing moccasin slippers and ancient sandals aside until she found what she was looking for. *There you are.*

'I'm taking Picasso out for a walk,' Gracie called up the stairs.

'OK, love,' called back Andrew.

It was mid-April, and a warm breeze pervaded. The low sun was setting the cloud-filled sky on fire in vibrant shades of marigold, lavender and cornflower blue, all reflected back in the still waters gently foaming at the shore. Very soon, the beaches would fill with holiday-makers and day-trippers as schools broke for Easter. In years gone by, she and Andrew would be getting ready for their own first trip of the season, counting down to the end of term and to wherever their travels would be taking them.

'This will do though, won't it eh?' Gracie enquired of Picasso as they descended the steps to the beach promenade. 'Not too shabby a view.'

And I'm bloody lucky to live in such a beautiful spot, and to be physically fit enough to enjoy it. These were the thoughts that had been invading her mind all day, along with the sinking realisation that she'd become rather selfish of late. Selfish to the needs of her husband, for instance, who languished at home alone, in pain, whilst she devoted her days to what now seemed to her like a frivolous and egotistical pursuit. Well, not anymore. She'd have to find a way to break it to Emily, but she was not going to compete in the marathon after all. There were far more important things to concern herself with, like Andrew's impending op.

In response to her statement, Picasso tugged on the lead, circling and jerking her head.

'Hold your horses,' laughed Gracie, 'wait until we get on the beach.'

Dogs were strictly only allowed to be off lead between September and May, so the window of messing about on the shore was slowly drawing to a close.

Gracie made to descend the few steps down onto the sand, but Picasso rooted herself to the spot.

'What's the matter, you silly billy?'

Still, Picasso dug in her claws and refused to budge.

Woof. Woof-woof.

'Oh, for goodness' sake. Suit yourself. Come along then, move your bum.'

But as they walked on, Picasso continued to tug, until at last, Gracie understood.

'Clever girl,' she said, bending down and ruffling her ears, 'you remembered. Shall we do our old route?'

It had been ages, realised Gracie, as she eased herself into a gentle jog, Picasso scampering along beside her, since she'd taken the dog on a run. She'd been so focused on racking up the miles that she'd rather neglected her canine friend, offering her increasingly brief walks in between training instead.

With each stride, the rejuvenating freedom of the outdoors seeped into Gracie's bones. This is what she'd missed. The nuts and bolts of a simple run, no gadgets, no fancy trainers, just her and her ancient Reeboks and just for the hell of it. Not because she should, but because she could. And because through running, she'd met wonderful people, who she was proud to call her friends.

Sometime later, when the night had deepened to an inky indigo, Gracie and Picasso climbed the steps from the promenade.

A lone figure sat on Gracie and Andrew's favourite bench, their silhouette in stark relief against the brightly moonlit sky. For a single moment, her heart stopped as the figure stood and turned to face her. A cloaked, backlit shape, legs apart and bearing a staff that emitted an orange glow. That was until she realised that it wasn't Gandalf the Great, guarding the greensward and commanding she *shall not pass*. It was Andrew, in his waterproof mac, with his special walking stick that he'd adapted with an LED bulb to light the way on night-time dog walks.

'Everything alright, love?' she asked, when she drew close enough to see his face. He looked tired and drawn; she could see it in the way his eyelids drooped.

'Fancied some air, thought I might be able to see you walking down on the beach, but it got too dark.' He didn't ask why she'd been out so long, or why she'd been elusive all day. Instead, he sat back down on the bench. Gracie sat next to him.

After a beat, he gestured at her old shoes. 'Ditched the go-faster stripes then.'

She smiled. 'Uh-huh. And the ankle tag. I've let myself out on good behaviour.' She looked sideways at him. 'Do you mind?'

'Of course I don't mind. But I'm not sure about the good behaviour. You didn't have any dinner.'

'Sorry.' Gracie grimaced. 'Did you make yourself something? I just. . .' She paused. 'I just needed some time to think.'

Andrew turned to her. 'Gracie, never apologise for not being around to babysit me. I'm more than capable of feeding myself, just like I'm more than capable of amusing myself. I'm more concerned about you. What's happened? You've lost the spring in your step, if you'll excuse the pun.'

'Andrew, you go out of your way to make puns.' She sighed. 'And yes. You are quite right. I have lost the spring in my step, but that doesn't mean I want you to start finding ways to replace it. Those bastard trainers were cumbersome enough without having to contend with another one of your technological improvements.'

He nodded and gave a wry smile. 'No more gadgets. Right. Understood. For what it's worth, I'm sorry about the hat. I thought it seemed rather promising.'

Gracie took one of his hands in hers. 'It was thoughtful, and I love the wacky way your mind works, and all your clever inventions, just not when I have to wear them. But it's not even about that. I had a run-in with Jill yesterday. She seems to have taken issue with my lack of commitment to her training plan. Virtually combusted with rage over me looking after Theo and Elsie. Lobbed all sorts of accusations at me about the past, which, of course, was a red rag to a bull.'

Andrew nodded along, listening but letting her speak.

'I really thought this marathon business might be an opportunity for us to put the past behind us, but of course you can't just go sweeping it away, can you? At some point that carpet needs taking outside for a jolly good beating and then it's all still there staring back up you, where it was waiting all along.'

'And did you try talking to her about it?' asked Andrew.

Gracie spluttered a laugh. 'You can't talk to Jill about anything, Andy, haven't you realised that yet? Jill talks at you and you listen, that's just how she is. I should have known this would happen. And that's why I'm putting an end to it.'

Andrew tilted his head in question.

'I've decided to pull out of the marathon. Running was fun before all this, when it was just me and the running club, or me and Picasso and I didn't have to worry about having the right gear, eating the right thing, drinking the right juice, working the right muscle groups, and kowtowing to Jill's regime. It was a stubborn, knee-jerk reaction, thinking I could step into Emily's place and wipe that sneer off Kat's face, but I'm afraid I'm simply not up to the task. I'm old and I'm exhausted. There, I've said it.'

Gracie let out a long sigh, letting her words settle briefly into the silence. 'And besides, it's not just my life that's been dominated by this, it's yours too and I'm sorry. Sorry for buggering off and leaving you on your own every day for the past three months whilst I chased after some foolish, nostalgic dream. I'm not twenty-two, I'm seventy-two and it's about time I accepted it. Now, we just need to focus on the twenty-seventh of April for the *right* reason: namely getting your new knee and becoming pain free.'

Andrew reached around and pulled Gracie into him.

'I don't think we should tell Nathan,' she added, 'about the op. He'll only worry and there's nothing he can do all those miles away. Much better to surprise him with the news after it's all over.'

'Whatever you think best,' said Andrew into her hair. 'And you haven't been neglecting me; on the contrary, you've inspired me. When I've got the new knee, we're going on another adventure, you and me – I've been thinking about it a lot. We could do a cruise like Eugene and Ray's, or the Norwegian fjords perhaps? There's plenty of exploring we can still do. But that's for another day. And for the record, it wouldn't matter how old you were, Gracie love; you've always had big dreams, and you always *will* have big dreams, that's why I love you.'

18

Jill

It had been twenty-four hours since Jill's altercation with Gracie and she hadn't heard a word from her. Tomorrow was going to be interesting. All those plans she'd put into motion, all hanging in the balance if Gracie didn't turn up to her running club, and more importantly, afterwards at Victory Hall.

Jill had kept replaying the argument in her head, her stomach twisting with guilt every time she thought of the things she'd said. That was not supposed to have happened. Gracie might have her faults, but abandoning her duties had certainly never been one of them. Jill had no right to throw that back at her, accusing her older sister of deserting her, when all she'd been doing was living her young life, following her dreams and ambition. It wasn't her fault, what had happened. She'd never even known.

On Friday evening, Emily arrived back in Frinton. She'd been back to London for the whole week, which had wracked Jill with guilt. Had she made Emily feel uncomfortable with her awkward questioning? Made her feel unwelcome? They hadn't discussed the matter of her flat in London again and it hung over Jill, this niggling worry that all was not well. This was the longest she'd been away since her accident, and from the minute she walked in the door, it was obvious something was up. It was as if an invisible cloud hovered over her daughter's head, darkening her usually sunny temperament and making her snappy and sullen.

Still reeling from her first clumsy attempt to talk about her living arrangements, Jill followed Emily into the kitchen and found herself skirting around the issue again, whilst she boiled the kettle for hot drinks.

'How was it to see everyone again then, love?'

'Hmm?' replied Emily, who was crouched down, loading the washing machine.

'Your flatmates? Was it nice to see them after all this time?'

'Oh, I didn't really see them.'

Nothing in her tone to suggest she was pleased or displeased about that. In fact, she seemed positively ambivalent about it. Perhaps Jill had been reading something into things that weren't even there.

'And work, that was OK, was it, love?' she persisted.

Emily pressed the button, and the machine began to fill; a slow, steady whooshing that filled the silence before she answered.

'Work was as it always is. But look, Mum, there *is* something I need to tell you.' She spun around and leaned back against the counter, clamping her arms across her chest as though steeling herself for what came next.

Oh.

So here it was then. Emily did have secrets after all. And she was about to find out what had been plaguing her sweet daughter all this time. What had been keeping her languishing about here in this sleepy coastal town instead of living the high life in the city. Jill braced herself for the worst, whilst trying to mask her fear with an open, receptive expression.

Emily let out a long, weary sigh. 'I had a phone call from Uncle Andrew last night.'

Jill did a double take. Andrew? Why would he be telephoning Emily? This better not be about her disagreement with Gracie because it really wasn't anyone else's business.

'Go on,' she said, stirring milk into their mugs of tea, unable to keep the trepidation from her voice.

'But first, you need to promise you're not going to get mad.'

Jill closed the fridge door and made wide eyes at her daughter. 'Honestly, Em, I don't know why you say that. I don't *get mad*.'

Was that really what her daughter thought of her? And if so, was it any wonder she didn't confide in her? Jill's thoughts were interrupted.

'Look, I'll just come out and say it. Andrew rang to tell me Gracie's pulling out of the marathon. She plans to cover any pledged funds herself and give it to charity and suggest I defer my place to next year, which I'll need to check I'm still eligible to do.' She met Jill's eye. 'I know you've done a lot of work yourself to raise money, money she doesn't even know about, but it looks like we're going to have to tell everyone it will be next year instead.'

Jill carried the mugs to the kitchen table and sank into a chair with a deflated sigh. She should have seen this coming.

'Did he say why?' asked Jill. 'Did Andrew say why Gracie's pulling out?'

Emily shrugged. 'She told him she wasn't finding it enjoyable anymore and that she probably wasn't up to it anyway – which is total crap by the way, she's been running fifteen, sixteen miles no problems. But Uncle Andrew doesn't think that's the real reason. He said his knee replacement operation has been scheduled for marathon day; suspects she feels too guilty to continue. He said he's tried to assure her he'll be fine, that she should go ahead with it anyway, but she's made up her mind.'

Jill nodded. 'Yes, I can see how that would be an issue for her.'

'Uncle Andrew asked me not to mention it to anyone yet, as she plans to tell everyone at running club tomorrow. Look, you won't be angry with her will you, Mum?'

At this Jill looked up. 'Angry? Why would I be angry?'

'Because you're probably going to be embarrassed, having to go back to all the sponsors and explain. Because you've put so much time and energy into it yourself.'

'Oh, Emily, of course I'm not angry. And I don't give a toss about explaining anything to anyone.' She gave a snort of derision. 'I'd like to see some of those ageing rockers run to the end of their garden, never mind a marathon. I am sad though, because this is all my fault.'

'How so?' said Emily, pulling out a chair opposite and sitting down.

Jill's sparkly pink notebook sat on the table between them, filled with her research notes on nutrition, warm-up exercises, cool-down routines, tips for the big day, and dozens of motivational quotes she'd copied down from the internet and painstakingly typed out in WhatsApp messages to bombard her sister with. She pulled it towards her and ran her fingers over its glittery surface.

'Because I said some unkind things to Gracie. Because I tried to wrestle my sister's indomitable spirit into my own pretty, ordered boxes, but mostly because I wasn't here for her when she needed me.' Jill gave a mirthless laugh. 'That's the funny thing about it. You think you can make amends after the event, but sometimes there's just no avoiding the truth and, as they say, the truth will always out.'

Emily frowned. 'I'm not really sure what you're going on about, Mum. You're talking in riddles.'

'Sorry, love. Ignore me, I've just finally realised what I have to do, that's all.' She reached across the table and covered Emily's hand with her own. 'Do you know, I thought you were going to tell me something terrible.'

'That wasn't terrible?' asked Emily, eyes widening in surprise. 'I thought you would hit the roof.'

'Pff. It's a minor setback in the grand plan, that's all. No, what I mean is, I've been feeling for ages as though you've been keeping secrets of your own. Because something isn't right with you, love, I know it. In the way a mother should know it, deep in here.' She pressed her other hand to her chest, as though she could push back down the regret that her own mother had been so blind to Jill's suffering.

Emily looked contemplative for a moment, then she tucked her hair behind her ear and gave her a small, sheepish smile. 'I don't have any big secrets, Mum. I'm fine, truly, you don't need to worry about me. I'm just working some stuff out. Work stuff. Life stuff. And I miss Dad, too. That's all.'

Jill nodded, smiled. 'Me too, darling. Me too. Well, so long as you know this is your home. It will always be your home. *Wherever* I am in this world, that will be your home, I need you to know that.'

Emily flipped her palm over and squeezed Jill's hand. 'Thanks, Mum, I do appreciate that, and I know you only ever want the best for me. As I do for you. So, er. . .' she raised her eyebrows '. . . if there's ever anything *you* want to tell *me*, I just want you to know that's cool.'

Jill opened her mouth then closed it again, momentarily lost for words.

Emily laughed. 'So then, about this setback. What are we going to do about Auntie Gracie?'

What were they going to do indeed?

Jill checked the time. Just gone seven o'clock. Everything was already in motion, and besides, it was too late to change that now, but there *was* someone she really did need to speak with. She would get Emily to message the runners, because it would fall to them to get Gracie to Victory Hall *before* she dropped her marathon cop-out bombshell.

Jill scrolled through the contacts on her phone and shot Emily a wink as she pressed call.

The phone was answered after two rings.

'Well, well, well. Good-time Jill. How are you, gorgeous?'

Jill smiled at the familiar low, rough voice. Pictured him reclined on the sofa with a spliff in hand, because if he still hadn't kicked the habit by his age, it was unlikely he ever would.

'Alright, darling. Listen, Logan, I need a favour.'

19

Gracie

With just over two weeks to go until 27th April, Gracie set off to meet her friends in the Coast Path Runners group with a heavy heart. She still hadn't told anyone other than Andrew that she no longer planned to run the marathon, but today was the day.

For the first twenty minutes or so, Sophia recounted in detail a home visit she'd made in the week to an elderly gentleman who had tripped whilst dancing the foxtrot with his wife on their patio and cut his head on the rockery. 'Ninety-six years of age and they were twirling around their backyard like Ginger Rogers and Fred Astaire – she was even wearing a ball gown. Apparently, they used to be regulars at the Blackpool Tower Ballroom.'

'That reminds me of this callout we had once,' Ray then chipped in. 'This old boy climbed the twenty-metre-tall oak tree in his back garden to rescue his cat, then got completely stuck when his belt hooked onto a broken branch. Apparently, he'd been up there nearly twenty-four hours before his neighbour heard him yelling. Of course, the cat had found its own way down by then.'

These tales of resilience and stamina quite put her off her stride, in more ways than one. What would they all think of her for giving up this late in the day? She'd be one of those annoying people who talked the talk but never walked the walk. She hated letting people down. Hated letting herself down, even though in her heart of hearts she did believe she could do it. Still, it didn't matter either way; the most important thing now was to concentrate on Andrew. She'd neglected him for far too long.

Today was the day; no point stringing it out any longer – it was time for her to come clean. Andrew had insisted on meeting her back at Victory Hall after the run, because, as he'd said, he didn't know how long it would be after his op until he was back on his feet, and he was owed a backgammon rematch with Eugene. As she ran, Gracie decided perhaps that would be the best time to tell everyone, when they had a cuppa in hand and there was no chance of Giles or Kat being in earshot. Jill, she'd just have to deal with another time. The thought made her grimace.

Perhaps the worst part though was that as she ran along the promenade behind Ray and Malik, all she could focus on was the words 'GRACIE JENKINS, THE LONDON MARATHON', bobbing up and down on the backs of their t-shirts. She'd felt like enough of a fraud as it was, pulling on her own kit that morning to run. Just another way in which she was letting people down: all Malik's work in designing this marvellous logo, her sister for stumping up the cash to pay for them.

She recalled the hilarious series of facial expressions that had passed across Kat's face when Ray had presented them to her and Giles.

'Official club kit,' he'd said simply.

Giles had given a nervous laugh. 'But we're not an official club. We're just a group of people who met on Facebook and took up running together. Why do we have to wear a kit?'

'Maybe it's time we became an official club! I'd be happy to sit on the committee. It would be nice to open this up to the wider community; I bet there's plenty who would be interested. We've all benefitted, isn't it time to give back?' Ray had looked to Gracie as he'd said it, an unspoken question in his eyes. *Are you in?*

'I'll be anything but treasurer,' she'd replied. 'Good with pictures, terrible with numbers.'

Giles had fingered the fabric of the top, then slipped it on over his vest. 'It's not bad, actually. Pretty good quality.'

'It's completely shapeless,' said Kat, holding it up, aghast.

'Oh, get over. You could wear anything and still look *amazing*,' Sophia had said, prompting several sets of eyes to widen in disbelief.

Afterwards she'd shrugged and said, 'So what? I'm not averse to a little shameless bribery. She's wearing the fecking thing, isn't she? That's worth its weight in gold.'

And it had been, for a few weeks. Watching Giles and Kat sprint into the distance with her name on their backs had never failed to put a smile on Gracie's face, until now. Now she felt like a failure, before she'd even begun. And deserving of all the snide, bitchy remarks that were certain to come her way once they found out she'd quit.

'Carrying on?' Ray asked Gracie, as the small group arrived back at the pavilion.

'I don't think so, not today. You go ahead though,' replied Gracie. Ten kilometres felt like a walk in the park to her now, but the truth of it was she was shying away from being alone with Ray. Putting off the inevitable.

'No, I'm good. Let's head straight for the cake then, shall we, gang?'

'Gosh, I hope there's some of that lovely lemon drizzle from Waitrose again,' said Sophia to Emily. 'Or has your mum got her mojo back?'

Emily laughed. 'Sorry, guys, respite over. She was baking the whole day yesterday; it smelled like Mr Kipling's factory when I got in last night.'

'What exactly does she *do* to make her cakes taste so bad?' asked Sophia, groaning.

Emily shrugged. 'I have absolutely no idea. They always smell good, they even look good, but that's where it ends.'

'Not got to get back for the kiddies today?' asked Gracie when she realised Malik was walking with them to Victory Hall.

'Nope. Kids are staying at their mum's this weekend; they are *very* excited about getting to feed the baby and read her a bedtime story.'

'About bleeding time,' said Sophia.

Malik pulled a face and admitted, 'The thing is, I feel really bad now for giving her a hard time. She admitted to me this week that she's been suffering from post-natal depression. Didn't happen with the first two at all, so it hit her like a ton of bricks.'

'Ah, right, I'm sorry to hear that, Mal,' said Sophia, her expression softening in compassion. 'I see it a lot, unfortunately. It can be a truly debilitating thing, and far more common than you might think.'

'Yeah, well, it sounds like she's getting back on track now. She was desperate to see the kids. And they were over the moon to see her.'

'So, you're footloose and fancy free then this weekend, is that what you're saying?' Ray quirked a brow.

Gracie caught Ray's eye and suppressed a smile.

'First time in months,' said Malik. 'I can't decide what to do first – sleep, play Fortnite, or catch up on the last three series of *Money Heist*.'

'Oh, I've seen them,' said Sophia, 'I wouldn't bother. Now *Slow Horses*, there's a show. Gary Oldman is *fantastic*. In fact, I've a date with him tonight – me, him and a giant-sized Toblerone.'

180

'Seriously? That's how you youngsters are both planning to spend your Saturday night?' asked Ray, his fire engine-sized hints falling on deaf ears. 'Things really have changed.'

'Which reminds me,' said Gracie, 'we need to talk about your settings on Netflix, Malik, before Elsie gets the kind of sex education no father wants for their daughter. Oh, hold up, what's going on here?'

They had arrived at Victory Hall to find the doors bolted shut, with a notice Sellotaped to the heavy front doors. Rita was hovering outside, fiddling with the front of her cardigan.

'Everything alright, love?' asked Gracie kindly. Rita's cardigan was on inside out, which explained why she was struggling to do up the buttons.

Rita looked up. 'I don't know where she is,' she replied, looking about uncertainly.

'Who?'

'Kathleen. I was supposed to be picking her up from Brownies. But it's all locked up. I don't know what this is all about.' She flapped a hand at the written sign.

Today, the Be Together Café is taking place at
Beachcombers Retirement Village. Pop across the road
and join us for a cuppa and a chat.

'Oh yes!' exclaimed Ray, tapping himself on the forehead. 'I completely forgot. Dad's retirement home is having an open day, so they've decamped over there. Bit of a recruitment drive if you ask me, to advertise for more customers.'

Gracie looked to Emily. 'Did you know about this?'

Emily stroked her chin theatrically. 'Um, not sure. Mum might have mentioned it, but to be honest I tend to zone out, you know how she goes on. Ah, perhaps that's what the mammoth baking frenzy was about.' Her expression was of someone who'd just had a light-bulb moment, but Gracie could see the pretence. Her acting skills were on a par with Cynthia's, in last year's Seashells Am Dram Society's production of *Death on the Nile*, which is to say, they were non-existent.

What was going on here? Well, whatever it was, poor Rita was in a right muddle.

'Rita, love. I'm Gracie Jenkins, do you remember? From school. I was Kathleen's Art teacher.'

Rita studied Gracie for a moment, before slowly nodding. 'Yes, I think so. And you're the lady that's running the marathon.'

'Well, I, er—'

'Come with us, Rita, they're all over there,' interrupted Sophia. 'All the nice people you while away a few hours with every Saturday. We're heading over there now.'

'But what about Kathleen?' she asked, looking confused. 'She won't know where I am.'

'Don't you worry about that, we'll let her know.' Sophia threaded an arm through Rita's and steered her in the direction of Beachcombers. 'That's a *fabulous* cardigan you're sporting now. I've been looking for one like that myself. Do you reckon I could maybe try it on? See if that shade suits my complexion?'

As they crossed the road, Gracie marvelled at the way Sophia put the distressed woman at ease, all whilst managing to right her cardigan when she returned it without Rita suspecting a thing. She glanced sidelong at Malik who was watching her with nothing short of admiration.

Beachcombers was a bright, modern complex, made up of several smaller residential blocks that were joined to the main reception building. A neat, landscaped lawn formed a crescent around the entrance, and fresh-cut flowers decorated a pine-effect table in the lobby.

'If you're here for the open day, could I ask you to please sign in here,' came the bored voice of the receptionist, Mandy, as her name badge stated. Seated behind a large, curved desk, she looked up from her computer keyboard. 'Oh!' The woman's cheeks blushed pink, and she gave a nervous laugh. 'As *Ray* will know, we take the safety of our residents and our guests most seriously here at Beachcombers,' she added with a coquettish smile, leaving the group with little doubt that Ray had a fan.

As Sophia scribbled both hers and Rita's names in the book, the receptionist continued, 'The community room is through the double doors, keep going until. . . but, silly me. Ray knows exactly where he's going. Follow him.'

'What, am I invisible here?' whispered Sophia, turning around to face the others. 'I'm in here three times a week. Am I that unrecognisable without a blue tunic and lanyard around my neck?'

'I think it's fair to say Mandy only has eyes for a certain visitor,' muttered Malik under his breath, causing Gracie to let out a snort of laughter. 'But for what it's worth, I reckon you probably rock a blue tunic.'

For goodness' sake. If one of these two didn't pull their finger out and ask the other on a date soon, Gracie was inclined to bang their heads together.

They all followed Ray, through the double doors and down a short corridor until they reached the common area; a large, bright and airy room bustling with activity. A set of glazed bi-fold doors were thrown open onto a patio area, beyond which lay a manicured lawn. It was all rather lovely, Gracie had to admit. Not a bit like she'd imagined a retirement home to be, although she strongly suspected Eugene was paying through the nose for the privilege.

Instead of old-fashioned, clinical, upright chairs, the liberally scattered seats around the outskirts of the room were beautifully upholstered and wing-backed, like something out of a Laura Ashley catalogue. A huge flat-screen TV dominated a corner of the room, and the brightly painted ocean-blue walls were lined with brimming bookcases. Dozens of residents had come to the community room, a place Eugene had repeatedly described as dull as dishwater, and yet, there he was, surrounded by a posse of pensioners, holding court in the centre of the room. Occasional tables had been set up with a selection of board games, and as with the Be Together Café, chairs were grouped together to encourage interaction. Many, Gracie noticed, were already happily engaged in games of draughts, or cards.

'There they are,' said Emily at her side, pointing at a row of covered trestle tables, mobbed with customers.

A banner advertised the Be Together Café, listing its meeting days and opening times, and Cynthia poured hot drinks whilst Jill served up hunks of cake to a snaking queue.

A tall woman in a lavender trouser suit spotted the newcomers and approached, her face breaking into a warm smile.

'Good morning! You must be the Coast Path Runners, and *you* must be *Amazing Gracie*. We've heard *so* much about you,' she beamed. 'I'm Debbie, the manager here at Beachcombers. Welcome to our humble home.'

Gracie tried to catch Emily's eye, convinced now that something was afoot. For starters, what the heck was all that Amazing Gracie business about? Not that she hadn't heard the play on words a million times before, but there had been something about the way she'd said it. . . However, Emily was too busy signalling to Jill over the top of a stooped gentleman's head.

Ray stepped into the uncomfortable pause that ensued,

congratulating Debbie on the good turnout and listening politely as she reeled off a litany of compliments about Eugene and what a pleasure it was to have him there. Gracie took the opportunity to scan the room for Andrew, taking in all the families with their elderly relatives, chatting with members of staff, on the cusp of making big decisions that wouldn't be easy for any of them – she'd had a similar choice to make, until Andrew persuaded her that her mother should live with them.

Gracie spotted a familiar forest-green sleeve and the flash of a walking stick in the garden.

'Excuse me,' she said, breaking away from the others and making for the patio doors.

Outside, more guests gathered on the perfectly tended lawn, where several pop-up stands were erected under gazebos; some kind of craft stall, another selling raffle tickets, a couple of others she couldn't see as people were in the way. Gracie searched the crowd for her husband, certain she'd just seen him. There were a few familiar faces out there, parents of ex-students and the like, as was usually to be expected with social events in town.

'Gracie!'

Ah, there was Andrew, standing with Harold. She glimpsed an ex-colleague in a long flowy dress who turned in her direction and gave an enthusiastic wave. Honestly, if she'd known all these people were going to be here, she'd have popped home to freshen up. She must look a right sight in her running gear, not to mention sweatier than she'd have ideally liked.

'Hello, love,' said Andrew as she joined them.

They were standing next to a stall whose bright pink and green banner proclaimed it to be Alzheimer's Outreach UK. The charity first Emily, then she, had been running the marathon for, and whom Gracie planned to donate her sponsorship money, now she was ducking out. Volunteers dressed in the charity's colourful uniform stood behind a table, handing out leaflets and small pin badges.

'Good run, dear? Lovely day for it.'

There was something mischievous in his voice. A kind of tinkle. What had he been up to?

'Fine, thank you.'

There was a brief silence.

'Anyone for a cuppa?' asked Andrew, his voice hitting an unusually high pitch.

'Darling, with the best will in the world, you aren't going to manage three cups of scalding liquid and your walking stick. I'll go, is it teas all rou—' Gracie faltered as heads turned sideways.

'Ladies and gentlemen,' called out Debbie, her voice ringing across the lawn with as much clarity as the string of pearls around her neck. 'If you could all make your way into the community lounge, please, there will be a short presentation and a fundraising update.'

Gracie narrowed her eyes as Andrew and Harold wordlessly turned to head inside. *Presentation? Fundraising update?*

Just what was going on here?

20

Gracie

Even as everyone shuffled into the crowded communal lounge, Gracie clung to the hope that the manager of Beachcombers simply wanted to thank everyone for coming along and supporting the retirement village, and to direct them to the relevant member of staff for potential enquiries. Yet, as she glanced around and found that none of her friends, and particularly Jill, would meet her eye, the sickening notion that she was about to become prey, caught in an innocent-looking trap, coursed through her veins.

'Hello, everyone,' enthused Debbie, glowing in the limelight. 'Thank you all so much for coming along to our first-ever Beachcombers Open Day, a tradition we very much hope to continue. *Togetherness* is important to us, here at Beachcombers. Our residents provide us with the honour of sharing in their twilight years and so we extend our deepest thanks to the wonderful volunteers of the Be Together Café for suggesting our collaboration and for making sure there is always somewhere for those who may not wish to be alone, to be welcomed among friends in the wider community.'

Debbie paused for the brief but heartfelt bout of applause that followed, both Jill and Cynthia grinning along like Cheshire cats.

'But we also have someone else here with us today, who is going above and beyond to give back. Someone many of you have known over the years in her capacity of teacher, neighbour and Frinton resident. Here to tell us more about what Gracie Jenkins' phenomenal marathon challenge will mean to them, is Nina from Alzheimer's Outreach UK.'

Gracie's cheeks reddened and she wished the polished floor beneath her feet would crack wide open, as a pretty young woman, with shades of purple in her long, blonde hair, squeezed her way to the front.

'Andrew. Tell me you did *not* know about this,' hissed Gracie angrily.

Her husband became conveniently hard of hearing and her attempt to repeat herself was lost as Nina gave a short introduction to the charity, its history and mission to continue providing support in the community.

'So that's us, in a nutshell, and now I'll tell you a little more about how we can help you. One in three people born in the UK will go on to develop dementia in their lifetime,' said Nina compassionately. 'This is the reality we are facing, and whilst huge developments are being made every day in medical research, our job is to provide an essential support network for patients, carers and their families, which without your help we could not sustain.'

Gracie scoured the room until she picked out Rita, who was sitting in a comfortable chair beside Eugene. She did not appear to be listening to the talk and was instead transfixed on a tasselled cushion she nursed on her lap. It was hard to escape the probability that Rita might well be one of the service users Nina was here to represent.

'The services and support we are able to offer to ordinary people like you and your loved ones is only possible, down to the efforts of people like Gracie Jenkins,' Nina continued, bringing Gracie up short, 'people who undertake the toughest of personal challenges to raise awareness and much-needed funds for our cause, and who are the literal fuel in our engine. So, without further ado, if I could ask Gracie to step forward, please,' Nina homed in on her, beckoned her with a finger. There was no escape in sight, so with little choice and in the manner of a schoolchild singled out for bad behaviour, Gracie stepped forward. 'It is our pleasure to present you with your official marathon kit, including your branded Alzheimer's Outreach UK running top for this year's London Marathon.'

Nina held out the small bundle and Gracie froze. What was she meant to do? There must be upwards of fifty pairs of eyes on her. How was she supposed to turn around and say she'd changed her mind? That this was all a mistake, she'd made a terrible mistake. She'd just have to gracefully accept the package for now, then make her excuses later, in a slightly more private setting.

'Don't worry, Gracie,' came Sophia's lyrical voice carrying across the room. 'We'll all be there in our CPR gear to fly the flag for our running club too.' A murmur of amusement rippled around the room.

Gracie narrowed her eyes at her friend, and at Malik beside her who fluttered his fingers in a wave, conveying in that small gesture that they had been fully expecting this turn of events today.

She'd murder them all later – interfering, meddlesome pains in the arse. They had no right to ambush her like this.

'Thank you,' said Debbie, stepping forward once more. 'Nina will be on hand throughout the rest of the day for advice and information, or just a friendly chat. Please do go and visit the charity's stand in the garden. Now. . .' She paused, looking around until she found her target. 'There is someone else here today, who would like to say a few words. Some of you may know the former Thorpington High student who went on to become the entrepreneur and brainchild behind the award-winning FastArt app, used worldwide by the public and professionals alike, so please give a warm welcome to Isaac Hunter.'

Gracie, who still stood there clutching her folded jersey, watched incredulously as her ex-student, whom she'd bumped into in Tesco just the other day, took to the centre of the room. She had no idea he'd done so well for himself.

'Thank you, Debbie,' said Isaac, shooting Gracie a curious look. *What was going on here?*

'I won't keep you long. I'm here to represent Thorpington High teachers and students, past and present, who, in the last few weeks, have been working hard to raise awareness of Gracie's marathon challenge. Along with sponsorship from the wider academic community, it is my greatest pleasure to announce that so far, they have raised a whopping five thousand pounds.'

Oohs and ahhs ensued, whilst Gracie stared in disbelief.

'But I'd like to share something else with you today if I may. Something that for me, when I heard about Miss Jenkins' marathon challenge, struck a personal chord. For much of my time at Thorpington High, I was concealing a secret. My mother, a single parent, was clinically depressed and an alcoholic.'

Gracie inhaled deeply, his words transporting her back a couple of decades to her classroom and the quiet, thoughtful boy often to be found there.

'Unlike many of my peers, my day usually began in the early hours of the morning, when I would drag Mum up to bed, settle her with water, a sick bowl and food for when she woke up, before getting myself ready for school. There was often nothing in the fridge. Mum could go weeks without shopping. When she did, I would hide tins of beans, soup and packets of pasta in my room, so that when she went on another bender, we would have food to eat. During those periods, *all* her benefits went on booze.

'I had few friends. Friendships were difficult to maintain when you couldn't bring anyone home. Besides, I never liked to leave Mum alone for long.

'I don't tell you this for pity. I was not the first and certainly won't be the last child with a difficult home life. I tell you this because there was only one thing that made school bearable for me, and that was Art lessons with Miss Jenkins. They were pure respite, a whole hour filled with hope and imagination, where anything seemed possible. I craved the emotional connection you get when immersing yourself in something completely. In the connections to be found in the making and consuming of art. In knowing that even before humans could read or write, they communicated through art. Miss Jenkins is a teacher who recognises a spark of interest and knows exactly how to fan the flames. And where no spark exists, she creates one with her infectious passion. I'm not sure she ever knew why I liked to go and sit in the art room at lunchtimes, doodling or gazing out the window, chatting sometimes, as she cleaned brushes and palettes, preparing for her next lessons. Perhaps she suspected I had a hard time with the other kids, but for me it was an escape to a world of possibility, one where I could simply be me.'

Gracie's throat tightened and Andrew's hand found hers at her side.

'A few years later, after Mum passed away from an alcohol-related illness, I went back to college. I won't bore you with the details, but my love for art never waned. I designed FastArt as a means for anyone, anywhere, to have the tools at their disposal to disappear into their own creative worlds at the touch of a button. No expensive equipment required, subscriptions or fees, just an everyday smartphone or tablet. That venture changed my life, in more ways than I could ever describe and now I want to give back. This cheque—' he held it up briefly '—is just one small way in which I can do that.'

Isaac smiled at Gracie.

'So, Miss Jenkins, I just wanted to say thank you. Thank you for always being such an inspiration. I'll be rooting for you every single step of those twenty-six miles.'

Eugene got to his feet and began to clap. Others joined in, including residents and staff, until the applause became deafening.

Nina looked gobsmacked.

Gracie reeled.

This was not how today was supposed to have gone. She experienced a peculiar out-of-body sensation as she looked around the room, finally locking eyes with Jill. Her sister had a peculiar, flinty expression, as though she were daring her to fly in the face of all this goodwill. Damned, insufferable woman. She'd gone and manipulated this entire situation.

'Excuse me, Mrs Jenkins?' came a new voice, as a slight, wispy young man in shirt and trousers stepped forwards. 'I'm from the *Frinton and Walton Chronicle*. I wonder if you'd be so kind as to let my colleague take a picture of you with the various stakeholders – we'd like to run the story in next week's issue.'

This had gone too far. She needed to say something. Needed to explain she wasn't running the marathon after all, that she would instead be with her husband when he went in for the life-changing surgery they'd been waiting on for nearly four years. She could say that Emily would be doing it instead, the following year. Nothing needed to change. Nothing would be lost. Except that Isaac's words kept circling round in her mind like a spinning potter's wheel; *an inspiration. . . infectious passion. . . your achievement.*

'Hold your horses,' called Jill, sliding out from behind the refreshments table. 'We're not finished yet. Then you can take your pictures, but in the meantime, you might want to watch this. Em, are you ready over there?'

Startled, Gracie spun around to see that Emily was standing in front of the huge TV screen, brandishing a remote control.

'Ready,' she confirmed, then, pausing to wait until everyone had shuffled into a position where they could see, she pressed play.

As it flickered to life, the blank screen was replaced with a snapshot of someone's living room, and whoever it belonged to had questionable taste in décor, which was to put it mildly. A large plush, purple velvet chaise longue sat stark against striped silver wallpaper, whilst above it there hung an enormous gilt-framed picture of a Highland cow sitting cross-legged on a throne, complete with jaunty crown.

Then, a figure in skintight jeans and a black t-shirt crossed the screen and sat on the velvet couch, hitching himself forward so he could talk directly into the camera.

Beside her, Sophia sucked in a breath.

'Bloody hell,' exclaimed Ray.

'Is that. . .?' Malik began. 'It can't be, surely,' he said in surprise.

'Yes!' cried Sophia, looking as though she might combust. 'That's only flipping Jet Logan! Bloody hell, he's so cool!'

'Ssh,' said Andrew. 'Listen.'

Gracie glanced at her husband and knew instantly he had been in on all of it. Including this, whatever this was; an intervention on a record scale. For if her eyes were not deceiving her, there on the TV screen in front of her was one of the country's most famous rock stars. The Jet Setters had been huge in the late Eighties, going on to enjoy lucrative revivals with each new generation, as demonstrated by starstruck Sophia, and, it seemed, Nina, who was gazing open-mouthed at the screen and couldn't be more than twenty-one.

'Jill, babe,' came the rough, gravelly voice on the screen. 'How are you doing, doll? I hope you have that awesome older sister of yours right there with you, because I've got something I want to say to her.' He stroked his silvered, bristly chin, as though centring his thoughts. 'My mate, Mad Gaz, was one of the sweetest, kindest most all-round awesome guys I've ever known. The kind of guy who'd look at a broken-down car, smoke seeping out of its engine, wheels rolling off down the road, and go, *You know what? That could have gone a whole lot worse.* The kind of guy everyone needs in their life, a chink of blue sky on a stormy day. Phenomenal guitarist, and *that* voice. Could have made it huge if he'd gone solo, but he already had everything he wanted – something a lot of us in the business would have given their right testicle for, truth be known, because he had Jill.'

Jet stretched his arms up and folded them behind his head.

'It's a rare thing. To find that kind of soulmate.' He gave a wicked laugh. 'And I should know. I've done a *whole* lot of searching. Them two together, were like, I don't know, gin and tonic, or rum and raisin – meant to be together.'

Gracie glanced at Jill, who was smiling with affection at the screen. She'd had no idea her sister was friends with this man.

'Seeing what them two went through together, in the last few years of my friend's life, at the devotion Jill demonstrated as we began to lose Gaz. Well.' He shook his head, emotions rising close to the surface. 'Let's just say, I hope one day to find a woman even half as true. But, of course, she didn't do it alone.' Jet rallied himself, visibly straightening. 'The charity you are supporting when you run that marathon in two weeks' time, Gracie, well, if I was a religious man I'd say it was God's work on earth, but I think I kinda burnt those bridges long ago,' he chuckled, 'so instead I'll put my money where my mouth is. On the 30th of April, the Jet Setters new album, *Seeking Out the Light*, goes on sale across the globe. It's our first album for nearly a decade, and in memory of our good friend Mad Gary Baker, we will be donating 10 per cent of all record sales to Alzheimer's Outreach UK. We're right here behind you, Gracie, we've got your back. Now, go get 'em.'

With that, Jet Logan saluted, then leaned forward and switched off the camera, leaving nothing but white noise.

A loud tittering picked up, as the excitement of what they'd just witnessed fizzed around the room. From the corner, where Rita sat, a gentle humming drifted over to Gracie, the distinctive tune of Jet Logan and the Jet Setters most instantly recognisable hit, 'No Crying Here'.

Eugene turned to Rita and grinned. 'Ah, one of my favourites.' He began singing along with her, his rich, melodic voice making her smile in delight.

Gracie understood then. Realised that the acts in this. . . show, or whatever it had been, today, had been choreographed some time ago. That Jill's plans had always been big. That whilst for Gracie it had just been about running, about the physical exertion of her body; for Jill it had been everything.

She turned to Andrew, who leaned on his stick and offered her a tentative, questioning smile. She could read his unspoken words. *Do you get it now? Do you see why all of this matters?* Oh, she understood. Knew without having to think about it – if it had been she who'd lost the love of her life, as Jill had, she *too* would have resorted to any means possible to make this all happen. There may be manipulation afoot, but how could she be cross with her sister for wanting to raise awareness about the illness that had stolen Gary away? An illness that would continue to rob husbands, wives, daughters, sons and best friends of their loved ones in the cruellest of ways.

'But what about you?' Gracie asked. 'How can I *not* be with you?' The very idea provoked a physical pain in her chest.

Andrew took her hand. 'It's just one day. One day apart. I'll be in marvellous hands, and you can't be there the whole time. Imagine how much *good* you could do with that one day, instead, love.'

He was right, of course. Knew just as well as she did; she'd been using it as an excuse when it all got too hard. But she was all out of excuses now. She couldn't even use the argument she'd had with Jill as an excuse. The incorrigible woman was never giving up. No matter what may have gone on before, one thing was clear as day: Jill might not have been around for a while, but she was here for Gracie now and didn't seem to be going anywhere.

She looked down at the running shirt in her hand. At her name in blue letters.

'Well then, I just hope this fits.'

21

Jill

The rest of the afternoon had vanished in a frenzy as the visitors to Beachcombers set about clearing them out of refreshments. It had been the most lucrative day they'd ever had and the proceeds, along with several generous donations from members of the public, would all boost the Be Together Café coffers, enabling them to offer a wider range of refreshments and snacks.

'Well, I think that was a successful day, don't you,' said Cynthia, as they packed away their equipment ready to return it to Victory Hall.

'I'll say it was,' agreed Jill wholeheartedly. Although her measure of success would be considerably different to Cynthia's. If she'd achieved her goal, of making Gracie realise how much she wanted to run that marathon, it would be as thrilling as the six-figure donation she'd discovered had been pledged by Isaac Hunter. And that was before the royalties from Logan's band were even taken into account.

'I can't get over that surprise appearance from Jet Logan,' said Cynthia, reading her mind, as she stacked crumb-scattered plates into a plastic tote. They would do all the washing up over at the hall. 'I must say, you are a dark horse, Jill. Fancy having friends in such high places and never letting on. If we're not careful we'll be mobbed next week, with potential punters hoping for more Jet Setter scoops. Perhaps we need to think about taking on extra help,' she mused.

'You know, I'm usually free on Mondays,' came Ray's voice from behind, making Jill jump. He had stayed behind after the rest of the visitors left, accompanying Eugene back to his room to fix a broken shelf. She spun around and found him smiling back at her. 'I'd be happy to help out. And of course I'm usually there on Saturdays too, if you can accept my help in my running kit.' He gave a self-deprecating laugh, his lovely eyes crinkling at the corners.

I'd accept your help in no *kit*, thought Jill, pushing down the unhelpful thought as she unlocked her eyes from his and purposefully folded the tablecloth.

'That would be *wonderful*,' crowed Cynthia. 'You know, with the amount of interest we've received today, I think there's scope for a third session. Perhaps a Wednesday, what do you think?'

Jill agreed that was a great idea, whilst secretly wondering how she'd manage all the extra baking.

'Right, Mum, what can I do?' asked Emily, appearing.

'Have all the others gone now?' asked Jill, looking around.

'Yep. Everyone's gone, apart from Rita. Does she normally make her own way home from the café?'

Jill glanced over to where Rita was sitting in one of the residents' armchairs.

'Most of the time, yes, I think she does.'

Jill drummed the top of the box she'd just packed.

'Tell you what, love, would you mind helping Cynthia get this lot over to the hall whilst I walk Rita home?'

Ray jumped in. 'Why don't I do that? You've done enough.'

'No, but thanks for offering. I'd quite like to find out a bit more about her set-up, see where she lives, if that's OK with you of course, Cynthia,' she hastened to add.

Cynthia held up her hands. 'Absolutely. We'll be fine, won't we, Emily?'

Emily nodded enthusiastically.

'Thanks, love. See you at home?'

Jill wiped her hands on a tea towel, retrieved her handbag from under the table and crossed the room to Rita.

'Rita, love?'

The woman slowly looked up, confusion and something else swimming in her eyes. She looked almost frightened.

'Time to go home. I'm walking in your direction, as it happens. Shall we, madam?' she said, proffering her arm in a comedic way.

To her relief, Rita's face broke into a wide smile, and she rose to standing.

Later that evening, Jill absently stirred the contents of a saucepan and reflected on the events of the day. And it had been *quite* a day. She'd set the wheels in motion for the open day at Beachcombers some time ago, inspired by something Eugene had once said – 'It's a nice enough place, but there aren't half of them as lucky as me when it comes to my boy. If it wasn't for him, I wouldn't even know about this café – always with his nose to the ground. If there's anything going on around here, Ray already knows. Always been the same, takes after my Winnie. Weren't no-one could sneeze in Peckham without his mother knowing about it.'

It had seemed obvious then, to take the Be Together Café to them, to show them what was available on their own doorstep. From there, the idea had grown and luckily the manager of

Beachcombers had run with it, including Jill's suggestion that Alzheimer's Outreach UK have a stand, because if there was one thing she was passionate about since Gary's diagnosis, it was in the education of others.

Of course, with Gracie's marathon undertaking, the stars had aligned, meaning the Beachcombers Open Day became a real opportunity to get the word out there. Perhaps tipping off the local media had been a step too far, but when Emily announced Gracie's intention to quit, she'd had to pull out all the stops, including the heartstring-tugging video from Gary's ex-bandmate Logan. Gosh, he'd really laid it on thick. Had probably smoked a big fat zoot right before filming that clip. She wondered when the right time would be to tell Gracie he was actually Emily's godfather and would have donated all he had in the world to still have his best mate, absolutely no marathons required.

Only time would tell if Gracie would forgive her for putting her under the spotlight. But in the end, it was just another grievance to add to an already teetering heap.

'Mm, something smells good,' said Emily, entering the kitchen. 'But will you be upset if I go out instead? Sophia asked if I wanted to go round and watch a movie with a takeaway.'

Jill frowned. 'Why would I be upset? That sounds lovely. Go! Have fun.'

Exactly what she'd hoped for her daughter: a social life and friends. She wasn't *entirely* convinced about Sophia, mind you, always felt a little wrong-footed around her, as though she wasn't quite smart enough. Still, it wasn't about her. And the two girls got on well. She turned off the hob containing the smaller pan; Emily's meat-free version could be frozen for another time.

Not long after Emily had left with a kiss to her cheek, Jill was giving the saucepan a final stir when the doorbell sounded.

That was odd, she didn't often have visitors, and certainly not on a Saturday night.

Cautiously, she hooked the chain onto the catch and opened the door ajar.

Standing there on the doorstep, huddled in a warm fleece against the cool spring evening, was Gracie.

'Are you *that* scared of me, after your little stunt today?' Gracie asked, one eyebrow cocked.

Jill would never admit it, but part of her *was* an incy bit scared. Gracie could be formidable. Still, she'd been expecting this moment. One didn't knowingly orchestrate the blatant manipulation of one's sister without expecting consequences. The hour of reckoning was, it seemed, upon them.

'You can never be too careful,' she sniffed, unlatching the chain and throwing the door wide. 'Come in.'

'Something smells good.' Gracie echoed Emily's words, as they walked through to the kitchen.

'Spanish chicken,' Jill replied, 'it's a favourite recipe.'

'Lovely,' commented Gracie. Jill saw her sister's gaze fall on the recipe book on the worktop, open at a sauce-splattered page titled 'Low-Fat Chicken, Spanish-Style'.

'Were you about to eat?' asked Gracie. 'I can pop round another time.'

'No, no,' fibbed Jill, whose stomach was audibly rumbling. 'Batch cooking.'

Gracie nodded. 'Mind if I sit down?' she said, not waiting for a reply, before pulling out a chair.

'Can I get you a drink? Tea, coffee?' asked Jill.

'Haven't you anything stronger? If I have one more cup of tea today, I'll start growing a spout.'

Jill tried to contain a smile. 'Glass of red?'

'Perfect.'

Jill poured two large glasses of Cabernet Sauvignon and placed one on the table in front of Gracie, then sat opposite.

'Cheers,' said Gracie, raising the glass.

'What are we drinking to?' asked Jill.

Gracie met her with a steady gaze, eyes brightening as the glass neared her lips. 'Me reaching that finishing line in one piece, naturally. Hopefully with all ten toes and my ligaments intact, never mind my nipples.'

Jill did her best to rein in the triumphant smile threatening at the corners of her mouth. 'You'll do it?' Her words almost tripped over themselves. 'You'll really do it? Because I know you were planning to quit.'

Gracie blew out her cheeks. 'Not *quitting*, Gillian. Resigning with regret. As though that would ever have been an option with you in the background, scheming and meddling as though we were in some bizarre version of *A Christmas Carol*. Here are some students from your past to remind you of what you once were, on your left you'll see your friends, pulling out all the stops to support you, and if you'd look over to the easy chairs on your right, here is where you could be in ten years' time, lonely and away with the fairies.'

'Dementia's nothing to joke about, Gracie,' said Jill sadly.

Sighing, Gracie nodded. 'I know that. And I'm so sorry for what you must have gone through. I want to run this marathon, Jill, for the charity, and for *you*. If it were Andy... I cannot begin to imagine.'

Jill looked up to the ceiling. 'He was fifteen years older than me. It was always going to be hard, however it panned out.'

'Still,' said Gracie. 'I should have been there. I should have known what you were going through, and I should have been there for you. I'm sorry for that.'

Jill's eyes began to prick and she rapidly blinked, hoping to keep tears at bay.

'It was hard, Gracie. The hardest thing I've ever been through, but do you know what made it harder? Knowing that after he was gone, I'd be all alone.' A strangled sound escaped her, and she swallowed back the lump in her throat. 'I have Emily, of course I do, she's my world. But orphaned *and* widowed. . . that's something else.' She looked up through blurred vision. 'I didn't have you anymore either. And that's what I wanted to change. That's why I came here.'

Gracie twirled the stem of her glass and Jill knew what she was thinking. That she could have changed that at any point, why wait until their mother was gone? Well, the time for silence had passed – it was now or never.

'Gracie, did Mum ever tell you what went on between us? Because I need to know what you think happened.'

Gracie frowned. 'I'm not sure I was ever aware of anything happening, as such. Mum always maintained you cut her off after Dad died, disappeared into the sunset with Gary and chose to abandon your family. She said you always ignored phone calls, birthdays and the likes. Made it clear you wanted nothing to do with any of us.'

Jill spurted. 'I'd hardly call Hemel Hempstead *the sunset*, would you?'

'No,' agreed Gracie. 'So, do I take that to mean something *did* happen? Something you haven't told me?'

Just as Jill had been growing to suspect. Why had she doubted her sister all these years? Why hadn't she had the backbone to confront her, or her mother?

Jill took a deep, steadying breath. She would take no pleasure in this.

'The bullying began after you left to go travelling,' she said.

Gracie's eyes narrowed.

'I told Mum about it, about the kids at school I mean, and do you know what she said?' Jill gave a mirthless laugh. 'That if I wasn't so podgy, maybe I wouldn't get bullied.'

'Sorry, what?' Gracie sat up straight in astonishment.

'You know what was the strangest thing? I could handle the name calling and lunch-stealing, but I could not get my head around Mum. It was as though as soon as you left, she looked at me and found me to be wanting. She'd been left with the lesser child, the one who was slightly overweight and nowhere near as smart, or pretty, or popular. Not to mention I was hampering their social lives. I was the accident that came along and disrupted their plans to spend weekends at the social club and fondue evenings with friends.'

Jill swallowed down a tight ball of emotion, aware her voice was trembling. This was the first time she'd spoken about her childhood in a very long time. Gary had been the only person she'd ever confided in, until now.

'Mum became cruel. Not in an obvious way, and never in front of Dad, but in a way only *I* would understand. Smaller portions at dinner, new clothes a size too small, missed pick-ups from school so I'd have to walk the three miles home.' She paused to take a fortifying glug of her wine.

'Jill, that's terrible. I had no idea.' Gracie was watching her intently, her eyes clouding in grim acknowledgement as she digested her sister's words.

'Receiving your postcards was the highlight of my weeks. I used to dream of the day I'd be grown up like you and living out my own adventures. Then as the years went by, and you trained to be a teacher, then got married, Mum said the best I could hope for was finding something I was good at, like child-minding, or typing.'

'What the hell?' remarked Gracie, anger creeping into her tone.

Jill met her eye. 'But then, the strangest thing happened. I might not have been clever, or good at school, and I never really had many friends, but almost overnight, it felt like I became a woman. Suddenly, when I looked in the mirror, I could see traces of you. The puppy fat that had plagued my childhood fell away, and I saw myself differently. At sixteen, I jacked in school, which sent Mum into hysterics, and took a waitressing job in a local bar, and that's where I first met Gaz.'

At this, Gracie's eyebrows furrowed. 'I thought you met him at seventeen, when you ran off together?'

'That's what Mum wanted you to think because that's the version that fitted her narrative. The truth of it was we'd become friends. He used to drink there incognito in a cosy corner, with his best mate Logan, many years before he started calling himself Jet; bloody ridiculous name that was. I was a little bit starstruck, flirted my arse off. It made me feel powerful, you know, for the first time ever. Like I was finally in control of my own life.' She laughed. 'Totally naive, obviously.'

'The facts speak for themselves, Jill. You were married for twenty-five years,' reminded Gracie.

Jill nodded. 'Then, a year later, the band were setting off on a UK tour and Gary asked me to go with them. So I did. I was mad about him.'

'And then what happened?' asked Gracie gently.

'Then, our lovely dad had a heart attack, and Mum blamed me. After the funeral, when we went back to the house for the wake, she pulled me into the bathroom and hissed into my ear. Told me I was the bane of their lives, causing them nothing but stress and anxiety since the minute I was born. That if I hadn't turned into a teenage slut, filling their house with shame, then Dad would still be alive.'

The colour drained from Gracie's face. 'She said *what*?'

'It gets better. When Emily was born and I sent her a letter with a photo of her granddaughter, she wrote back to me, returning the photo. Said as far as she was concerned, she only had one daughter, and one grandchild, Nathan.' This time, Jill didn't even try to stop the tears from filling up her eyeballs and spilling down her cheeks.

'I gave up then, Gracie. I'm sorry. I could never have forgiven her for that. So, then, I did cut her out of my life. But in doing so, I lost you too. Perhaps I should have told you, but part of me wondered if she was right – if it really was me that had caused Dad's heart attack. And part of me wondered if you felt the same. I tried to keep up contact, calling you from time to time, making sure I attended all the big events, but it wasn't enough. I should have tried harder and I'm so, so sorry.'

Jill buried her face in her hands and sobbed, no longer caring about keeping up the glossy, careful front she shielded behind. What was the point? Her mother was gone, even if the scars her words had left behind still itched a little every day. A chair scraped against the floor, and then Gracie was there, wrapping her arms around her.

'Ssh,' she soothed, stroking back her hair. 'It's OK, darling. Everything's going to be OK. And you'd better believe me when I say, you have absolutely *nothing* to be sorry for.' Gracie squeezed her shoulder tightly. '*Never* for one moment think you are responsible for any of it. If anything, it's me who should be apologising. And I do, Jill, sincerely. I'm your big sister; I should have been looking out for you. I should have seen the signs back then and every day since. If I'd made more effort over the years. If I'd asked to hear your side... But I'm here now, and I promise you, I'm not going *anywhere*.'

The grit and strength in her big sister's voice cut through Jill's tears. She closed her eyes and soaked up the feeling of having her close. The years fell away, and her mind lodged on a memory so clear, it could have been yesterday. She'd been lying on her bed in her school uniform, after another gruelling day of bitchy remarks and misery. Gracie was perched beside her, a woman of twenty-eight back to visit, a woman newly married and thinking of starting her own family. She'd brought Jill a present, delivered in an instantly recognisable green and black plastic bag, something Jill had nagged her for the last time she'd visited, believing that just by owning the coveted, trendy new perfume it would help her fit in with the other girls. That she'd become relevant and cool. She should have told her big sister then, that even twenty bottles of White Musk could never have made her happy. She should have told her the truth. Perhaps if she had found the words back then, she might have found a way to navigate life without the paranoid anxiety that pushed everyone away. Making friends, true friends, was something she'd never truly mastered. Not until now, perhaps. Perhaps, finally, she was laying her ghosts to rest. Letting down the facade, letting others in.

'Jill, love?' came Gracie's voice, cutting into her regret.

'Mmm.'

'Do you think we could have some of that delicious-smelling Spanish chicken before the pot boils dry. I'm bloody ravenous and I know you are too. Either that or you've got rowdy gremlins living under the floorboards.'

Jill snorted with laughter and a stream of snot hit Gracie's sleeve.

Gracie pulled away and examined her sleeve in horror, whilst Jill dissolved into hysterics.

'The. . . the kitchen roll's over there,' she managed to spit out between bouts of giggles. 'Oh my goodness, grab that wine,' she hooted, 'I think we'll need the bottle.'

Gracie topped up their glasses, then Jill got up and fetched two plates from the cupboard.

'It's a bit burnt,' she said, grimacing as her wooden spoon hit a sludge in the bottom of the pan, 'we can eat the top part, but this pan will take some soaking. Which reminds me,' she said, spinning around to face Gracie. 'We need to talk about Rita.'

22

Gracie

After finishing off the bottle of wine, and starting on another, Jill convinced Gracie that walking home alone at gone eleven on unsteady legs wouldn't be one of her finer ideas, so she rang Andrew to come and pick her up.

Their car was an automatic these days, so that Andrew could still drive, although how long it would be before his other knee gave out and he could no longer use the brake pedal remained to be seen.

'Thanks for coming out so late, love,' she said, as they let themselves in.

'Don't give it another thought. I was sitting up waiting anyway, lest news of a grisly revenge murder reached me. I could even picture the headlines: "Local Marathon Woman Bludgeons Sister to Death with Nike Trainer". Even wondered if there was enough in the savings account to meet bail.'

'Daft old fool,' said Gracie. 'I'd choose something far more effective than a rubber sole. Cup of cocoa for bed?'

'Sounds perfect.'

Snuggled under the duvet with two steaming mugs of hot chocolate, Gracie updated Andrew on the evening's events.

'I think I always knew Mum had a callous side; it would come out occasionally if she was watching the news, for example, and it featured food banks or the homeless. "Bring it on themselves and then expect the rest of us to pick up the pieces," she'd say. But I'd always put it down to ignorance. How could any mother treat their own child so cruelly? And more to the point, how come I didn't see it?' Gracie shook her head miserably.

It was going to take time to process Jill's revelations this evening. Time to reconcile her own memories of a relatively happy childhood with Jill's very different experience. To re-evaluate her uptight mother who'd had a tendency for snobbery and scorn, as the cold and selfish woman who ruthlessly cut Jill and Emily from her life.

'She made sure you didn't see it, Gracie. That's how. No point blaming yourself. Best to look forwards, not back.' Andrew gave her hand a reassuring squeeze.

But that was easier said than done. Already, Gracie was casting her mind back to before she'd left the family home and gone off to university. Had there been any signs of her parents' resentment towards Jill? Could she have done more? There certainly hadn't been on her father's part; Jill had been the apple of his eye. He'd been a gentle man, able to calm his wife's hysterias with his easy manner. And Jill had been so easy to love, with her big innocent eyes and kind, loving nature. Sophia's words about post-natal depression drifted back to her: *it's far more common than you might think*. Had that been the cause of her mother's rejection of Jill? Or had it been jealousy, pure and simple? Someone stealing the limelight and her husband away from her, just when she thought he was all hers once more.

All the haughtiness and obstinance she'd displayed in later life took on new meaning, as Gracie's view shifted uncomfortably. She may have been a grumpy old woman with declining health, but she had also had a wicked streak.

'We have a lot of lost time to claw back,' said Gracie eventually, realising that her focus should be on the here and now and in rebuilding her relationship with Jill.

But Gracie wasn't sure any amount of sisterly love was going to undo the more subtle damage that had been done to Jill. So much made sense to her now, from the gregarious veneer she portrayed to the world, to the insecurities and paranoia that made her seem aloof or judgy. And it hadn't been lost on Gracie either that there was an entire shelf in Jill's kitchen dedicated to dieting cookery books, everything from Weight Watchers to Slimming World and a whole lot in between.

It just went to show that you really never could know what was going on behind closed doors. Like Rita's door, for example.

She thought back to the conversation earlier, when Jill had confided her concerns to her, and experienced another torrent of blood roiling fury.

'Even in the short time I've known the woman, it's obvious she's become consistently more confused and bewildered,' Jill had said. 'At first, I thought it was great, you know, that her daughter was bringing her to the Be Together Café, to get her out and socialising in a safe environment. With a little light cajoling, she'd sit with the others and Eugene usually managed to raise a smile or two, well let's face it – he could charm the hind legs off a donkey.' Gracie had laughed at that, because it was perfectly true, and his son had been blessed with the same gift.

'But then, I realised, that apart from one time Kat appeared – do you remember, you and the other runners were there? Of course you do, she was particularly unpleasant about you taking Emily's place in the marathon, well, that day was the only time she's ever collected Rita from the hall.'

'Yes, we found her standing outside today, as forlorn as a child who'd lost their parent. She seemed to think she was collecting Kat from Brownies. So clearly something's not right there,' supplied Gracie.

'Hmm, Emily told me. Well, I thought I'd better walk her home this afternoon as it was getting late and there was no sign of Kat, even though Emily had sent her a WhatsApp message to tell her where she was.' Jill narrowed her eyes. 'Do you know the poor woman couldn't remember where she lived. Became completely distressed, not to mention embarrassed. I had to ask if I could have a quick look through her handbag to find something with her address on, which made me feel like a criminal, and then when we got there, it's to find she is living completely alone. I'd assumed she must live with her daughter. I mean, she clearly has symptoms of a worsening neurological condition, but I'd *assumed* her daughter was looking after her.' Jill had shaken her head, as though it were somehow her fault this was the case. 'But that's not the worst of it. Gracie, believe me when I tell you, I have never seen such shocking living conditions, and I lived on a tour bus with five men for six months.'

Gracie had listened to her sister in concern as she had gone on to detail the chaotic mess and filth of Rita's home and the obvious signs that she wasn't looking after herself; from the rotten, mouldering food in the fridge, to the pervading stench of unwashed clothing and layers of grime.

'Did you know, she's only four years older than me?' Jill had remarked in astonishment. 'She looks seventy-five at least.'

Gracie had done the sums in her head; yes, she supposed that sounded about right. Rita had been a fairly young mum when Kathleen was at school. A young, timid mother who'd always seemed out of her depth when it came to her bullish, domineering daughter.

'Anyway,' Gracie said to Andrew, having relayed to him the conversation about Rita, 'I decided, all things considered, I would tell Jill what really happened to Emily on New Year's Eve.'

Andrew sucked in a sharp breath. 'Blimey, Gracie. Are you sure that was wise? Jill can be a loose cannon; you've said it yourself. And you can't prove anything.'

'Perhaps not. But after hearing about the years of bullying Jill endured as a teenager, it struck me that she would want to know. Imagine if something like that happened again, to Emily, or someone else. And imagine if Kat's despicable behaviour in sabotaging Emily's marathon manifests itself in other ways, a little closer to home? What if her vicious streak comes out with her mother, for example? It's something we should perhaps consider.'

Andrew lowered his mug and shared a grim look of concern with Gracie. 'Blimey. That doesn't bear thinking about, love.'

'Quite,' agreed Gracie. 'And no need to worry; Jill said the same as me. Absolutely nothing to be gained in telling Emily she was tripped on purpose. Especially as she seems so much happier now and is back to being active again.'

'And you? Are you happy?' he said, quirking a brow. 'About running a marathon two weeks tomorrow, I mean?'

Gracie took the empty mug from Andrew's hand and placed it together with hers on the bedside table. She snuggled into his chest, and he folded an arm around her.

'I'm happy to have such wonderful friends and family,' she said. 'And to have you. That's what today has really shown me. It's highlighted something I think I'd lost sight of along the way. This whole thing isn't *about the running*. Not really. Anyone can run, physical limitations permitting, of course. It doesn't matter where you're from, what you look like, what you wear, what you've got or whether you are fast or slow – you just put one foot in front of the other and you do it for you. But running *for* something is a different beast entirely. It's an idea that gathers momentum, until it's no longer about you, it's about what can be achieved when *one* becomes *many*. You only have to think about Captain Tom's achievements during lockdown to see that.'

'That's rather profound, dear,' said Andrew, giving her a squeeze.

'I'm feeling profound. I'm also feeling lucky. Jill's lost so much, yet somehow she digs deep every day and finds the strength to not only keep going, but to give back too. I think there's an awful lot to learn from my little sister.'

'Oh, I completely agree.' Andrew cleared his throat theatrically. 'So, er, when can we expect leopard-print boob tubes to make an appearance in your wardrobe then, because I'm *particularly* looking forward to that,' he asked, only to receive a smack on the thigh.

'We're all stylish in our own way, dear. I heard Harold ask where your jumper came from today; who knew the humble sawdust-flecked fleece could be such a desired paragon of senior-citizen apparel?'

Andrew chuckled into Gracie's hair, and they remained like that for a while, enjoying the comfortable, contented peace that comes from being with someone whose thoughts are so entwined with yours there seems no need to voice them.

As a sleepiness began to wash over Gracie, she mumbled, 'One more thing though, Andy?'

'Hmm,' he murmured back.

'No more gadgets please. I just need to run this my way, no distractions, no *improvements*.'

'Absolutely. No more. I promise,' he said, and Gracie could hear the smile pressed to her head. 'Although I did have a brainwave the other day, I was thinking – when you need the loo, mid-marathon. . .'

'OK. And let's leave that there, shall we. Night, night.'

23

Gracie

On Sunday morning, Gracie bounded out of bed with conviction. Today was going to be her last opportunity for a really long run before she would need to start the tapering process Jill had told her about, gradually decreasing her mileage and conserving energy for the big day. The furthest she'd managed to date was sixteen miles. Today, she was aiming for eighteen.

An hour before setting off, to allow time for digestion, Gracie had her pre-run breakfast of choice – a bowl of muesli and a banana – then sent a quick selfie to Jill showing her grimacing at a spinach-coloured smoothie, which she duly guzzled.

A thumbs-up came back instantly, along with a motivational motto: 'Be Your Own Hero'. Actually that was rather good, adaptable too – she'd try and remember it next time she was confronted with a giant bar of Galaxy.

She tugged on her CPR running top, freshly washed since yesterday morning, courtesy of Andrew, and slipped into her favourite white trainers. She sent Jill another message asking if she could meet her at three designated spots along the route to provide her with water, energy drinks and calorific snacks, in as close a simulation to the real event as possible. The only thing she wouldn't have access to was a Portaloo, and if she'd given Andrew free rein, goodness knows what hideous contraption she'd be sporting to accommodate that need. As it was, a couple of pubs along the seafront would provide perfectly good pitstops.

Gracie popped her head into the shed. 'See you in a few hours then. And hands off that deep-pan meat feast in the fridge. It might be the only thing that gets me through, the thought of biting into all that cheesy, gooey loveliness.'

'Understood. I wouldn't want a *pizza* your mind now would I, love?'

With a groan, Gracie pecked her husband on the cheek and mentally catalogued herself as she made her way to the street. Warm-up stretches, check. Slow-release carbs, check. Comfy trainers, check. Battered old baseball cap, check. Sunscreen, check. Lip balm, check. Well then, all that remained was to take in a long, lung-filling breath of fresh, briny air and. . . she was off.

This time, when Gracie reached the greensward, she turned left to follow the Coast Path Runners' usual Saturday morning route to Walton-on-the-Naze. She needed to push herself today, harder than she ever had before, and those initial few miles before doubling back and powering through to Clacton and Jaywick beyond that were going to count.

The first surprise of the day was a small support party in the form of Ray, Malik, Elsie and Theo, all enjoying a bacon roll on the decking of Ray's beach hut. As they saw Gracie approach, the children scrabbled to hold up a homemade sign, displaying the words 'You can do it, Gracie' in large felt-tip pen bubble-writing.

'I'm only a mile and a half in!' Gracie laughed in delight as she drew closer.

'Doesn't matter,' insisted Ray, 'every one of those miles counts, girl.'

The smell of cooked bacon drifted from the hut and made her mouth water. 'Blimey, you lot, now all I want to do is sit down with a mug of tea and a bacon sarnie too.'

Malik jumped up. 'Oh no you don't! Here you go,' he said, lifting the lid of his bun and handing Gracie a rasher of bacon between thumb and forefinger as she slowed up. 'Off you trot, no hanging about!'

Gracie did as she was told and carried on moving forwards, to the sound of Elsie and Theo calling after her, 'Off you trot!' and descending into squeals of laughter as though it was the funniest thing they'd ever heard. *Bloody cheek of it*. She smiled to herself and crunched on the crispy bacon. Then not ten minutes later, she was treated to another chorus on the return journey past them, the boost of which kept her going all the way past Frinton, through Holland-on-Sea, and as far as Clacton, before her focus drifted to her dry lips and the aching impact of each stride upon her thighs, knees and the balls of her feet.

Lots of runners listened to playlists as they ran. Some used the rhythms of carefully selected songs to set and match their pace. She'd tried it in the beginning but found she was focusing so hard on the music, she was missing out on the connection with her environment that fuelled her to run at all. She often felt as though she were a three-pin plug, earthed to the ground, wired to hear, see, and inhale her surroundings as she, herself, became a part of the landscape. Mindfulness wasn't something Gracie necessarily prescribed to, but she was increasingly arriving at the conclusion it could take many forms. Some liked to write in a gratitude journal, for instance; some liked to meditate. When Gracie ran, she was mindfully feeling and experiencing the present. She tuned in on the chattering seagulls overhead, a man calling his dog back from the lapping water's edge, the rumble of traffic on the road above, the crunch of her trainers as they connected with the concrete. The scent of seaweed, washed up on the beach. The aroma of coffee drifting from a beach-front kiosk. It was all thoroughly wonderful to her.

By the time Gracie admitted defeat and came to an exhausted stop, accepting that if she pushed herself further, even *with* regular walking breaks, she ran the risk of injury or burn-out, she had managed a whopping seventeen miles. It had been her best-ever run. Jill had been there, as promised, at strategic points along the way to cheer her on and provide a much-needed boost, which this time, Gracie had been grateful for. Jill had even managed to restrain herself when she clocked the tatty old trainers, a revision to her attire Gracie was certain would invoke comment.

Back home, as Jill chopped and sliced fruits and vegetables to blend her a recovery smoothie, Gracie looked around her kitchen. It felt so homely with the extra company and the easy chat. It had been too long since she and Andrew had enjoyed the company of others here, in a house that used to be full of life. An idea sprang to mind.

'Are you and Emily doing anything next weekend, Easter Sunday?'

Jill paused in her chopping.

'Um, not sure. . . why?' She sounded cautious.

'Because I'd like to cook for my family and friends, a proper Easter lunch, with all the trimmings, to say thank you for the support.'

Jill beamed in delight, but her smile quickly sagged. 'Gracie, that sounds amazing, but can I get back to you?'

Gracie had so hoped that she and Jill had turned a corner, that this was the beginning of a closeness she'd always craved and, if she was being perfectly honest, a family-shaped dollop of love to help heal the raw edges of the hole Nathan always left around the table on such occasions. Yet it was there in Jill's expression, an uneasiness that put an instant dampener on the moment.

Jill resumed chopping, then suddenly slapped her knife down on the counter with a long sigh.

'Sis, I'd love absolutely nothing more than for us to be together at Easter, and I'm sure Emily would too. It's just that. . . I worry about the customers of the café. About whether they would be alone. Cynthia and I hosted Christmas lunch for them this year and we haven't yet discussed Easter, but. . .' She tailed off.

Gracie could kick herself for confusing complacency with compassion.

She nodded. 'Absolutely, and I agree, it's extremely important that nobody is alone.' She looked around her kitchen again. Did a mental calculation.

'How many did you have on Christmas Day, at the café?'

Jill twisted her mouth, thoughtfully. 'Perhaps eight in the end. Not many.'

'This table seats eight,' announced Gracie. 'And we've plenty of extra chairs. I think it's about time Andrew made something useful in that workshop of his, don't you?'

Jill grinned. 'Let me ask around at the café tomorrow. Get an idea of numbers before you have Andrew taking your doors off for use as makeshift banquet tables.'

In the end, it was just the usual suspects. Eugene had jumped at the invitation, as had Ray. Harold had despondently admitted that one of his boys was on holiday in Thailand and the other hadn't been in touch, so yes please, he'd love to come. Rita had just looked back at Jill blankly.

Come Easter morning, there was a moment when Gracie regretted inviting twelve people for lunch, right around the time she was peeling the fiftieth potato. 'Only another twenty to go,' she muttered to herself. Gracie had always preferred to over-cater, on the off chance there was an extra guest, or, as invariably happened, some were lost to the kitchen floor.

'Right, where do you want me?' asked Andrew, rubbing his hands together and leaning heavily on one leg.

Gracie glanced up. He was wearing his usual smile, but she could see past that to the pain he was endeavouring to conceal. Thank goodness the op was just a week away.

'I think you've done enough, dear, don't you? Why don't you go and rest up for a bit.'

Andrew had crafted an extension to their dining table from a rickety old oak patio set that needed replacing. Once it had been given sturdier legs at the right height, a good sanding, then covered over with tablecloths, the result was an enticing-looking banquet table, laid up for all their guests. The work had been considerably more physical than usual, and he was paying the price of it.

'No,' he said, an argumentative edge creeping into his tone, 'I want to help.'

Gracie knew it for what it was, a stubborn determination not to give in, and who was she to argue with that? 'If you really must help, take these carrots and sit at the table to do them. Batons, not circles.' She handed him a small chopping board and a knife.

Jill and Emily were the first to arrive, Jill sweeping into the kitchen in a blur of turquoise satin and an overpoweringly floral scent, dressed more appropriately for the BAFTAs than a roast lamb lunch.

'I've brought two of every colour,' she said, unpacking wine bottles onto the already cluttered worktop, 'and I know you said dessert was covered, but I couldn't let the side down now, could I?'

She whipped the plastic dome from a cake stand with ceremony, as though unveiling a town statue, to reveal a buttercream-plastered masterpiece worthy of a *Bake Off* final.

'Wow,' said Gracie, studiously ignoring her niece who was drawing a finger across her throat behind Jill's back and miming choking to death. 'That looks more fitting for the Tate gallery than my table. Are you sure you wouldn't rather save it for the café?'

Jill flapped her away with a dismissive wave, then opened the fridge door to find space for the wine.

'There's no room. Shall I pop these desserts in the freezer, so you can have them another time?' she called back over her shoulder.

Gracie, Andrew and Emily exchanged loaded looks of longing and regret at the decadent and delicious-looking boxed cheesecakes from Waitrose in Jill's hands, cheesecakes they *had* been having for dessert.

'Uh-huh,' squeaked Gracie, using more willpower than she'd need to get her across that finish line next week not to sprint across the room and rescue the coveted puds from her sister's grasp. But unlike over recent months, Gracie didn't feel as though Jill were being pushy or meddlesome. She wanted only to boost her sister's fragile confidence. 'Why would we want shop-bought, when we've got something you've made with love.'

Jill rewarded her with a look of pure, surprised delight.

Sometime later, as the last of the serving dishes were placed in the centre of the table, and everyone began to tuck in, Gracie appraised her guests.

OK, so perhaps she should take back her thoughts about Jill being meddlesome because the woman had unrepentantly ushered each guest into an obviously contrived seating plan, which placed Malik opposite Sophia and, unsurprisingly, herself squeezed in beside Ray. Doubtless the low-cut satin number had been engineered for that very purpose. Twelve friends and family members, eleven of whom Gracie couldn't even have conceived of having in her life this time last year. Of course, there were always going to be people missing from a get-together like this. Nathan was probably tucked up in bed by now, having enjoyed Easter with Beth and the girls, on the other side of the world. She tried not to let her mind linger on how much she missed them all.

'These roasties are delicious,' declared Emily. 'We never have roast potatoes at home.'

'What's the point?' asked Jill. 'You don't eat roast dinners, you're vegetarian.'

Gracie felt rather guilty about the sorry-looking red onion and goat's cheese quiche on Emily's plate, when the rest of them were tucking into succulent roasted lamb with mint sauce, but she seemed to be enjoying it.

'Newsflash, you don't need meat to have a roast dinner. Case in point right there,' replied Emily, pointing across the table.

All eyes drifted to the plates of Theo and Elsie, who were munching on (at Malik's request) carrots, peas, honey-roasted parsnips, roast potatoes and. . . fishfingers.

'It's inspired,' said Sophia. 'That's what it is. I'll take fishfingers with anything.'

'What, *anything*?' asked Theo, who was clearly giving that some thought.

'*Anything*,' insisted Sophia. 'Even chocolate ice cream and sprinkles,' she added with a wink. 'You should try it. Yum.'

Theo looked to his dad. 'Seriously, Daddy?'

'Oh, I wouldn't be surprised, son,' he replied, fixing Sophia with a grin, 'she's bonkers enough.'

Rita gave a long, appreciative sigh, prompting everyone to look her way. She'd completely cleared her plate whereas everyone else had barely started and was dabbing her finger into the leftover gravy and sucking it from her fingertip with pleasure.

'I take it you enjoyed that, Rita,' laughed Sophia. 'Will I get you some more?'

Seeming to notice the eyes upon her, a slow, shy smile crept onto Rita's lips, and she gave a small nod.

How long had it been since she'd had a proper meal, Gracie wondered, experiencing a rush of gratitude for her husband, her family and for friends like these who she knew without a doubt would never turn a blind eye to someone else's suffering, as Rita's own daughter had done to her.

When the sound of cutlery scraping on china was replaced with the hum of chatter, Ray pushed back his chair and reached for Jill's plate. Except, Jill, who had clearly had the same idea, levered herself to standing in the same split second and her torso collided with his, hands, arms and plates clumsily connecting, before swiftly, they both righted themselves.

'Er, sorry about that,' said Ray, looking uncharacteristically embarrassed.

'Not at all,' trilled Jill, who Gracie could tell even from the other end of the table had greatly enjoyed the encounter. 'Let me help.'

Ray replied with a brief smile and continued collecting up dishes.

In fact, Gracie realised, Ray had been unusually quiet today. The usual stream of banter that passed between him and his dad had been lacking, with Eugene mostly chatting with Harold, all the way through lunch. Surely they hadn't fallen out?

Andrew went to get up too, but Gracie placed a hand over his.

'Why don't you take everyone through to the lounge, love? We can eat pudding in a comfy chair, maybe crack out the Trivial Pursuit?'

'Not fair,' laughed Emily. 'You two know all the answers! You even told us that!'

'Knowing them and remembering them, darling, are two entirely different things. I can barely remember my way upstairs these days,' retorted Gracie, then as her gaze moved along the table to Rita, who was looking down at her lap, she regretted the flippant comment. 'Will you give Andy a hand getting everyone settled, Em?' She made eyes at Rita, so Emily would understand what she meant. 'And I'll help with finishing up out here.'

Chairs scraped on the floor tiles and the assembled party dispersed one by one, accompanied by groans of full bellies.

Elsie skipped over to Gracie, clearly nominated as leader by Theo, who hung back slightly. 'Gracie, can you play hide-and-seek with us?' she asked.

'I think I'd better wait until my lunch has gone down before I go crawling around on the floor, looking under beds,' Gracie laughed.

Not to be deterred, Theo threw out another option. 'Can we play the drawing game?'

Gracie pondered for a moment. 'Come with me, I want to show you something.'

She led them into the small sunroom she and Andrew had used when they were teaching. Somewhere quiet to mark work or plan lessons, or simply sit with a cuppa and enjoy the sunshine. Nowadays it was a bit of a junk room, every inch of wall space crammed with bookshelves full of faded books, and boxes of files to sort through one day. But it had also always been Gracie's favourite place to paint, when the muse took her, and her old easel was still set up in the corner, a trolley of paints and brushes beside it.

She leafed through a stack of old canvases and found two that were fairly clean.

'I wondered,' she said, running her finger along the bookshelves until she found a battered, old reference book, 'seeing as you two are such accomplished artists, whether you might like a go at painting your portraits.' She opened the well-thumbed book to a page featuring *Girl with a Pearl Earring*. 'These are examples of famous portraits, but you can do anything you like. Stand on your head, pull a funny face, or gaze out of the window dreamily. You can take it in turns, one can be the sitter, and one the painter, then swap over to give the other one a go, what do you think?'

Theo's eyes widened. 'But I don't know how to do proper painting.'

Gracie got down to his level. 'No such thing, my love. If you paint what your mind sees and what you feel, in here—' she pressed a hand to his heart '—that is art.'

Elsie shrugged. 'OK, can I be painter first?'

As Theo shuffled onto a wicker chair, and Elsie stood at the easel drowned in one of Andrew's old shirts to protect her dress, Gracie withdrew from the room with a smile. She'd set up her own granddaughters with a similar challenge the last time they'd visited, and they'd been at it for hours. Made an unholy mess, but the results had been worth it.

Back in the kitchen, Jill was wearing Gracie's apron and a pair of washing-up gloves.

'Can't find any dishwasher tablets,' said Jill, 'and what the heck is this? I found it in the cupboard.' She pointed at Andrew's showerhead attachment. 'It looks like an instrument of torture, or something you use for anal douching. In fact I'm not sure I *want* to know, come to think of it.' She shuddered.

'Just another of Andy's unnecessary inventions, and *I'm* not sure I want to know how *you* would know what an anal douche looks like. Where's Ray?'

'Went outside for some air. Don't blame him, it's boiling in here.' Jill fanned her face with the J-Cloth, splattering her rosy cheeks with bubbles.

Gracie slipped out of the back door and scanned the garden.

'I'm here,' came Ray's deep voice from behind.

He stepped forward from where he'd been leaning against the side wall.

'That's quite the man cave,' he said, nodding towards Andrew's shed.

'Isn't it. I really should have bargained harder. I got a night at *Phantom of the Opera*, and he got an aircraft hangar.' She qualified her statement. 'Retirement gifts to ourselves.'

Ray nodded. 'Most men, in my experience, need some kind of den. Look at me with the beach hut. Don't know why that is. Perhaps we're all just cavemen at heart, dreaming of a simpler life.'

After a beat of silence, Gracie asked, 'Is everything alright, Ray? You don't seem yourself.'

Gracie could see the internal battle as a shadow crossed his eyes. Something was wrong, she was certain of it. And he seemed to be debating whether to open up to her. In the end, he gave an apologetic smile.

'Thanks for lunch, it was delicious, and a really lovely thing to do. Look, I hope you don't think me rude, but you know what, I'm not feeling too great. I think I'll go for a walk. Clear the head. Then I'll come back for Dad and Harold, take them home.'

'Of course,' insisted Gracie. 'But if you're not feeling well, wouldn't you rather go home? Andrew can drop Eugene and Harold back whenever they want to go.'

Ray stalled for a moment, then, as though he hadn't even the energy to discuss it any further, he just nodded.

'Thank you. I'm sorry. Please pass on my apologies to the others, I'm gonna. . .' He began to back away. 'Thanks, Gracie.'

Gracie watched her friend walk away, his shoulders slumped against a mighty weight, until he disappeared from view, then she sighed and went back inside.

24

Jill

'Leave that now, Jill, I can finish up tomorrow,' said Gracie as she went back into the kitchen. 'Let's go and get a show of hands for some of your lovely Easter cake.'

Jill didn't need telling twice, tugging the rubber gloves from each finger with a satisfying ping. She'd broken the back of the dishes, at least, and the roasting tins needed a good soaking.

'Great idea. I'll bring the cake. You bring the plates and forks and a nice big knife. There are four layers of chocolate sponge to get through!'

Then, she realised Ray hadn't followed her sister indoors.

'Ray still outside?' she asked.

'No,' said Gracie apologetically. 'He didn't feel well so he's slipped off home.'

The smile sagged on Jill's face, before she checked herself. *It's nothing you've done.* And yet she couldn't get Ray's awkwardness around her today out of her mind. He'd seemed so distracted all day. Perhaps it *was* her, perhaps he'd rather have been seated next to Andrew or Malik so he could have enjoyed a bit of male banter. 'That's a shame. Right then, shall we?' She lifted the weighty cake stand from the worktop and pushed down the flicker of disappointment.

In the lounge, a contented fug had settled over the lunch guests. Harold was asleep in an armchair, his chin touching his chest, Emily was curled into a beanbag she'd brought down from the spare room and Malik lay flat on his back on the rug with his eyes closed. It was only when Jill said the words, 'Anyone for pudding?' that Sophia's guilty gaze jerked upwards from where his t-shirt had ridden up, exposing smooth, brown skin.

'I thought we were playing Trivial Pursuit?' remarked Gracie, gesturing with open hands at Andrew. 'This looks more like a scene from *Village of the Damned*.'

Eugene hooted with laughter. 'As much as I'd love to see Harold wake up impregnated with an alien child, I've got five pounds riding on that game, so we'd better wake him up.'

'Oh, you think you can win now, is 'that'? it?' said Sophia, swivelling around.

'Now, I didn't say *that*,' said Eugene, raising his hands, 'only that I will beat *him*.' He grinned with mischief.

Harold suddenly stirred, jerking upright. 'The porpoise is in the wardrobe,' he said, making a small, snuffling noise, before his head dropped back to his chin.

'See what I mean?' Eugene shook his head in exasperation.

Andrew tapped the lid of the box beside him on the coffee table. 'We'll have to split into teams, or we'll be here until next Easter.'

'In that case, where's my Raymond, he's with me,' said Eugene, hitching forward on the sofa and rubbing his hands in anticipation. 'Who else wants to be on the winning team?'

'Ray's not feeling well, love,' said Gracie kindly. 'I told him to get off home. Will you have me instead?'

Eugene, far from looking surprised at his son's disappearance, merely nodded knowingly and tapped the space beside him. 'Sit yourself down right here, Gracie. In the corner of champions and athletes.'

Whilst everyone organised themselves into teams, Jill sliced the cake' her most ambitious creation yet, a layered double chocolate sponge, smothered in vanilla buttercream and decorated with Cadbury Mini Eggs.

She handed around the plates, noticing a certain reluctance as she did so. *Everyone had space for pudding, surely?* There was always room for sweet stuff. Something she'd battled all her life to resist.

'Whose team are you on then, Jill?' asked Andrew, taking his plate.

Jill looked around. Emily had partnered with Eugene and Gracie and Andrew had pulled up a chair next to Harold, which left Malik, Sophia and Rita yet to decide.

'Budge up then, Rita,' said Jill, 'you and me are going to take this lot on.'

Rita blinked back at her, then shifted up on the sofa as Jill squeezed her way in.

'Right, I'm coming with you two,' announced Sophia, shuffling over towards them. 'Girl power, right.'

Malik sighed and accepted his fate to join Andrew and Harold' like a schoolboy remaining on the sidelines after everyone else had been picked.

'Mmm,' said Emily. 'Mum, this tastes amazing!'

'Really?' asked Sophia in surprise, who sat holding her untouched plate, then realising everyone was looking at her, she spluttered, 'What I meant was, I'm not surprised, it looks *really*, really good.'

Jill watched as Emily attcmpted to stifle a giggle, by stuffing more cake into her mouth. What was going on here?

'Bloody hell,' said Malik, licking his fork. 'You're right. This is actually gorgeous.'

Sophia shrugged and cut into the cake, popped it into her mouth, then after a few seconds grinned and gave Emily the thumbs-up.

'This is delicious. Thank you, Jill,' said Gracie, holding her own fork aloft. There was a sparkle of amusement in her eyes. 'Can I ask what your secret is? I've never been any good at baking.'

Jill felt wrong-footed but couldn't put her finger on what was going on. Everyone seemed to be wolfing down the cake, so it certainly wasn't that. Perhaps she had a piece of cabbage stuck in her teeth or something; she'd pop up to the loo and check in a minute.

'I'm not sure there's a secret, as such. I usually use baking soda to get them super fluffy, although I ran out of that this week and used baking powder instead; it wasn't quite as effective, I thought. And I usually use artificial sweetener to make them healthier, but I ran out of that as well and had to use granulated sugar.'

Eugene beamed. 'Your best yet, Jilly. Stick to those substitutions, huh? You've created something *magical*.'

Magical. Gosh, this was praise indeed. If only Ray had still been here to enjoy her bewitching wares. Even as the thought passed through her mind, she recoiled from it. Her husband had only been gone a year for heaven's sake, what on earth was she thinking. Although the truth of it was, she'd been losing Gary gradually for several years before he took his final breath.

Half an hour into the game, a couple of things became apparent. Eugene, Emily and Gracie were a powerhouse team that were wiping the floor with everyone. . . all apart from Jill's team. Because Jill's team had a secret weapon, and that secret weapon was Rita.

Longest river in Europe. BBC Sports Personality of the Year in 2008. The two chemical elements that combine in an alloy to form brass. These were just some of the questions Rita had voiced an answer to whilst everyone else had been scratching their heads.

'Are you a secret quizzer, Rita?' Sophia had asked in awe. 'You could moonlight as one of those Chasers on the telly.'

But that had been a question seemingly too complex to answer, and so instead she'd given a girlish laugh, and continued playing with the twiddle muff Jill had kept from Christmas Day. She'd found Eugene's unwanted gift the other day, lurking, forgotten, in an old shopping bag, so she'd brought it along today and had given it to Rita earlier.

'Anyone for another drink?' asked Andrew, holding his empty glass aloft.

'You stay there,' said Jill, 'I'll get them.'

'I'll help,' said Sophia, pulling herself to standing.

'And I'll check the children haven't redecorated your conservatory,' said Malik.

As Jill waited for the kettle to boil, she stared down at Gracie and Andrew's tiled floor, her thoughts straying to bittersweet territory. To the memory of a familiar and yet achingly distant smile on a handsome, much-loved face.

'One coffee, one white wine, a gin and tonic and a lemonade for Andrew because he's driving later. I think I've got that right,' said Sophia, counting them off on her fingers as she entered the kitchen. 'Penny for them, Jill? You looked miles away.'

Jill looked up; she'd been thinking about Gary. About how he'd still had the capacity to surprise her right to the end, just as Rita had today. How even when he no longer knew who she was and referred to her as 'that woman' when speaking to Emily, he'd still let her hold his hand and gently circle his palm with her thumb, like he always had for her when she was having a dark day. Gary had been her bright, shining rock. Her only rock, until recently.

Sophia waited patiently for her to speak. She had what Gaz would have called 'sparkle', essential in the music business – an energy and something else indefinable that ensured her presence was felt in every room. But Sophia was not in showbiz, she was a district nurse who spent her days administering tenderness, care and treatment to the elderly, the sick and the vulnerable. She was also Emily's friend; she was loyal and kind. It struck Jill then exactly what she should do.

'Sophia,' Jill began, aware that once she'd voiced her thoughts, there would be no taking them back. 'I'm not sure *how* to go about it, but I think an intervention might be needed.' She met the young woman's eye. 'And I think I'm going to need your help.'

'You're talking about Rita,' said Sophia. 'I've been thinking the same, myself.'

As she poured the drinks, Jill swiftly filled in the younger woman on what she'd gleaned from visiting Rita's home, namely that she wasn't coping, was living in terrible conditions and that there seemed to be little sign of any assistance from her only daughter.

'Jeez,' hissed Sophia, snatching up a glass of wine and swigging it back, 'I knew the woman was a cow, but seriously? That's bordering on neglect, what you've described, you know?'

'Is it though?' Jill had given this some thought. 'I don't think children have any duty of care to their parents.' And if they did, where did that leave *her*? She'd remained estranged from her own mother, right to the bitter end. 'As I understand it, Rita lives alone, therefore nobody else is responsible for her. Rita and Kat's relationship is really nobody's business, but the fact of the matter is, she *does* need help.'

'Well, it might not be my business, but I swear to you, Jill, if that bitch so much as breathes in my direction, she's got it coming.'

At the disdain in Sophia's words, Jill decided now definitely wasn't the time to bring up Emily's supposed accident. She would deal with that herself.

'So, what would you suggest?' encouraged Jill. 'How do we get Rita the help she needs?'

'Well, the first thing to do won't be easy, but we need to have a sensitive yet practical conversation with Rita and express some of our concerns because from what I've seen, she's already worried, and we don't want to scare her. Then, assuming she is willing, first thing Tuesday morning we ring the GP and get an appointment. A doctor's assessment is always the starting point, as there could be one of many underlying causes for her confusion, so that's got to be the priority. Will you come with us?'

'Absolutely,' agreed Jill. 'I want to help.'

Sophia appraised her. 'You know, you'd make a good nurse. Have you ever thought about care as a career?'

Jill barked a laugh. 'Honey, I'm fifty-eight. Think I'm a little bit past starting out on a new career path, don't you?'

'That's where you're wrong. There's more to healthcare than doctoring and nursing you know. Heck, half of the patients I visit each day, they just want a chat.'

Jill laughed. 'Well, I've been told I'm quite good at that.'

'It's a talent, that's what it is, and I should know – back home, you're the black sheep of the family if you can't spin a good yarn, a bit like in *Pride and Prejudice*, only your mam and dad are scared of being saddled with an unweddable mute, rather than an ageing spinster.'

Jill dissolved into laughter, wondering why it had taken her so long to warm to Sophia. Yes, she was fiery and blunt, but also funny and incredibly kind. Although, deep down, she knew it had only been due to her own insecurities that she'd always expected Sophia's razor-sharp wit to be turned upon her. Jill was disarmed by assured, confident women and she knew it was something she needed to work through.

'Any sign of those drinks? I cannot listen to another discussion about model railways without at least of litre of wine,' said Gracie, walking into the kitchen. 'Oh, hello? So, this is where the party's at is it. Excellent stuff. Pass me one of those, will you.'

'Who has a model railway?' asked Sophia.

'Harold. We've been treated to a lengthy and detailed depiction of his replica Greater Anglia showpiece, such was his devotion to his former career as a train driver. Sadly, he can't get up into the loft anymore. So, guess who's now considering turning his shed into the equivalent of Liverpool Street Station?'

'Old boys and their toys,' tutted Jill.

'You're joking, aren't you? Malik's all over the idea. Always wanted a Hornby train set apparently, even admitted to playing with Theo's Thomas the Tank Engine after he'd gone to bed.'

'Oh, my, *God*,' said Sophia, horror-stricken.

'Well,' said Jill, grinning, 'at least the men can be making tracks, whilst you're, you know, making tracks.'

Gracie groaned at her joke.

'Speak of the devil,' said Sophia, into her glass.

'The kids want to show us all their masterpieces,' announced Malik from the doorway. 'Bit difficult to tell where the paintings end and their faces begin, mind.'

'Oops,' muttered Gracie. 'Good job I swapped out the oils for water-based paints.'

As Sophia trailed after Malik, and Gracie turned to follow, Jill caught her arm.

'Thank you for such a lovely day. And I want to say how proud I am of my big sister. Even if you weren't running a flipping marathon, I'm still so proud.'

233

Gracie smiled, then pulled her into a tight hug, filling Jill with such love she thought she might burst, until her sister pulled away and said, 'It *has* been lovely. But I'm afraid that before I can let any of you leave, I must insist you get your bottoms back in the lounge, so Eugene and I can battle our way to victory and win our five pounds. Forget the marathon – for today that is *all* that matters.'

'You're not competitive at all, are you, sis?' said Jill, rolling her eyes and traipsing after her.

25

Gracie

Easter Monday brought warmth, sunshine and, to Gracie's horror, a belly full of jangling nerves. The countdown was well underway, with only six days left until the marathon, and only two mall training sessions left.

Today she had a short run planned with Emily and Sophia, just three miles. Her final run would be Thursday, leaving Friday and Saturday free to rest up. Though how she was supposed to rest when filled with a nervous energy that was preventing her from even getting a good night's sleep, was anyone's guess. Perhaps she'd tap Jill up to help with some relaxation exercises, or recipes for calming teas; both things she'd previously pooh-poohed.

'Everything OK, Mum?' Nathan enquired, frowning into the camera. 'You look a bit jittery?'

Darn it. She should have made an excuse, avoided him until after it was all over, by which time it would be too late for his objections.

Gracie had felt confident Nathan wouldn't find out about the marathon, right up until Jill's publicity stunt at Beachcombers a

235

fortnight ago. And even now, she was fairly sure he wasn't in touch with anyone from school, having lived away for so long, but mostly owing to the fact that as well as living fairly self-sufficiently, both he and Beth prescribed to what they called 'digital minimalism'. Neither of them had social media accounts and the only computer in the house was Nathan's work laptop. In spite of their off-grid way of life, however, Gracie had worried about word reaching them, particularly now that Jet Logan was involved. And perhaps even worse than the ticking-off she'd receive about that, was the fact they were also keeping shtum about Andrew's op.

'Everything's completely fine,' she fibbed, 'why wouldn't it be?'

'That'll be the sugar rush from the Thorntons Easter egg she gorged this morning, son. I wouldn't upset her, she's not to be truffled with,' interjected Andrew.

Nathan grinned in the long-suffering way they all did at Andrew's jokes, and Gracie squeezed her husband's thigh in gratitude to his quick deflection.

'How about the girls?' she asked, eager to move the conversation on. 'Did Beth set her annual Easter egg hunt?'

'Sure,' nodded Nathan, 'plenty of eggs all round.' He looked away for a moment, then readjusted the screen, angling it slightly away.

Gracie detected a slight reticence in his voice and wondered if he was keeping things back of his own. There had been no sign of the girls – they were out with friends, he'd said.

'Beth gone to pick the girls up, has she?' asked Gracie, seeing as her daughter-in-law was absent too. 'Must be close to Olivia's bedtime.'

'Uh-huh,' said Nathan, stifling a yawn. 'Close to mine too, I reckon,' he joked.

When the Skype call ended, Gracie pushed the laptop lid closed and looked to Andrew.

'Now was that me, or did he seem a bit distracted?'

'Oh, I don't know, love, he seemed OK to me.'

'Hmm,' said Gracie, unconvinced. 'Something seems off.'

Andrew laughed. 'You're a fine one to talk!'

'You know what I mean. Its barely eight o'clock over there and I swear he was in bed; I could see a pillow sticking out behind him.'

'For goodness' sake, woman. A man's entitled to relax on his own bed – don't be so suspicious.'

Agreeing that perhaps she was simply projecting her own anxiety, Gracie went upstairs to change into her kit.

Ten minutes later, she poked her head round the living room door, where Andrew still sat on the sofa, the laptop open on his lap. He'd been using the computer a lot lately; to research beer-making, so he said. He'd always been more of a look-it-up-in-a-book kind of man, and she wondered, not for the first time, if he was more worried about his health than he was letting on. Was he googling his prognosis? Preparing himself? A fresh wave of guilt pricked at her conscience. She shouldn't be leaving him to deal with this alone!

'You off then?' he asked, without looking up.

'Yes. I'm popping to the café with Emily afterwards, love, in case you wonder where I've got to.'

'The café's on today, is it? On Easter Monday?'

'Yep. Cynthia didn't see any reason not to run it as usual. A Bank Holiday Monday is no different to any other Monday for some of the customers, after all.'

'True,' agreed Andrew. 'Take it steady then, love, we don't want any injuries this late in the day.'

Briefly the idea of a broken ankle to match Emily's drifted enticingly across Gracie's mind, before common sense prevailed. She could do this. She wanted to do this. She was just blinking terrified of the magnitude of it all, particularly since Thursday had yielded a double-page spread in the *Frinton and Walton Chronicle*.

The journalist's photography skills left much to be desired, Gracie having been snapped whilst listening to Isaac Hunter's testimony and wearing an expression of astonishment. It wasn't the picture she'd have chosen to reinforce the strapline 'Amazing Grace Sets the Pace for Dementia'. She looked more like a doomed and elderly rabbit in *Watership Down* poised to flee from a predator, than a mature, determined woman, taking on the challenge of her life.

As Gracie strolled down to the seafront to meet Emily and Sophia, she was struck by how much had changed since those first tentative steps back in November. Prompted by a nostalgic yearning for her adventurous and active youth, she had only set out to inject a little vigour into her increasingly sedate lifestyle and look at her now. Six months on and she had developed a level of endurance and stamina she'd never previously believed possible, and that was just for the running, never mind Andrew's inventions or Jill's 'help'.

Smiling at the memory of her sister lecturing the sales assistant in Planet Run as to why compression socks were something those of a certain age knew plenty about already, she crossed the greensward to meet the girls.

'You're looking remarkably cheerful today, Gracie,' said Sophia with a sly grin, '. . . considering.'

'I don't know what you mean,' said Gracie, feigning innocence.

'Let me help you remember,' laughed Sophia, forming a 'L' shape with her fingers and placing it to her forehead, before skipping off across the grass in peals of laughter.

'She's never going to let us live that down, is she?' asked Gracie, sighing and falling into step beside Emily.

'Don't blame me. I said it was Jane Seymour and I've never even *seen* a Bond movie, but Eugene was adamant.'

Gracie tutted. 'There's absolutely nothing "trivial" about that game, trust me. Wars have been fought over less. But dear girl. . . you've *never* seen a Bond movie? What, not even the ones with Daniel Craig?'

'Nope,' Emily pulled a face, 'am I missing much?'

Gracie side-eyed her niece. '*Oh yes.* Trust me. You should educate yourself immediately.'

As the three women ran along the promenade, side by side, Gracie realised she *did* feel cheerful. The nerves she'd woken up with dispersed along with the sunny haze that shimmered above the water, leaving her feeling thankful, for having these wonderful young women in her life and for being here to enjoy this moment.

Never lose sight of this, she reminded herself. Because, in the end, all it came down to was the feel of the wind in her hair and having good friends at her side.

'Hey!' came a call from the beach. 'You're the lady who's running the marathon!'

All three of them stopped chatting and looked to the young woman in a maxi dress with a brood of kids. The Easter holidays were underway, and the beach was busy with hardy families, hunkering down beside windbreaks to embrace the bright, dry day, whilst children ferried buckets and spades to and from the water's edge.

'I recognise you from the paper,' she called again, then put her fingers to her lips and let out an ear-splitting wolf whistle.

Heads popped up all over, as she jerked a pointed finger towards Gracie.

'It's Amazing Grace!' she hollered to anyone who'd listen. 'The old lady who's running the marathon!'

Gracie sucked in a breath, and Sophia spluttered a laugh.

'*Old!*' Gracie hissed under her breath, whilst trying to maintain a sunny smile, especially when around them, people began to clap.

'Smile and wave, Auntie, smile and wave,' giggled Emily at her side. 'Ooh, Queen Gracie, now that's got a lovely ring to it.'

'Go on, girl,' croaked a white-haired gentleman, leaning heavily on a walking stick as he strolled the promenade. He untangled his arm from that of his companion to shakily pump the air with his fist. 'You can do it.'

Yes, she decided. Yes, she could. Because she already knew she'd carry with her the boyish glee in his rheumy, pink-rimmed eyes.

'Well, that was fun,' said Sophia, as they filed into Victory Hall. 'I wonder if we, mere mortals of the CPR, will get that level of support on our usual Saturday morning runs.'

'We'll probably be inundated with requests to join the club,' said Emily.

'I jolly well hope so! If I achieve nothing else, it would be marvellous to have inspired people from all walks of life to get out there and enjoy some exercise,' said Gracie. 'Something *everybody* could benefit from,' she added, taking in the scene of customers munching and slurping.

Eugene was at his usual station, a chessboard between him and Harold. No sign of Ray.

Jill paused in her slightly off-key accompaniment to Elvis Presley on the radio. 'With you in a mo,' she called through the hatch. 'Cynthia's popped home to deal with a dead mouse brought in by the cat. Roger's hiding in the loo – won't come out until it's gone. Dreadful phobia.'

Sophia and Emily joined the men, and Gracie wandered over to the serving hatch.

'Need a hand in there?' she asked, noting the saucepan of baked beans on the stove thickening by the second, whilst Jill buttered wholemeal bread for sandwiches.

Jill looked up, her cheeks flushed from holding the fort during the busy lunchtime rush.

'If you're sure you don't mind? The young lad in the corner over there ordered a jacket with beans, spud's in the microwave, it just pinged.' She lowered her voice. 'Can't help feeling it's the cheap grub that's brought him in here, rather than the scintillating conversation on offer. Made me think of your ex-student's story.'

Gracie looked around. A boy of no more than fifteen was hunkered over his phone, sleeves pulled down over his knuckles, hood pulled up on his jumper. He was a boy who should be hanging out with his friends, not sitting at a Formica table in an old community hall. She went through into the kitchen and began plating up his food, under Jill's direction.

'You know,' said Gracie, thinking aloud, 'I think sometimes it's just important to know you're in a place where people care, whether you choose to engage or not. Look at Rita. She might not be here today, but something keeps bringing her back, and that's certainly not down to the nurturing guidance of her daughter.'

'Perhaps she fancies Eugene,' said Jill, prompting a stern look from her sister. 'What?' she said, laughing. 'I'm sure she wouldn't be the first – he's an attractive man.'

Gracie brushed past her with the lad's lunch. 'Funny that, because I could have sworn you only had eyes for the younger version.' She hotfooted it from the kitchen before Jill could respond.

'Jacket with beans, love?' said Gracie, approaching the table.

'Ah,' came Eugene's musical voice carrying across the room. 'A man after my own heart. Bit of grated Cheddar on top and. . .' He threw a chef's kiss into the air.

A blush bloomed on the lad's acne-plagued cheeks, as he picked up his fork.

'Can't eat cheese, innit. Lactose intolerant,' he mumbled.

Gracie's heart went out to him. Whatever his circumstances were, he was in good hands here.

As she walked back to the kitchen, the door flew open and she expected to see Cynthia return, but to her surprise, it was Malik. Usually he was dressed for running, in joggers and his CPR top, sometimes his work-branded NewTek hoody that drowned his slim frame, but today he wore black jeans and a crisp white tee, beneath an open, checked shirt.

'Didn't expect to see you here today,' remarked Gracie, taking in his smart appearance.

'Hi, Mal!' called out Sophia and Emily, having spotted him too.

'Oh, just thought I'd pop by on the off chance of finding some friendly faces.' He seemed unusually flustered.

'No kids?' asked Gracie, who had expected to see them appear behind their dad.

'Nah,' he said with a small shrug, intended to look carefree, 'they're staying with their mum for a few days, so you know how it is—' he rubbed his hands together '—footloose and fancy free, as Ray says.'

'Is that right?' asked Jill, who had crossed the room to deliver Harold his cheese and pickle sandwich. She gave Gracie a meaningful look, before turning back to Malik. 'Because as it happens, I have two tickets for a gig tonight, but sadly Emily and I can't make it. Why don't *you* have them?'

Emily's eyebrows shot up. 'Sorry, what's that, Mum?'

'Remember, Em?' said Jill, imbuing each word with an unspoken threat *don't argue, just agree*. 'We double-booked ourselves with that other thing. Said we'd rather do the other thing.'

Emily eyeballed her mother as if she'd just fallen out of a spaceship.

'O-kaaay,' she said eventually, though it was clear from her expression she had no idea what was going on. Poor love, for such an intelligent girl, she was being exceptionally slow on the uptake.

Gracie decided to step in and assist.

'Sounds like it's your lucky day, Malik. Footloose, fancy free and now the proud owner of tickets to a gig. Hey – why not take Sophia? You said you didn't have any plans tonight didn't you, Soph?' she asked, bringing her into the conversation.

'Er,' Sophia floundered. 'No, I've no plans. But what's the gig? And *where's* the gig? I've work in the morning.'

'Where? Oh, um, not far.' Jill collected up the empty cups as a distraction technique. 'Milton Keynes.'

'Milton Keynes?' exclaimed both Malik and Sophia at the same time.

Malik checked his watch. 'That's a couple of hours' drive away. I thought you meant something local. Perhaps you can get your money back instead?'

Jill shrugged. 'No, I don't think so. Oh well, never mind. It probably wouldn't have been your thing anyway.' She turned her back and gave Gracie a wink.

'Well don't leave us in suspense here, Jill,' said Sophia, intrigued, 'who's playing in Milton Keynes?'

'Duran Duran, probably not your kind of thing at all,' said Jill apologetically. Honestly, the woman was totally shameless. Gracie was impressed.

'Hang on. Are you *serious*?' shrieked Sophia. 'THE Duran Duran?'

'Perfectly. My Gary was good friends with Simon Le Bon, back in the day.'

Sophia pushed back her chair.

'Pick me up in an hour, Malik. I'm going home to wash my hair.' She shook her head in amazement. 'And what the actual bejesus am I going to wear?'

Without even waiting for an answer, she fled the hall, leaving a thoroughly bamboozled Malik to gawp in her wake.

'I'll, er, I'd better, well, I'll be heading off too then,' he stuttered.

'You'll be wanting these!' called Jill, thrusting the tickets into the air, plucked from her handbag like a rabbit out of a hat.

He paced over to take them, blinked in disbelief at the tickets in his hand, then with a resigned shrug he was gone.

'Oh. My. God. *Mother!*' cried Emily. 'What the hell?'

'What?' frowned Jill. 'Don't tell me you wanted to go after all? You've never been interested before.'

'No, I didn't want to go. I didn't even know you had tickets! But did you have to be *so* obvious? That was the most blatant attempt at matchmaking I think I've ever seen!'

Jill shrugged. 'I don't know *what* you mean. Gary's old agent sent them to me with a bunch of other stuff to auction. I think you'll agree I found a far better use for them.'

Jill folded her arms across her chest and looked so pleased with herself it made Gracie grin from ear to ear.

A grin that was wiped clean off her face as the door swung open again, and Kat stomped into the room, fur coat flapping, heels clacking, and a look of pure scorn plastered across her face.

The room fell silent, except for the radio in the kitchen, which by some ungodly misfortune was playing Tom Jones' Sixties belter 'What's New Pussycat?'

Kat made straight for Jill, stalking across the room like an angry catwalk model.

When she arrived in front of her, she pulled something from her oversized bag and shoved it into Jill's chest.

'What the *hell* do you think you're playing at, you interfering old bat?' she hissed.

Gracie narrowed her eyes and moved purposefully closer.

Kat had thrown the colourful, knitted twiddle muff at Jill, the comforter that Rita had been playing with most of yesterday, satisfyingly running her fingers over the different textures, ribbons and buttons.

'Where do you get off, handing out stupid toys to grown adults as though they're pathetic little kids? Isn't it enough that you're ripping them all off to come in here and eat shit cake and drink cheap tea, when they could be at home? You're just a sad lonely old woman yourself, really, aren't you? Leeching off vulnerable people to make yourself feel better.'

Gracie's jaw dropped in shock as she witnessed this heinous defamation of Jill's character.

Emily gasped in outrage, and Eugene shouted angrily, 'Who the hell do you think you're talking to, missy?'

But Jill simply stood there, staring Kat down.

Slowly, she placed the twiddle muff on the nearest table.

'I'd think carefully about what you say next, if I were you,' said Jill. 'There's a room full of witnesses here who care very much about your mum, and, believe it or not, not one of them comes in here for the tea and cake. Someone like you might struggle with that notion, that there's more to life than what you can buy.'

Kat snorted, her face contorting in derision. 'Just mind your own business in future alright. My mum might be dumb enough to fall for your nonsense, but I'm not, so watch it.'

She turned to leave, but Jill caught hold of her sleeve.

'Do you think it's acceptable to barge in here, throwing around all manner of accusations and threats?'

'Get your hand off my coat,' barked Kat.

'I *see* you,' Jill sneered, nostrils flaring. 'I know exactly what makes someone like you tick and, believe me, it's not pretty. Do you sleep well at night, knowing that everyone around you is dispensable? Friends? Partners? Parents? Is there nothing you wouldn't do to get whatever shallow thing it is you think you want at the time?'

'What are you talking about, you mad old bitch?'

At this Jill jerked an eyebrow towards Emily and hissed in a voice so low even Gracie struggled to hear and she was standing right there. 'Oh, I think you know. And if you thought your little stunt that night went unnoticed, you're very mistaken. So, if anybody needs to watch it, lady, believe me, it's you.'

Kat recoiled from Jill's venomous glare and appeared ever so slightly taken aback, before swiftly recovering herself and letting out a nasty cackle.

'Whatever,' she said, flouncing out of the hall.

The classic teenage retort, thought Gracie, who'd heard the much-used comeback a million times before, often from the young Kathleen Banks. What an empty vessel that woman must be.

And what a brilliant woman her sister was, recognising her for what she was: a thirty-seven-year-old bully, no different to all the other playground bullies she'd encountered in her life; jealous, bitter and resentful, just as their own mother had been. And there was no way on earth Jill was letting anyone get away with behaviour like that on her watch.

Because what she'd said was true, the Be Together Café wasn't just a café. It was a community and to be in a caring community was to be strong.

'That was awesome,' came a small voice from the corner. 'This place ain't as boring as it looks.'

Gracie and Jill turned to see the teenage lad grinning from ear to ear.

'Reckon I could get some of that chocolate cake now?'

26

Gracie

The last time Gracie had packed an overnight bag, it had been for a spa break with Linda; a birthday treat from Andrew and something he loathed to do himself – *All that sitting about in a robe, sharing skin cells and athlete's foot, no thank you.* Now she was hunting out two holdalls, one for her hotel stay in London and one for Andrew's hospital stay in Colchester, where he would, ironically, be sitting about in a robe.

'Spots or stripes?' called out Gracie.

Andrew poked his head out of the bathroom, flannel in hand, face covered in soap. 'What was that?'

'Pyjamas, do you want your spotty ones or the stripy ones? The spotty ones are brushed cotton, might be a bit too warm. Mind you, it's blowing a hooley out there today, you might be glad of them.'

'You choose,' said Andrew, ducking back into the bathroom.

Gracie folded the stripy pyjamas and placed them into the bag, along with underwear, a clean set of clothes, Andrew's slippers, his washbag, a towel, a spare pair of glasses, his medication, his phone charger; now, what else? Her gaze swept the room, hunting for anything she'd missed, and landed on the book on his bedside table, her dog-eared copy of *A Room with A View*. Andrew had been reading it, a few pages at a time each night, because as he'd said when he plucked it from the bookcase, 'Your favourite book – a part of you. I think I'd like it to be part of me too; after all, we share pretty much everything else.'

Gracie picked up the battered old paperback that she'd owned since her university days, and inexplicably, her eyes filled. She sank down onto the bed and was stroking the wrinkled cover when Andrew came back into the room, drying his chin on a towel.

His hand dropped away as he saw her face.

'Gracie? Whatever's the matter, love?' He padded across the carpet and lowered himself beside her.

She looked back into his concerned eyes and was powerless to stop the tears from rolling down her cheeks and plopping into her lap.

'Hey,' soothed Andrew, twisting to face her and taking her hands in his. 'What's this all about then? Come on, love. You can talk to me.'

'Sorry,' she sniffed, wiping her face with her sleeve. 'Gosh, I'm so sorry. Ignore me. The nerves are getting to me, that's all.'

Andrew stroked her hand. 'That's perfectly understandable, tomorrow's a big day, and I wouldn't mind betting every single one of the fifty thousand entrants are feeling just as anxious as you are right now.'

Gracie swallowed back the lump of emotion. 'It's just. . .' she choked out a small laugh '. . . it's silly really, but I can't face the thought of you not being there with me tonight, at the hotel, or in the morning when I wake up. You make truly terrible jokes and overcomplicate the simplest of tasks, but I don't know how I'm going to haul myself to that starting line, when I should be with you at the hospital instead. I wish. . . Oh, I don't know.' She let out a frustrated sigh. 'I just wish it hadn't worked out this way. We shouldn't have to be apart.'

She looked up and found him smiling with such tenderness, her chest clenched. He rested his forehead briefly on hers.

'Is that your way of saying you'll miss me?' he asked.

Gracie squeezed his hand and sniffed loudly. 'Don't be foolish. I won't have *time* to miss you. I've got a marathon to run, remember.'

'Exactly,' he said, wiping beneath her eye with his thumb.

She offered him a weak smile and he gently kissed her on the lips.

'Anyway,' he said, breaking away, 'you've got Jill to nag you and force-feed you slow-release carbs for breakfast. I'd only get in the way.'

'This is true.' She nodded, then grimaced. 'Do you think she snores? She strikes me as the sort who does.'

'Earplugs. Pack some.'

Gracie nodded, then pulled Andrew into the tightest hug. 'But who's going to look after you?'

'I'm rather hoping the doctors and nurses will,' came his muffled reply. 'And Eugene's threatened to visit, God help the rest of the ward.'

Gracie giggled, eternally grateful for her husband's gift to take everything in his stride, to always know just what to say. She pulled away.

'Right then,' she said, rallying herself. 'That's enough of that. We're due at Victory Hall for two o'clock for a quick send-off, before our train leaves at four. Then Harold will be here to pick you up in the morning at seven o'clock sharp to get you to Colchester General. Got it?'

'Got it,' he saluted. 'It's awfully kind of him to help out. And for walking Picasso and feeding Banksy.'

'He seemed rather flattered to be asked. And of course, now you're thinking of installing a model railway in your shed, he'll want to be your best buddy. Eugene and Malik too. Perhaps you should charge an entrance fee, could be highly lucrative.'

'Well then,' said Andrew, levering himself off the bed, 'best I help you with this packing.' He tapped the neat pile nestling inside her purple flowery wheeled suitcase. 'Because if I left you to your own devices, it looks as though you'd be running the marathon in my navy-blue striped pyjamas, and I'd be lying in a hospital bed dressed as Paula Radcliffe.'

Gracie glanced at the bags in horror because there indeed was the official marathon event pack Emily had collected on her behalf from the ExCel exhibition centre in London on Thursday, tucked into Andrew's canvas holdall along with his washbag. Perhaps it was time for a cuppa instead.

A couple of hours later, Gracie and Andrew wrapped themselves up against the lashing rain and gale force winds, and set off for Victory Hall.

'Bloody hell fire,' muttered Gracie, battling to keep her hood up, 'this better blow over by tomorrow morning or I can forget the hat and sunglasses, I think a motorcycle helmet may be more the order of the day.'

'Forecast looked fine when I checked,' called back Andrew, the small suitcase bumping along behind him, 'you know what it can be like here. We've our own coastal microclimate: hurricanes followed by heatwaves, all within half an hour.'

'Yes, well, I don't want a heatwave either, thank you. A nicely overcast but clement April day will do me fine. Here, give me that,' she said, taking the case handle from him, 'just you concentrate on staying upright please, you're going to need that good leg.'

As they bustled into the hall, Cynthia fussed around them, relieving them of rain-soaked coats and hanging them up to dry by the radiator.

'Blimey,' commented Gracie, glancing at the various suitcases and rucksacks stacked against the wall. 'You lot don't believe in travelling light, do you?'

'I'm really excited,' said Emily, who was dressed in her usual faded jeans and her battered old Converse, looking every inch the traveller, 'it's like we're all going on a school trip.'

Ray laughed. 'It's been a heck of a long time since I went on one of those.'

'But, Em, you're not even staying with us at the hotel tonight,' exclaimed Jill.

Emily shrugged. 'Doesn't mean I'm not excited. Just don't see the point in paying out for a room when I already rent one a couple of tube stops away.'

'How are *you* feeling, Gracie?' asked Eugene, rubbing his hands together. 'Like an Olympic champion waiting on the starter blocks?'

'If plodding around the track a hundred times looking like a drowned rat is an Olympic event these days, then I'd say I'm primed for it,' sniffed Gracie, taking a tissue from Jill to wipe the drizzle from her face.

Suddenly, the door opened, and caught by the wind, it crashed back on itself, causing everyone to jump in alarm.

'Rita!' exclaimed Jill, hurrying over to the small figure standing dripping in the doorway. 'I'm so glad to see you, but you're soaked through! Shall I take this for you?'

Gently, Jill helped the shivering woman from her ineffective jacket, then led her over to a chair by the radiator to warm up.

'Here, Rita,' said Sophia, jumping up. 'Would you like to borrow my fleece?'

'Are you Brown Owl?' asked Rita, taking the offered garment and folding herself into it. 'You're so kind. All the Brownies must love you.'

'I'll get the kettle on,' said Jill, heading into the kitchen.

Gracie followed her.

'How did it go at the surgery this week?' she asked, indicating Rita behind them.

Jill considered. 'Quite well, I think. Sophia thought it was positive anyway. The GP explained there would be a referral to a memory clinic, for tests, and depending on the diagnosis, we can help Rita apply for some extra help, around the home and with personal care, that sort of thing.'

Gracie nodded. 'And all of this can be done without her daughter's consent?'

'Absolutely, although obviously it would be better for everyone if the damned woman woke up to the fact her mother needs help. The doctor was reticent to be drawn on the matter, but I got the distinct impression this wasn't a new situation.'

'You can only do your best, Jill. Well done,' said Gracie, squeezing her sister's shoulder.

'Well, it's one thing being a friendly face for a chat twice a week, but imagine how much good work the dementia charities do.'

The group fell into its usual rhythm, with Eugene and Harold sparring over *The Times* crossword, everyone seemingly too wired to settle into board games today. An elderly lady, who had started coming to the café a few weeks ago, took herself over to Rita and pulled her knitting from her bag. She didn't ask anything of her, just gently chatted away about her grandchildren and her garden as she stitched, Rita watching her and listening, seeming to enjoy her company.

After several fortifying cups of tea and some delicious angel cake, proving Jill had taken Eugene's advice on board and ditched the artificial sweetener, Ray stood and zipped his jacket.

'Right then, gang. I think it's time.'

Gracie's stomach whooshed.

Her eyes darted to Andrew.

This was it. She was heading off to London to face the biggest challenge of her life, and Andrew wasn't coming with her.

'Knock them dead, love,' he said, pulling her into a hug, then giving her a quick kiss on the cheek.

'Just you behave yourself, do you hear me? Do exactly what the doctors say,' she said, surprised at the strength in her voice.

'Ah, don't you worry about Andy,' said Eugene, folding his newspaper in half. 'He'll be in good hands.' He gave her a fat wink.

'That's what I'm worried about,' she muttered, letting herself be ushered away by Jill.

Rita surprised everyone by calling out, 'Good luck!'

It was the boost Gracie had needed, and she doubled back to the woman, and planted a kiss atop her forehead. 'Thank you.'

'Did you want your fleece back?' Malik asked Sophia, as they collected up their rucksacks.

'No, let her keep it. I've got another one,' replied Sophia.

Then with goodbyes from everyone, including Cynthia who'd recruited Roger to help clear up, they filed out of the hall into the street to begin their grand adventure.

'At least it's stopped raining,' said Ray, hooking his bag over his shoulder and holding out his hand to take Gracie's case. 'May I?'

'I can manage, love.'

'I *know* you can manage but let me take it.'

Gracie handed him her case.

'We look a right motley crew,' said Ray.

Emily had steamed ahead with Jill, whilst Malik and Sophia had stopped to look in the window of a vintage clothing shop. Gracie was desperate to hear how their trip to Milton Keynes had gone, but the opportunity to ask hadn't yet arisen.

'I'm so grateful to everyone for coming along. It feels like a real adventure,' said Gracie.

'It *is* an adventure. And anyway, someone's got to make sure you make it to that starting line.'

'Oh, I've absolutely no doubt Jill will get me there. She'll drag me there by my hair if it comes to it.'

'She's a determined woman,' agreed Ray. 'Look, Gracie, I'm glad to have got you on your own. I want to apologise about the other day.'

Gracie turned her head to see her friend looking unusually coy.

'You've nothing to apologise for. Everyone's entitled to feel under the weather or overwhelmed. You don't need to explain yourself, love, I only care that you're OK.'

Ray shot her a grateful smile. 'I *am* OK, now, but for a long time I wasn't. I always find Easter Sunday hard, probably shouldn't have come. I guess I was hoping that being with everyone would be a welcome distraction. But the truth is, wherever I am and especially if I'm with families, I'm always thinking about one family, in particular. Catastrophic RTC on the North Circular, Easter Sunday six years ago – that's a road traffic collision in laymen speak. My crew were first on the scene, never attended anything like it in my life. Took its toll on my career, my health, and eventually, my marriage.'

Gracie glanced behind her to check who was in earshot. Sophia and Malik were following slowly, engrossed in conversation. The others were way ahead.

'I'm so sorry to hear that. If you ever want to talk about it. . .' ventured Gracie.

Ray looked up to the sky. 'I think I will, sometime, if that's OK. You're a good listener, Gracie.'

Gracie snorted. 'Perhaps that's because we usually chat whilst running, and it takes everything I've got to breathe.'

Ray laughed. 'You don't give yourself enough credit. I've seen how far you've come, remember. You're an inspiration, Gracie. It does me good to be reminded I'm still here, that it's never too late to get out there and live. That there's always second chances, new goals, new friendships.'

'Perhaps, one day, a new relationship too,' said Gracie, following his line of sight to her sister, as she threw back her head in laughter at something Emily said.

'Perhaps.' He flashed Gracie a knowing smile, one that said she hadn't been as subtle as she'd thought. 'Who knows what the future holds. But I *do* know that if we don't get a shift on, we're going to miss that train. Hurry up, you two!' he called behind him.

Up ahead, the others disappeared from view as they turned left into Station Approach. Moments later, Gracie, Ray, Malik and Sophia caught up with Jill and Emily in the small ticket office to find them huddled around a screen.

'What's wrong?' asked Gracie, immediately clocking the anxious expression on her sister's face.

Jill pointed to the digital screen.

All trains cancelled

'What?' gasped Gracie. 'But why?'

'It says a tree came down on the line earlier, that no more trains will run today.'

Gracie looked around – surely there had to be someone they could speak to. Perhaps they could catch the train from a different station, but the small ticket office was closed up, the platform deserted.

'We'll have to take my car instead,' announced Jill.

'Er, you only have two seats,' reminded Emily. 'And for some reason you've brought a suitcase big enough for a week in Spain that will need a seat all of its own.'

'Well, let's take two cars then!' Jill flapped her arms in exasperation. 'We're wasting time here. Gracie needs to check into her hotel, have a decent meal and a good night's sleep.'

'I think you can forget that,' muttered Gracie. 'I haven't slept in days.'

'My car's in the garage having a new clutch fitted,' said Malik, scratching his neck.

'I can walk back to get my van, but it'll take me half an hour and it's also only got two seats,' offered Ray.

'There's Andrew's car,' said Gracie cautiously. 'I'm not sure how I feel about driving into London, but I'll have a go. . .' Silly really, she was about to put her body through the ultimate endurance test, yet the thought of jostling her way into the city in a car she rarely drove had her coming out in a cold sweat.

'How about yours, Sophia?' asked Emily, coming to her aid. 'Your house is only round the corner from here.'

They all watched as a flush of pink highlighted Sophia's cheeks.

'Er, sorry, my car's not at home. I, um, left it at a friend's house last night.'

A matching blush warmed Malik's cheeks, leaving the group in no doubt whatsoever as to which 'friend' Sophia referred.

Ray jumped in to save anyone further embarrassment. 'Look, I vote we head back to Victory Hall before the heavens open again, and ring for a taxi, travel together in style. We'll only be a couple of hours later than planned but at least nobody will have the hassle of driving and finding somewhere to park and all that business.'

'Good plan,' remarked Gracie, 'and before anyone says a word, I'm paying.'

They exited the ticket office and set off back down the street, an air of disappointment dampening the group's earlier good spirits. Even Jill seemed to be lost in thought.

At Victory Hall, Eugene was stood on the threshold, head bent against the first spots of drizzle, zipping up his jacket.

Looking up to see Ray approaching, Eugene frowned. 'What are you doing back here?' His voice travelled up a few notches as he registered Gracie and then the others. 'You should be on a train!'

'Change of plan,' muttered Gracie, huddling under the porch as a crack of thunder split the sky.

'Come on, Dad, I'll walk you over to Beachcombers,' said Ray, pulling up his collar.

'No!' exclaimed Jill. 'I mean, wait there a sec,' she blurted, dashing inside, then emerging again with a large golf umbrella which she pulled open with a whoosh. 'Good old lost property cupboard. I'll walk you back, Eugene,' she said, taking the older man's elbow and tugging him away before anyone could object. 'There's something I need to do.'

'What was that all about?' asked Gracie, puzzled.

'Don't ask me.' Ray shrugged.

Perplexed, they watched on as the huddled pair crossed the street and into the grounds of the retirement village, a flash of lightning illuminating the sky as they disappeared from view.

27

Jill

Jill squinted, straining to see a damned thing through the rain-battered windscreen as she parked up in the street outside Victory Hall. Even with the wipers at full speed, they struggled in their fight against the heavy torrent. This was going to be an interesting journey. And yet, her elation at finding a solution to the group's setback couldn't be dampened by a few April showers.

Debbie, the manager of Beachcombers, had baulked at her request at first.

'Oh, it's out of the question I'm afraid, Jill. Our driver isn't rostered to work today and not just anyone can drive a minibus – as you may already know, you need a special licence.' She'd picked up her pen as though putting an end to the discussion, but Jill wasn't to be deterred.

'Which, I have,' said Jill, pulling her purse from her handbag. She thrust her driving licence under Debbie's nose. 'Years of ferrying my Gary's band and their kit around. I've driven many a minibus in my time. Not recently, exactly, but you don't forget these things.'

Debbie had tapped the page of her notepad with the nib of her pen.

'But there's the insurance to think about, and. . .'

'The work of a phone call,' interrupted Jill. 'And I'll pay any premiums due.' She stepped further into the office. 'And there's all the extra publicity too. Think about it: Gracie, fresh from the finish line in her official Alzheimer's Outreach UK kit, medal in hand, stepping into a Beachcombers sign-written minibus. What better advert for your motto "luxury retirement living by the sea" than a sprightly pensioner completing her first-ever marathon?'

Jill had seen the exact moment the penny had dropped, a flash of gold sparking in Debbie's eye.

'Well, when you put it like that,' she'd said, placing her pen back on the table. 'Do you think there will be. . . much media interest?'

Jill had flashed her a beatific smile, knowing she'd sealed the deal. 'Oh, I'd say so.'

Now, with the engine still running, Jill delighted in honking the horn five times in quick succession with the heel of her hand.

First to poke their head out of the door, grimacing into the grizzly weather, was Malik.

He turned left, then right, scanning the street, before his gaze alighted on Jill's vehicle, and finally Jill herself, waving at him frantically through her wound-down window.

'Get the others!' she shouted, through the horizontal rain.

'What?' Malik screwed up his face.

'Get the others!' Jill repeated, cupping her hands around her mouth and leaning out of the window. 'And hurry up, I'm getting soaked.' She wound the window back up and wiped the rain from her face.

Thank goodness the BBC had forecast seventeen degrees and clear skies for tomorrow; if it carried on like this, it would be more of a swimathon than a running race.

Gradually, the others appeared in the doorway, peering into the rain.

Gracie pulled up the hood on her jacket and ran over to the driver's window.

'Why are you all standing there like ornaments instead of getting into the bus?' said Jill.

'Seriously? We're borrowing this to take to London?'

'Too right we are. Grab your bags, sis, we've got four wheels and one, two, three, four. . . twelve seats, and I'm not afraid to use them.'

One by one, everyone scrabbled into the minibus with whoops and cheers.

'I can't believe I didn't think of this,' said Ray, looking impressed.

'Oh, I *thought* of it,' remarked Sophia, 'I just didn't think there was a cat in hell's chance of Debbie saying yes. What did you offer her, Jill? Fame and fortune?'

Jill laughed. 'You know what, you're not too far from the truth there. Right then! Everybody in?'

'Yep,' came the replies.

Jill twisted around to look at the eager faces. 'And. . . was anyone planning on keeping me company up here? Do I smell or something?' She pointed at the empty passenger seat.

'Oops,' said Emily, who'd automatically piled, giggling, into the back with the others. 'Sorry, Mum.'

'Stay there, I'll take shotgun,' said Ray. 'More leg room.'

Jill glanced in the rear-view mirror and caught Gracie's eye. Her sister winked, which threw her into a blind panic as the passenger door opened and Ray slid into the seat beside her. She began pressing buttons and flicking switches. 'Now, if I could just work out how to demist the windscreen. . .' She tailed off as Ray reached across, his fingers brushing hers as she fumbled about.

'That should do it,' he said, as a fan kicked in.

'Ah, good,' spluttered Jill, 'as I was going to have to ask you to stop breathing.'

'There's a good chance we'll be holding our breath all the way anyway,' called Gracie, proving everyone could hear perfectly well in the back. 'I've experienced your driving, remember Jill.'

As everyone chuckled, including Jill who could see the funny side and for once didn't feel as though everyone were laughing *at* her, but *with* her, she tugged off the handbrake and pulled away.

It was a long, slow drive to London. What should have taken two hours on a normal day, took three and a half in the torrential rain, with traffic crawling at a snail's pace the entire length of the A12. They stopped en route in Hackney for Emily to jump out, promising she'd see everyone the next day. Jill wished there'd been time to see where her daughter had been living, or rather where she *hadn't* been living, these past few months, but in the dying evening light it was impossible to make out anything beyond the glistening of wet pavements and overstuffed bins.

Exhausted, Jill pulled into the underground car park of their budget hotel near London Bridge. All the advice online had pointed towards staying closer to the finishing line than the starting point, whilst still being easily accessible by train. They could reach the starting line near Blackheath Station within thirty minutes in the morning, so all that remained was to check in, grab some food and head to bed.

'Well done, Jill,' said Ray, as she killed the engine. 'That was a tough drive.'

Jill blinked as her vision adjusted to the floodlit car park. 'Thanks, I'm just happy to have got us all here in one piece.'

She glanced up at Ray and found him watching her. 'Yeah,' he said, with a strange, sad smile. 'That's all that matters.'

For the briefest of moments, his hand covered hers, where it still rested on the handbrake. The warmth of his touch seeped into her skin, sending shock waves along her arm, and then just as quickly it was gone, and he was unclipping his seatbelt.

Turning around to address the others, it became apparent that everyone, except for Gracie, had fallen asleep. Malik's head rested against the window, and Sophia, who had snuggled into his side, stirred and sat up straight, attempting to mask the slip-up by yawning and stretching.

'Huh, my driving can't be that bad eh, sis?' quipped Jill.

'There's truth in that old adage you know, ignorance *is* bliss,' said Gracie, pulling herself upright and wincing.

'What's the matter?'

'Leg's gone to sleep. Pity the rest of me won't follow suit.'

The five weary travellers disembarked from the Beachcombers minibus with their luggage and made their way up to the hotel's reception.

'Guys, I'm heading out for a quick drink with an old colleague from the service. Catch you all at breakfast?' said Ray, taking his key from the receptionist.

Jill felt suddenly and inexplicably coy, as he seemed to search her face for an answer. This was just Ray, for goodness' sake. He was polite to a fault, and more to the point he was here to support her sister.

'Absolutely,' said Gracie, jumping in to fill the pause. 'Have a nice evening.'

'Who's next please?' asked the receptionist.

Sophia stepped back. 'I'm just, er, I need to find the ladies'. Early night for me, see you all at breakfast!' Then she turned and paced off through the lobby before anyone could comment.

Jill looked at Gracie and widened her eyes.

Gracie's lips twitched in amusement.

'Next please?' repeated the receptionist.

'Malik? Would you like to go next?' asked Gracie.

'Oh, no, no. Ladies first, please,' he said, giving a mock bow and stepping away.

This was hilarious, thought Jill. However, as much as it would have been fun to loiter and watch Malik and Sophia pretend to check into separate rooms, time was of the essence, so she stepped up to the counter and completed the necessary paperwork to check into the twin room she'd booked for her and Gracie.

'Presuming you, *also*, plan on having an early night, Malik, we'll see you in the morning. Nighty-night,' said Jill, taking her sister by the arm and heading towards the lifts.

Gracie sniggered. 'How long do they intend to keep up the *just good friends* pretence, do you reckon?' she asked.

'No idea, but it's brilliant fun to watch so let them get on with it.'

The lift pinged open, and they stepped inside. Jill selected the third floor.

'The set-up with the Duran Duran concert was inspired, I must say. Do you often get sent free concert tickets?' asked Gracie.

Jill grinned. 'Not so much these days, and Gary's agent's long retired – that was just a one-off. But, er, there *is* something I should tell you. Jet Logan is actually Emily's godfather – absolutely dotes on her, and he's always been a good friend to me too.'

Gracie's eyes widened in surprise.

'Mm, and I *suppose* I should apologise for pulling that stunt with the video.' Jill winced, realising it was time to come clean. 'Truth is, I was willing to try anything to get you to change your mind. And Logan was totally game. He'd have donated money for Gary without anyone running any marathons. But it's a great thing he's done with the album's royalties; it will really raise the charity's profile.'

Instead of being annoyed, Gracie laughed out loud. 'Well, I never.' She shook her head. 'I had no idea you had such friends in high places, Jill. And don't be sorry – it was absolutely inspired. Hearing him speak about Gary really hammered it home. Made me realise what this is really all about, and why it's so important to you. And why it's so important to me.'

The lift pinged and the doors opened.

Stepping into the grey carpeted corridor, Gracie asked, 'So are there any other perks to having these famous friends?'

Remembering what else was on the cards for the evening, Jill stifled a sudden urge to laugh, instead saying, 'Oh not really, just the odd ticket to a gig or invitation to a party. But after a lifetime of being a groupie, I'm afraid I can't be bothered with it much these days – is that bad?'

'Not at all. Give me a nice meal, a glass of red and a snuggle on the sofa with Andrew, and that's about as high octane as my evenings get these days.'

'Well,' said Jill, giving Gracie's arm a squeeze, 'I'm not Andrew, but there's an Italian restaurant next door and I'm bloody starving. Fancy loading up on the carbs?'

At eight o'clock, Jill and Gracie were shown to a table for two with dramatic views of London Bridge. Lit up against the night sky, the iconic landmark reflected purple, silver and gold across the gently rippling water of the Thames. Absolutely no sign of the horrendous monsoon and forty-six miles an hour winds that had brought a tree down on the track earlier that day.

'Gosh, what luck,' said Gracie, gazing out at the spectacle. 'I can't imagine these tables are easily come by at such short notice.'

Jill smirked. There had been absolutely no luck involved at all. Gracie seemed blissfully unaware that obtaining a table for dinner in this place on a Saturday night was tantamount to getting tickets for Taylor Swift. She'd booked it a long time ago, back when she first heard about the marathon and when the idea of spending an evening like this with her sister had felt like a dream. As it happened, it wasn't the only thing happening this evening that Gracie was ignorant of, but for now she just needed to relax. She didn't need to know, she just needed to focus on preparing herself for the big day. Jill just had to make sure Gracie didn't turn on the television, which should be easy enough seeing as she'd hidden the remote control whilst her sister was in the loo.

'I think I'll go for the mushroom risotto,' said Gracie, removing her reading glasses. 'And bruschetta to start. Nothing risky on the tummy, but plenty of slow-release glycogens.'

'You *have* been swatting up, haven't you?' said Jill with a raised brow.

'I've even packed protein bars,' said Gracie. 'But I draw the line at those revolting performance energy gels. Why would anyone want to squeeze gloop purporting to taste of apple crumble into their mouth directly from a sachet?' She shuddered. 'No. I'll be stopping for a good old-fashioned banana, a drink of water and a pee in a proper loo, thank you very much and to hell with the lost time.'

'I quite agree. Your marathon, your rules,' said Jill scanning her menu. 'I think I'll go for the house calzone. That was always Gary's favourite. He always said why choose between pizza and meatball marinara, when you could have both.' She smiled at the memory. 'He was a terrible procrastinator. Would have been late to his own funeral if he'd had the choice.'

Gracie's face crumpled in sympathy.

'I wish I could have got to know him, Jill. And I really am so sorry that I didn't. He sounds like a good man.'

Good, kind, thoughtful, sensitive, infuriatingly laid-back. He wasn't hugely dissimilar to Andrew, Jill realised. Such a missed opportunity. How much fun the four of them could have had together. How close Emily and Nathan might have been. The what-ifs were a list that could be added to forever.

'He was,' agreed Jill with a quiet nod. 'But there's no use dwelling on the past. I've made my peace with it. I don't even feel anger towards Mum anymore. At the end of the day, she was an insecure, inherently selfish woman who suffered a heartbreak so terrible she did the only thing she could to keep going: she found someone to blame for it. Although I'm sure hating me brought her little comfort in the end. If anything, I feel rather sorry for her.'

Gracie twirled the stem of her glass. 'Sadly, I think you're right. She wasn't one for a positive outlook; *grumbling* was her default setting. Lord knows how Andrew put up with it for so long, he could never put a foot right.'

Jill shook her head in disbelief. 'What a life. Well, I propose a toast,' she said, raising her glass. 'Here's to *all* the good men out there, especially Andrew who loves you more than anything, and to his new knee!'

Gracie laughed and clinked her glass. 'To good men, and new knees!'

28

Gracie

When Gracie woke the next morning to the sound of rustling, it took her a few moments to remember she wasn't at home. Her eyes snapped open, taking in the unfamiliar crisp white bedding, and her sister propped against pillows in a neighbouring twin bed flicking through a magazine.

'Good morning,' said Jill, 'I was starting to think I'd have to come over there and shake you awake. Thought you said you hadn't been sleeping?'

Gracie rubbed her eyes, trying to shake off the fuzziness of a deep, dream-filled slumber.

'I haven't,' she said. 'Blimey, what was in that tea last night, chloroform? I don't remember dozing off.'

Jill looked pleased with herself. 'Chamomile and lavender. Works a treat, doesn't it? I chugged my way through gallons of the stuff after Gary died. Figured it was better for me than gin, which was how it started off.'

'What's the time?'

'Just before seven,' replied Jill.

Gracie sat bolt upright and reached across for her phone. 'Andrew! Harold will be picking him up any minute; I promised I'd call.'

Jill swept back the covers and climbed from bed.

'You give him a try and I'll have a quick shower, give you a bit of privacy.'

Jill gave Gracie an encouraging smile, then disappeared into the bathroom and the door clicked shut.

The phone was answered after two rings.

'Gracie?'

'Oh, Andy, I thought I'd missed you. I overslept!'

Andrew chuckled. 'Late night? I knew your sister would lead you astray.'

'Hardly,' snorted Gracie. 'We had dinner then drank tea in bed and reminisced on the good old days. Jill wouldn't even let me watch telly!'

'That's good, love. So. . . are you full of beans and raring to go?'

The very thought of what lay in store today made her want to dive back under the duvet and play dead, but she swallowed down her nerves. 'I wouldn't necessarily go that far, but I *think* I'm as ready as I'll ever be?'

'Of course you are,' he said gently.

'And you?' asked Gracie, running her nail across the fabric of her pyjama bottoms in concentric circles.

'Absolutely,' he said. 'Not long now. You know what, I've been thinking that maybe for next year's resolution, I might sign myself up to the Coast Path Runners too, what do you say about that?'

Gracie smiled into her phone. 'I say you'd be bored within five minutes. Probably get home and build yourself a set of wings to streamline the whole process, knowing you.'

The warm, treacle-like sound of Andew's laughter was enough to galvanise Gracie into action.

'Best get on, love. I've got a marathon to run.'

'And there's a new kneecap with my name on. I love you. Go smash it.'

Gracie put down the phone as Jill came back into the room, wrapping her hair into a fluffy white towel.

'All good?' she asked.

'All good.' Gracie smiled. 'Well, I suppose I'd better get ready and then try and eat some breakfast.'

Already sitting at a table laden with coffee cups and orange juice, were Sophia, Malik and Ray. Ray was working his way through a full English breakfast, and judging by the remnants of toast and jam, it wasn't his first course.

Spotting Jill and Gracie approach, he set down his knife and fork, hastily wiped his mouth on a serviette and stood to pull out chairs for the women.

Gracie waved away the gentlemanly gesture, whilst Jill, she couldn't help but notice, preened at the chivalry.

'Sit yourself down and finish your breakfast, Ray,' said Gracie. 'Gosh, that looks nice. I might order one of those myself. Can't remember the last time I had a fry-up.' She picked up one of the breakfast menus to peruse.

'Uh-uh,' countered Jill, 'transit time, remember!'

Gracie rolled her eyes.

Malik looked blank. 'Uh?'

'She means how long until your woman needs a poo, isn't that right, Gracie?' supplied Sophia, ever helpful with her medical knowledge.

Ray paused in the cutting of his sausage.

'Do you think we could get through breakfast without discussing my bodily functions?' snapped Gracie.

'We've been through this before. These are important considerations for *anyone* running the marathon today,' assured Jill. 'Choose something easy to digest with plenty of carbs; I'd go porridge if I were you. Absolutely no caffeine or chocolate, unless you want runner's trots.'

At the glare Gracie threw her sister, Malik cleared his throat to suppress a laugh.

'I had a smoked salmon bagel with poached egg,' supplied Sophia. 'Protein, carbs and it *tasted* nice.'

'That will do perfectly,' said Gracie, snapping the menu shut. 'Alright with you, boss?' She raised a brow at Jill.

After breakfast, the group dispersed with hugs, wishes of good luck and reminders of their various spectator spots. It would be a good few hours until she saw them again, but Gracie suspected it would feel like days.

Following Jill through the large reception lobby, heading for the street, Gracie suddenly halted.

'What?' asked Jill, when she turned and realised Gracie had stopped walking. 'What's up? Did you forget something?'

My nerve? My common sense? These were the thoughts running through Gracie's mind, along with the far more urgent sensation of needing to wee, again. It would be the fifth time that morning.

'With you in a tick,' she said, handing Jill her bag and the cosy sweatshirt she planned to wear before offloading onto her sister at the start line. She pointed to the ladies' loos and crossed the room. On second thoughts, her nerve was very much present and ensuring her body knew it.

As she went to push on the swing door it was jerked open. The woman stepped back and held it for her with a wide smile.

'Good luck!' she said as they passed each other. 'I don't know how you do it.' She shook her head in amazement as she let the door close.

I haven't done it yet, thought Gracie, stepping into the tiled room and coming face to face with her reflection in a full-length mirror.

For a split second she was blind-sided. Didn't recognise the anxious woman staring back at her: heavily freckled arms hanging rigid at her sides, legs lean with muscle but wrinkled with age, protruding from blue contoured shorts. But as her gaze took in the pink and green vest, emblazoned with the logo for Alzheimer's Outreach UK and beneath that 'GRACIE', she sucked in a sharp breath.

This was it. She was really doing this. The five-digit number pinned to her top was testament to it. Bringing her hands up to cup her mouth, she inhaled and exhaled deeply. Blinked slowly. Then she let her hands drop and couldn't stop the smile that tugged on her lips, or the giggle that escaped her. It was a stomach-flipping sensation that melted away the tension in her cheeks, which despite the daily sunscreen, were as sun-kissed as the rest of her. *Yes*, she was doing this. And it was time to go.

The atmosphere on the train as it departed London Bridge station was electric. Gracie's event guide gave detailed instructions of where she needed to be and Jill was accompanying her to her designated starting point as far as possible, whilst the others bagged themselves a good spot further along the route. The carriage was packed, but unlike during the mid-week commute when passengers swarmed on autopilot, avoiding eye contact at all costs, runners and spectators alike were buoyant with excitement and chatting to one other as though all heading to one enormous party, which Gracie supposed, in a way, they were.

'Excuse me,' said a young woman, getting Gracie's attention with a little wave. 'You're the lady they were talking about on TV last night, aren't you?'

Gracie blinked in surprise. 'Oh, sorry! I think you must have me mixed up with someone else,' she said with a polite smile. 'Is someone you know running today?'

'No, I mean, yes—' she grinned '—my husband's running, but yes, I'm positive it's you. You're running for an Alzheimer's charity too, aren't you? Harry's dad had Alzheimer's, awful disease. We saw it last night and both thought, *wow*. I've always thought I could never do something like this, but you've inspired me to have a go. I'm going to apply next year!'

Gracie's brow creased in confusion. 'That's wonderful, but truly I'm puzzled about the TV part. . .' She sought out Jill across the carriage, who was sandwiched in the aisle between two beefy chaps in tracksuits and looking mighty pleased about it too. Jill caught her eye and let go of the rail to give her a thumbs-up.

'Here you are, look I found it on YouTube – it was on *The Graham Norton Show*. So cool that the band are donating the royalties from their album. Wish I had friends in high places like that!'

Gracie watched as the woman pressed play on a video clip. The instantly recognisable Graham Norton faced the camera, hands clasped in his lap.

'And now, here to tell us all about their latest UK tour and perform a song from their new album *Seeking Out the Light* are the fabulous, multi-award winning Jet Logan and the Jet Setters!'

Graham, along with the studio audience, gave a deafening round of applause, as the camera panned around to take in all four members of the rock band sitting on the sofa, book-ended by two A-list Hollywood stars.

'So, Jet Logan, before you take to the stage, tell us about the inspiration behind your decision to donate 10 per cent of royalties from all sales of your new album to Alzheimer's Outreach UK.'

Gracie watched on, dumbstruck, as Jet Logan crooned about his former bandmate Gary Baker and the 'awe-inspiring' relative who was undertaking the challenge to run a marathon for the first time ever at the ripe old age of seventy-two. Then, to Gracie's abject horror, the awful photo that had been printed in the *Frinton and Walton Chronicle* appeared on the big screen above Graham Norton's head.

A hand slid to her mouth.

'See, I told you I recognised you,' said the woman, 'I'm good with faces.' She looked up as the train pulled to a stop. 'Ooh, this is me,' she chimed, ending the video clip. 'Good luck!'

The woman squeezed her way to the carriage doors and Gracie stared after her, wondering how many more people on this train had recognised her. With a gulp she realised there were several sets of eyes swivelling in her direction. Her own gaze slid across to Jill, who was wearing a distinctly sheepish expression. Her sister's insistence that they didn't watch TV last night was now making perfect sense.

At last, the train pulled into Blackheath Station and everyone poured onto the platform. Fortunately, the day had dawned bright and clear, with a slight nip in the air, which Gracie knew she'd appreciate later.

'Are you terribly mad?' asked Jill, grasping at her sleeve from behind as they were jostled along with the crowd.

Gracie halted so she could catch up, then levelled her with a questioning look. 'Mad? Our charity has just had national television coverage, not to mention Jet Logan's fundraiser. When I think of all the good that will do, how could I possibly be mad?'

Jill threaded an arm through Gracie's. 'You called it *our* charity,' she said.

'Well, it is, isn't it. I just wish it was *our* marathon too,' said Gracie, feeling bewildered as they emerged into the street, along with the thousands upon thousands of bodies, all being shepherded and directed to where they needed to go. 'I'm a bit scared of doing this on my own,' she admitted.

'You're not on your own,' said a man dressed as a carrot who leaned across and grinned through the face-sized hole in his restrictive-looking costume. 'Sorry, I couldn't help but overhear. This is my tenth marathon and if I can give you one piece of advice, it will be to enjoy yourself. Make friends. Chat to people. Have fun. Everyone is in this together and I promise you, it will be one of the most rewarding experiences of your life. It can't be that bad, can it, if I keep coming back?'

'I suppose not. Thank you,' said Gracie, slightly taken aback by the stranger's friendliness. 'What's your name?'

'Ian. Ian Gardener. And every year I come as a different garden vegetable. Reckon this one might be the most challenging yet, mind,' he said, demonstrating how tight the pointy part of the carrot was around his legs as they walked. 'Better quality than last year's though, all the kernels kept popping out of my corn on the cob so by the time I got to the end I was a husk and I'm not just talking about the outfit,' he chuckled. 'Well, best of luck,' he said, waddling off.

'Looks like this is where I have to leave you,' said Jill, as they crossed Blackheath and drew closer to Greenwich Park. Hot air balloons hovered above the ground and huge signposts directed runners towards either the red, blue or green starting pens they'd each been assigned by their bib colour. Gracie wore red.

'Remember, look out for me at the *Cutty Sark*, then I'll try and make it across to join the others at Tower Bridge,' Jill said, as Gracie removed her jumper and handed it to her. 'I still can't believe that bib has a tracker in it. How times have changed.'

'I know,' agreed Gracie. 'Andrew was most impressed, and of course it added weight to his argument that I should have been wearing his all along, until I pointed out this one is invisible, weightless and not flapping around on my shoe.' Gracie looked down at Jill's own feet. 'First time I've ever seen you in flats, sis.'

Jill grinned. 'Didn't fancy my chances much, power walking the South Bank in my Kurt Geigers.'

'Thank you,' said Gracie with feeling. She experienced a rush of affection for her little sister, who was fidgeting from foot to foot, and looked just as pent up with the same nervous energy that was quickening her own pulse by the second. 'For everything. Wish me luck!'

With bright, watery eyes, Jill pulled her into a firm hug. 'You don't need luck – you'll smash it. You're Amazing Gracie, remember.' She tightened her grip. 'And, I love you.'

'Love you too,' said Gracie, squeezing her eyes shut against the butterflies in her belly and finally pulling away to give Jill one last tremulous smile, before turning to join the humming throng of runners. She resisted looking back over her shoulder at Jill's retreating form. She might have been tempted to run after her.

Instead, Gracie brought up the email instructions on her phone that she'd received, providing her with details such as her starting pen colour, start time and wave number. Owing to the many thousands of participants and to avoid overcrowding and bottlenecks, the runners were split into waves of staggered starting times, with the elite runners setting off first and the final wave at eleven thirty. Because Gracie's expected race time was on the longer side, she was in one of the later waves, so there was going to be a little bit of waiting around before she could finally get going. She glanced around at the bewildering number of people, many of them saying goodbye to friends and relatives, posing for photos, unzipping jackets or sipping from cardboard coffee cups. Should she get herself a hot drink? There were several kiosks dotted around. But then she spotted the long queues snaking towards a row of Portaloos and decided against it.

What she needed to do was find the truck that corresponded with her bib number and deposit her official plastic kitbag, which contained things she'd need when she finished the race: a drink, some snacks, a change of shoes and a lightweight sweater, as well as her mobile phone. She scanned the vast grassy area, spotting the curtain-sided lorries and fell into step beside two women also heading in that direction.

'Hi,' said the tall, fair woman, her arm linked with her friend. On second glance, Gracie realised they shared strikingly similar features, though one was much older than the other. 'How are you feeling?' she added brightly. 'It's exciting, isn't it?'

Gracie gave a nervous laugh. 'Exciting – that's one way of putting it!'

The other woman leaned forwards; her neat grey crop of hair secured back from her face with a headband.

'Ah. Your first time?' she asked with the distinctive sing-song pitch of a Scandinavian accent.

Gracie nodded, intrigued.

'My granddaughter's too. As I keep telling Meg here, try to relax and enjoy it. After all, when else will you have all of London come to a standstill just to watch you?' Her eyes twinkled.

Meg grinned good-naturedly. 'This will be Gran's eleventh marathon. I finally plucked up the courage to have a go myself.'

Gracie's eyes widened. 'Eleven marathons! Crikey. I'm not sure I'll even make it through this one.'

The older woman cocked her head. 'Of course you will. I'm eighty and I ran my first marathon at sixty. Best thing I ever did. You'll see.'

Eighty. That put things in perspective. Whilst Gracie had never considered her age to be a barrier, or even a motive, in setting out to achieve this goal, she'd definitely presumed that the vast majority of participants wouldn't look like her. But, glancing around, she noticed many mature faces among the sea of bibs. Briefly, she wondered what a collective noun for thousands of runners might be: a legion? A stampede? Ooh, how about a *river of runners*, coursing through the streets of London. Yes, she rather liked that idea. As though they were a force of nature to be reckoned with.

'Well then,' said Gracie, an anticipatory hum building momentum inside her, 'I think I'll stick with you two for the time being if you don't mind.'

Eventually, it was time to filter into the starting pen and wait for the race to start. Never before had Gracie found herself among so many exhilarant people; an ocean of bobbing heads, wishing each other luck and nervously ticking off the minutes. If Gracie had been yearning for a new adventure, by heck had she found it. This was the biggest kick she'd had in a long time – possibly ever! And to think she'd believed her days of exploring pastures new were behind her. What hogwash. At this moment in time, it seemed to Gracie as though a whole new chapter of her life was only just beginning.

Suddenly, the loudspeaker crackled into life.

This was it. . .

'Are. We. *READY*, London!' The disembodied voice was friendly, yet full of gravitas, like an international pop star addressing a packed Wembley Stadium.

Loud cheers erupted all around and a thrill shot through Gracie's veins. In front of her, the veteran Scandinavian runner turned and caught her eye. She winked.

Beside her a young woman with tightly woven cornrows danced on the spot.

'Are we *SET!*'

To her right, a man muttered away to himself, repeating a mantra, '*You got this.*'

'Then have a great race everyone! *ON YOUR MARKS!* Three. Two. One. . . GO!'

29

Jill

As Jill picked her way through Greenwich Park towards the iconic *Cutty Sark*, one of the first famous landmarks along the route, she began to realise her chances of getting anywhere near the front of the rows of spectators already lining the route were slim. Marathon-mania was in full swing as runners powered their way around the course. It would be a while before Gracie came through though, so Jill took her time and soaked up the whooping and whistling, enjoying the feel-good music and race coverage that pumped from a PA system. She bought herself a latte from one of the many coffee shops lining the street and looked up to see a helicopter circling overhead; collecting footage to livestream on television, perhaps. In front of her, a woman stopped and pulled a helium balloon from a plastic bag, then tied the long string onto her belt so it hovered high above her head. It was in the shape of SpongeBob SquarePants; a bright yellow, goofy face with spindly legs – something that would be most bizarre on an ordinary day yet perfectly sensible today – the woman would be easy to spot in the crowd now. Perhaps whoever she was here to support was running in a SpongeBob costume too;

or perhaps it served as nothing more than a beacon. Either way, it put a smile on Jill's face.

Wondering whether Emily had met up with the others yet, she pulled out her phone and sent her a text to confirm Gracie was safely in situ and she'd see her at their meeting point in Butler's Wharf as arranged.

A reply came swiftly back.

Whoop, Whoop! Can't wait to see Auntie Gracie smashing it. Slight change of plan here. I'll see you all at the finish line; there's something urgent I need to sort out.

Something urgent? What could be more urgent than being here to cheer on Gracie? Jill tried not to feel disappointed. Perhaps she should have insisted Emily stayed with them at the hotel, paid for her to have a room. She'd hoped they'd all be experiencing this epic event together, not spread out across the city in clusters, although considering how busy it was, perhaps it was just as well because she suspected travelling across town en masse was going to be tricky.

Jill wasn't a regular visitor to the capital these days, but all the flag-waving, singing and multi-generational crowds lining the streets reminded her of a street party or a royal event; a family-friendly occasion where just for one day, entire communities came together. She had hazy childhood memories of the Queen's silver jubilee street party in the Cambridgeshire village where they'd grown up. Lots of bunting, jam tarts and Union Jacks, as she recalled. But these days, it was sadly just so irregular to receive jolly smiles from strangers, with everyone going about their business in dogged isolation.

Every so often, the cheering and calls of encouragement for the runners would reach fever pitch as friends and family spotted their loved one running past. The buzz intensified as Jill reached the busy stretch of the Thames that housed the imposing tea clipper, with her towering masts and world-famous museum. She opened the app to track Gracie and saw she was approaching mile six. *Cutty Sark* sat between miles six and seven. It was time to put the skills she'd acquired all those years ago as a groupie to good use, because when she'd wanted to get to the front of a gig, there really wasn't anything, save a six-foot bouncer perhaps, that would get in her way.

But as Jill began to slowly edge her way forward, she wasn't met with the usual pointed elbows and rigid wall of those who wished to cling to their hard-won places at the front of the queue.

'Is someone you know coming through?' asked a woman standing with her friend, a Miniature Schnauzer wrapped in her arms. 'Here, take my place.'

Jill squeezed through. 'Thanks,' she said, showing the woman the moving dot on the tracking app. 'Looks like my sister isn't far off now.'

Another man turned around. 'Our friend's still three miles away, quick – come through to the front.'

'Thank you so much,' said Jill, stepping in front of the couple and finding herself at the barrier. 'I was starting to panic I'd miss her.'

'We've been coming for years, people are usually really helpful. And the runners go past so quickly, there's no point hogging the front row all day.'

Agreeing, Jill took in the scene. As far as she could see in either direction, it was wall to wall with bodies. Spectators roared and clapped as the runners looped around the ship and into Greenwich Church Street. Someone banged a drum and music drifted from a nearby sound system. The runners passed in a riot of multicoloured vests. There were wigs, masks, face paint, onesies, bright ribbons and bandanas. Wonder Woman streaked past, flanked by Spiderman. There were blind runners with their guides, wheelchairs, racing chairs and assisted chairs. The whole place had a carnival vibe to it, whilst at the same time feeling poignant and sincere. It was impossible not to be moved by the thousands of charities emblazoned on running shirts: cancer, heart disease, child welfare, the list was endless. All the sheer goodwill brought an inexplicable lump to Jill's throat.

Then suddenly she caught sight of something between the flashes of colour; a familiar formation of letters in brightly painted block capitals being waved on a giant banner across the road:

YOU CAN DO IT MISS JENKINS!

The only people who would ever call Gracie 'Miss Jenkins' were her students, a peculiar British tradition that persisted even when an entire school knew the marital status of a teacher.

Pride swelled Jill's bosom to bursting as she surveyed the banner-wielding group of spectators. They looked to be in their late twenties, a group of friends who had heard about their old teacher's fundraiser and had come out to support her. It spoke not only of how popular and loved Gracie had been as a teacher, but of how much good she was *still* doing in putting herself through this ordeal. Jill was so caught up with the moment that had it not been for the rowdy ex-students, she might have missed her sister entirely in the throng. A rousing cheer erupted, along with the blast of an air horn, as they called out Gracie's name. Even those in the crowd beside her added their voices to the calls of encouragement for Gracie.

'You didn't say Gracie Jenkins was your *sister*,' remarked the woman holding the mini schnauzer, joining in with the round of applause that accompanied the group of runners as they plodded past. 'We saw *The Graham Norton Show* last night. Blooming well done to her.'

Jill scoured the moving human mass and finally spotted the

striking pink and green of Gracie's Alzheimer's Outreach UK top adorned with her name and almost jumped over the barrier in her eagerness to catch her attention. It was Ian the human carrot who spotted her frantic waving and touched Gracie's arm to alert her; it looked as though they'd become friends. 'GRACIE!' Jill yelled. 'YOU'RE AMAZING!' At nearly seven miles in, Gracie still looked relatively calm and collected, her cheeks flushed and eyes bright as she sought out Jill in the crowd. 'DO YOU WANT A BANANA?' hollered Jill, rootling around in her bag and thrusting one over the barrier, almost taking out a runner. 'Oops, sorry,' she said, pulling her arm back in. The banana was then whipped from her hand, and like a relay baton, passed forward to Gracie who had by now moved beyond where Jill stood. She waved it above her head like a trophy and Jill whooped with delight.

'Oh yes,' said Jill aloud, pride warming her cheeks. 'That's my sister.'

30

Gracie

As the runners had slowed to negotiate the hectic bottleneck of the infamous *Cutty Sark* stretch at mile seven, Gracie had found herself running beside none other than Ian Gardener the carrot, which was pretty remarkable considering there were 50,000 runners, but then again, he was easy to spot. He was also making amazing strides, despite his restrictive costume and gave Gracie a cheery wave as they drew level.

'How's it going?' he asked, his words slightly muffled by the orange neoprene.

Gracie grimaced. 'I've tried to slow down a bit before I run out of steam; got off to a rather overenthusiastic start by attempting to keep up with an octogenarian who left me for dust.'

Ian nodded. 'It's hard not to get carried away with the party atmosphere, isn't it? But believe me, you'll be glad of it further along; gives you a real boost when you need it most.'

'I can well imagine; the marching band back there made me feel like royalty!'

'One of my favourite bits is coming up,' he'd said. '*Cutty Sark* and

Tower Bridge make it all worth every stomach cramp and blistered heel.'

Gracie laughed. 'I'll take your word for it!'

But, as they'd rounded the corner of the towering clipper and funnelled through the spectator-lined course, the deafening cheers cloaked Gracie in a warm glow that made it hard not to grin like a loon. A feeling that was further enhanced when she spotted several ex-students waving banners bearing her name. There hadn't been time to scan the sea of bodies, put names to faces, or seek out loved ones, but she knew they were there, rooting for her and it was like rocket fuel to the soul. Then her sister had bellowed out her name and she'd spotted her flailing her arms about like someone marooned on a desert island with a plane circling overhead.

'Blimey, you've got quite the fan club!' chuckled Ian, as a slightly bruised banana was handed to Gracie by a passing runner.

'That will be my sister,' explained Gracie, finding it harder than anticipated to peel and eat a banana on the move. 'You can usually hear her before you can see her – quite handy today.'

After the bustle and excitement of *Cutty Sark*, the track began to thin out and Gracie and Ian settled into a comfortable rhythm. Frequently, other runners would fall into step to ask Ian about his eye-catching costume, or take selfies, something Gracie found mind-boggling, all those Go-Pros and selfie sticks; it was enough of a bother simply keeping moving, let alone trying to capture it all with technology. Still, she smiled and posed and gave the thumbs-up and rather enjoyed knowing she'd been captured for posterity doing something spectacular.

At around mile ten, the aching calves kicked in. This was something Gracie had battled with on every training run and knew she could run through it, but it didn't stop the sense of panic in knowing she wasn't even halfway through. She paused at a drinks station for a drink of water and gave her aching calf muscles a quick massage, whilst Ian entertained the crowd by dancing along to the disco music blaring from an overhead balcony. They were becoming quite the double act, and not for the first time, Gracie experienced a wave of gratitude for the kindness and solidarity of strangers.

'Alright?' enquired Ian as she broke back into a run.

'All the better for watching a carrot perform the "YMCA", thank you, Ian.'

'I'm here to serve.'

Boosted by the brief stop and a good laugh, Gracie's ancient trainers ate up the next couple of miles, until long before the imposing spectacle of Tower Bridge at mile twelve came into view, a roaring, exhilarant crowd announced its proximity.

Adrenalin spiked Gracie to attention.

With each step, the frenzied buzz grew louder and her aching muscles quieter. Then, a sharp right turn revealed the soaring turreted stone and blue steel bridge ahead, linking both sides of the Thames and standing guardian above London's waterway, as it had done for over a century. The pavements throbbed with applauding spectators who filled every inch of space as far as the eye could see, a palpable energy humming in the air, along with the rhythmic beating of drums and jingling bells. Gracie's breath hitched as she crossed the threshold onto the famous suspension bridge, the runners in front slowing slightly to soak up the scene. She turned to Ian in wonder.

'Best feeling in the world, eh?' He grinned.

It was. . . *remarkable*. Unexpectedly, Gracie's eyes stung with emotion. Sentiments she couldn't even put a finger on. . . nostalgia, patriotism, pride, belonging and, above all else, joy. As though she'd become part of a sprawling, yet close-knit family, all bonded in the act of being here today, in this jaw-dropping place. Complete strangers calling out the name printed across your t-shirt made you feel as though *they* were family too. After all, they were rooting for you, standing out here all day to watch, support and encourage all the marathon runners, not just their loved ones. It was quite the most extraordinary thing Gracie had ever experienced, she realised, scanning the smiling faces for any she recognised.

Around halfway across the packed bridge, Gracie spotted a neon pink placard held aloft, featuring the words 'AMAZING GRACIE, LET'S GET RACY'.

A chuckle escaped her as she recognised the familiar cluster of heads beneath the placard: Ray, Malik, Sophia, and somehow, there was Jill too, looking red-faced and flustered, as though she'd run a marathon of her own, which come to think of it she must have done to get here ahead of Gracie from *Cutty Sark* six miles back.

Gracie pointed at her friends. 'This lot's with me, Ian. I'm going to stop for a tick, you go on ahead.'

Ian saluted and called back over his shoulder, 'See you down the line!'

'Whooooop!!!' bellowed Sophia and Jill in unison, as Gracie veered off towards the railings and halted in front of them to high fives and outstretched hands.

'I wouldn't get too close,' said Gracie as Sophia leaned in to hug her, 'bit clammy.'

'I don't care,' retorted Sophia, squeezing her tight around the shoulders, which was as close as she could get. 'I could snog you I'm so proud right now.'

'Look! You're famous!' said Malik, thrusting his phone screen in Gracie's face.

Gracie took in the screenshot of a BBC news page and shook her head in disbelief; there she was, pictured running alongside a waving Ian the Carrot with the biggest grin plastered across her face and a half-eaten banana in hand. It must have been snapped at *Cutty Sark*.

'They're calling you an inspiration to pensioners everywhere,' announced Malik proudly.

'Oh marvellous, there's me feeling invigorated and empowered, when apparently I'm just an advert for eating your five-a-day and getting your steps in after the age of sixty-five.'

Ray chuckled. 'Worse things to be remembered for. You're doing brilliantly.'

Gracie beamed at her friends, then noticed someone was missing. 'No Emily?' She looked to Jill.

'Meeting us further down the line instead,' she said with an odd, forced brightness. She passed her an energy drink, changing the subject. 'How are you feeling?'

'Like someone cut off my feet at the ankles and welded breeze blocks on in their place,' replied Gracie, having neither the time nor energy to dwell on Emily's absence. There would be a good reason.

'You can do it! If anyone can, you can,' assured Ray.

'Well. Best push on.' Gracie steeled herself, then turned to weave back into the heaving throng.

After the euphoria of Tower Bridge, Gracie eventually settled back into a rhythm. She passed the marker for mile fourteen, then counted off another, and another.

But, as intoxicating as it had been to see her friends and family, it had also reminded her that instead of being there on the bridge beside them, Andrew was in a hospital bed.

Whilst she was pounding tarmac using her strong, yet smarting knees, he was having his cut out and replaced with a synthetic part.

A solid lump rose in Gracie's parched throat and a small, pained cry escaped her as an unexpected wave of desolation engulfed her. A visceral longing to be with her husband bloomed within her chest and despite the spectators and runners beside her, she suddenly felt dreadfully alone. The crowds were much sparser here, as the route burrowed deeper into the city's financial district; not as much jollity to distract from thoughts that darted dangerously in different directions. *I should be with Andrew. This is too hard. What am I trying to prove. I can't let everyone down. I can't let Jill down.*

Up ahead a runner lumbered along with what looked like a gigantic packet of cornflakes strapped to his back. He looked ridiculous. The box obscured him completely, but as she drew closer, she could make out the words in a font designed to look like a recognisable breakfast cereal brand – *City Central Foodbank Needs You* – and beneath that a weblink and the word 'DONATE'.

To Gracie, the contrast was palpable: here in the banking district among the steel and glass skyscrapers of Canary Wharf, a stark reminder of all those in need. *This* was why she was doing it.

She gave the red-faced, sweating man a big thumbs-up as she overtook him and then turned her attention to drinking in her surroundings, as she had done during training and throughout every dog walk and hill climb. She shifted her focus from aching limbs and self-doubt, to the towering buildings that rebounded cheers from the thin line of spectators below. Occasionally, the wall of vertical glass was interspersed with enclaves of green and the fizz of pink cherry blossom, small pockets of oasis that reminded her these were homes as well as offices. It went some way to distancing her from the hefty acreage between her and the finish line, especially as her mind drifted to wonder at the people who lived and worked in these buildings, at the people from all over the globe who ran alongside her today and to what a great leveller the marathon was. Celebrities, athletes, supermarket cashiers, students, office workers, you name it. It didn't matter if you were a city banker or a home carer, whether you shopped in Waitrose or visited a foodbank, you were all in it together – same stakes, same distance, same goal.

It was with such philanthropic musings in the forefront of her mind that as Gracie passed the marker for mile seventeen, she happened upon a familiar figure up ahead. The well-toned physique of a man who should be miles ahead of her in this race, but who was labouring forth with a weighty, lopsided gait. The man who'd been aiming for a sub three-hour finish, a feat no less than wizardry, as far as Gracie was concerned.

'Giles?' she called out, coming up behind her fellow Coast Path Runner. 'You're limping, are you hurt?'

Puzzlement streaked briefly across his pain-etched features as he turned to see who'd addressed him, until recognition settled in.

'Oh, Gracie, it's you.'

It was hard not to hear the subtext in his disappointed tone. *I've cocked this up so royally, even the galloping granny has caught up.*

He sighed deeply. 'Stupid new trainers. They're crippling me.'

Gracie tried not to let surprise show on her face. Giles was the self-proclaimed aficionado of the running club, he was the gadget man, tech man, ridiculously expensive running shoe man.

'When you say *new*, you have run in them before?' she ventured.

'Yes,' he snapped, 'of course I have. I trained in identical shoes. Ordered a new pair of the exact same make and size, so why the hell does it feel like I'm running with bear traps clamped to my feet? It doesn't make any sense. My feet haven't grown overnight.'

How was it possible that a man as knowledgeable as Giles had made such a schoolboy error? There wasn't a woman in Christendom who didn't know you never went anywhere important in brand-new shoes. New shoes needed breaking in – it was bad enough with heels, but even the humble flat could be a weapon of torture on the high street, many steps from home. And just because you thought you were buying an identical product didn't necessarily mean you were. A marathon was *not* the time to put that theory to the test.

Gracie decided not to give Giles the benefit of her wisdom; the poor man was lurching along like a drunk sailor in a sea storm.

'I don't think I can go on,' he said miserably.

Gracie glanced around. They were approaching a point where several runners were queuing to use the Portaloos, and where there was a break in the barriers.

'Come with me over here,' she said, pointing to the kerb.

Giles limped meekly alongside her like a chastened student, a mere shadow of the alpha male of the CPR she'd come to know.

'Sit down and take your trainers off,' she instructed, unzipping the bum bag that was strapped to her waist and fishing inside for the emergency first-aid kit she'd packed.

Gracie tried not to wince at Giles's bloodstained socks, as he peeled them from his feet. No wonder the poor man was in agony. Silly, silly boy.

'Now,' she said, crouching down and trying to ignore the screaming in her knees, 'here's an antiseptic wipe. Give the affected areas a quick going over, we don't want any infections. Then, these,' she said, peeling back the paper packaging of a cushioned sticking plaster, 'should help with the rubbing.'

'Are you alright there?' called a woman from behind a nearby barrier.

Gracie gave a thumbs up. 'Quick spot of TLC,' she replied, thinking that actually, T*PC* would be the better option, and if that didn't make the poor guy scream, nothing would, but it usually did the job.

'Take some of these,' called the woman, and Gracie looked up to see her reaching out with a tray. 'I baked them this morning.'

Gracie handed the plaster in her fingers to Giles and stood, to see the saintly woman was offering them deliciously sticky, icing-sugar-dusted chocolate brownies. If that wasn't a sight for sore eyes, *and* sore feet, she didn't know what was.

'Thank you so much,' said Gracie, gratefully taking a couple of brownies. 'What a treat.'

The twinkling-eyed woman in the headscarf smiled. 'I ran it once myself, many years ago. Couldn't stop thinking about sugar all the way around. This is the fourth batch today, I only live over there,' she said, pointing to a block of flats.

Thanking the woman again, Gracie sank back down to the pavement and passed one of the cakes to Giles, along with a couple of chewable ibuprofen from her bag.

'Better?' she asked, as he swallowed the last of the brownie and began tugging his sodden socks back on.

Giles gave a small, incredulous nod towards her bag. 'What else have you got stashed in there? The kitchen sink?' His eyes crinkled in amusement and Gracie was pleased to see him rally.

'Habit. I have a son a bit older than you. He was quite the tearaway, always getting into scrapes. I'm afraid I fall short at carrying clean socks though.'

'Thank you,' he said, levelling her with an earnest look. 'Seriously. I'm not sure I deserve your kindness. I haven't exactly been very encouraging, or sociable for that matter.'

Gracie shrugged. 'Just because you like to run, doesn't mean you have to be buddies with everyone too. We all like different things. I happen to like hanging out with the others and eating cake, much to my downfall today, I expect.'

Giles shook his head. 'No. You're doing amazingly well, I haven't given you enough credit. This isn't easy. In fact, it might be the hardest thing I've ever done. And, contrary to what you and the others might think, I would quite like to hang out sometimes too. It's just that. . .' He paused, then began lacing up his trainer. 'I bet you all think me and Kat are having an affair, don't you?'

Gracie's inability to think on the spot betrayed her.

293

'It's OK,' Giles said. 'I don't blame you. I'd think that too.' He tied a knot decisively. 'I can't get away from the damned woman. I go to the pub with my wife, she's there. I take my kids to the park, she's there. She follows me everywhere, even started getting the same train into the city and I only go in once a week. I had to change my working hours in the end, to shake her off.'

Gracie tilted her head in surprise. 'But we saw you, Jill, Emily and I, coming out of the cinema. Are you saying there *had* been something between you and that now she's stalking you?'

Giles let out a snort of laughter. 'That night? That was a trap. She said she'd been given free tickets for the new Leonardo DiCaprio movie from one of her fitness clients, said she'd invited the others from the CPR, as a social event. I thought we were all going together, until nobody else turned up. And then, of course, I realised it had been a ruse when I saw you all coming out of the hall opposite with Pilates mats and a distinct look of disapproval.'

'I'm not sure I was disapproving, per se, it's really none of my business. . .'

'Well, *I* disapproved, strongly. I love my wife and have absolutely no desire to be seen as a cheat. I've tried everything. I chat endlessly about my family when we run; I'm careful not to send the wrong signals. I even started skipping sessions in the run-up to this when I should have been training as much as possible, because it was just getting too much. I thought she'd get the hint, but so far, it's not working. She'll be here somewhere, you know, loitering on the sidelines, she said she was coming up for the day. It's incredibly embarrassing to admit, but I just don't know what to do about it.'

Giles looked miserable.

'And are your family here too?' asked Gracie.

At this Giles looked up, nodded. 'They'll be at The Mall. Where I should have been by now.'

Gracie eased herself upright, massaged her legs and rolled her aching shoulders.

'Best get on then, love. Can't keep them waiting all day.'

Giles hesitated, then pushed up off the pavement. He tentatively tested one foot, then the other.

'How do they feel?' asked Gracie.

'Remarkably better,' he said, eyebrows lifting in surprise.

'Hydrocolloid gel,' explained Gracie. 'The plasters, best ones for blisters, and I should know, I spent an entire career on my feet in class.'

'Oh, right.' He nodded, testing his feet further with a little jog on the spot. 'I'll have to remember that.'

'You know,' said Gracie, 'it's not always the men. What I mean is, any kind of unwanted attention is bullying, whether it's in the playground, the workplace, or in the bedroom. *Sometimes* the bullies are mothers and daughters. And it *is* a form of bullying, what she's doing. You're not alone, you know, Giles. Reach out – it might surprise you to learn how many friends there are around to listen and offer their help.'

Because if Gracie had learned anything in the past few months, it was that secrets only protected the bullies, and hurt those who had suffered, even more.

Taking Gracie by complete surprise, Giles wrapped her into a hug. He smelled of fresh sweat, mixed with a sporty, masculine fragrance that reminded her of fifteen-year-old schoolboys and their cans of Lynx Africa.

'Thanks, Gracie. You are an absolute superstar.'

He gestured to the road ahead. 'Shall we?'

Smiling, she picked up her heavy feet, and resumed the race.

31

Jill

'Still not answering?' asked Sophia, after taking a long swig from her pint.

They had crowbarred themselves into a tight corner of a busy pub whilst Gracie ran the seven-mile Canary Wharf and Isle of Dogs loop, and were now perusing a bar menu whilst hoping the pub wouldn't run out of food before they got their orders in.

'No,' said Jill, sliding back into her chair and placing her phone on the table where she could see it. 'I hope she's OK.'

'Perhaps she's got poor signal too, she'll be on the underground or something,' said Sophia, but Jill wasn't so easily assured. It really wasn't like Emily to go off the radar like this, especially on such an important day. The marathon had meant as much to her daughter as it did to Gracie, and she didn't think for a moment that she'd want to miss any of it. Something must have happened, but what?

'Right, I'm going up to order,' said Sophia. 'What are you all having, we can sort the money out later.'

'Pie and chips for me,' said Ray, snapping his menu shut.

'I'll come with you,' said Malik.

Jill scanned the sticky menu again but she barely had any appetite she was so on edge, what with worrying about Gracie and now Emily. She stared at the various options blankly.

'Are you alright, Jill?' asked Ray in a low, butter-smooth voice that was almost swallowed up by the background noise of the packed pub. He was perched on a windowsill beside her, there not having been enough chairs for them all and the earnestness in his kind face made Jill's heart play hopscotch.

'I'm OK,' she replied, giving herself a mental shake-up. 'Just a bit anxious, you know. I'll have the toasted cheese sandwich please, Sophia,' she replied to her waiting friend.

'Hey look, Gracie will be fine. If she needs to stop at any time, she can. If she wants to walk, she can. She's a tough cookie, you know that.' Ray reached out, as though he were about to lay a hand over hers. It hovered there tantalisingly close to hers; so close she could feel the warmth radiating from his skin, before he let it come to rest on the table instead. 'She's strong, like you,' he said, giving her a reassuring smile.

Jill flicked her eyes to Sophia and Malik, who were standing whispering at the bar like two loved-up teenagers and not paying them the least bit of attention. Which was good because she was certain the heat travelling up her neck and into her cheeks would give away her own current crush.

Lifting her glass and cooling her thoughts with an ice-cold sip of Coke, she said, 'It's not Gracie so much I'm concerned about. It's Emily. Where is she? Why isn't she answering my calls? There's been something going on with her for a while, I just. . . I don't know,' she shook her head. 'I feel like there's stuff going on in her life that she keeps from me, and I worry about her. It's as though she has two lives, and I only see one of them.'

Ray looked pensive for a moment. 'Hmm. Well, I'm not a parent, so I'm not sure I'm qualified to comment here, but you know what I think? I think Emily is a wonderfully warm, sensitive and considerate person who would hate to know you feel this way. I also think perhaps you should give her credit for having a valid reason for being a little secretive. Sometimes a person needs to work things out by themselves for a while. Trust me, I know exactly how that feels.'

Yes, thought Jill, searching those velvety conker-brown eyes that seemed to look right into the nucleus of her soul, *I think perhaps you do.*

The food arrived surprisingly quickly in the end, delivered to their table, piping hot, by a harassed-looking server in a splattered apron. Jill was thankful they'd discovered this ancient, peeling, spit and sawdust hostelry hidden away from the bustle of Tower Hill, rather than one of the trendier gastro pubs. This place was cosy, cheerful and the food was simple, but plentiful and good.

'Well, I'm ready for a kip after that,' said Malik, pushing his plate away and yawning.

'I'm ready for another pint,' said Sophia, 'anyone else?'

As Ray opened his mouth to answer, his phone blared on the table before them with an incoming video call.

He frowned at the screen. 'It's Dad, I better take it.'

Jill glimpsed Eugene's cheeky face on the screen and smiled to herself, loving that the sprightly gentleman used FaceTime to chat with his son.

'What's up, Dad?' asked Ray, holding his phone screen out in front of him.

'Nothing's up. Why would there be anything up? Where are you? I can't see any marathon runners in the background, in fact that looks *suspiciously* like a pub to me.' Eugene squinted and drew closer to the camera, peering at Ray's surroundings.

'Is that you, Jill?' he asked, giving away the fact she was nosily craning in to look at the screen.

Jill shrank back, then leaned forward again and gave a little wave. 'Hi, Eugene.'

'We've had a pit-stop for lunch, if that's alright with you, and we're heading off to watch Gracie cross the finish line shortly,' said Ray.

Eugene turned his head to address someone else. 'They're going to the finish line now. We're not too late.'

'Who are you talking to, Dad?' asked Ray.

Eugene pulled a face, as though he found his son to be an idiot, then swung the camera around, revealing that he was in fact sitting beside a hospital bed, where Andrew lay propped against pillows, and Harold slurped tea from a paper cup on the opposite side.

'Ohh,' cried Jill, announcing to anyone in earshot. 'Andrew's out of surgery!'

Sophia and Malik moved to huddle round the screen too.

'How is he?' asked Ray.

'What am I? An interpreter? He can hear you perfectly well, ask him yourself.'

Jill tried to suppress a giggle at Eugene's blunt manner, which rolled straight off Ray's remarkably muscular shoulders.

'How are you doing, Andrew? Feeling groggy?' Ray directed his question at Andrew instead, as the picture bumped around and finally landed on Andrew; Eugene perched beside him.

'I'm OK,' came Andrew's cheerful voice, 'not sure about the others on this ward though. These two have been making everyone play Who Am I, with bits of wet paper towel stuck to their foreheads. It's a wonder they've not been kicked out.'

Eugene beamed and moved closer to the screen. 'I told the nurse she must be related to Julia Roberts, as the resemblance was too uncanny. She brought us sandwiches left over from lunch and even joined in the game.'

Harold harrumphed. 'And then you went and stuck Benny Hill on her forehead and she's been snappy ever since.'

Sophia snorted with laugher.

'Dad!' Ray chided, whilst also struggling not to smirk. 'You're a nightmare. But seriously, Andrew, how did the op go?'

'The doctors seem pleased with me, so that's the main thing. But tell me about Gracie, have you seen her yet? I could hardly believe it when these two showed me the pictures on the iPad. My Gracie, on the BBC!'

'Yes, we've seen her, she's doing *so* well. We're all very proud,' Jill replied, pulling out her own phone. Andrew's words had reminded her she'd better check the whereabouts of Gracie on the app; they'd been in the pub quite a while.

Malik enthused about the incredible atmosphere on Tower Bridge as Jill waited for the app to refresh; her network signal in here really was terrible, perhaps Emily *had* been trying to get hold of her. She pushed back her chair and leaned closer to the window, holding her phone to the small glass panes. Eventually, along with the one struggling bar that appeared in the corner of her screen, came the flashing initials GJ – a good deal further around the course than anticipated.

'Er, guys,' said Jill, refreshing the app again in case there was a mistake. 'Gracie's on target to reach the finish line in less than an hour? Shit.' Jill looked up. 'She's motoring along, and we're sat here supping pints in the pub!'

'Blimey,' said Ray, 'I know she was hoping for anything under seven hours, but that will be. . .'

Before he could make the mental calculation, Jill cut in. 'Six.' She met his eye in disbelief. 'She's going to smash this in under six hours.'

Sophia pushed back her chair with a loud scrape. 'Well don't just sit there then, you eejits. Have you seen how many people there are out there? We have to get all the way over to St James's Park, and I don't fancy our chances of flagging a cab, do you?'

'Sorry, guys,' said Ray to Andrew, Eugene and Harold, laughing as he got to his feet. 'Looks like we've got a bit of a sprint of our own to do.'

'Go! Go!' called Eugene excitedly.

'Wait!' added Andrew with an impassioned plea. 'Can you video call us when you get there, so we can watch too?'

'We will,' they assured in unison, then Ray ended the call.

As they bundled out into the street, which still hummed with the sound of cheers and applause, Jill looked right and left. 'Where's the nearest tube station?'

Of the four of them, it was Ray to whom they deferred when it came to the logistics of getting across town. As a Londoner by birth and as someone who'd lived and worked in the city for most of his life, he zipped around like a local.

'This way,' he nodded, before ducking right and leading the way. 'The Circle Line takes us straight to St James's Park.'

At Monument underground station, the westbound platform for the Circle Line was at least ten people deep. In fact, there was an actual queue at the foot of the steps to even get on to the platform.

'Shit,' groaned Malik. 'This is going to take forever.'

Even as the words left his mouth, a train pulled into the station and there was a civilised jostling as the mass of people moved forward, but they still barely made it as far as the platform before the doors shut and the train moved off.

'We'll never make it in time,' said Sophia, wincing.

'There has to be another way,' said Jill firmly, looking to Ray. She refused to accept they could miss Gracie crossing the finishing line. As far as she was concerned, it simply wasn't an option.

Ray nodded. 'Follow me.'

He turned to squeeze himself back through the tightly packed crowd, then reached for Jill's hand to pull her along too. Heart thumping, she dashed after him as they all retraced their steps through the cavernous underground to adjoining Bank Station, and to the far less crowded Northern Line.

'This seems counterintuitive, but if we go one stop south to London Bridge and change for the Jubilee Line, we can hop off at Westminster and hotfoot it down to The Mall. The tube won't be as busy on the other side of the river.'

Ray was right. There were still plenty of passengers waiting to board the train when it swept into the station, but they squeezed themselves into the packed carriage as the doors beeped shut. For the entire sixty-second journey, however, Jill didn't even notice the many bodies packed around her like sardines in a can because all she could focus on was the warm, solid wall of bloke pressed against her front and Ray's distinctive aftershave, a faintly spicy scent with citrussy undertones. When the doors hissed open and they disembarked for the Jubilee Line, Jill felt giddy. It could have been the airlessness of the London underground but was more likely the fact she'd held her breath as the long dormant sensation of lust had hit her squarely between the eyes.

As she stumbled slightly, Ray caught her arm.

'Alright?' he asked, face creasing in concern.

'I'm fine. Everything's fine,' she gabbled. 'Just, you know, I don't want to miss it.'

'We won't. Trust me,' he said, with his trademark winning smile.

Oh boy. It seemed it wasn't just Sophia and Malik with their (not so) secrets of the heart. Thank heavens she was the undisputed queen of putting on a good front; she'd need it to get through the rest of the day without dissolving into a lovestruck, girlish mush.

Her phone buzzed in her pocket. She tugged it out and squinted at it, whilst hurrying after the others. It was a text from Emily.

Sorry I missed your calls, Mum. Will explain all later. Where are you guys? I'm at the finishing line waiting for Auntie Gracie!

Thank goodness. Jill's chest sagged in relief. Whatever it was, it could wait, but she was here, she was safe and they'd all be together soon.

Twenty minutes later, the group emerged from Westminster tube station into the bright afternoon, and without stopping to consult each other, they all broke into a run. The roaring sound of the finish line on the other side of St James's Park was audible, even above the hordes of cheering spectators on the embankment and lining the streets of this, the final stretch. High above Big Ben, the late-afternoon sun finally burst its way through the thick white cloud cover that had kept the day cool and fresh, bathing Westminster in golden light. Breathless, Jill slowed to pull her phone from her pocket and check on Gracie. It took a few seconds for the GPS to update and then suddenly there it was, the red dot that was her sister, just a few hundred yards from this very spot.

Except, the red dot wasn't moving.

32

Gracie

By mile twenty-one, Gracie hated running more than she'd hated anything.

For four miles, Giles and Gracie had run together, side by side. Gingerly, Giles had tested the water with light, tentative steps, bolstered by Gracie's gentle encouragement and the sugar rush of some delicious brownies.

'Forget about the time for now, love, just focus on putting one foot in front of the other. I'm right here, and I've got a few plasters left, so we can patch you up again if needed,' Gracie had said, jogging beside him.

'Thank you,' Giles had said, with meaning. 'I'm not sure what I'd have done without you. I might have given up.'

'Nonsense. We're the CPR, we don't *give up*.' She'd smiled wryly.

As they fell into a gentle, comfortable stride, Giles chatted animatedly about his children, he had two – Archie and Freddy – and clearly doted on both them and his wife. There was none of the macho showiness, or 'dick swinging' as Ray had so aptly put it, and Gracie suspected he and Malik might have more in common than either of them realised, if they ever behaved like grown-ups long enough to find out. With children of a similar age and both with a love of gaming, they might even become pals.

But as the miles tripped by and Giles's mojo returned with a fanfare, Gracie's seemed to have sung itself hoarse. She'd read about this stage of the race. Marathon runners called it 'The Wall'. And she could understand why. The deflation in her mood became a physical pain of its own. In fact, her entire body began to feel like an orchestra of ailments. Over on strings, her hamstring wailed, and her Achilles screeched. In wind instruments, her battered lungs struggled to raise so much as a parp, utterly drowned out by the percussive thrum of scores of feet hitting the ground.

'Do you know,' said Giles chirpily. 'I might see if I can make up some ground. Would you mind?'

Gracie frowned. 'Mind? Why on earth would I mind?'

'Well, you've been so kind, waiting with me and running with me, and you could have been so much further ahead.'

'I'm raising funds by being here. All I need to do is finish. That will be challenge enough, thank you. Please, Giles, go on ahead, don't pay me a thought, this is a comfortable pace for me.'

Giles gave her a grateful smile. 'Only if you're sure? Keep going, Gracie, you're doing something special here. I'll see you on the finish line.'

She gave him a small wave and watched as he accelerated into the stream of runners, which had now thinned out. Leaving her with no one to conduct the symphony of agony, but the magnificent supporters on this grueling stretch leading out of Limehouse, and the thought of her sister nursing Gary through a terrible disease. It would have to be enough.

But by the time she passed the twenty-five-mile marker on the Victoria Embankment, Gracie's ravaged body could take no more, and she staggered to a sluggish limp. All she had to do was get across that finishing line. It didn't matter if she didn't storm across it, chest thrust forward like a hundred-metre sprinter. Visions of collapsing onto the pavement for a nice lie-down began swarming her mind. Perhaps she could find a hotel and simply check straight into a room and go to bed. Forget all the celebrations and jubilations, all she wanted was sleep, and maybe a nice packet of smoky bacon crisps. Why did she fancy crisps all of a sudden? Her mouth was like a cat litter tray, but she really craved something salty.

As runners overtook her, it seemed that no matter the exhaustion evident in their faces and their bodies, they each seemed to muster a little extra something in response to the thick tunnel of whooping spectators that lined the final mile. The regal sound of bagpipes drifted from somewhere nearby, adding weight to the momentousness of the occasion and reminding all that they skirted close to Buckingham Palace. Yet despite all this, Gracie's limbs were like sandbags anchoring her to the tarmac. She had nothing left. All calories burnt, every muscle overworked, lungs spent and raw. Even her mind was depleted of thought, other than the all-consuming need to rest.

Feeling like one of the remote-controlled cars Nathan had loved as a boy, Gracie accepted she had finally run out of speed. Her batteries were dead. She lumbered to a stop and stooped over, resting her weight on her unsteady knees. The sun warmed her back, and the scent of sweat filled her nostrils, whether it was her own or that of the passing runners, she couldn't possibly tell.

Behind her, Big Ben began to chime, striking off the hours she'd been counting with each painful step. One. Two. Three. Four. Five. Then time stood still. It had been six hours since she'd set off that morning, brimming with nervous energy. Six hours to *almost* complete the London Marathon. In the wake of the bells, her name rang out, a supportive call from someone in the crowd, a well-wisher urging her to keep going. More voices joined in. Cries of 'You can do it, Gracie,' and 'You're almost there,' echoed in her ears. She wanted to call back; to tell them it was impossible. But she didn't have the breath.

Then, suddenly, a familiar voice cut through the noise, pleadingly calling her name, followed by an ear-shattering wolf whistle.

Disorientated, Gracie raised her head and scanned the crowds. Runners swooped past to victory whilst all she could do was stagger forwards.

Then, she saw her. Or rather, she saw the commotion being caused by what looked like a woman attempting to climb over the metal barriers, one leg almost over and the other stuck at an awkward angle, before she was lifted by a couple of cheering men and passed over the barriers as though crowd-surfing at a rock concert.

Her sister was now sprinting in her direction against the human traffic, ample chest bouncing and leather jacket flapping.

'What are you doing?' gasped Gracie, as Jill reached her. 'You'll get arrested!'

'Pff,' shrugged Jill, slinging an arm around Gracie and hugging her tight. 'I'd like to see them try! It's like you said earlier, sis, this is *our* marathon, and we are going to run this last tiny bit together, you and me. Come on, you can do it, you know you can, darling.'

Jill looked so ridiculous standing there, in her silver jeggings, bright pink Skechers, and black leather jacket, it caused a hiccup of hilarity to rise in Gracie's deflated chest. Unbidden, laughter burst out of her. At the absurdity of it all, and at the relief of strong arms around her and love, for this incredible woman who she was *just so lucky* to have back in her life. Fuelled by the warmth and love, as though simply by being there at her side Jill had gifted her with some of her own vibrant energy, Gracie picked up her feet and began to walk. Jill grinned and fell into step, as the crowds around them erupted into applause.

'Look,' said Jill, tapping Gracie on the arm.

Gracie followed Jill's eyeline. Sophia was easy to spot, for she was sitting on Malik's shoulders holding her phone aloft. She wore her CPR running shirt back to front, so it bore Gracie's name. Beside her, Ray beamed. His support was more subtle, but no less passionate, and she saw the look that passed between him and Jill; there was no disguising the admiration, or adoration for that matter.

'Aren't you going to blow Andrew a kiss?' grinned Jill. 'He's on the other end of that phone, watching, with Eugene and Harold.'

'You've spoken to him?' Gracie asked in surprise.

'Mmhmm, he's absolutely fine. Trust me, the hospital will be quite keen to send both him *and* his visitors home.'

It was as though Gracie found another gear she didn't even know she had. They passed a sign stating 800 metres to go. She was almost done. This was almost done. And then she could go home, home to her wonderful husband and to making sure he had everything he needed. Which wouldn't be hard really, because honestly, if today had shown her anything, it was how much they already had. The only thing missing from her life was Nathan, Beth and the girls, but they were safe, and they were happy, which would just have to be enough.

'I have *got* to get fit,' panted Jill, who had clearly been rushing around. 'Perhaps I should give the CPR another go.'

'Only if you want to,' said Gracie sternly. 'It's supposed to be enjoyable.'

Jill laughed. 'Enjoyable? Is that right?'

'Ask me in a few weeks. I'm hoping it might be a bit like after childbirth, when the good far outweighs the bad, and when I can sit down again without wincing.'

After a few beats, Jill breathed a sigh of wonder, 'Wow. *Look* at this. I mean I've seen it before, but never like this.'

Gracie had to agree. Buckingham Palace loomed ahead, presided over by the majestic Queen Victoria Memorial, all glistening gilt and marble. Yet it wasn't the buildings and statues that gave the moment gravitas, it was the ocean of whooping spectators crowding the iconic landmark, cheering them on as though they were the royalty they'd come to see. It was the fists pumped in the air as Gracie and Jill hobbled past. The calls of encouragement from onlookers and the ceremonial fanfare of a live brass band. It was the camaraderie of other runners who shared knowing smiles of relief and determination as they all covered these final few yards. And it was the breathtaking sight as the track veered right, into The Mall; a route traversed by Kings, Queens, Heads of State, and now the London Marathon finishers.

Flanked by manicured lawns, the wide, austere, tree-lined road was transformed with Union Jacks fluttering on flagpoles in the breeze. A tunnel of banners in a riot of colour promoted marathon sponsors and giant screens zoned in on the triumphant faces of runners crossing the finish line, to the feel-good sound of party music. A young man limped painfully past, trailed by two women; arms linked, wearing matching pink running-club vests. The sight of them tweaked at something in Gracie's chest. How lovely to run with your own club; the people you've trained with, bonded with and become friends with. Like her own friends, who were right here on the sidelines, following her every step; in spirit if not in practice.

'Almost there,' said Jill excitedly as a huge overhead banner proclaimed there was just 385 yards to go. 'And this is where I'm going to leave you.'

'What, no, come on, you're here now,' said Gracie, seized with panic. She could do this, with Jill at her side. Could she do it alone?

'Uh-uh,' refused Jill. 'No way am I stealing your limelight now. You deserve this. You've *earned* this.' She gave her hand a quick squeeze. 'Just a few more steps and I'll see you on the other side. Horse Guards Parade at the Meet and Greet, remember. Now I'm going to find Emily, she's right here somewhere – look out for her!'

Gracie nodded, watching her sister veer off to the barrier and signalling to someone in a hi-vis vest that she should actually be on the other side of it, which considering she wasn't wearing a running bib, sports gear or fancy dress, was pretty blooming obvious.

Smiling faintly to herself at the sight of her, she picked up her feet again and fixed her gaze firmly on the finishing line ahead.

Damn it.

She'd just run twenty-six miles, for heaven's sake. She could run a few more metres.

With Herculean effort, she threw her weight behind her leading leg and into the momentum of a slow, exhausted jog.

Photographers' lenses began to flash. She was far too tired to care what she looked like – as though she'd just run a twenty-six-mile marathon, probably, which no flattering camera angle was ever going to improve. Her hair had worked itself loose from its tight braid, long strands welding themselves to her face and neck. *If I do this again, I'm lopping the whole lot off.* Wait a minute, what the hell was she thinking – *do this again?*

With a matter of metres to go, something in Gracie's eyeline made her breath catch in her throat. Or rather, *someone*, in her eyeline.

Her heart skittered in her chest.

It couldn't be.

But there was Emily, beside him, furiously waving a sign to attract her attention:

And there also was *his* sign, waved proudly by a red-headed little girl in his arms, her older sister now standing far taller than when Gracie had last seen her, almost as tall as her smiling mother.

MUM, NANA, GRACIE JENKINS – WE ARE SOOOO PROUD

Gracie's hand flew to her mouth in shock.

Nathan. *Nathan.* All of them – Nathan, Charlie, Liv and Beth, they were *here*. Right here in London. As her brain grappled with this new reality, her eyeballs pricked with stinging tears. She faltered. She wanted to run over to them. She wanted to abandon this silly running race and cross the tarmac to where her son and his family stood behind barriers, to hug them all to her and hold them tight.

But as Nathan cupped his face and bellowed, 'I love you, Mum, almost there!' she remembered where she was. On the cusp of the finishing line of the London Marathon. She was so close; she could even see the officials handing out the medals beyond.

Galvanising herself once more, she waved to her family, then fixed her eyes ahead. Just a few more steps. Nathan was here and they were going to have the mother of all celebrations.

Crossing under the official, overhead finishing line of the London Marathon to thunderous applause, Gracie's battered legs almost gave way. It was emotional strength alone that propelled her forwards, kept her walking unsteadily towards the tents handing out finisher t-shirts, past medical and water stations. It was the overwhelming wave of pride, mixed with triumph and relief' which robbed her of speech when a volunteer handed her a bottle of water, which she unscrewed gratefully.

Next, Gracie accepted her medal from a congratulatory

gentleman who burst with enthusiasm, even though he must have been doing this all day. She stared down at the metal disc in her hands. Proof: engraved there forever. She was a London Marathon Finisher. She fingered it lightly, ran her quivering thumb over the embossed braille. *This is for you, Jill*, she thought, slipping the lanyard over her head. It might have started out as a whim, but it had evolved into something vital. This was for Jill. For Gary. For Andrew and Emily. And for all the generous souls who had donated their hard-earned money.

Breathless, yet exhilarated, she followed the marshals who directed her to the waiting trucks to collect her bag, soaking up the scenes around her. A young woman sat on her bottom, happy tears streaming down her cheeks, her friend's head in her lap, flat on her back, chest rising and falling like a pair of bellows. A man stood, wrapped in a foil blanket, as though he'd broken down by the side of the road and was awaiting vehicle recovery; he smiled at Gracie as she passed by.

'We did it,' he said, as though only saying it aloud could make it true.

'Yes,' she replied, unable to stop the silly grin spreading on her lips. 'We did.'

Gracie wondered how the remainder of Ian the Carrot's race had gone, and if she'd ever see him again. She thought of Giles too; would he be reunited with his family yet? Well, that was one marathon runner she *would* be seeing again and was determined to include from now on in social events, even if she had to drag him there herself.

The remaining walk up The Mall and round to Horse Guards Parade felt like the longest walk of Gracie's life. Every step shot agonising bolts of pain through her ankles, calves, knees and hips; yet it also took her closer to her loved ones. She paused briefly along

312

the way and rooted around in her bag for her phone. There was one thing she wanted to do before she reached the busy square where family and friends would be waiting.

'Gracie? I just saw you on the livestream! I saw you cross the finishing line. Well done, my *incredible*, amazing wife.'

'Oh, Andrew,' breathed Gracie into the phone. She scrunched her eyes shut against the pleasure of hearing his familiar, loving voice. 'Did you know?'

There was a beat of silence on the other end. 'Did I know what?'

'Andy?' she warned playfully. 'I saw them.'

Andrew chuckled. 'I *didn't* know anything about it, not until about an hour ago when Nathan called from the car. They've had a heck of a job getting here, delays left, right and centre. Emily ended up borrowing one of her flatmate's cars and driving across to Heathrow to pick them up so she could get them there in time. They must have made it with minutes to spare.'

Gracie's brow creased in confusion. 'Emily? What on earth has Emily got to do with it?'

'I think perhaps you'd better speak to her about that. But how are you? I can't believe you've done it.' There came the muffled sound of clapping down the phone line, and she swore she could hear Andrew's smile. 'That's everyone here on the ward. They've all been watching on their phones and iPads. Apart from Arthur, he didn't have one, so Eugene put some credit on his TV so he could watch on there.'

She could picture Eugene geeing everyone along, whether they fancied watching a load of sweaty runners or not, and she experienced a wave of gratitude, understanding with certainty that, whilst she couldn't be there with him, Andrew was in good hands.

'Brilliant,' she said. 'And what about you, love? Are you terribly sore?'

'Not too bad. A bit tired. Looking forward to getting home and seeing my runderful wife.'

Gracie added, 'And not forgetting your runderful son, daughter-in-law and granddaughters.'

'Ah, so you see that doesn't work, because. . .'

'Yes, dear. I understand how puns work,' Gracie laughed, in only the way a patient and doting wife can. 'And probably best I hop along and find them now, seeing as they've come all this way. Love you. Call you later.'

Ending the call, Gracie picked her way into the square and sought out the pre-arranged meeting point.

Before she'd even spotted them, the scream gave them away.

'Nannnnaaaaa!!'

And there they were, Liv scampering towards her, pigtails flying, Charlie hanging back with her mum, displaying the tell-tale signs of teenage shyness, and Nathan casually bowling towards her with the biggest, most beautiful grin.

'Mum,' he mumbled into her hair, as he wrapped her into a hug with Liv hanging from her leg.

She couldn't even find the words to reply, just closed her eyes and breathed him in, the achingly familiar smell of rugby bags, soap and a hint of coffee. Poor buggers would have been travelling for over twenty-four hours; he must be practically inhaling caffeine to stay awake.

Wrenching herself away, she attempted to shake the emotion from her face but couldn't control the glassy film that coated her eyes. She reached down for Liv's hand, the little girl clasping it in her own small clammy fist.

'It's been quite a day, huh?' he drawled, the Australian accent thicker than ever.

'Hi, Gracie,' beamed Beth, leaning in to kiss her mother-in-law on the cheek. 'Surprise.'

Gracie shook her head, freeing herself from Nathan long enough to squeeze a slightly sheepish Charlie into her side. *Surprise* was the understatement of the century.

The others all lurked on the periphery, not wanting to impinge on this important family reunion. They were all there – Emily, Jill, Ray, Sophia and Malik. All her supporters, friends and new-found family.

Finally, when she felt she'd mastered her vocal cords, Gracie called out, 'Nearest pub, anyone? I think I need a very large glass of wine.'

33

Jill

'Look at her,' said Jill, handing Emily a Diet Coke when she returned from delivering all the other drinks to their table, 'she's so happy.'

Emily followed her mum's gaze to where Gracie sat in the most comfortable chair they could find in this packed and happy pub, ensconced by Nathan and his family.

'Exhausted, but happy,' Emily agreed.

Jill took a sip of her drink, gazing enviably upon Gracie's goldfish bowl of wine, but she was driving them all home in the minibus that evening, so orange juice it was.

'I still don't understand how any of this came about,' she said, shaking her head in confusion. 'Gracie was quite determined that Nathan shouldn't know about the marathon, she didn't want him to worry. And how on earth did *you* know they were coming? I didn't know you were in touch with your cousin, you've only met him twice.'

Emily batted away the question with a noncommittal, 'It just kind of happened,' but Jill could see the secrecy lurking beneath a tentative smile. Her daughter had been up to something for a while now, and she suspected it wasn't quite over yet.

'Shall we go and join the others,' said Emily, not waiting for a response before moving away from the bar.

Jill raised an eyebrow and followed Emily. She sensed that whatever it was, it wasn't going to remain a secret for much longer.

'Come and sit down you two,' said Ray, giving up his chair. Thankfully, they'd had the foresight to book a table, a good job too, as every pub within a square mile seemed to be hosting euphoric marathon runners and their friends and family. But they hadn't banked on having four extra members in their party.

'I'm OK, you sit down, love,' Jill said, steering Emily towards it.

Sophia sprang up. 'Here, you have mine, Jill. I've a far more comfortable seat in mind.' And with a wicked smirk, she lowered herself onto Malik's lap. A blush crept up Malik's neck, but it didn't stop him from snaking his arms around her waist, in what appeared to be their first public display of affection.

Ray began to clap, Emily falling into suit, along with the others, whilst Nathan, Beth and the girls watched on with bemused expressions.

'Don't mind us,' laughed Gracie in explanation to her son, 'it's only taken about five months for these two to finally get their act together.'

'And a little helping hand along the way, too,' added Jill, unable to stop her lips from curving into a smug grin. 'My guess is it wasn't only Duran Duran that night who was feeling hungry like a wolf.'

'Mum!' cried Emily, agog, whilst Gracie snorted into her wine glass.

Actually, thought Jill, perhaps she should keep an eye on her sister's wine consumption; all the exertion and excitement of the day seemed to be making her delirious. It was probably a blessing she was stone-cold sober.

Sophia slid an arm around Malik's neck, her sea-glass blue eyes shining, though whether from the endorphins of love or beer, it was hard to tell. 'Your man was a perfect gentleman, as ever. Me, on the other hand. . .'

'Alrighty, I think that's enough sharing for now, don't you?' interjected Ray, shaking his head at the two lovebirds. 'We're all super happy for you both.' His gaze shifted, subtly, as he sought and met Jill's eye. 'There's nothing lovelier than finding someone special when you least expect it.' Jill's heart skittered. The way he looked at her. As though she was the only person in the room. She answered his silent question with a small, secret smile. 'A great news day all round – cheers!' he added, raising his glass.

'Well, since we're sharing news,' began Nathan, looking to his wife for a reassuring nod, before turning back to Gracie, 'we thought we'd keep it as a surprise, but this isn't a regular holiday, Mum. We're staying for six months, if you'll have us. I don't mean *have* us to stay at your house; we've rented somewhere locally, but, hopefully, you'll be happy to have us all around for a good while.'

Gracie clamped her hands to her face in disbelief.

Nathan laughed. 'Well, there's no need to look so horrified about it!'

'Can I have a sleepover at your house, Nana?' asked Liv, her earnest little face completely oblivious to the effect of the bombshell her father had just dropped.

Gracie reached out a shaky hand and stroked her granddaughter's hair. 'Absolutely! We'll have as many sleepovers as you want, *both* of you.'

Charlie shrugged in ambivalence, but was clearly intrigued in the goings-on around her because she kept glancing up from under her floppy fringe.

Then Beth piped up, her Aussie accent rising at the end of each sentence, as though she were testing the water. 'We figured it was a good time, before Charlie starts at the high school, and what with Nathan being eligible for long-service leave. It'll be a great opportunity to see some of Europe too, you know?' she said, prompting lots of nodding of heads.

'This,' said Gracie, beaming with delight, 'is the *best* news I could have had. Oh, your dad is going to be beside himself.'

'He kinda knows,' admitted Nathan with a guilty smile. 'I had to get him to help with a bit of research on rentals and schooling. Swore him to secrecy, mind. And he didn't know we were arriving today, for the marathon. I didn't want him to think I knew about that, or the op. Although we only found out about *that* on the drive here today, to be fair.'

'So that's what he was being all secretive about,' said Gracie, as though she'd just slotted the last piece of a puzzle into place. 'All that nonsense about looking up beermaking recipes online, as if your father wouldn't know how fermentation works; he was a scientist for goodness' sake.'

Nathan continued, 'The hardest part, actually, was trying to prevent these two motor mouths from giving the game away.' He ruffled the hair of his eldest daughter, who shrugged him away. 'Had to keep them off camera in the end.'

Jill couldn't keep the smile from her own face as she watched her sister light up with happiness. What an emotional rollercoaster of a day this was turning out to be.

'Um,' came a small voice, followed by a throat being cleared. 'I have some news too.'

With surprise, Jill turned to Emily, whose cheeks had turned the colour of a ripe tomato.

'So, as Nathan mentioned earlier, we got chatting on Instagram after he saw one of my posts about the marathon. I made sure your face wasn't in the picture Auntie Gracie, but, of course, Nathan knew it was you.'

'And there was me thinking you lived in a. . . what did you call it? Social media blackout?' Gracie tutted.

'I did for a while, I mean that would be the ideal world, but we have the girls, so, you know. . .' replied Nathan, earning himself an eyeroll from Charlie who, true to form, was sitting scrolling on her phone.

'I made Nathan swear he wouldn't say anything but kept him in the loop with how you were getting on with the training,' said Emily.

Gracie added good-humouredly, 'You mean you bribed my son into silence with regular health updates?'

'Most insightful, Mother,' said Nathan with a playful eyeroll. 'But, a fair assessment, wouldn't you say, Em?'

Emily nodded. 'Pretty much.'

'Well anyway, it was a blessing in disguise. Because the more I chatted with Emily here, the more we realised how much we had in common. I mean, I know we're cousins, but we didn't really know each other at all.'

Jill flinched at Nathan's words, but a quick, reassuring wink from Gracie told her she had nothing to feel guilty about on that front.

Emily picked the thread back up. 'And Nathan's job sounded so amazing, like exactly the sort of thing I wish I'd gone into, instead of selling my soul in the finance world.'

At this, another frisson of unease swept through Jill.

'The whole renewable energy industry is so fascinating, and compelling and *important*,' enthused Emily, her passion for the subject galvanising her, the flush on her cheeks fading. 'It's like, I have this idea of how I think we should be living and I do my best to live by those ideals, but working in an industry like that means that you're *actually* doing something about our future and working for the planet, instead of against it, which is how it feels for me at the moment, trudging mindlessly through each day only to line the pockets of the wealthy. I can't do it anymore.'

320

Oh. God. Was this it? Was Emily going to leave? Was she going to up and leave and head off to Australia, as Nathan had all those years ago, when he left Gracie with a hole in her life that could never quite be filled. Was this to be her fate too?

'And she's totally wasted,' added Nathan. 'In this industry, you need all the passion you can get, and Emily has it in bucketloads, all that untapped potential.'

'Which is why I've made a decision,' said Emily, leaving a weighty pause.

Oh *please* no. Not *my* baby. Visions of upping and following Emily to Australia flooded Jill's mind, along with panic – don't you need a skill to live there? Don't you have to be a doctor or an electrician or something useful? How quickly could she retrain?

'Because I've been *so* inspired by Auntie Gracie, and all the incredible things she's done in her life, I've decided to quit my job and go travelling for a year. . .'

Sorry, what? Travelling? Jill's mind reeled. Not emigrating, but still. . .

'. . . I want to see the world, to see how other people live, to learn from other communities and climates and then, when I come home, I'm going to retrain. I might try for an apprenticeship, or I might go back to uni. Either way, I know what I want to do now and that feels life-changing for me.'

'But how can you just *go* travelling?' asked Jill, a manic edge to her voice that she tried to get under control. 'I mean, don't you need money, how will you live?'

Nathan leaned forwards in his seat. 'Ah, well, the best bit is, there's an entry-level research opportunity within my firm for a three-month placement in Romania. So, Emily will start off there.'

'And there's on-site accommodation, so I can save up my salary for the rest of the trip.' Emily fixed Jill with an excited smile. 'I'm sorry I haven't said anything until now, Mum, it's all just kind of. . . fallen into place, thanks to Nathan. I still can't believe I've been given this opportunity.'

'Wow,' said Gracie, eyes swimming with pride. 'Congratulations, Emily, this is *incredible* news.'

Trying to shake off her stunned reaction, Jill rallied. Because this *was* incredible news. It was scary and unsettling, her baby was going to go off and travel the world – alone! No friends or family on hand, no running club. Yet, it was also exciting and brave and thrilling. Jill remembered being totally in awe of her big sister when she'd announced her own travel plans back in the Seventies, how she'd practically glued herself to the bottom stair until the postman had been most mornings, in case another exotic postcard landed on the doormat, with tales from afar. It was time to step back and let her daughter carve out a path for herself, one that would make her truly happy.

'I'm really happy for you, love,' said Jill, pulling Emily into a hug. 'You're going to do amazing things, I know it.'

'Really?' asked Emily, pulling back and inspecting her mum's face. 'You're not disappointed? About me giving up my job and the flat? You don't think it's going backwards?'

'Disappointed? Why would I be disappointed? I only want you to be happy, Em, and you haven't been, not truly. I thought you were building up to tell me something awful had happened, that you'd been a victim of some kind of bullying, or. . . worse. I thought *that* was why you didn't like your job, or staying in London, that maybe a flatmate was intimidating you, or I don't know, stalking you or something. I'm bloody over the moon that's not the case, quite frankly!'

Emily looked stricken. 'Oh, Mum. I'm so sorry. I hate that you've been worrying. My flatmates are lovely, but Noor works nights and

TJ's always round his boyfriend's, so it's pretty dull really. I preferred being with you crazy lot.' She smiled sheepishly at the table.

Jill squeezed Emily's hand, not able to articulate the feelings that threatened to burst from her chest. There was a light pressure on her shoulder, the gentlest of touches, and she knew without glancing around that it was Ray, standing behind her, watching her back.

'So then, don't keep us in suspense,' said Malik, 'when do you go?'

Emily returned Jill's squeeze, gripping her fingers tightly.

'Well,' she said, wincing, 'that's what I was going to ask. Is anyone available to lend a hand with moving my stuff out of my flat? I leave in two weeks' time.'

Jill swallowed hard, using everything she had to keep her strangled feelings in check.

'Of course we'll help,' promised Gracie, 'and hopefully by then I'll be able to walk again, because I'm not confident my legs are working right now, which is problematic, as I really need the loo.'

'I'll come with you,' said Jill, jumping up, thankful for an excuse to leave the table and compose herself, get a grip on her emotions.

After installing Gracie in a toilet cubicle, with the promise of being on hand to yank her off the loo seat if required, Jill braced herself against the sink unit and examined her shellshocked face in the mirror. There was nothing there to suggest the rug had been pulled from under her. No new creases at the corner of her eyes to indicate the turmoil her nervous system had been through, all within the space of one day; the nerves, admiration, pride, elation, desperation, desolation and the sweet, terrifying realisation that you were freefalling towards love. Although perhaps that last one had been brewing for considerably longer than she'd dared to admit, fermenting away in an unlabelled demijohn like Andrew's homemade beer.

The toilet flushed, then the cubicle door eased open and Jill watched in the mirror as her sister emerged. She was dishevelled, stiff and lumbering in her movements, but at the same time majestic, like a queen returned from battle with her head held high, which in a way Jill supposed was true. Gracie was a warrior. Yes, she might have run a marathon, but she'd also endured this hollow ache, the gearing up of oneself to bid farewell to your child as they embarked on adventures of their own. And she was still here, still enduring, still winning.

'God, I look like our grandmother did after she'd been embalmed,' remarked Gracie, grimacing at her reflection. 'An experience you were spared from, being only three years old. She had thick silver hair that had been brushed into a frizz ball, and they'd rubbed rouge into her cheeks. Grandma Polly *never* wore make-up; she was as matronly as they came.'

'And she certainly never ran a marathon. Although I think that's the wine warming your cheeks now, rather than the running,' added Jill with a grin.

Gracie turned on the tap and washed her hands.

'I'm not going to pretend it won't be hard, Jill, when Emily goes away. It will be horrible. But you're strong. Look what you've already been through. And now you have all of us.' She looked up and met her eye.

Jill agreed with a barely perceptible nod. 'Ironic, isn't it, Nathan back here, Emily going. But I'm so happy for you, Gracie, having him and the family home. I know it's not forever, but what a wonderful year it will be, all together at last.'

Gracie tipped her head to gently rest against Jill's. 'Darling, nothing's forever. All we have are the nows. That's why you have to make them count.'

All we have are the nows. It was quite an exhilarating thought, when you put it like that. As though there were no time to waste.

'Then we'd better get back out there and carry on celebrating,' said Jill, 'before you fall asleep under a table. And then, we need to retrieve our minibus from the hotel car park and perform one last duty.' Jill pulled a face, remembering the deal she'd struck with Debbie to procure the vehicle. 'Best polish your medal, sis, it's almost time for your close-up. Tell me, how do you *feel* about being the face of Beachcombers Retirement Village?'

Jill didn't wait to see Gracie's response, but turned and ran for the door, laughing like a schoolgirl, whose best friend in the world was her own, brilliant sister.

34

Gracie

It took almost two weeks and a couple of soothing sports massages for Gracie to decide she might be up to a short run. And a short run, by her new standards, was around the length of a standard Coast Path Runners' Saturday morning run with her friends.

As she strolled towards the pavilion, the planted borders of public spaces exploded in vibrant shades of cerise and scarlet, showcasing the hard work of volunteers for Frinton's entry to Britain in Bloom. It was early May, and it seemed like the entire town was gearing up for summer, for the long, hazy days and busy calendar of community events that made living here on the Essex Sunshine Coast such a uniquely magical place to be.

The North Sea shimmered a perfect blue as children skipped across the neatly manicured greensward towards a day of paddling and picnicking, whilst adults lumbered behind, weighed down with windbreaks, blankets and buckets and spades. Gracie and Andrew had been those parents once, their garage a treasure trove of faded beach paraphernalia, colourful kites, Frisbees and dog-eared deckchairs. All of which were coming in terribly useful, with

Charlie and Liv on their doorstep, since both girls loved nothing more than getting down onto the sand in their sun-kissed bare feet.

Nathan and Beth had taken a flat on the seafront, a short-term rental, as they wanted to be close to Gracie and Andrew, yet able to move around easily by train for sightseeing and short European trips, so Frinton fitted the bill perfectly and Gracie could not possibly be any happier. Here they were now, strolling towards the pavilion, her handsome son and his teenage daughter, who also, it transpired, liked to run. Two extra-special members of the CPR, which had seemingly grown overnight to include dozens of new members, young and old, all inspired by Gracie's journey and a desire to see what all the fuss was about. *What exactly was it about going for a run?* Gracie wasn't sure she could ever answer that question but knew in her heart that for as long as she was physically able to, she would continue to pick up her feet and feel the wind in her hair, to experience the here and now and the thrum of her blood in her veins.

'Lovely day for it,' commented Nathan as they met at the roadside.

'It's a beautiful day,' agreed Gracie, kissing them both on the cheek. 'But I expect you're used to having lots of those back home.'

Charlie screwed up her nose. 'I don't actually like it too hot. This is the perfect temperature for me, Nan.'

Gracie took in her pale granddaughter, self-consciously tugging her long sleeves down past her wrists, her slight, slender frame about to burgeon into womanhood, and felt a pang of love. She was so lucky to be getting all this time with them, to enjoy all the comfortable, unfilled quiet moments that lay between the family gatherings and hectic arrangements that usually accompanied every trip. The normal ebb and flow of familial life that was now commonplace between her and Jill – Emily too – and which had been absent for so many years. Too many years.

They crossed the grass and made their way over to the others who were grouped about, chatting and laughing. They were all there, among the newcomers, Ray, Malik, Sophia and Giles. All except for Emily, who was probably frantically packing at this very moment, before her flight to Romania the next morning. No sign of Kat, of course. The ghastly woman had become curiously absent since Jill sent her packing with a flea in her ear a fortnight ago. Hopefully she'd retreated for a period of introspection and reflection on her abysmal conduct and was even now resolving to be a better daughter, neighbour and friend, although somehow, Gracie doubted it. But, if there was something Gracie had learned of late, it's that often, you never really knew the whole story. Who was to say Kat's behaviour hadn't been shaped by events in her past – relationships and experiences none of them knew anything about and had no right to judge. All you could do was look out for those around you, no matter who they used to be, or who they may become.

Giles broke off from an engrossed conversation with Malik, a new development Gracie was delighted to bear witness to.

'Hi, Gracie,' he said jovially. 'We were just talking about our kit. With all these new members we're going to need more, and Malik's firm NewTek has offered to sponsor us, isn't that cool?'

Gracie looked back at Malik in surprise. 'Really? How did that come about?'

Malik grinned. 'I had an interview for a promotion, higher pay grade, more training, a fantastic opportunity. Somehow, we got onto the topic of community projects and I told them about Alzheimer's Outreach UK and the amazing total you raised, and how proud I was to be a small part of it.' He glowed with pride and Gracie noted how different he looked these days; gone were the dark shadows under his eyes and the sightly gaunt look that spoke of sleepless nights and a heap of stress. Now that parental duties were more evenly split between him and his ex-wife, he had more time to unwind, as well as spending time with Sophia. 'Anyway, I got the job, and they offered to sponsor the CPR. We can get beanies and hoodies done for winter too. Win-win.'

'Oh, Malik, that's wonderful news! Congratulations!' Gracie pulled him into a brief hug. 'We'll have to celebrate properly. You are coming along later, aren't you?'

'Wouldn't miss it for the world. How about you, Giles? Are you coming to Emily's leaving do?' asked Malik, to Gracie's surprise.

'Absolutely,' he said, 'it's high time I saw what all the fuss was about at this café of yours. And I've heard amazing things about Jill's cake – can't wait to try it.'

At this, Gracie caught the twinkle of mischief in Malik's eye. Oh well, she supposed it *was* early days, after all. But she'd be keeping a close eye on Jill; if those sugar-free abominations reappeared, there would be an intervention.

'Right, come on then,' said Gracie. 'Let's find Ray. Seeing as we've all elected him club leader, we'd better let him practise his welcoming spiel on the newbies.'

A couple of hours later, invigorated from the run, freshly showered and dressed in her favourite shorts, a new pair of fancy pink Birkenstocks, which Nathan and Beth had brought with them as a gift, and an airy cotton blouse, Gracie went to find Andrew.

Predictably, he was in the shed. The stubborn man was leaning heavily on a crutch whilst trying to pack tools, rolls of tape, knives, packets of screws and all sorts of detritus into a series of plastic tote boxes, where they were to be labelled and stacked tidily, making way for next week's big arrival – the train set.

'I told you to wait for me to help, Andy,' said Gracie, sighing at the sight of him, covered in dust and iron filings. The operation had been a great success, and he was already walking better. The other knee would also need doing eventually, but for now they were going to make the most of things. *Perhaps* even book that cruise.

Gracie looked around. 'There's plenty of time to do this' and now you've gone and got yourself all grubby.'

'Oh, have I?' He glanced down and began to brush at his trousers. 'Sorry, love. Thought I'd make myself useful. You know, I think I might give it a lick of paint in here, before we start building the track. Harold was telling me about this brilliant set-up he saw on the telly, some celebrity – I forget who – turned his attic into a scaled-down version of his hometown. Painted scenery on the walls, the sky on the ceiling, the whole shebang. Imagine that! A miniature Frinton-on-Sea, right here in this shed. The sea over there, the railway station over here, what do you say?'

Gracie looked around at the cavernous space that had so often irked her, imposing upon the garden and stealing away her husband in retirement to happily potter whilst she grew bored and restless.

'Do you think I could be in it? And the CPR? Tiny figures running along the seafront?'

'Absolutely. And Victory Hall too. It will be like a celebration of home.'

'A home, within a home. I love it.' Gracie smiled.

Andrew grinned back. 'Time to get a wriggle on, is it?'

'Mm-hm, Nathan will be here in five minutes. I've stacked the crates by the door ready.'

The virgin batch of Andrew's craft beer was accompanying them to Victory Hall, for a celebratory tipple with friends and family. They'd decided to name it Thirsty Work, in homage to the last few months. Because it hadn't just been Gracie who'd put in the legwork – yes, she actually ran the marathon – but it had also been a community effort. What with Harold looking after Picasso and

Banksy for the weekend, taking Andrew to hospital and visiting with Eugene. Then there had been all the fundraising, all the extra time and effort people put in to raise awareness and support Gracie. Today was a fantastic opportunity to honour all of that, whilst wishing Emily well on her exciting new adventure.

Nathan arrived, helping his dad into the front seat, then fetching the crates of beer and stacking them into the boot, whilst Gracie settled herself on the back seat with the huge bouquet of flowers she'd picked up that morning for Jill from the local florist, gorgeous sprays of purple stocks and big blousy peonies that filled the car with the scent of spring. It wouldn't take away the sadness when Emily bid her mum farewell the following morning, but it would brighten the house a little and Gracie fully intended to keep Jill busy with a new fundraising idea she hoped to run past her later.

At Victory Hall the doors were propped open invitingly wide and letting in the sunny afternoon. Andrew had made a small wooden sign, at Cynthia's request, which hung proudly from the doorknob:

The Be Together Café – Everyone Welcome

Inside, was a comfortingly familiar scene. Eugene held court, as usual, flanked by Harold and several new faces from Beachcombers. A discarded game of Scrabble littered their table, along with cups and saucers and plates. Rita was there too, sitting quietly in an easy chair, with another lady beside her. A carer perhaps, or a new friend? Jill had updated Gracie a few days ago to say that extra support was already in place, and that she was able to stay at home with the help of various services and adaptations, many of which came courtesy of the tremendous wealth of knowledge from charities such as Alzheimer's Outreach UK, which Gracie had been able to play a tiny part in helping.

The battered old table tennis table had been pulled out from the back room and had been commandeered by four children, who squealed in delight as they ping-ponged the ball back and forth. It seemed Malik's two, Elsie and Theo, had taken the two new Aussie girls under their wing, which filled Gracie's heart with joy, a feeling further deepened when she spotted Malik and Sophia standing hand in hand, chatting and laughing with her daughter-in-law Beth.

'Dad! Come and play!' called out Charlie when she spotted him.

'Yes, Daddy, come and play!' cried Liv.

'In a bit,' he replied, 'best get your practise in first before I show all you kids how it's really done.'

Gracie marvelled again at the easy manner he had with his family, and how alike his own father he was. So kind, sensitive and thoughtful. A brilliant father, husband and son.

As Nathan helped Andrew settle in a chair, finding a small footstool to prop his leg on, Gracie looked around for Jill so she could find somewhere safe to put the flowers for now.

'They're in the kitchen,' called Cynthia, from where she was clearing and wiping down tables. 'It's a busy one today, we needed the extra pair of hands!'

Assuming Cynthia meant Emily, Gracie pushed open the kitchen door and found herself face to face with a canoodling couple, who leapt apart, startled at the interruption as though teenagers caught by their parents.

'Oops,' she said, not even trying to suppress her delight.

Ray looked abashed, then gave a small shrug as if to say, *what the hell, no point denying it now.*

'Gracie,' acknowledged Jill, her voice going up a few notches. 'Uh, we were just. . .'

'Yes?' Gracie prompted, enjoying herself immensely.

'Ray's just lending a hand. With, um, making salad garnishes.'

'How kind. Nothing worse than a bit of limp old lettuce. Have you got somewhere you can put these? They're for you,' said Gracie, thrusting the bouquet at her sister, completely unable to wipe the smug smirk off her face.

After a beat, Jill took them and returned the smile with one that lit up her entire wonderful face. 'Thank you, they're gorgeous.'

'I'll go check on Dad,' said Ray, excusing himself from the kitchen.

Gracie raised an eyebrow in question.

'We went on a date. Last night. An actual *proper* date, with dinner and wine and everything.' The girlish joy in Jill's hushed words was infectious.

'And *everything*?' enquired Gracie, giggles of hilarity threateningly close.

'Oh shush, you.' Jill turned serious. 'Do you think it's too soon? You know, after Gary.'

Gracie covered the remaining metre between them and took Jill's face in her hands.

'You deserve to be happy, little sis. That's *all* that matters. Now, what say I give you a hand so we can get everyone fed, then we can really get this party started?'

Later, when Emily, who had popped to the shops for last-minute toiletries, returned rosy-cheeked, wired and jangling with nerves, bottles of Thirsty Work were handed round.

'Cheers, everyone!' said Andrew, holding his drink aloft. 'Here's to my Gracie for raising a phenomenal £200,000 for Alzheimer's Outreach UK. . .' he paused to accommodate the ensuing whooping and clapping '. . . She really went the extra mile.'

There were several loud groans, as well as a '*Dad!*' from Nathan.

'And that's not even counting the proceeds from Jet Logan's

record,' added Jill. 'It's incredible. When I think how that will help people like Gary and their families.' She broke off as Emily rubbed her shoulder.

'But of course we have another toast,' continued Andrew, raising his glass again. 'We're going to miss her, but she's off to do good in the world. Here's to Emily and her exciting new adventure. *Bon voyage!*'

'*Bon voyage*, Emily!' chimed everyone, before taking tentative sips of their beer.

'Not too bad, not bad at all,' proclaimed Harold. 'I'm getting caramel and something else. Do I detect a nutty note?'

At this Gracie joked, 'Andrew made it, dear. There is *definitely* a nutty note.'

Everyone laughed, including Andrew, who, Gracie suspected, rather liked being viewed as slightly eccentric; after all, it allowed you to get away with almost anything. *Almost*, but not quite, for there was no way she was trialling any more of his wearable gadgets, no matter the physical demand. Which reminded her of something. . .

'So, as we're all together, there was something I wanted to run past you all, another big fundraising idea for next year.' She paused, taking in the intrigued expressions, and waited for Emily to meet her eye, because she had a feeling that out of everyone here, it would be her adventurous niece who was up to the challenge.

'How do we feel about Ben Nevis?'

Author's Note

The coastal town of Frinton-on-Sea is the setting for this story, and whilst many of the geographical locations and landmarks referenced within this story do exist, all people, places and establishments mentioned are entirely fictional.

Alzheimer's Outreach UK is a fictional charity in this story, but there are many incredible organisations out there committed to providing care and support, along with undertaking valuable research, to tackle this disease. At some point in our lives, many of us will be touched by the devastating effects of Alzheimer's or dementia in some way. If you, or someone you know, has been affected by any of the issues raised in this book, support is available. Here are some of the charities you could contact for help and advice:

Alzheimer's Society	www.alzheimers.org.uk
Dementia UK	www.dementiauk.org
Age UK	www.ageuk.org.uk

Jill's Favourite Motivational Mottos

'You never regret a run.'

'There's no such thing as can't, if you haven't tried.'

'Strength comes with belief.'

'It doesn't matter where you're going,
the joy is in the journey that takes you there.'

'Nothing worth having ever comes easily.'

Jill's Pre-Run Stamina Smoothie

(Enjoy one hour before exercising)

Handful spinach

Handful cooked kale

½ avocado

Handful frozen mango chunks

200ml Oat milk

Honey, to sweeten to taste

Gracie's Post-Run Scrumptious Smoothie

250ml Coconut Water

1 x banana, chopped

¼ fresh pineapple

Handful blueberries

Juice ½ lime

3 x frozen strawberries

1 tsp chia seeds

Acknowledgements

Thanks are due to many individuals for their involvement and hard work in the publication of *Gracie Jenkins Runs a Marathon*.

I was lucky enough to have not one, but two brilliant editors whilst working on this book: Maddie Wilson and Rachel Hart. I can't thank either of them enough for their enthusiasm, insightful suggestions and creative vision. Also working on the novel were the following talented professionals: Copyeditor Sandra Ferguson, Proofreader Clare Wallis, Illustrator Bodil Jane, Designer Toby James, Emily Hall and Jessica Whitehead in Marketing and Katie Buckley in Sales. Publishing with Avon really does feel like teamwork, so thank you also to the wider team: Helen Huthwaite, Emma Grundy Haigh, Amy Mae Baxter, Anna Nightingale and Jess Zahra.

A shout out to fellow Avon authors too, you are all *great*.

Huge thanks to the bloggers, reviewers, authors and early readers who have given their time and support for publication. And to *all* readers, everywhere, for picking up a copy, thank you so very much.

Thank you to my literary agent Kate Nash, and the whole agency team, (*P.S. thanks for tipsy train snacks. Note to self: have dinner*).

Thanks to Lianne Hogan, Communications Manager at London Marathon Events Ltd for her incredibly helpful insights into the admissions process for the London Marathon (any mistakes are my own). Thanks also to Rachel Dell and Tracey Vickers for fielding a million questions and telling me about their experiences of running the London Marathon. I am in complete awe of them both for their amazing achievements. Thanks again to Rachel Hart, for her valuable insights as a London Marathon spectator. It wasn't until I got to attend the London Marathon for myself that I truly appreciated what a humbling and awe-inspiring event it is. Each and every participant deserves the utmost respect for setting out to achieve one of the toughest of physical and mental challenges. I can only hope that within this book, there is at least a flavour of the vast spectrum of human emotions experienced by both the runners and the spectators.

Thanks also to my dad, David Goff, who knew an *awful* lot about the intricacies of building an air-conditioned hat. I'll say no more about that . . .

Lastly, thank you James, for being as supportive as ever on long walks to iron out sticky plot points, Aimee for being my Marathon Day buddy and to Squirrels for another fun location recce and braving the sea for a chilly dip. So, where to next. . .?

Loved
Gracie Jenkins Runs a Marathon?

Why not read Penny's other novel
The Unretirement?

It's never too late to chase your dreams...

the Un-Retirement

PENNY MIRREN

'Uplifting, funny and warm' Phillipa Ashley

An uplifting story about the joy
of pursuing dreams at any age, full of warmth,
heart and community spirit.